ONE DAY, ONE DAY, CONGOTAY

ALSO BY MERLE HODGE

Crick Crack, Monkey
For the Life of Laetitia

For Nnamdi:
Patois researcher, Patois teacher – cultural activist.

MERLE HODGE

ONE DAY, ONE DAY, CONGOTAY

PEEPAL TREE

First published in Great Britain in 2022
Peepal Tree Press Ltd
17 King's Avenue
Leeds LS6 1QS
England

ISBN13: 9781845235246

Supported using public funding by
ARTS COUNCIL
ENGLAND

ACKNOWLEDGEMENTS

My thanks to:

Prof. Funso Aiyejina, colleague and friend, who generously made time to read the manuscript and give sound advice.

Eddie Hart, whose life is one of the sources of inspiration for this story. Like the boy Sonny in the novel, Eddie was raised by elderly sisters – my great-aunts – one of them a teacher. Eddie grew up to be a grassroots mover and shaker at community level, notably in sport and the steelband movement, and served also at the national level, as a member of Parliament.

Teacher Cathy Adams, Mother Marjorie Anderson, and all members of the Spiritual Baptist church Brotherhood of Time Spiritual School, guardians of heritage. "Blest be the tie that binds".

Kim Johnson, for his unparalleled work on steelband history, as well as his helpfulness in personally providing me with information.

Eintou Springer and Prof. Bridget Brereton for some crucial insights regarding our culture and history.

Nnamdi Hodge, for reconnecting me with the Patois heritage, and for IT first-responder assistance to the techno-peasant.

Peepal Tree publisher **Jeremy Poynting,** for his ongoing encouragement, and for unshakeable grace and civility in spite of this writer's cantankerousness.

NOTES ON LANGUAGE

Definitions
The word "Creole", often appearing in this text, has more than one meaning. In its broadest definition it refers to "livestock, trees and other living things, *born or nativized in the Caribbean, but of foreign parentage.*" (Lise Winer, *Dictionary of the English Creole of Trinidad and Tobago,* McGill-Queen's University Press, 2009).

Technically, therefore, the whole human population of the Caribbean is Creole, except our First Peoples. However, the term is most often applied to *the African-descended person*. In this novel, as in the society it portrays, Afro-Caribbean people are referred to variously as "Creole", "Negro", or "Black", and in a few instances, the racist epithet "Nigger".

A Creole is also a language, born out of contact between two or more languages. The Creole languages of the Caribbean were created by Africans transported to the region in the era of the slave trade, from the contact between European and African languages.

The term "Patois" refers to French Creole in the Caribbean. In the spelling system devised for Lesser Antillean French Creole, it is spelt "Patwa". This is not to be confused with the use of the word "Patwa" in Jamaica. There it refers to the English Creole spoken in Jamaica.

Racist epithets in this novel
Regarding the appearance of racist terms in a literary text, writers of fiction are not called upon to reflect only sweetness and light. They may also reflect ugliness. One might even consider it an obligation of the creative writer to confront and challenge us with undesirable human behaviour. Fiction may be a lens through which people get to look behaviours such as racism in the eye. The practice of sweeping racist words under the carpet – hiding them or hiding from them – does not help to eradicate racism.

M.H.

CONTENTS

1

"Is me, Phillip."

He was brought to her one morning in the middle of the Easter term by his irate father. While the man spoke to Gwynneth he held the boy by the back of his pants, almost lifting him off the ground, so that he was jacked up in the most uncomfortable way. The child was in uniform – Boys' R.C. School – and was clutching his three tattered books: reading book, arithmetic book and exercise book. His father had, to all appearances, frogmarched him there from school, all the way over on the other side of Turagua.

"Madam!" the man sputtered. "I want you take this boy in you school. He ain learning a damn thing over there. Them teachers just drawing pay and ain teaching the chirren a damn thing. I cyaan believe I make a dunce, a stupidee. The teacher say all he want to do is beat drum on the desk. Madam, this is a wotless child, and I give you licen to do what you want with him. Doan forget to cut he skin. This is a child need plenty licks, so doan fraid…"

At this point, Gwynneth held up her hand to silence him.

They were standing just inside the gate to the backyard. Gwynneth took the child's hand and the man released him. She directed the child to the bench under the mango tree and returned to the father for a brief conversation. Then she went into the shed and settled the other children. "I will be right there under the mango tree," she let them know, giving *the look* to those most likely to create ruction while she was outside. "Remember, I can see you and hear you."

She went to talk with the new child sitting on the bench under the tree, mango blossom dusting his hair. He was crying, without a sound, just one long tear proceeding down each cheek. When he saw her coming, he hurriedly wiped his face with both hands and with so much force that he seemed in danger of gouging out his own eyes. Gwynneth sat down next to him. She put her arm around his shoulders and gave him a squeeze.

It took her some time to draw him out, but eventually he moved from just nodding or shaking his head or shrugging, to answering with indistinct sounds, to one-word answers, then at last to actually chatting, though in a guarded way. Gwynneth learned that he was nine years old and in Standard 2. When he seemed more at ease, she asked him: "And what about the drumming, now?"

He looked up at her, nervously, but saw that she was smiling, so he explained: "Is when we get hard sums to do, Miss, and I cyaan get out some of them. I doesn even know I beating on the desk, until Sir bawl at me to stop that."

He told her that his uncle often let him beat the foolay in his tamboo bamboo band, and sometimes he got to be the scratcher-man. He also beat a goatskin drum when he went with his uncles to Shango-feast. As he spoke, his face lit up, but then clouded over again, and he stopped talking.

"What's wrong?" Gwynneth asked.

He answered in a small voice: "My father ain want me go up by my uncle and them."

She waited for him to talk. The problem seemed to be that the father was not happy with the boy and his mother keeping close ties with her family. There was clearly no love lost between these parties. The boy related to her how his two uncles had come to the house one evening and quarrelled with his father. As they left, one of them looked back and said: "Next time you raise you hand for she, they go find you in a canal next morning."

By now sounds of restlessness and imminent ruction were beginning to come from the shed, so they got up off the bench and went in. A whole plan had formed in Gwynneth's head. This boy was in a tamboo bamboo band. Her children would learn to play tamboo bamboo, and they would form a band. She would gather the instruments. Some of the empty bottles under the house, the thicker ones, would do just fine until she could get hold of gin bottles. She might well find a pitch-oil pan under the house, too, otherwise she could get one from the shop. A grater would be used for scratcher. The children would make the shac-shacs right there in school, bringing the materials from their yards – whole calabashes, dry seeds, and sticks for the handles.

Getting the bamboo would not be that simple. There was a right time to go and cut it down – only on dark-night – and you had to know the widths and lengths of the pieces in a tamboo bamboo band. The uncle would have been an obvious source. She had heard about his band, up in San Miguel Road. It was on the long list she had carried about in her head for years, of things to do and places to visit one day when she got the time.

But at the moment it might not be a good idea to approach Phillip's uncle. It could seem like putting herself into the quarrel within the boy's family, which would only bring down the wrath of the charming father. She would have to talk to Ollie – he was sure to know someone who could provide the bamboo for them.

Tamboo bamboo, under the direction of Phillip, became part of the class they called "Music Time". He grew in self-confidence. And there was nothing wrong with this child's brains. He read very well, and after he was introduced to the storybook table, he discovered that he actually liked reading. His handwriting was not the neatest, but that improved. Gwynneth's children were encouraged to write and illustrate their own stories. These were sewn into little books, with covers cut from cardboard boxes, and placed on the storybook table for everybody to read, side by side with the fancy storybooks from Away. Nobody was inclined to present crapaud-foot handwriting to such public view, so everybody worked hard on their penmanship.

New pupils would often begin by writing stories modelled on the ones in books, illustrating them with rosy-cheeked children, snowmen, apple trees and houses that sported chimneys atop their roofs. It was the same with children she had taught at Oropuna and St Paul, until she could convince them that Cayerian children and their lives were just as worthy of being written about, drawn in pictures and put into storybooks, as the children who peopled every storybook they had ever seen.

All of Phillip's stories were about a boy who spent happy holidays with his grandmother, uncles, auntie and cousins, in a yard of two houses, with plenty trees and bush around them. Among the adventures this boy had there were: going into the bush with his grandmother to collect wood for the fireside and coming upon a pretty coral snake under a stone and his grandmother pulling him away from it; climbing to a high branch of the orange tree, where he braved sharp pikka and marabunta nests to get hold of a big, big orange that he would take home for his mother; practising in his Uncle Chester's tamboo bamboo band; and going to Shango-feast with his Uncle Chester and Uncle Melville... Phillip presented each of these stories to Gwynneth with a radiant smile on his face.

Phillip had great difficulty with arithmetic, but so did Gwynneth when she was his age. It was only with some special attention from Puppa that she had learned to make better sense of numbers. Puppa would sit at the dining-room table and ask her in his kindliest voice to bring her exercise book. He looked through all her latest work and complimented her on the high marks she had got in spelling, dictation, parsing, comprehension, penmanship and composition. He acknowledged, too, that she was not doing too badly in scripture and geography, either.

But a frown came over his face as he contemplated her pitiful attempts at working out sums, the majority of which sported a large red-ink X. The frown would creep into his voice: "So what is this here, now? A simple little sum like that and you have to get it wrong? Take your time with your work, girl!"

It was then that Mumma would begin to hover pointedly nearby.

Mumma always said that she had got enough licks in school to last for all her coming generations, so nobody was going to beat any child of hers. Days before Gwynneth first started school, at Morain R.C. where Puppa was teaching at the time, Mumma warned him that if he let any teacher beat her child, and worse, if *he* were to put God out of his thoughts and raise his hand for her child, she would have to pay a visit to the school. Mumma repeated the admonition when she sent Viola off to school with Puppa and Gwynneth, and again years later, as Roy's first day of school approached. On each of these occasions she thought it fit to remind Puppa of how her mother, Sarah, had earned the title "Crazy Obeah-Woman".

Whenever Mumma retold the story to the grown-up Gwynneth

and Viola, it might start off with indignation, but this soon melted into a fond remembrance of her mother.

"The teacher lash me with the belt, and the buckle ketch me cross these two finger – watch them good. See how they crooked? Is break that *salaud* did break me finger them. Me hand start to feel hot and swell up one time. I wait till the bell ring for recess, and then I just pelt out from there and put foot down the road. I run home. Mammy take me hand and kiss it and blow on it. Then she make a poultice and she plaster it on the finger them."

Mumma demonstrated the gentle, caressing motion with which her mother applied the poultice to her fingers.

"Then she band them up with cloth. But same time, she quarrelling about the teacher, the school, the Father-priest, and how she go do for them people, how she go make them fart. Next morning she full the tub and send me to pick what-and-what leaf and flowers for we to bathe with. She bathe me first and tell me go and put on me school uniform. Then she bathe and put on she spiritual clothes. Mammy take up she bell and she cocoyea broom, and we march down the road."

Pilgrim R.C. School was a mile and a half away, out on the main road. The two of them walked briskly and in silence, not wasting breath to talk.

"Mammy leave me stand-up in front the school, on the two piece-a board they did put down over the canal for bridge. She tell me doan move from that spot. First thing she do is go and lean up the cocoyea broom upside down gainst the front door step. She say that is just to confuse them Catholic."

For a while nobody noticed the two of them. Not yet. Gwynneth could imagine the scene – children galloping about the schoolyard, fully absorbed in playing, until Sarah's bell rang out from somewhere behind the building, and the children froze in their tracks. They would have been quite puzzled, for it was early still, not yet time for the morning school bell. But just as quickly, they unfroze, and with much chattering and shrieking all rushed towards the pump to wash their feet before going in.

Meanwhile two teachers had come to the door and poked out faces knotted with bewilderment, which turned to raw fear at the sound and sight of Sarah (wrapped in a whirlwind, they swore) emerging from behind a corner of the building, having made her first round.

By this stage of the story, Mumma would be shaking with amusement.

"My mother circle the school seven times, ringing she bell, praying, talking in tongues and singing at the top of she voice. Same time the headmaster and the teachers and them grabbing chirren and pulling them inside, whether or not they foot wash. Before Mammy finish make she seven rounds, school door lock up tight, and *tout moun* inside, like Adam in the garden hiding."

Gwynneth pictured them cowering indoors, from headmaster to ABC pupils. Nobody would have been able to even peep outside, for they had shut all the windows, and this was no luxurious glass-paned or jalousie-windowed school. The window flaps were made of solid board.

"When Mammy done, she pick up she cocoyea broom and call me come stand-up on the step. She brush me down from head to toe with the broom. Then we come out they yard and take a cool walk home."

Gwynneth had to start Phillip on arithmetic almost from scratch, but within a year or so he had caught up – he had conquered the dreaded sums. At school he was mostly in good spirits, but on some days he brooded. On those days, although he did everything that was required of him, he would work in an absent-minded, mechanical way, showing little interest.

Then one morning his grandmother brought him to school. She had the same radiant smile as Phillip when he was himself, the smile that was on his face, too, that morning as he stood in the yard tightly holding her hand. She introduced herself as Ruth Benoit. She had come to inform Teacher Gwynneth of Phillip's new address, and to let her know that her family was now responsible for him. Phillip couldn't stop smiling, even after his grandmother had left. Nor could he wait to tell Teacher Gwynneth more of the story.

"Miss! We gone back up and live by Gang-Gang and this time is forever, you know! Because this time, Uncle Chester and

Uncle Melville bring a cart and pack up all we clothes and thing in it and carry everything up in Gang-Gang house!"

For the rest of his time at Gwynneth's school, Phillip was an evenly cheerful child who gave her no cause for worry. She never saw the melancholy spirit take hold of him again.

He had to go back to big-school for Standard 5, to sit the College Exhibition exam, which would give him a shot at winning a free place at high school. Boys' R.C. was not inclined to take him back, however, because they remembered, and did not appreciate, his father's habit of visiting the school periodically to upbraid whoever was Phillip's teacher at the time. The whole school would fall silent, and the children's heads would turn to Phillip's class as they frankly enjoyed the spectacle. On the day that the father came into the school, grabbed Phillip by the scruff of his neck and practically dragged him out, shouting abuse all the way across the schoolyard and announcing that he was putting his son in another school, headmaster and teachers were sad for Phillip, but really quite relieved.

Phillip had to go over to St Paul Government Primary School, where he sat the exam. As for the free place in high school, however, no such luck. Leaving the mirage of high school behind them, Phillip and his classmates settled into Post Primary to sit the school leaving exam. The day Phillip received his Primary School Leaving Certificate, he rushed over to Gwynneth and called out to her from the gate, excitedly waving the document in the air: "Miss! Miss! Teacher Gwynneth! Look I pass, Miss!"

And he had passed with flying colours, arithmetic and all.

Gwynneth would meet Phillip from time to time in the years after he left her school; and whenever he passed along Farfan Road, he would call out a greeting. She knew that he was working in Carl's mechanic shop where his Uncle Melville had got him placed as an apprentice. Out of the blue one afternoon, not long after the contentious Mothers' Union meeting, Gwynneth heard Phillip's voice at the front gate. She looked out, and there he was, his face aglow with the endearing smile. "Evening, Miss. Is me, Phillip. I could talk to you a minute, please, Miss?"

Once more he seemed to be bursting with some news. As soon

as they sat down in the gallery, he leaned towards her in a conspiratorial way, and said, "Miss, we make a iron band, Miss. You could come and hear we? Sounding good, Miss!"

Her first reaction was alarm, for all she could see was danger for Phillip – police beating him, locking him up, dragging him before the court. And what about his job? He could lose his job simply because of the poisonous mauvay-lang that people like Valda Pierre and her gang were spreading about boys who played in iron bands. Just remembering the contention in Mothers' Union was enough to quicken her response – *of course* she would come and visit their band! Indeed, she would appoint herself protector of this band.

Nobody in that rowdy Mothers' Union meeting of July 1940 was aware that the iron-beating had found its way into Turagua, right under the scornful noses of Valda Pierre and her chorus. Gwynneth herself did not know until the day Phillip turned up at the front gate, just about two weeks after the meeting. She discovered, then, that all the while she was making hopeless plans to travel to town and visit iron bands, right here in Turagua, unknown to her, an iron band had come into being; and who was it that had achieved this?

She should have guessed, she should have known, that Phillip would be among those who answered the call of this unfolding marvel. Phillip told her he had joined an iron band started by a friend over in St Paul; but they practised during the week, and making his way over there and back on workday evenings was a strain. His Uncle Chester had suggested that Phillip start a band himself, up in his great-grandfather's old Shango palay, which was also the headquarters of the uncle's San Miguel Road Bamboo Band.

2
"Better you look for husband!"

The new world war, that (again) some said would be over in two twos, had been raging for almost a year already, with no sign of stopping. It was hard times once more. People ketching they royal. Eating the bread the devil knead. Mumma's health had also taken a turn for the worse. The three of them had to count themselves lucky for the roof over their heads and the pennies in their purse.

Viola was working at the telephone exchange, and Gwynneth now had thirty-seven schoolchildren in the shed (she called it "the schoolroom" when in the presence of said children). Almost half of them were five years old, ready for big-school, but big-school wasn't ready for them. Come January, there was never enough room in ABC class at Anglican School, Boys' R.C., Girls' R.C., or sometimes even the Government schools over in St Paul and Oropuna, so to Teacher Gwynneth they came.

Some of the children were not yet school age, but their families insisted on sending them to Teacher Gwynneth for them to get a head start on Book, so she had a benchful of four-year-olds to contend with. She had pupils right up to Standard 4. Most of these older ones were children who had not fared too well in big-school, and their families had plucked them out and given them to Teacher Gwynneth, who, it was agreed, could work miracles with the world's worst duncey-heads. After Standard 4 they had to go back to big-school for the College Exhibition exam.

People didn't mind too much that she had their children play tamboo bamboo in school, and sing oldtime Cayerian songs, even Patois songs, and calypsos, though why she would do so was a mystery. They turned a deaf ear because if Teacher Gwynneth did it, there had to be some good reason; and anyway, they knew that she wouldn't let them sing any song that had rudeness in it. More puzzling still, she had neither tamarind whip nor guava stick, not the littlest leather strap, not even a sewing-machine cord hanging

17

up anywhere in her schoolroom to strike the fear of God into their hearts.

Teacher Gwynneth asked a fee of one dollar a month for children up to Standard 1, and $1.50 for the older ones. On the fourth Friday of the month, some of the younger children would press a sweaty shilling or two into her hand with the message: "Mammy say she sending the rest next week."

A week later another shilling might follow, or two shillings. Sometimes people sent a shilling every week for four weeks and considered the matter closed. But four shillings was still four cents short of a dollar, and four cents was a pound of flour – when you could get flour to buy in war-days. For some of the older ones, Gwynneth might collect six shillings by month-end if she was lucky; but that was a whole six cents short. Six cents was a train ticket to Kings Port and back, or a pound of rice.

Even before the rationing came they were making do with three pounds of rice a week, and sometimes just two pounds, because, like everybody else, they were eating more dasheen, yam, green-fig, cassava, eddoes and tannia. It was clear that far from being over in two twos, this war might go on just as long as the last one. Earlier that year, as June approached, Gwynneth had given notice: "This Corpus Christi we have to put down a serious kitchen garden, eh, Viola. Not just chooking a cassava stick here and two grain of corn and peas there."

"So we sending and call Orville, then," Viola replied.

"Hm. We cyaan take Orville from his home Corpus Christi day. He and he family go be doing they planting, too."

"Yes, but we could get him to come before the day and prepare the ground. I know you think you could weed up all that ti-marie and bull grass, and fork up soil that dry-season turn into concrete; but not me, not this Viola."

Puppa used to hire Orville, a young man at the time, to work in the yard one day in every month. He would thin out the undergrowth up in the land, then cutlass the backyard and leave it looking like a soft green counterpane covering the ground. In Puppa's time that same greenery could quickly get out of hand as soon as rainy season set in. With just one heavy downpour it would sprout into a low jungle. Now, with thirty-odd children trampling the ground for the past fourteen years or so, it was only during the August vacation that the backyard needed any major cutlassing.

There was a time when Gwynneth would do some of the yard work herself, and with great relish. She would haul on one of Puppa's old trousers to go outside and wield hoe and cutlass to her heart's content, at least once a week. Now she considered herself lucky whenever she got the chance to go outside and pull up some of the ti-marie and rabbit grass that were beginning to overrun the beds Mumma had planted along the side of the house and faithfully tended, in her able-bodied years. Mumma's garden still provided them with all the green seasoning they needed – big-leaf thyme, fine-leaf thyme, chive, shadon benni, pimento....

Though the beefed-up kitchen garden would be a big help, they would still need to go to the market, and to the shop, for goods like salt-meat, smoke-herring and saltfish that came from abroad, and that in war-days you had to pay a pound-and-a-crown for.

They bought their milk from Sookram. It was delivered every morning by ten-year-old Kalowtie, who sometimes would sit on the step for a few minutes before continuing on her way up Wilson Trace to deliver another bottle of milk. Later on, when the rationing came, Kalowtie's family would not only supply them with milk. The Sookrams had more family members in their household than Mumma's, and there was a ration card for each person, so Dolly would let Gwynneth use one of their cards to get an extra pound of rice or flour, as needed, from Aleong's shop.

Mumma refused to become totally bedridden; but it was difficult for just the two of them to manage, now that the arthritis had begun to seriously hamper her movement. Roy came to see her regularly, and he would hug her up and kiss her and sweet-talk her, telling her she was going to live to be a hundred and fifty years old. When Roy was little, Puppa used to quarrel with their mother, saying: "Cut that boy's navel-string, Estelle, or he will never be a man!"

Mumma would answer back: "You leff me and my lagniappe!"

Roy was her unexpected little bonus, coming as he did when

her two daughters were almost grown-up. Gwynneth was a seasoned pupil teacher at Oropuna Government School, knocking on the door of the Teachers' Training School. Viola was a big girl going to Alpha Commercial School and making new boyfriends just as fast as Puppa could chase them away. Puppa had continued to chase boyfriends away even after his daughters had entered their early twenties.

~

When, in 1912, Joseph Cuffie's older daughter wanted to build a room of her own onto the back of the house, he had readily given his permission, for in that time he was still quite proud of this daughter who had followed in his teaching footsteps. She had finished Training School and saved up money from her first year of teaching as a fully certificated schoolmistress. Joseph suspected (but did not know for sure, as they always conspired to keep him in the dark), that she had also got some monetary assistance from her mother.

He remarked to Estelle that the room could be rented out to a decent lodger after Gwynneth was taken to her husband's home. He also expressed the hope that it would not be too long before this event took place, noting with grave concern that neither daughter seemed to have any such goal in her sights.

In Gwynneth's case, it could be that she was postponing marriage for the time being, because the minute she got married, she would have to leave the government teaching service. That was the regulation. But Gwynneth, he could see, loved teaching. And she was contrary enough to wilfully remain a spinster all her life in order to remain a teacher. But surely someone like her, a graduate of Training School, with years of teaching experience behind her, could be employed in one of the private schools in town that people of the better classes had established for their children?

And what was Viola's reason for flouting Holy Matrimony? The two girls were just too happily ensconced in his house. Each of them now had a whole room to herself, for when Gwynneth moved into her own room, Viola was left in Roy's room.

Joseph had added a room at the back of the house for Roy in 1910, but thought it best not to move him into it just yet, for that would have placed the boy too far from the rest of the family at

20

night. Up till then, Roy and his sisters had been sharing the bedroom that was called "the children's room", next to their parents. He had moved the double bed and the girls (or young ladies) into Roy's new room for the time being, leaving Roy in the old room.

Joseph complained that his daughters were yet to present him with any acceptable suitors, and declared that he was not surprised. Gwynneth had the decorum of a marchand woman in the fish-market, and Viola, though more ladylike, was not far behind. Viola had a sharp tongue, unbecoming of a well-bred lady.

He had pointed out to them that unless they changed their jamet ways, they would not be courted by men of good breeding, and he put his foot down firmly on the unending procession of worthless young loafers coming to warm his gallery chairs. Then he noticed that Gwynneth and Viola had stopped entertaining suitors, but were now perpetually out. At large. They would announce their going; but at what ungodly hour they returned he could never tell. They came and went through the back door, where their rooms were. Heaven forbid, they might even be sleeping out!

He couldn't very well interfere with their going and coming, however. They had both passed the age of twenty-one, were working and giving part of their pay to their mother to help with the expenses of the household. So he could think of them as lodgers. He could evict them. But how would that look? They were not lodgers; they were his family. And family putting out family was the worst kind of barrack-yard commess. Furthermore, he knew that whitepeople, no doubt observing how many Negro men did not look after their children, were in the habit of speaking of Negroes as "improvident". He would give nobody reason to class Joseph Cuffie with The Improvident Negro.

Sleeping out was one thing, but then, another alarming possibility had crept into his mind. It was not unusual for lodgers to receive guests in their rooms. Indeed, it was normal practice for a person renting a room in someone else's house. The two bedrooms occupied by Gwynneth and Viola were like an independent kingdom at the back of his house. Therefore... Was that why the parade of loafers through the gallery had come to an end?

21

Were Gwynneth and Viola now receiving guests in their bed-rooms? He had crossed himself repeatedly, seeking to cancel out this possibility.

He would speak to Estelle… But, if this was taking place, it might be with her knowledge. Estelle could be in cahoots with them, and she would never let him know. And suppose it did turn out that they were bringing in boyfriends? Better to shield himself. He preferred not to know. He would not raise this matter with Estelle.

Wearily, he accepted that he could do nothing about his daughters' actions except worry about what disreputable liaisons they might be finding themselves in behind his back, and shudder at the thought that they might one day bring shame upon him. Especially Gwynneth. She was born in Pilgrim, and she was almost a year old before he was finally transferred out of that hole. Were he superstitious, he would have been convinced that the place had blighted her. If any of his children was going to bring him down, Gwynneth would be the one. No use taking this problem to Estelle. He had repeatedly asked her to speak to her daughters about the importance of getting a good husband; but it seemed that they were doomed to suffer the pitiable fate of becoming old-maids.

~

Ollie could still send them into stitches with his story of how, a week after he and Viola met, Puppa scuttled their first rendezvous. "So this young-lady tell me to come and pick her up half past four, and doan be late, because her father does reach home five o'clock on a Friday. She say he would surely run me outa there, because he doan want no fellas come warming up he chairs. Her mother let me in, though. Nice lady, ain show me no bad-face. Put me siddown in the gallery and tell me Viola coming out just now.

"I wait. I wait. Nervous like hell. Every time I hear a sound in the road, I jump. I keep looking up and down the road. Looking at my watch. Sweating. And where the girl I come to pick up? Viola inside, dollsing up.

"Well, I didn know where he pass. I ain even hear he come in the yard, but all of a sudden, a man standing up in the door-mouth, watching me blue vex, like he ready to cuff-down somebody. Well, you know I make sure the somebody wasn go be me!"

And here the story veered off into fiction, as Ollie's stories often did. Puppa let out such a roar that Ollie – so he claimed – jumped clean over the bannister and didn't stop running until he'd found a safe hiding-place – the seminary – leaving Viola all dollsed-up in vain. Mumma added to the Ollie-story Puppa's version of the event.

"He say that from the road he see somebody in the gallery, so he pass through the side gate and come in the house through the back door. He go to the front door and see this skinny Potoguee boy siddown in the gallery, so he turn he head to call out to me, 'Estelle, who is this?' and betime he turn back to the gallery, the fella done disappear, clean outa sight!"

She said Puppa was haunted for days by this apparition – the skinny Potoguee boy who vanished from the gallery in one second and without a sound. (In years to come, when Ollie's size had doubled and tripled from what it was in those days, he was quite happy for the household to refer to him now and then as "the skinny Potoguee boy".)

And the fact was that a year or so after his encounter with Puppa, Ollie did actually renounce the world and enter the seminary. But that was nothing to do with Puppa. He and Viola had started going out together just a few days after Puppa frightened him away, and they went out as often as they pleased for that whole year. Puppa could not really get in their way, not with Mumma aiding and abetting the escapades of her daughters.

Ollie seeking to take the cloth was to do with pressure from his own father. The senior Mr Oliveira was pushing Ollie, not to be a priest, but to marry the nice Portuguese girl he had picked out for him. Viola did not seem overly upset as she broke the news that Ollie was going off to the seminary. Gwynneth was at a loss for words. "*Bondjé*, Viola!" she exclaimed, and could only sit gaping at her.

"Wha you go do?" Viola said with a shrug. "Man gone, man dey."

But in just over a year Ollie was out of the seminary, declaring that the air was too rare up on that mountain, and, furthermore, the food didn't agree with him. Viola provided the real story. Brother Jerome had called Ollie into his office one day to have a kindly chat with him. He told Ollie that the Brotherhood didn't think he had any vocation to be a priest, especially as they had found out he was writing letters to a girl (named Viola) and getting the seminary cook to dispatch them from the post office down in the village.

Ollie settled back into working in his father's drugstore and trying to get Viola to marry him.

"Married to your family?" she would say to him. "With my two eye wide open, I will leave my mother good house and put myself in a marabunta nest to get sting up? I good, thank you very much. I good right here where you see me – nobody to watch me cut-eye; nobody to gimme scorn..."

"But you know that is not how my family is," Ollie pleaded. "You still mixing up Portuguese people with them English and French-Creole people. We come from Madeira as ketch-ass people, Viola, and even if my father generation manage to climb out from the ketch-ass and today we could eat four square meals, we doan scorn nobody."

Ollie begged Gwynneth to talk to Viola on his behalf.

"Hm," Gwynneth responded. "I doan know that I could persuade anybody to get married, nuh, Ollie. I meself not exactly waiting and wishing for man to put me in house."

Then Ollie's father began dropping hints for him again. One day he put it bluntly. The bride he had lined up for him was now taken, but he had found another girl – almost as nice as the other one – who was available. She was going to be at the Portuguese Association's Christmas function with her parents...

Ollie's next refuge was the First World War. He lost no time in signing up for the British West India Regiment. His mother was distraught, and his father pleaded with him to join the private contingent being recruited by planters and merchants, rather than the public contingent that was the BWIR – if he absolutely must distress his family by going and putting himself in danger thousands of miles away from home.

"The planters' and merchants' contingent," his father argued, "might put you in the rank of officer, and that will mean you stand a chance of coming back home alive."

Ollie was not inclined to take up the option of joining what he called the All-White and Negrophobic Contingent. Fellas he had known since his primary school days in Morne Cabrite were enlisting in the BWIR – so he followed suit, and off he went to the war.

As it turned out, Ollie's family need not have worried too much about him getting killed in battle. When Ollie came home from the war, he had no tales of combat to tell, for he had seen no action on the battlefield. His war-stories were about digging latrine-holes and cleaning latrines; carrying heavy loads, like a beast of burden; washing the white soldiers' dirty bedding, and more. He had written to Viola from Egypt, where his battalion was parked:

> *We thought we coming here to fight as soldiers, but we are more like a band of criminals serving a sentence of hard labour. Our dearly beloved Mother Country will not send BWIR soldiers to fight the Germans, for, it seems, the British army thinks that putting black men to fight against white men would be a disrespect to the white men. So here we are, we "British citizens," not only doing the bull-work for the white British soldiers, but suffering the most shameful discrimination and bad treatment – getting lower pay than the white soldiers; living in quarters worse than any shanty town; eating food fit for dog, and swallowing insult for tea-breakfast-and-dinner…*

~

Now, another world war was on. Mumma was ailing, her "lagniappe" was in his mid-thirties and the navel-string still held, for Mumma, anyway; he remained the apple of her eye, through thick and thin. But when it came to helping her eat, spoonful by spoonful, sip by sip; giving her the tablets and the tisane; turning her in the bed on those days when she preferred to stay in bed; helping her bathe and change her clothes; combing her hair; washing her clothes and the sheets and the towels – it was the daughters who did all of that. Roy would now and then stay long enough to rub her legs, or her back, or sap her head with bay rum, but could not be called upon to do much more. Left to Roy,

Mumma wouldn't live to see her next birthday, far less a hundred and fifty years.

The more Mumma went down in age, the clearer it became to Gwynneth that she couldn't keep up the school *and* look after Mumma, *and* be chief-cook-and-bottle-washer in every Mothers' Union undertaking. She was also helping with choir practice – two Saturdays in every month. If Gwynneth wasn't there to play the organ, Mrs Knight insisted, the choir took a long time get into voice; then the younger members would start skylarking and in the end nothing was achieved. Every time Gwynneth hinted that somebody else could come out of their house on a Saturday afternoon and accompany choir practice now and then (for she was not the only living soul in St Hilda's congregation who knew how to play the organ), Mrs Knight would become a little sulky and almost wouldn't speak to her.

November would make it two years since St Hilda's Mothers' Union had given Gwynneth honorary membership, over the objections of Mrs Pierre, Mrs Gill, Mrs Inniss and Mrs Ferguson who all felt that Miss Cuffie should not be given such an honour because she had a *past*…

~

Gwynneth's thoughts drifted back to the evening when Earline came over to give her the score. Gwynneth listened with a wicked delight, picturing what Valda Pierre's face would look like if she could overhear Earline's report. She would have been most offended, for Earline translated what "Mistress Pierre" had said at the meeting into language that would never come out of Valda Pierre's hoity-toity mouth if she could help it.

"Mistress Pierre say doan forget what it was that woman did get sheself mix-up in. And furthermore the man didn good cold in he grave yet before she take up with a next rabb – gone in Kings Port and live with he, if you please! Some say she father did put she out. Then when she do get a decent man, was like casting pearls before swine. How she go appreciate a gentleman like that? Kobo cyaan eat sponge cake. She did done ain no spring-chicken already. But that woman so lucky. She coulda married this man and go up in England with he to see about he betime he studying but no, Mamzelle refuse. She ain want that, and what you expect, the man go and study and come back with white-wife, and Gwynneth Cuffie never get a husband.

"Everybody know Mothers' Union is for mothers, decent married ladies, not for any and everybody, Mistress Pierre say, and with that, she throw cut-eye for me, Janice and two-three others whay living in sin. And Mothers' Union is for *Anglican* ladies, she say. The woman is a Catholic. Gwynneth Cuffie never christen in a Anglican church. Then Mistress Knight put up she hand and say Mothers' Union is not for we to mauvay-lang one another. None of we in here could hold a candle to Gwynneth Cuffie, and I vote in favour of the motion. And Mistress Pierre say…"

Here Earline put on a hoity-toity face and voice: "Mistress Pierre say, 'Well, orm afraid orl have to vote against.'"

Gwynneth and Earline collapsed into a laughing fit, gasping for breath and wiping their eyes. Gwynneth laughing, but at the same time asking herself what nansi-story Valda Pierre giving people about her and Gaston? That old macco – always know everybody business or think she know. As for the "next rabb", clearly she didn't know anything about him, for had she known, that was something she would have been most happy to run her mouth with. Loyal, selfless Ainsley. Valda Pierre didn't know the half of it.

The same Valda Pierre, who had voted against letting Gwynneth into Mothers' Union, was nowadays throwing words for her that Mothers' Union falling away because Gwynneth Cuffie not pulling her weight. The gall of the woman. First you doan want Gwynneth Cuffie in you Mothers' Union; now, if Gwynneth not there, Mothers' Union cyaan do a thing? Look at the jumble sale in April month – a jumble of confusion, and whose fault? Gwynneth's. The same Good-Friday-bobolee Gwynneth, because she couldn't be there to help organise it from start to finish. And the latest charge: that she, Gwynneth, was the one to blame for the uproar in the July meeting that nearly mash up Mothers' Union for good…

A surge of dismay soured her insides. Phillip! She had not kept her promise to Phillip. Was no more than a fortnight after the meeting in July that Phillip turned up on her doorstep – the meeting that end-up in kangkalang over Valda Pierre and Esme

Gill and that cabal running they mouth on "badjohn boys" and "rabbs" in town beating iron, and what the authorities should do with them.

Now it was nearly September, school vacation coming to an end and she had not found the time to keep her promise. With the reopening of school she would have even less time. By now Phillip and the other boys must be thinking that she didn't really want anything to do with them. They would be well aware that some people bore ill will towards the iron bands, and they would have heard about what happened to the St Paul band. She must get a message to Phillip. She would have to go and hear them. She would have to make the time.

For the past two or three years Gwynneth had been singing a weary song: "Enough. This is the last. Next year, God-spare-life, I am closing down the school. Time to rest my bones and look for pension. These rambunctious little imps will kill me."

"Pension?" Viola would snort. "Better you look for husband! You have some years still before they will give you pension, so close down the school and do what until then – beg you bread by the side of the road?" (And to Ollie, Viola said, "Talk, pure talk. Only mouth. More they rambunctious, more she love them. Gwynneth wouldn know what to do with herself if she didn always have some lil imps round her to make her fret and cluck like Mother Hen. And is not she that thinking about starting a Cub Scout pack and a Brownie troop right inside here?")

Every year Gwynneth swore it would be the last, but every January first-day-of-school there would be a little crowd of women outside the front gate, each with a newly-scrubbed child, little girls with their hair tightly plaited and be-ribboned, little boys shorn almost to baldness, tender faces upturned and shining with coconut oil. They waited patiently for Teach to appear in the gallery. She would look out, sigh (unconvincingly), and direct them to the side gate on Wilson Trace that opened into the backyard.

3
GIVE THE BOYS A CHANCE

It was in June 1939 that Gwynneth had first heard an iron band. She had gone to town for the celebration of Ainsley's fiftieth birthday – Ainsley, her comrade-in-arms, a stalwart of Moun Demmeh. It was he and Pelham who had been the safe haven for her recovery after the nightmare of late November 1919. She had lived with them, lived on their kindness and their care, for almost eight months, right there in the house on Bedeau Lane, Morne Cabrite, until she moved into the room on Catherine Street. For the birthday celebration, Pelham had organised Sunday lunch as a Dutch party. The guests were sworn not to say a word about it to Ainsley, for it was to be a surprise.

Ainsley, none the wiser, cooked lunch for three – Pelham, himself, and his godmother – as he would on any other Sunday. When he was almost done, just cleaning watercress to add to the salad, friends began to stream in bearing food and drink. Before long, every inch of the table was covered with bowls, bottles, little mountains of fruit… till they had to clear off the sideboard, the centre table, and the kitchen counter, to make space for the overflow. The company piled their plates high and sat all over the place to eat – the drawing-room, the gallery, the front steps. Some carried chairs and stools outdoors and settled all over the yard, some under the mango tree at the back. Others readily sat down on the bare concrete paving that skirted the house.

They had finished eating, and, with glasses in their hands, were talking in little knots inside and around the house, when a hush came over the front yard. It travelled up the front steps, through the gallery and into the house. All talking stopped and people looked quizzically at each other. Gwynneth was in the gallery, so she was among the first to catch the intriguing sound in the air that had put an end to conversation. It seemed to be coming nearer. She cocked her ear. Metal. A contagious polyrhythmic sound, beaten out on metal. Plenty of metal, not somebody in the road Jouvay morning beating on a pitch-oil pan or a milk tin in between the tamboo bamboo…

~

In their house, Jouvay was forbidden fruit. Gwynneth was nine years old, Viola was eight, and they were living in Coryal. Rousing noises in the road – tamboo bamboo and tin pans, lusty singing, chanting, shouting. Groups of people on the move, adults and children dancing their way through the village, some dressed in ragged clothes or crocus bags; a man wearing a big panty over his trousers and a po-chamb on his head; others dressed up as the governor, or his wife, or some other lofty personage. And you knew what was coming when you heard the chanting: "Look the Devil dey!" or "Pay the Devil!" or "Jab molassi! Look one dey!"

Gwynneth and Viola were as fascinated by the molasses devil as they were afraid of him, even watching from the safety of their bedroom. They stayed in a half-crouching position, their eyes at the level of the windowsill, ducking every time he cracked his whip, until he and the little imps chained to his waist had moved past the house, he dancing scandalously to the rhythm that one of his imps was beating on a pitch-oil pan…

Puppa had laid down the law years before, while they were living in Morain: on a Jouvay morning they were not to even look outside. That, of course, was too much to ask of them. This heady ruction started in the fore-day morning half-dark, while decent people, according to Puppa, were still in their beds, so Gwynneth and Viola could risk peeping out from their bedroom window, ready to dart back into their beds if they thought they heard Puppa stirring.

The two of them looked on with envy as other children got to dance and parade in the road, beating on powdered-milk tins with sticks, knocking bamboo on the ground, and singing as boisterously as their big-people. A wistfulness would come over Gwynneth as she gazed at these lucky children her age and younger, who held in their heads all the words of these songs, and were free to be belting them out to their hearts' content. She felt that these children owned something from which she was unjustly barred; indeed, they were owners of a whole world she wished she could fully enter, because no matter what Puppa said, she was convinced that it was hers, too.

On Jouvay mornings children would call at the gate, hoping for someone to come out and give them money. That Jouvay morning Gwynneth stood at the window with three farthings and a cent – her savings – clasped in her fist, and a terrible pounding in her chest. She had made up her mind to dash out and give the coins to the first set of children to come to the gate. Viola nearly suffered a stroke as Gwynneth informed her of the plan and then in the next minute abruptly left her side, announcing, "I going and give them."

Viola sank to the floor, stuck her fingers in her ears, and closed her eyes. Time seemed to stop. She was just about to pass out from not breathing, when Gwynneth hurtled back into the room and flopped down next to her. The two of them stayed stock still for a while, fearing that Puppa might have heard Gwynneth's movements; but he did not stir. Gwynneth was triumphant.

After Puppa got up on a Jouvay morning they could do no more than sit and listen to the tempting sounds outside. Puppa always kept the front door closed until Jouvay died down under the mid-morning hot-sun...

~

Now what was coming up the lane towards Ainsley's house sounded like a substantial collection of metal, keeping up a steady beat.

At first there was nothing and nobody to be seen, up the lane or down. There was only this sound approaching. A jubilant, cheeky sound, the likes of which she had never heard before. It was getting closer and closer, until, down the lane, a posse of youths suddenly burst into view from behind the bend. Young men and boys. A dozen or more of them. Now, along with the rhythm of sticks beating on metal, you could hear singing:

> *Pwizonnè lévé*
> *Mété limyè bay*
> *Congo Barra*

For Gwynneth it was a most exciting moment, never to be

forgotten. She had heard about this thing that happened at Carnival, just months before – the band of young men who had come out onto the road making their rhythm with scrap metal only, no bamboo, and the excited crowd that had followed them, growing larger and larger as it made its way jumping-up through Kings Port. The men had not only tin pans, but also pieces of iron and steel, bedposts, all kinds of things made out of metal. Their band was the talk of the Carnival.

Since then, there had been reports of other such bands sprouting here and there in the town. Truth be told, she had heard that some of the metal they were using wasn't scrap, but people's good buckets and dustbin covers that disappeared out of their yards overnight. Some of the burgesses of Kings Port, including the police, did not take kindly to the young fellows forming these bands, and no doubt there were some lawless ones among them. Gwynneth's view of the matter was that if indeed badjohns were turning into makers of music, then everyone should be happy.

The company inside Ainsley's house moved to the gallery and front steps, while those outside converged at the front of the yard. Some went out into the road to get a better view, but had to make way when they realised that the group was heading purposefully towards Ainsley's gate. Ainsley stood among the guests in the gallery, scratching his head in bemused awe as these boys and their music streamed into his yard. Under Pelham's direction, the band filled up the space on one side of the steps.

At close quarters, now, Gwynneth could see that in addition to metal objects such as a biscuit pan, a pot cover, a bucket, and what seemed to be parts from motorcars or heavy machinery, they were also using ordinary Cayerian instruments: bamboo, bottle-and-spoon, scratchers, and shac-shacs.

Ainsley's guests danced and joined in the singing, which went from Shango praise songs to sankeys to calypsos. (Because there were children present, they had to stick to clean calypsos, or calypsos whose bawdiness was artfully disguised). Some of the guests went to the kitchen and took up spoons to beat on bottles. One woman took a comb out of her handbag, got silver paper from somebody's cigarette packet and folded it over the comb to make a mouth organ. Neighbours collected in the road for a jump-up. After a while Pelham had to call intermission so that the band could get something to eat and drink.

Party guests relinquished the front steps and their seats in the front yard to the band members. Gwynneth helped with serving them, and then she sat in their midst to engage them in conversation. She found out that the name of the band was "Squadron 7", and that Franklin was the leader. On that day, Gwynneth set herself the task of finding out more about this music.

Ainsley and Pelham arranged for her to meet with Franklin at their home one Saturday. As she sat and talked with him in the gallery, she became even more convinced that what these boys were doing was not to be taken lightly. Franklin invited her to visit his band, and offered to introduce her to other iron bands around the town, in LaCour Danglade, Bourg Ravine, Jericho, and Rat Hole. Although she did not know how she was going to find the time, Gwynneth was quite excited at the thought of these visits. She would be giving life once more to the "cultural reconnoitre" that she and her colleagues in Moun Demmeh had embarked upon twenty years before.

Before the plan to visit town bands could materialise, however, Gwynneth would again find herself right in the middle of an iron band, this time closer to home. Bernice Callender, whom she had taught at St Paul Government School many moons before, asked her to stay for her baby. Gwynneth already had more godchildren than she could count, Viola observed. "Anglican godchildren, Catholic, Presbyterian, Shouter Baptist godchildren, and even a Hindu one."

Five babies were christened that day, early in the new year, 1940, at St Paul Anglican Church, amid a chorus of squalling at the font, as all had lain fidgeting and protesting on their mothers' or godmothers' laps for the whole Sunday morning service, dressed in fussy clothes that chafed, or itched, or made them feel hot.

When they got back to Bernice's home, Gwynneth took the baby, Garnet Adolphus Christopher Oliver, still much displeased and making it known, and stripped him down to vest and diaper.

Immediately he became a gurgling, congenial little butterball, more taken up with Gwynneth's spectacles than with the festivities going on all around him and all because of him.

And there, once again, the festivities included an iron band. This one was called the St Paul Syncopators. They played outside, in a basic ajoupa put up for the occasion – just bamboo poles and the top covered with coconut branches. Gwynneth couldn't resist the sound. She went to the gallery, where some guests sat looking out on the band, and took a seat with the baby on her lap. Other guests had taken up vantage points around the shed to get closer. When one of Garnet's aunts took him to feed him, Gwynneth made her way out into the yard and went to sit inside the joupa with the band.

The floor of the joupa was dirt, softish from a recent shower of rain, so they had placed a flat stone on the ground for a youth to thump the bamboo on. Two other boys were clinking spoons on gin bottles with water in them. The boy beating a short metal rod on what he told her was the brake hub from a motorcar wheel, allowed her to take a turn on it. Gwynneth immersed herself in their music, their enthusiasm and their energy, clapped and sang, and called out her encouragement.

She chatted with them when they stopped for refreshments, and learned that even though some people showed them bad-face and the police were giving them a hard time, they were getting invitations to play at parties and other functions. They had even played on a bus excursion to Diamond Beach. The boys were eagerly looking forward to playing on the road for Carnival, which, at the time, was not too far off. And just like Franklin, these youngsters in St Paul spoke about their iron band with a glowing passion, as though some irrepressible fire had been lit within them.

As Gwynneth headed back into the house, a man standing in the gallery spoke to her in an ominous whisper: "Two of those boys have court cases coming up, you know."

"All right," Gwynneth said, and continued on her way into the house to see what Garnet was up to.

~

Had anything like this iron band phenomenon emerged in the

days before Johnstone and company left Moun Demmeh, Gwynneth mused, it would surely have produced one more brawl on David's veranda. Most members of the group would have warmly welcomed the new, home-grown music, but she could picture Johnstone and his supporters recoiling from it in disdain.

Months after Garnet's christening, that brawl did take place, but not on David's veranda. Moun Demmeh was long gone – banned and disbanded. It happened at a Mothers' Union meeting in July 1940, where she had a run-in with Valda Pierre and company on the topic of iron bands. That meeting threw her back more than twenty years, to the arguments that had flared up from time to time in Moun Demmeh meetings. Especially the one in June 1918 where she suggested that name for the group. Her suggestion touched off a serious quarrel, and some of the members never came back: the ones who had looked aghast, or fixed their faces into a sneer before they made their views known.

"Hog language," said one. "Glorifying backwardness," said another. And Augustus L. T. Johnstone, the writer of bad sonnets, delivered a speech.

In their discussions, Johnstone always got up from his seat to speak even a sentence, as though he was in school. Among the group he was considered "old". They didn't know his exact age, but most of the other members were in their twenties and thirties, from where any number beyond the forties seemed like well over the hill. To Gwynneth, Johnstone and his clothes *looked* musty. He wore a jacket that had seen better days, and once-white shirts with wrinkled collars. She could not remember ever seeing him take his jacket off, not once, not even on those days when the cooling breeze on David's veranda gave way to a hot, hanging stillness.

"Ladies and gentlemen," he said, clearing his throat. "Are we serious, or are we not? Are we for the upliftment of this colony, or are we not? If we are, then we cannot look down into the pit of ignorance to find a name that befits our standing and our noble purpose."

There were groans of despair as Johnstone began the drill of lifting himself onto his toes after every few words – a bad sign. It meant that he was revving up for a flight of pompous oratory and it was going to be a task to get him to just say his piece and sit down. At some point they were going to have to pull him down. The opportunity presented itself sooner than expected.

"The goodly lady has put an idea to us," Johnstone lectured on. "The idea is to call ourselves 'tomorrow's people', but in Patois? Ladies and gentlemen, let us not lower ourselves. Patois is the language of ignorant people, Miss Cuffie, people who did not go to school. And you a big teacher."

Gwynneth flew at him. "Foolishness! You just *have* to come with some dotish talk, eh? And I done tell you already: take meh name out you mouth!" Then, in a low grumble, "Damn old jumbie."

Johnstone looked towards David: "Did you hear what she just called me?"

(Looking back and remembering this exchange with Johnstone that took place when she was 30, Gwynneth cringed with embarrassment at her own words.) David intervened, trying to look appalled while visibly fighting down a grin as he sought to rescue Gwynneth's victim. "Ladies and gentlemen! Comrades! Let's keep it friendly, please. Gus, you have two more minutes."

"Your idea is not a bad one, Miss Cuffie," Johnstone continued, "if we translate it into proper French, or, better still, Latin! That would be a fitting name for a group of intellectuals looking to the future, not some uncivilised illiterates from a barrack-yard."

Johnstone's speech was cut short by the indignant howls that came from most of the people present, but he and some others failed to see what could possibly be so wrong with his comment. Bedlam ensued, with exclamations of "Take that back!" or, "Insulting!" or, "Apologise!" or, "Snob!" and even "House-slave!" and "Uncle Tom!"

Others asked, in puzzlement, "Something wrong with what he said?" or, "What's the problem?" or challenged hotly: "So those people are not illiterate?" and, "Truth is truth!" and, "*Of course* 'uncivilised' goes with 'illiterate'!" and, "That's just calling a spade a spade," and so forth.

The quarrel blazed for quite some time.

During the uproar, it became clear to Gwynneth that people had forgotten what it was they were arguing about. The name was no longer the main point of dispute. There was more in the mortar than the pestle. This quarrel was really a continuation of the one that had erupted two or three months earlier around da Silva's article on the size of black people's brains, published in the magazine of Phaedrus Literary and Debating Club. For the sake of peace, the topic had not been touched since, at least not in a meeting. This quarrel, therefore, was not only about the Patois name that she had just thrown into their midst.

David calmed them down. He brought the meeting to order and put Gwynneth's suggestion to the vote. Eleven people voted Yes with a show of hands and by the next meeting it was clear that some of the others had voted with their feet, never to grace David's veranda again. Those were the members whom the rest of the group had been referring to as "The Johnstone cabal", but only behind their backs. Johnstone, however, had never put water in his mouth to call his adversaries, in their presence, "Bolsheviks", and "rowdies", and "Philistines".

The name stuck: Moun Demmeh Social and Cultural Society. "Purgative" was the word David used afterwards to describe this quarrel. It was the end of tiptoeing around the question of who they were, what they were about.

~

Now, twenty-something years later, she had stirred up the same consternation and raging war of words by suggesting to St Hilda's Anglican Church Mothers' Union that they invite the iron band from St Paul to play at the Harvest Fair. Afterwards, when Gwynneth told Mumma about the contention in the meeting, she steupsed and asked drily what Gwynneth was doing still up under that cabal of *poto légliz*. Churchposts. Pharisees. "And you working youself to death for them. Let they make they Harvest for theyself."

But not all the members were against the suggestion. From the beginning of the dispute there were many who, provided they were not in Valda Pierre's direct line of vision, nodded in agreement with Gwynneth, and with Mrs Knight and others who found that inviting the band was a good idea.

For a while all you could hear was Valda Pierre's imperious voice, shrilly assisted by her chorus – Esme Gill, Gertrude Inniss and Audrey Ferguson – for in St Hilda's Mothers' Union, when Valda Pierre spoke, no dog was expected to bark anything different. Mrs Pierre had not quite got over Gwynneth's being in Mothers' Union, and worse, expressing opinions not shared by Mrs Pierre, so, as often happened, she responded to Gwynneth by speaking as though Gwynneth wasn't there. "Of course Miss Cuffie wouldn't see anything wrong with bringing some young blackguards in among decent people. Not me and those vagabonds. They always in trouble with the police."

"You mean the police always troubling them," Gwynneth remarked. "Making music is not breaking the law. They outside the law because the law cast them out, just like the Shouters. Sometimes when you hear 'badjohn behaviour', is just young men standing up for the right to make their music."

Gwynneth was startled by a little burst of applause, muted and short-lived because Valda Pierre beamed a scowl around the group.

"Hmph," said Mrs Pierre. "Music? You call that 'music'? No tune, just knocking old-iron, making noise… Taking dustbin to say they making music. What good music could come out of a nasty dustbin?"

"You ever hear a iron band, Mrs Pierre?" Gwynneth asked, in a sugary voice.

"Me? Why I would want to hear that?"

"Oho! So you just talking from hearsay. Let me tell you. An iron band is a rhythm band, beating sweet, sweet rhythms for people to sing and dance to. Like tamboo bamboo." Gwynneth cocked her head to one side, mischievously: "You know tamboo bamboo, Mrs Pierre?"

Mrs Pierre opened her mouth to say something, but Gwynneth raised her voice slightly to discourage her from interrupting, looked her straight in the eye, and continued. (Valda Pierre's back-up singers were no use to her at this point, unwilling to engage when it came to a one-on-one verbal contest with Gwynneth Cuffie.)

"Doan worry – they say some of the young men looking to

make notes on the iron, now, Mrs Pierre! One day they'll be able to play any tune you want, on that same 'old-iron' you talking about. But even after that, we will still have bands that make pure rhythm. We always had rhythm bands, with all kinda drum – skin-drum, tamboo bamboo, pitch-oil pan – and we will always have rhythm bands, long after you and me dead and gone, Mrs Pierre. That's the African in us."

Gwynneth smiled smugly with this last remark, relishing the sting it would give Valda Pierre.

Mrs Pierre screwed up her face and mumbled something about "Garveyite foolishness", not quite under her breath. "And who is 'us'?" she asked out loud. "Who here born in Africa? Instead of we thank God for bringing our forefathers out of there so we could better ourself, you-all want us to be 'African'? All who encouraging those young men in their wotlessness, they will regret it. No ambition. Negro people have no ambition. You see any high-colour boys in that? No! Is only black-hen chicken. Wait till you see those warahoons in St Paul start breaking bottle to stab one another, like the ones in town."

Valda Pierre continued to hold court, until some of the women began to object, politely at first.

"Mistress Pierre," Earline ventured. "That not nice, Mistress Pierre. How you could be washing you mouth on poorpeople chirren so, calling them all kinda 'rabb' and 'ruffian' and 'hooligan' and 'dregs'? Janice! Stand up for you godchild!"

Janice was only too happy to offer Mistress Pierre a piece of her mind on behalf of her godson Mervyn, who was a member of St Paul Syncopators iron band.

"Yes!" She scowled at Valda Pierre. "My godson ain no vagabond, you hear? He's a decent youngboy who does respect everybody, so you will please to respect him, and mind how you talk about people chirren – like they is rubbish in the road."

What had started as a low, brooding murmur was giving way to sharply raised voices.

"My sister in town have two sons playing in a iron band," Gemma Bobb informed Mrs Pierre, wagging a finger in the air, "and nobody ain have no right to talk about my nephews like that!"

There was loud agreement.

Gwynneth joined in the counterattack: "'Warahoons', Mrs Pierre? In between all those insulting names, you putting in 'warahoons'? I am disappointed in you, Mrs Pierre. You are an educated woman, and you think 'warahoon' means 'hooligan', and 'ruffian' and such? Doan get tie-up, Mrs Pierre. If you calling the boys 'warahoons', you actually complimenting them. The Warahoons are the most peaceful people you could think about. I doan know where Cayerians get this idea that they wild and they aggressive. Those people used to just come over from the Main in they canoe, trade they fish, and they hammock, and they basket and thing, and go back. They never trouble a soul. Nothing ruffian or hooligan about them, Mrs Pierre."

The lecture was lost on the group of offended women (who very likely called their children "warahoons" when they misbehaved) for those women were, at that moment, otherwise engaged, gesticulating to each other as they railed about the faasness of Mrs Pierre. Then Earline and Octavia and some others stood up and stayed on their feet, the better to let Mistress Pierre know just where to get off. By this time Valda Pierre's voice could no longer be heard above the din, and she had to give up trying to be chairman of the meeting. She put her handbag on her lap and sat clutching it.

Earline's voice rose above the rest: "Okay, Mothers' Union! So we want to bring the iron band in Harvest Fair?"

There was cheering. Earline conducted a vote, assisted by Mrs Knight, and Mothers' Union voted in favour of inviting St Paul Syncopators to perform in the Harvest Fair concert.

Suddenly, Valda Pierre's voice, cold with offended dignity, "So who is in charge of the Harvest Fair committee?"

A brief silence in the room before Earline answered, "Well, *you*, Mistress Pierre!"

Mistress Pierre was, indeed, the automatic and undisputed overseer of everything to do with Harvest Fair, the grandest event on the calendar of Mothers' Union at St Hilda's.

"Well," retorted Valda Pierre, "you-all will have to find somebody else to take on this task. I will not be available this year."

A moment of silence in the room once more. Then a burst of

agitated voices, people again addressing their commentaries to each other, all at the same time; and again, emerging bell-clear out of the din, Earline's voice: "The best person to put is Mistress Knight."

Gwynneth raised her hand and said, "I second that motion." Most of the gathering applauded. For as far back as anybody could remember, Mrs Knight had been in charge of entertainment for Harvest Fair; but everyone knew that Valda Pierre had been dumping much more responsibility on Mrs Knight for the running of the event than entertainment alone. The whole meeting was now looking at Mrs Knight.

"What you say, Mistress Knight?" Earline prodded.

"Yes, I don't mind," Mrs Knight answered. "But there may be others willing to chair the committee. You should find out, and then put it to a vote."

Everybody looked around the room, but there were no other candidates, and the meeting voted to appoint Mrs Knight head of the Harvest Fair committee.

Mothers' Union sent a message to St Paul Syncopators via Janice's godson, but what came back to them was disappointing news. The St Paul police had so harassed and hounded the boys over the past few weeks that their band was no more. The last straw was when a party of officers, batons in the air, cornered them behind the pavilion in the savannah, and rained blows on anybody who didn't manage to slip through their hands and run.

Gwynneth was incensed by this report. She had not sent a letter to the newspapers for quite a while, but now she lost no time in writing to both *The Kings Port Sentinel* and *The Listener* (*The Voice* had gone under by then). Her letter condemned the folly of police persecuting young men and boys who, for all who had eyes to see and ears to hear, were clearly bringing forth an important invention. In time to come, her letter warned, the persecutors would have to turn around and pay tribute to these young pioneers. She quoted Psalm 118:22, "The stone which the builders rejected is become the cornerstone." When would there be an end to the dishonouring of everything created by black Cayerians?

~

David used to tease her about the pseudonym she had chosen

when, in 1916, the group decided on the strategy of letter-writing campaigns. It was Sylvia's idea. "Revolution is fought not only with marches and guns," she reminded them, "but also with words that change minds." They would write individual letters to the newspapers on an agreed issue, within a set period, in the hope that some of their letters, or even just one, might appear in the press, injecting their view into the public discussion on that particular issue.

This was in the early days, when they were still a group of like-minded people. Then they were joined by people who had a different view, or none at all, on matters that were of deep concern to the original gathering on David's veranda. The new people labelled such matters "too political". They were more interested, they said, in "cultural progress". The original members, however, had continued, undeterred, on their letter-writing thrust. The government employees among them had taken pseudonyms. Gwynneth's choice was "The Pen is Mightier", which got her nowhere, barely one in five of her letters carried in the Press (not that the other members had any better luck). David began to joke about changing her pseudonym. "What about if you turn your fuming pen into a flaming sword?"

And when she started signing her letters "Flaming Sword", both *The Voice* and *The Kings Port Sentinel* had printed more of them.

"You see!" David commented. "And bet your bottom dollar the editors think 'Flaming Sword' is a man, a white man, and a expatriate at that. So even if he putting out radical ideas, that's okay, man. Is just eccentric he eccentric – charmingly eccentric. No danger to peace in the colony."

She dropped the alias when, in 1922, she started writing letters to the newspapers again. By then she was no longer teaching in the government system, so there was no need to be hiding behind an imaginary person.

~

In the years since then, her success at getting letters into the papers was as variable as that of any other letter-writer who was seen as challenging the existing order. That is to say, most of her letters did not get published. She had laid off writing to the press because she had less time, now, for wasted effort. She was therefore pleasantly surprised when she leafed through *The Kings Port Sentinel* of August 25th, 1940, and discovered that they had not only printed her letter about the treatment of iron bands, but in response to her letter they had devoted the day's editorial to the same topic, with the headline **GIVE THE BOYS A CHANCE.** Even if their support, which they extended only to "the law-abiding members of the iron bands", was rather grudging, and the editorial gave an inordinate amount of space to condemning "the criminals among them", the writer did suggest that, like the Boy Scouts and the Cadet Corps, the iron bands could, perhaps, help keep these young men from getting into trouble.

The new music should be given a chance, the editorial argued, but these boys, coming as they did from the lowest stratum of the society, would need to be supervised with a strong arm. Many had no fathers, and when the father is not present in the home, there is no moral guidance. ("Damn foolishness," Gwynneth said aloud, to no one. She was reading the newspaper in the gallery, all by herself. "So women are incapable of giving moral guidance, and every man on Earth is a shining moral guide?")

The editorial recommended that retired schoolmasters, policemen, Boy Scout masters, and officers of the Cadet Corps step forward, take charge of these bands, and guide them in the right direction, the path of God-fearing honesty, industriousness, and respect for authority.

Gwynneth decided to be just amused by the recommendation, and to be thankful for the small mercy tucked away in this editorial – the voice of the ruling class acknowledging that there might be some value in the iron band phenomenon. She could hear David, all those years before, egging her on: "Go brave, Gwynneth. If *one* of your letters changes *one* mind, that's a crack in the wall of Jericho. We know that in the long run, the pen *is* mightier than the sword."

4
"Culture? What culture?"

Moun Demmeh's letter-writing project of 1916 never properly got off the ground. They continued to submit letters to the newspapers, while they also tried to get a regular newspaper column. They first approached *The Voice*, which some people saw as the more broad-minded of the two. *The Voice* seemed to give the request some thought before declining; and *The Kings Port Sentinel* refused without delay. Early in 1917 they came to the conclusion that their best course would be to start a periodical of their own.

At first they named their publication, rather pompously, *The Cayerian Quarterly Review*. As it turned out, "quarterly" denoted intention rather than achievement, for it was clear, after their experience with the first issue, that their review was likely to come out not every three months, but whenever they could muster the funds for printing. They had scrounged around for advertisements to pay the printer's bill, but did not have much luck. The first issue, which was due to come out in the third quarter of 1917, did not see the light of day until the end of December – renamed *The Cayerian Review*. They had given up on their quest for advertisements to fund that issue. Instead, they pooled their personal funds for the printing bill. Johnstone forked out the largest donation, for which they had to let him put in four of his awful poems, taking up almost a whole page.

When the issue was printed, they each took a batch and fanned out, some to place copies in shops and parlours along the Eastern Main Road, others going south along Grand Chemin. They would walk as far as their feet could carry them, take the bus or train back, and then come out another day to cover a further two miles or so. Ainsley and others living in town were able to place copies in some of the stores lining the downtown blocks of James, Albert, and King George Streets, but had more success with humbler establishments like parlours and street vendors stalls. Some members took the *Review* to whatever market they went to on the weekend and

44

persuaded their pwatik, and any other vendors there with whom they had a good relationship, to take a little pile and put a stone, a yam, or a shaddock on it to secure it from the wind.

Some of the shopkeepers scrutinised the contents with a suspicious eye before agreeing to take copies, and one or two asked outright whether it was something that would bring the police down on them. A few of them raised their eyebrows at the editorial, headlined **A CALL FOR REPRESENTATIVE GOVERN-MENT**; but Johnstone's verses, prettily rhyming about nothing at all, seemed harmless enough to win their trust.

Ravi and Kenrick went to place some copies at Capitan's Dry Goods, Rest. and Bar, an establishment on the Eastern Main Road where members of the group often went after their meetings. Capitan readily took a batch. As they lingered over a drink, they told him their tale of woe, how they had gone to Rostant's, Cumberland's, Agostini's, D'Abadie's, Humfrey's, and others, asking for advertisements, and had come away empty-handed. Capitan looked at them reproachfully. "So allyou did only want the big-shot businessman and them money. Capitan money ain good enough?"

Ravi and Kenrick apologised profusely, embarrassed that the group had not thought to approach small business owners like him. The second issue was funded by money collected from sales of the first one (not a staggering haul, at 6 cents per copy, with a commission going to the seller); a contribution from members; and a proud announcement advertising Capitan's Dry Goods, Rest. and Bar. They managed to bring out that issue in April 1918, and already Bharath's Drugstore had pledged an advertisement for Addison's Tooth Powder, a new brand on the market, to support the third issue.

Members of the group were chatting casually while they waited for others to arrive, so the meeting of May 1918 had not yet started when the impromptu discussion arose – on culture. Rawle expressed the view that the culture of Cayeri needed to be made visible to the Cayerian people, so that they would recognise the forest made up by the one-one trees of their daily living. If Cayerians could not see their culture, he said, it could actually disappear before it had any chance of coming into its own.

Johnstone guffawed and asked, "Culture? What culture?"

Completely ignoring him (or seeming to), Rawle continued: "How does a people learn what their culture is? I mean, in a conscious way. A person grows up participating in a culture and learns it mainly by just absorbing it – like osmosis. But that is 'knowing' in an almost subconscious way; and that is where it ends with us Cayerians. We don't think that we have a culture. Ours is not a culture that knows itself, and therefore cannot appreciate itself. If you say to a Cayerian 'Tell me about your culture', you are likely to get the response that our resident wiseman just gave us: 'Culture? What culture?'"

Johnstone was offended by the comment and the laughter it produced; but he only scowled, holding his tongue.

"How does a people learn what their culture is? School plays a part, surely?" someone said.

"And family?" someone else suggested. "Children gain some awareness of their culture from school – but that is not the experience of Cayerians. Long before the institution known as 'school' became part of human civilisation, there was family."

"And religious leaders," Sunil added, "shaman, imam, pundit, priest…"

"And then there is anthropology, of course," Gwynneth said. "But anthropology is not often fed back to the people that it studies. I think that one very important way that people get to see their culture is through their stories – a people's own, home-grown stories about themselves. In the beginning, stories were handed down by word of mouth, in storytelling, songs, proverbs, and so on. Today it's written literature, and movies, and plays…"

"Yes!" Sylvia agreed. "And that is why we, living thousands of miles from Britain, can see the way of life of the British more clearly than we see our own, and have more respect for their way of life than for our own. We are brought up on their stories – their fairy tales, nursery rhymes, novels, plays…"

"So much so that we actually believe we're British! 'Children of the Empire…' we sing lustily at school."

"And it's also us we're singing about when we sing: 'Britons never, never, never shall be slaves'!"

This was met with wry chuckles.

"Anybody here ever learn any Cayerian songs in school?" Sylvia asked.

People looked around the gathering at each other, shaking their heads.

"The two-three Cayerian songs I know," somebody said, "was my granny I learn them from."

Others nodded.

"So, in school we're taught traditional English, Scottish and Irish songs, yes, but nothing of our own," Sylvia pointed out.

"Because we think we are nothing." Gwynneth was shaking her head as she spoke. "Back to Rawle's point – we do not think that there is any such thing as a Cayerian culture. Or, we do not think that what we have is of any worth. Better to adopt what is presented to us by our superiors. In every field, we need to find out about ourselves; and on the matter of songs, we should consider putting together a Cayerian songbook. That is something we can do – gather what we can find of our own heritage of song, to help ground our children in their own reality. That does not mean parting with the songs of other peoples; it just means that Cayerians must know their own, too. Indeed, Cayerian children should also be learning some songs of their ancestors across the ocean – songs of Africa and India."

"Meanwhile, what literature has come out of Cayeri?" David asked. "Decorative drivel about our 'azure sea' and 'balmy zephyr's breath' – imitating the exotic view of our reality. Monkey see, monkey do. *Makak wè, makak fè.* That kind of writing will not help us find ourselves.

"Where is the great novelist, playwright, or poet of this colony who will choose to look inwards and write from within Cayerian life? That writer may well be sitting among us. But while we wait for the man or woman who will write that story in which we can recognise ourselves – and others will surely be emboldened to follow – there's more than one way to chart the forest. What if we became our own, home-made anthropologists? What if our group were to go on a… something like a… reconnoitre… a *cultural reconnoitre*? Eh?"

This idea took over the meeting. The agenda, which included the long-deferred naming of the group, was abandoned, and the meeting became one of those discussions that went on so late that David felt the need to put a one-pot on the fire – pelau, or oildown, or sancoche – so that they could be fed. That evening it was oildown; Gwynneth would never forget. After more than twenty years her mind still held on to some of the most ordinary things that David had said and done in that period, and especially that Sunday evening.

The group was meeting, as usual, on the spacious back veranda of David's family home, quite possibly the largest space in the house. At the front of the building was a little dolly-house gallery, and the drawing-cum-dining-room was also dolly-house in size, compared to the veranda, where David's parents often ate, and entertained guests.

While someone else was speaking, she saw David lean over and confer briefly with Ainsley, who got up and went into the kitchen. Then David headed towards the side steps, motioning Gwynneth to come with him. They went out into the failing light. In the yard David took the long, skinny bamboo rod with the cocoa-knife at the top and jabbed at the stems of two or three breadfruit. Each fell heavily to the ground and lay still. Then he directed the rod to another one, but when it fell it rolled down the little incline into some bush. He did not pursue it. "Oh, well," he murmured. "That one is for the spirits."

Gwynneth was in the kitchen garden nearby, picking seasoning. Then she went to the dasheen patch and broke off some tender leaves with their stalks. On their way back into the house they crossed Johnstone coming down the sidesteps in something of a huff. He raised his hand in an irritated gesture of goodbye, made his way around to the front of the house, and left.

In the kitchen the saltfish was boiling on the stove. Ainsley was pounding garlic with the grinding stones that Gwynneth and David had picked up at the river-mouth on Tucupita beach. The round one – almost a perfect sphere, just a little bit lopsided – was dark grey. The other one, the slab, was a lighter grey, criss-crossed with white streaks. It was about an inch thick, with one flat surface and the other slightly sunken. The sink in its middle made that side of the slab a perfect cradle for the round stone, and ensured that the garlic (or whatever you were pounding) was restrained, to some extent, from flying all over the place.

There was a little heap of coconuts, already husked, in a corner of the kitchen. David took two outside to crack the shells, while Ainsley and Gwynneth peeled and cut up the breadfruit. David began the task of grating the coconuts. Gwynneth left Ainsley to deal with the seasoning, and took turns with David on the grater. All this could have been yesterday, so vivid was it in her mind's eye.

The three of them soon got the big iron-pot of oildown going. They left it on a low fire and rejoined the discussion on the veranda, where they discovered that some other members had excused themselves and left. They were all Johnstone's people, and they had been notably quiet in this meeting, except for Johnstone's contemptuous guffaw and brief admonition: "Hm. A nameless group putting out a review, and now, still nameless, embarking on yet another project. Hm."

By the end of the evening, those who remained had come up with a plan to go and sit with people, learn from them, and inventory Cayerian proverbs, Anansi stories, tales of *Konpè Lapen* alias Brer Rabbit, songs, dances, musical instruments, Carnival traditions, food, hairdressing, medicine, religions, languages, patterns of family, and more. These were things that nobody learned about in school. Indeed, for Cayerians, school was where one went to have such habits scrubbed off one's person. They would begin the project by drawing on the knowledge of the older people in their own families.

The Moun Demmeh meeting of the following month, June 1918, at which Johnstone and his troops turned out in full force, was the one in which members had clashed over the naming of the group. This meeting had also led to part of the group walking out, this time, for good. Gwynneth, David and others speculated afterwards that Johnstone's people had all come out because they knew the naming could not reasonably be postponed again. That agenda item would have to be tackled this time; everyone understood the shaping power ("the obeah," David said), that lay in a name. Instinctively everyone had been dodging the discussion to choose a name. They knew it would be a sure road to contention, and there had been too much of that already. But there was no escaping it.

Johnstone had, at the ready, a whole list of possible names for the group. Someone suggested that nobody should be allowed to present more than one name, and this ruling was passed by a show of hands. Johnstone therefore distributed some of the names to his troops for presentation. Each name would be discussed and voted on, until the list was whittled down to one name. All of Johnstone's suggested names were thrown out without much discussion. (The only one Gwynneth could remember now was "Noblesse Oblige", which still made her want to giggle.) When Gwynneth put forward her suggestion, core members who had other names to proffer withdrew them and enthusiastically supported hers. That was how in the end it boiled down to arguing, and then voting, for or against the name "Moun Demmeh", followed by the definitive Johnsonite walkout.

Before the split in the group, disagreement – open strife – had become the order of the day in their meetings, always with the same line drawn: on the one side Johnstone and those who could see no further than his rancid colonial views, and on the other side, the rest of the group. Gwynneth had more than once tried to blame the disruptions in the group on David. She griped and grumbled about his harbouring "those aliens" who had brought disharmony to their group. Now and then he had to rescue one or another of them from her exploding at them for something (admittedly crass) that they had said. David would make a silly joke of it afterwards: "Good thing I was there, or you woulda bite-out Greta throat!" or, "So when you done chew-up Nelson fine fine, what we going to do with all that mincemeat?"

"I doan know how you could tolerate those foolish people in you house," she said to him after one of the disagreements. "They just getting in the way."

"And you doan suffer fools gladly. I know."

It was impossible to strike up a quarrel with David, but she shot back at him all the same: "You just too damn tolerant – Mr Hail-fellow-well-met!"

He chuckled. "And it couldn't be, could it, that milady is just a little intolerant?"

She gave up, with a loud steups and a roll of the eyes.

"Gwynneth," he said. "We doan have to chase them out. They are a pain in the neck, yes, but they will leave of their own accord, sooner or later. We just have to tolerate them until they go. But, more importantly, when they leave, they will all have learnt something from sitting with us. Some will stay because they have grown; they have gained some understanding that they didn't have before. And for these very reasons, some will leave and come back. Mark my word."

A couple months after the walkout of Johnstone's colleagues, a few of them did come back. The cultural reconnoitre had been set in motion, and they turned up at a meeting, eager to be part of the project. Gwynneth noted that their return was ample grounds for David to deliver an "I-told-you-so" lecture to her; but when the meeting had dispersed, all he said to her on that topic was, "See what I mean?"

The two projects would proceed side by side – The *Cayerian Review* and the cultural reconnoitre. Issue No. 2 was already out, and they were working on issue No. 3. With the departure of the Johnstone cabal, there was no more wrangling over what should go into the *Review*. No longer were they obliged to include any of the bad writing offered by some members – ludicrously stilted, imitative poems; adventure and romance stories set in regions of autumn and snow, with characters who tossed blond or auburn hair; and superficial articles that avoided anything serious that was taking place in Cayeri.

Grave matters such as malnourished children too drowsy to learn anything at school; the legions of breadwinners working for 12 cents a day; the Shouters living under official persecution; the soldiers returning from the war destitute, wounded in body and soul, unemployed and often no longer employable, with no-where to turn for relief – all such realities the Johnstonites declared "too political" for their taste.

Moun Demmeh was gratified to receive mail from people who had read one or both of the previous issues of the review. Readers sent congratulatory letters, two articles, a poem, and a story. Some

51

of these items went into the third issue. There was a wealth of material coming out of the first few months of their culture project, and from this they selected 13 proverbs with their meanings; some chants used in children's games; a piece on how to make the best dhalpouri and curry-aloo, written by Ravi after an interview with his mother; and a Warau folk tale about how the world began.

They had twin editorials on religious persecution in Cayeri, one by Shiraz on the refusal of the colonial government to recognise Hindu and Muslim marriages, the other by Gwynneth on the treatment of the Shouters. That issue, No. 3, appeared in July 1919. It sold well, and before long the group again began to receive appreciative letters and material offered by readers for publication in the *Review*: more proverbs; calypso lyrics; a short story with a tragic ending about love between a Creole boy and an Indian girl...

Gwynneth had begun her information-gathering for the cultural reconnoitre by questioning her mother. Mumma was a near-inexhaustible source. (Puppa would have none of this digging up of things that brought no credit to the Negro man.)

She had also interviewed some of her Mothers' Union sisters, and arranged for herself and Joycelyn to visit Sookram's mother, Savitri (whom everybody called "Aajee"). Joycelyn was in charge of the Cayerian cookbook that was part of the project. They would interview Aajee about the Indian foods that had become part and parcel of the Cayerian diet. Joycelyn had been making roti for years, and curry channa, aloo pie, beigan chokha, and much more. But these were all run-of-the-mill Cayerian fare. She wanted to also put into the cookbook the more complicated items from Indo-Cayerian cuisine, like saheena, and delicacies like gulab jamun...

Gwynneth was planning to take some members of Moun Demmeh to Pilgrim for a weekend, as part of the cultural reconnoitre. Her original plan had been to set out on this expedition the weekend after issue 3 of the *Review* was put to bed; but it was decided that given the positive response of the public to issue 3, the group should get cracking right away on issue 4.

"The paper is getting attention and approval," Sylvia remarked. "We mustn't risk losing this momentum. At this point there are no other outlets like this in Cayeri for people who want to write about the everyday lives of Cayerians."

The *Review* team was Sylvia, Gwynneth, Ainsley and David. It would be their job to solicit material, from Moun Demmeh members and other sources. Someone suggested that the Workers' League should be invited to submit an article. The team would have to sift and select from what they gathered, and get an editorial written. Gwynneth was responsible for the editing of the finished product. By late October they had compiled the contents of issue 4, and Gwynneth took the sheaf of papers home to give it a final look-through. She was not able to tackle that immediately, for she had forty-two exercise books to mark for her pupils – the exhibition class at St Paul Government School.

At the November meeting, Moun Demmeh discussed the hunger march that the Workers' League was organising, set for Saturday, the 29th of November. There was unanimous agreement that they would participate.

Now, with the children's assignments marked, and issue 4 almost put to bed, she could, at last, take the cultural reconnoitre to Pilgrim. She would deal with issue 4 on her return. On a Friday evening in the middle of November, Gwynneth and five other members of Moun Demmeh took the train to Pilgrim, carrying rolled-up crocus bags and sheets, as well as food supplies. They stayed at Uncle Albert and Tantie Grace, but declined Tantie Grace's plan for them to take over the family's two bedrooms. Just as Gwynneth and Viola and their cousins used to do when they were children, the group happily camped on the floor – in the drawing-room and in the gallery.

On Saturday morning after breakfast, Gwynneth, Raj and Fitz interviewed Uncle Albert and Tantie Grace. Meanwhile Ainsley, Sylvia and David went to the kitchen – an ajoupa outside the back door of the house – and cooked lunch, with Gwynneth's cousin Lyris on call, for managing the fireside of a country kitchen was a cooking skill the visitors did not possess.

After lunch they split into three pairs and went out into the village, which consisted of Pilgrim Road with side roads (more like tracks) branching off it into little settlements where people quietly went about their living. Gwynneth and Sylvia took one segment of Pilgrim Road and its branches; David and Ainsley took another; and Raj and Fitz yet another.

They walked through the place, sat with people in their galleries or on their front steps, and hung on their every word. They got recipes. They collected cryptic proverbs, like: "Moon does only run till day ketch him", and "Is the yam-vine does tie-up the yam", and "Shroud doan have pocket"... They were given advice on the medicinal powers of the most innocent-looking weeds around them. Mumma had already provided information on some of these plants – shandilay, fever-grass, *zèb-a-fam, zèb-a-pik, bwa-kano*, shining-bush, *géritout*...

Mother Queen Lottie had sent word that if they intended to visit the church on Sunday and speak with her, they would have to get up there no later than one o'clock. Tantie Grace insisted on cooking Sunday lunch for her guests, and so she was out in the kitchen before they woke up that morning.

They had an early lunch, and then Gwynneth led the way up the hill to Queen's church, past her house where the church and Shango-yard used to be. Pilgrim Road disappeared into rough scrub strewn with boulders, through which the group picked their way carefully as they trekked up and up into mountain bush. The Lion of Judah Mystical Tabernacle had moved up there in the wake of the Shouter Baptist Prohibition Ordinance, to escape the attention of the police, who were breaking down Shouter churches all over the colony.

They came upon the compound suddenly, for as they made their way up through the bush, there was nothing to see before or beside them but more bush. Then they were standing in front of a fence made of dry coconut branches. There was no visible entrance, but Gwynneth and her party had already been seen. On their right someone appeared from around the fence, and stood beckoning to them. He led the visitors to the side of the enclosure. There they entered, one by one, through a gate positioned behind a huge cedar tree that obstructed easy access.

Just as Gwynneth expected, Queen made no mention of the narrow breach in the fence at the back of the compound, designed for escape in the event of an approach by police raiders coming up the hill. That exit was camouflaged with loose coconut branches hanging from a wire that could decapitate the unwitting. The fence at the back was almost up against the dug-out mountainside, so to get in or out through that opening, you would have to scrape your way along the wall of earth.

Going onto the compound, you entered a space cooled and darkened by the overhanging branches of leafy trees and other vegetation crowding around outside the fence. Church members were busy cleaning for that night's service, sweeping the ground between the buildings with cocoyea and bush brooms, pulling up grass and weeds that had barely pushed out a baby leaf. Queen walked with the visitors among the tight little cluster of tapia buildings and smaller structures, all with carat roofs, as she explained the meaning of some of the things they saw.

Some things she did not explain. "That," she would say, closing her face, "is not for everybody to know."

The first structure they met she had identified as the palay, which looked as innocuous as the ajoupa on a gardener's provision ground. She pointed out the seven stools ranged along the inside of the fence. On one side of the gate was the stool dedicated to Eshu who guarded the compound, with Ogun and Shango further along that side of the fence. Along the fence on the other side of the gate was a stool for Kali, and one for Mother Lakshmi. Yemanja and the Virgin Mary kept company along another part of the enclosure. Queen showed them the chapelle, but brushed past it, telling them it was a sacred storeroom containing things not for everybody to know.

"We ain have no mourner-room up here," Queen told them, almost apologetically.

The church was still using the mourner-room down on her home compound. She led them around to the back of the church to show them the clump of bamboo poles with flags of different colours on top, planted in a back corner of the compound. Then she took them to the door of the church and let them peer inside. She pointed out the centre pole – the *poto mitan* – surrounded by a collection of articles placed on the ground. Brass receptacles, clay goblets, calabashes. Some of these had flowers and candles in

55

them. A bell. A cocoyea broom. A conch shell. Bottles, containing olive oil, kananga water, florida water, lavender water, and other liquids, clear or coloured. There was an altar. Incense was burning somewhere, but nobody could see where. Perhaps it was just the aura of this place. Somebody enquired about the chalk markings on the wall, but that was another of the things not for everybody to know.

On the train afterwards, Gwynneth explained, "Some of what we saw in there you wouldn't see in all Shouter-Baptist churches. This church is one of those that people call 'Shango-Baptist', because they embrace much more of the African tradition than other Baptists do."

"And some of my Hindu heritage, too!" Raj noted. "I was amazed to meet up with Mother Lakshmi and Kali up there."

"Oh, yes," Gwynneth said. "That's not uncommon. I remember Queen reading to the congregation from the *Bhagavad Gita* at Sunday service. We will have to visit different Baptist churches to get a more complete picture. Some of the churches doan like you to mix them up with Shango at all – to them that's anathema – while others are quite comfortable moving among Christian, Shango and Hindu traditions, and their spiritual life is all the richer for it, just as Cayerian culture, generally, is the richer for its multiple ancestries."

Ainsley's godmother was a Shouter and he was no stranger to her church, although his family was Methodist. Gwynneth had taken part in activities at Queen's church from her earliest years. One of David's colleagues in teaching, a Shouter, had invited him to thanksgivings at his church. David had also attended the colleague's baptism on L'Anse Marron beach. But it was the first time that Sylvia, Raj and Fitz had ever come anywhere near such a place, or entered such a presence.

The visit had left them overawed. They marvelled at their own ignorance, their own oblivion. They had lived all their lives in Cayeri, growing up alongside this heritage, yet completely sealed off from it. They had only the haziest notion of this world. Gwynneth and Ainsley they eyed almost reverentially, for the two of them had been privy to it from childhood.

"All I know about Shouters," Sylvia said, "is seeing and hearing a grappe of people by the side of the road singing and praying and preaching, and a bell ringing. And now you doan even see that any more, since the government outlaw them."

"And what does the Creole Cayerian know about Hinduism, or Islam?" Gwynneth asked. "What does any Cayerian know about Shango, unless he or she is a Shango devotee or Shango-Baptist? All Cayerians should have a basic understanding of, and respect for, the religious faiths of their compatriots, for they are as much part of our cultural landscape, our cultural heritage, as Christianity. The cultural reconnoitre needs to visit some mandirs, mosques, Shango-yards…

They talked excitedly about the visit to Queen's church, but in hushed voices, not only because of their strong sense of having entered an other-worldly sphere; they were whispering also out of caution. Wasn't this what the authorities had banned, two years before? Wasn't that ordinance meant to wipe off the face of the Earth everything they had seen on that compound? Wasn't this Mother Queen lady, as well as her members, and others like them all over the colony, under heavy prohibition? The police could swoop down at any moment, demolish church, palay, stools, everything, and put Mother Queen and all her congregation in jail. Yet this serene person was going about her business with no inclination to look over her shoulder, not the least bit intimidated!

They wished with all their heart that they could have stayed on for the service that night, but they had to catch the last train back, to go to work in the morning. They vowed to come to Pilgrim again, on another Sunday, bringing their workday clothes, so that they could attend Mother Queen Lottie's service, take the earliest train out on Monday morning, and head straight for work.

That return expedition would not come to pass, for Moun Demmeh's tours were about to come to an abrupt and premature end.

The grand plan for the next stage of the project was to have been the creation of booklets on various facets of Cayerian culture, never mind they had no idea how they would find the money to get these printed. But their optimism knew no bounds, since at that time they had already succeeded in keeping their little paper going for three issues. The cultural reconnoitre had been a most exhilarating time, and all those involved would remember it with a sad fondness. But when tragedy struck, even if the authorities had not placed the ban on Moun Demmeh, with David gone, no one had the heart to regroup.

Not content with having trained their guns on a peaceful march and wantonly snuffed out a man's life, two days later the police would go on to raid her family's home in the middle of the night. They carried away piles of her books and papers, including the bundle of pages lying in plain sight on her desk – issue No. 4 of *The Cayerian Review*. She had not yet finished the editing.

They did not look under her bed, it seemed, or, if they did, they were not impressed by the cardboard boxes they would have seen there. Safe and sound in one of those boxes were some school exercise books, carrying King George V's face in an oval frame at the centre of the front cover, and inside, material gathered in the cultural reconnoitre. In particular, there were the lyrics of traditional Cayerian songs, and the sheets on which she had done the musical notation. Thankfully, the last exercise book, with material she had gathered in Pilgrim just before the march, was there. She had taken it off her desk to make room for the editing of issue 4, and placed it in the box with the others.

~

It was not until 1926, after she came home from her exile in town and was starting up her school, that she could finally bring herself to pull the boxes from under the bed and fish out some of the exercise books. During all the years she had lived in town, on her visits to the family home she had never so much as peeped under her bed. The very thought of what was in those boxes gave her a stab of pain. But she knew that sooner or later she would have to tackle them. She couldn't shy away from them forever. With the opening of her school, the time had come. Time to give life to what had been lying patiently in those boxes for years – home-grown stories to tell the children; proverbs for them to live by; songs for them to sing.

The songs were to have been put into a book – "Songs of Cayeri" – so that all Cayerian children could one day sing the songs of their own land, alongside the others. She needed to complete work on the ones she had gathered in Pilgrim. She had written down the lyrics, but had never got around to doing the musical notation, because it was right after the Pilgrim tour that her world fell to pieces. Some of the songs were not new to her, and for those she would have no difficulty writing up the music sheets; for the others, however, those she had heard for the first time in Pilgrim, she could not now remember the tunes.

In the time of the cultural reconnoitre, in 1919, Mumma had helped her to pin down the music for some of the songs brought in by other members of Moun Demmeh. Once more, Mumma was a great resource. It was during Puppa's last illness that she and Gwynneth would sit together at the piano again, both listening out for any sound from his room, while Mumma sang the remaining songs, and Gwynneth played the melodies on the piano before committing them to paper. Gwynneth also chatted with Mumma about the plans she had, besides the songbook, for bringing forth the songs. "I want to form a children's choir that will hold concerts and perform at functions, to raise money for printing the songbook."

"Okay, *Doudou*," Mumma said. "Take you time!"

Gwynneth recognised in her mother's tone the familiar warning not to bite off more than she could chew. When she told Mumma that oldtime Cayerian songs such as these would one day be put onto gramophone records, as far-fetched as that might seem, Mumma replied with a sceptical "Hm!" and then added, "I not going live to see that!"

"Sound like nansi-story, eh?" Gwynneth said. "But doan fraid. One day, one day, congotay."

"And Monkey say, 'Cool breeze'," Mumma concurred.

5
Dammit, Roy will have to pay.

Now, fourteen years later, Mumma had become bedridden, but if she called during the day, Gwynneth could hear her, provided her imps were not making too much noise. Every now and then she would leave the buzzing schoolroom to go inside and peep at her. However, staying inside for even the time it took to give Mumma a cup of water was a risk. Just because Teacher Gwynneth had turned her back, somebody could jook somebody else with a slate-pencil, or an unidentified spirit might wander into the shed and break the new stick of chalk, just for spite. So far no serious harm had come to life or limb, but a week or so before school closed for the 1940 August vacation, Darnley Matthews had given her a scare. He went to the latrine and dawdled so long, because Teacher Gwynnie had gone into the house to check on the old lady, that his pants managed to find their way down into the pit.

Nothing could get him to open the door. He had latched it on the inside, and he stayed in there, howling with rage until the two children that Gwynneth sent running to his home returned with a pair of pants. Meanwhile, almost every child in the school suddenly wanted to pee-pee. One after the other they came to Gwynneth, finger on forehead: "Permission, Miss?" then ran to join the happy queue wriggling up the back steps to the inside WC.

Gwynneth reflected that it could have been worse. Instead of Dudley Matthews's pants falling into the latrine pit, it could have been him or one of the other lawless ones falling off the doudouce mango tree and breaking his neck. Before something serious happened, she would have to either get a girl to help look after Mumma, or close down the school. It was an idea she had been turning over in her head for months. She had even bounced it off Viola.

She could close down the school and go back to private tutoring… on weekday evenings, and on Saturdays, perhaps, times when Viola would be at home to see about Mumma.

Neighbour Marjorie and her nephew Lennox, too. Lennox loved to come over and sit with Mumma. He had grown into a quiet and thoughtful youngster, not speaking much, but with Mumma he turned into a chatterbox. He made Mumma cackle in the most scandalous way.

Town-people had never stopped asking Gwynneth to please come and tutor their children. Bigshot people: lofty British civil servants; an American missionary; Potoguee people who owned stores in Kings Port. Yet, to go back to that, she had first to be sure that the money would be enough, what with Hitler and his damn war making everything so dear. Mumma's pension and the shameful pittance that Roy gave towards her upkeep could barely feed her and buy her medicines.

Mumma couldn't eat too much solid food now, and the things they had to get for her had gone up in price – Cream-of-Wheat, Marmite, Armstrong's Extract of Halibut Liver. Everything was black-market. The war was preventing ships from coming to Cayeri as often as they should, so every cargo that arrived was like good gold, and the businessmen weren't ashamed to take advantage. They were free to charge any price they pleased. One of Gwynneth's ill-fated letters to the newspapers was on the subject of greedy merchants committing highway robbery against the people, with the protection of the government. *The Listener* did not see fit to print that one, so she sent it to *The Kings Port Sentinel,* where it died a natural death.

She could close down the school, take up tutoring again, and also continue with the piano lessons… but the war had hit that, too. Times were so hard that not many families could spend their money on piano lessons. She only had two music students left. She could take them to their Grade Five exam and then close down the piano lessons for the time being. But, the thought of going back to that life… teaching the children of the Kings Port well-to-do… some so haughty she had to first bring them down a peg or two before she could teach them anything. One little girl stamped her foot to demand that Gwynneth call her "Miss Abigail" and call her three-year-old brother (who wandered in and out of the mahogany study making a nuisance of himself) "Young Master Jonathan", because all the servants did.

"Well, they shouldn't" was all Gwynneth would say, and as hand-to-mouth as she was living at the time, she gathered up the learning aids she had made especially for this little girl, and dismissed herself forthwith from the employ of Miss Abigail and family.

Some were high-school students who couldn't fathom long division, or write as fine a composition as some of her pupils in the shed were capable of, children who would never see the inside of a high school. *Money could buy education, but it cyaan buy brains.* Disband her imps and turn herself over to their counterparts in town who had shoes and socks for every day of school, and were innocent of jigger-toe, or head-lice, or mirasme? In another time it was the children of the well-to-do who had brought her a living; but they were part of what were not the best days of her life.

Getting to their homes, now, would not be as easy as when she lived on the edge of town and could just walk out from her home on Catherine Street to the bottom of James Street, and take the tramcar up to the fairer quarters of the town. Now it would mean taking the train from Turagua to Kings Port, then the tramcar, as she had done for those three months in 1926 when she first came back home...

As for hiring a girl...

Dammit, Roy will have to pay. Why should she be forced to disarrange her life when one of Mumma's children, Mumma's eyeball, to boot, could easily do better for her? A man with a good government job could afford to give his old ailing mother more than sweet-talk and the few miserable coppers that, come month-end, we have to fight you for, have to squeeze out of you. Stingy, ungrateful wretch. You coulda never reach where you reach today if the oldpeople didn band they belly and do without, if they didn sacrifice to send you up through the world. Especially Mumma. You think you just wake one morning and find youself up there?... They would get somebody to help look after Mumma, and Roy would pay the wages.

There was an argument, of course, and they had to keep pulling their voices down for fear that Mumma would hear them. Viola properly washed her mouth on him. Roy had made it clear that he had no intention of taking on any added responsibility for Mumma. He had a family to support ("So Mumma is not you family?" Gwynneth enquired, with mock mildness) and although his wife was working ("In the bank!" hissed Viola. "Her Majesty not picking cocoa! She working *in the bank!*"), even though Helen had a bank job, what did they really think it cost to have both Gordon and Freda in high school? He was already giving money for Mumma, more than enough to pay a servant.

What were they doing with his money, anyway, and why couldn't her daughters make a contribution, too? After all, they had nobody to spend their money on, for they had neither chick nor child. Two old-maids with nothing to do and nobody to spend their money on... Viola lunged at him, but Gwynneth put out an arm and barred her, asking hotly, "What the France you mean 'make a contribution'? Who seeing about Mumma? You ever sponge you mother face or put a spoon of porridge in her mouth?"

"Oho," Roy replied, "so now I must leave my office, tell the clerks 'Continue with your work, ladies and gentlemen. I am just going up to Turagua to give my mother some porridge'..."

Gwynneth was shaking her head with sadness. "Well I only hope your mother not hearing a word of this contention. I am not going to carry on any war with you, Roy. I am just telling you that we have to hire somebody to help take care of our mother, and the money coming into this house right now can't stretch that far. You earning much more than the two of us put together, so we asking you to pay. As for the ton-load of money that you bring and give Mumma every month – *when we remind you* – lemme show you where it gone."

And while Viola took him on again, telling him how he would roast in hell for his selfishness, Gwynneth went inside and came out with her arms full of pill-boxes, medicine bottles, a half-empty tin of Cream-of-Wheat.

"Doan bother with him, Vie. You only sending up you pressure. You will end up flat in you bed, and he will go his way hale and hearty."

Gwynneth sat down, and placing the items on the bannister one by one, patiently told him the cost of each.

"Roy," she said quietly. "One day you will come looking for you mother and you will meet this house close up tight. You will find all three of us down in the Poor-House."

This picture gave him a little jolt, but of course she was exaggerating, so he laughed and shook his head. It was no use. Roy strode off with Viola's curses ringing in his ears, slightly ruffled, but determined that they were not going to milk him of his money.

Then Mumma fell off the bed. Gwynneth didn't hear a sound. A batch of children were counting to a hundred when it happened – about fifteen of them, all bellowing, and not quite in unison, so there was no split second of quiet between one number and the next. Because Gwynneth had left Mumma sleeping soundly when she checked on her some time after lunch, she did not look in again for the last hour or so of school. After the children were dismissed and she went over to the house, as soon as she entered the back door, she could hear the sound of groaning.

Mumma was lying on the floor with the coverlet trailing from the bed and partly wrapped around her middle. Her left leg was at a strange angle, her face, her head-tie and her hair bathed in sweat.

"*Bondjé*, Mumma! What happen?"

"*Mwen pa sav, machè*. Me ain know, me dear. To tell you the truth, me ain know wha happen," Mumma said weakly, "but I giddy, and me foot hurting me like blazes." And she went on groaning.

Gwynneth leaned out of the bedroom window and called out to Marjorie, who deftly parted the barbed-wire, eased her body through, and was there in a flash. The two of them hoisted Mumma back onto the bed. Then Marjorie rushed up to the exchange, where Viola put a call through to Dr Carmody, and then to Roy.

"You'll have to treat her like an egg, now," Dr Carmody told them. "Nothing broken, but the knee will give her some trouble, and she has a little concussion. We oldpeople don't recover so easy from knocks like these, you know, so we will have to see that nothing of the sort ever happens to my *makoumè* again." He boxed her playfully on the arm: "Estelle, *Doudou*, you have some good years left in you still, but we will have to take care of you. We don't want you to turn your back and leave us yet!"

Roy had come in, huffing and puffing, a few moments before, and now he looked as if he would burst into tears.

He was there every evening for the rest of the week. He even paid the joiner Ollie engaged to put side-bars on Mumma's bed. Sometimes he brought Gordon and Freda, and one evening their mother, Her Royal Highness, came with them, smiling absently at everyone, and looking, as usual, as though she couldn't wait to get away because something here was offending her nose. When Viola went in to make up a waiter of drinks for the visitors, Gwynneth followed and stuck her head in the kitchen door with a wicked look on her face. She spoke in Patois.

"What you giving HRH to drink, girl? All the champagne finish, you know!"

"Doan fraid," Viola answered, also in Patois. "Mumma chamber-pot have anything in it?"

The peal of laughter that came from the kitchen would have puzzled the visitors a little, and Gwynneth had to rearrange her face before she went back out to them.

Gordon and Freda were a pair of tall and well-dressed town-children. Freda was looking more and more like a red version of Roy (and Puppa) as she grew. Gordon, too, remained red-skinned like the mother, but the touch of Spanish in the hair that she had given him was wearing off, and now, Roy would remark with dismay, Gordon was beginning to look like any little red-nigger. Gordon was in Third Form at Government College (not the College of the Ascension, to Roy's eternal grief), and Freda had just started at Maria Regina Convent High School. They both spoke as if their mouths could open only so much and no more, addressing their aunts as "Ornt Gwynnie" and "Ornt Violer."

These youngsters were strangers, now. But then, Roy and Helen had always kept their children to themselves. Like Puppa, they didn't believe in all this rubbing up between Tan-Tan and Nennen and *Makoumè* and *Konpè* that low-class Creole people were given to.

In years past, Roy's children were brought to visit their grand-mother at Christmas time and on her birthday. Sometimes on their way to or from the beach the family would stop off and spend a little time. Roy was a mango-peong, so in mango season he visited more often, sometimes bringing Gordon and Freda with him. The children would disappear up into the land, armed with buckets. There was mango on the parcel of land when Puppa acquired it, mainly "common-breed" kinds like mango vert and mango rose. But Puppa had planted more trees – for his grand-children, he said – high-class mango like Julie, starch, and Graham, as well as other fruit trees.

Sadly, Puppa never met his grandchildren, never saw them emerge from the bush with their buckets full and mango juice on their faces and down the front of their clothes, never heard them shriek with glee as they darted about the yard and ran round and round the house like animals released from a cage. Sad, too, how these children, in their whole life, had never been allowed to spend a night in their grandmother's house, no matter how much they begged.

When they were little, Gordon and Freda would rush in through the front door and all but strangle Mumma, Gwynneth and Viola with hugging-up and kissing. They would chatter loudly and both at once, until the walls rang with their excite-ment. Now, they stiffly pecked Mumma on the cheek, stood around her bed for a few minutes among the adults, and then went and sat upright in the drawing-room chairs, where they soon began to fidget and look peeved.

Something about them now reminded Gwynneth of how Roy, after a month and a half at Ascension College, didn't want to come home on weekends any more, when they were already struggling to pay Mrs Gouveia for the five weekdays' boarding in town…

~

There was no earthly reason for Roy to be boarding in town to begin with. People who lived in Turagua and went to school or to work in Kings Port were taking the train to town and back every day. Even the Estate Manager's son, William Laurent, had trav-elled by train to school and back for his entire five years at Ascension, willingly, as far as anybody knew (first class, of course, and by the tramcar between the terminus and the college).

Roy did start off going to school in town by train, albeit without the luxury of the first-class carriage, or the tramcar for the last leg. He had to walk from the terminus to school, and back again on evenings, but the distance between Kings Port railway terminus and Ascension College was not all that much more than the distance between home and Turagua train station, which Roy had walked for most of his primary school years.

He went to Trois Rivières R.C., the primary school where Puppa was stationed at the time. At first, Puppa would put him on the bar of his bicycle and ride to the train station, where he parked the bike for the day. But when, at age seven, Roy left the infant level of primary school and went into Standard 1, Puppa decided to park the bicycle at home, and the two of them started walking to the train station, in keeping with a father's duty to toughen up his boychild so he wouldn't turn out weak and soft and girlish, Puppa said.

In Roy's first three weeks or so at Ascension, he discovered that some boys from the country were boarding in Kings Port, either at relatives, or in boarding-houses run by respectable ladies. Roy fancied the latter. He didn't have any relatives in town that he knew of, and if it should turn out that he did, he was not sure he would want anything to do with them. Trouble was, the Ascension boys who stayed in the respectable boarding-houses were the sons of planters and others for whom boarding out a child was a negligible expense. Not so for the parents of Royston Joseph Cuffie.

Roy began a campaign of complaining, with the aim of getting to board in town. The complaints, or reasons why he should board in town, could change from day to day. Getting up early on mornings (the same time he used to get up for the journey to primary school) was hard for him because all that travelling was making him so tired. He couldn't do his homework properly because he was getting home so late on evenings (4.50 p.m.). There were some bullies on the train who harassed him every day. There were so many beggars along James Street where he had to walk, and they frightened him. Downtown James Street was so dirty that the smell made him feel sick. There were pickpockets on James Street, etc.

But Puppa seemed to understand what really was amiss, didn't make a fuss, and squeezed the extra money out from somewhere, most likely Mumma's well-guarded Friendly Society stash, saved from her sewing. Without Mumma's money, Roy could not have been at Ascension in the first place. Though the church had awarded Roy a bursary, as a reward for his father's tireless work in the vineyard of Catholic education, it paid only part of the exorbitant school fees. The balance was still a struggle, not to speak of uniform, books, stationery, money for lunch and travelling at first, and later, the boarding.

Mumma kept the Friendly Society record book hidden and Puppa was never privy to the exact amount of money she had there. This was in keeping with a tenet of womanly living that Estelle drummed into her daughters' heads: make sure you have you own money so you could stand up on you own two foot and never have to ask no man for nutten.

Gwynneth, by then, was working at St Paul Government School, earning the salary of a qualified female teacher. She helped with Roy's expenses, buying his books and putting a hand with the fees when the family was hard-pressed to make up the amount. But she made it clear that not a cent of her money was to go into this wasteful foolishness of boarding Roy in town.

When a week or two after Roy started boarding at Miss Gouveia's, he came up with a fresh set of complaints, reasons why he should stay there also on weekends, Mumma dipped into her own-money again. She tried to let Roy have his wish even though they could see that his wish was breaking her heart. Mumma tried her best, but there wasn't enough money to keep him at Miss Gouveia's for every single weekend of the term. Mumma strove to let him stay there every other weekend, and even that was not always possible.

From then onwards they almost only had Roy home for the school vacations – Christmas, Easter and August – a sulky, restless visitor. For most of his high-school years the room was left standing empty, the room that Puppa had added on to the house for him when he was five. Roy's sisters (both of them at first and then just Viola) had occupied the room for all of his primary school years, up until Roy turned twelve and Puppa installed him in it with much fanfare, bringing in the priest to bless it, handing Roy the key, making a speech, and so forth. Now, for most of the year, nobody lived there. Viola had settled back into the old "children's bedroom", which was also where Mumma did her sewing.

They suggested to Mumma that she could safely set up her sewing-machine in Roy's room. It was not, they hastened to add, that Viola wanted to put her out of the room, but that Mumma would have more space to work in. Moreover, her customers could then come up the back steps and straight into the sewing-room, instead of passing through the gallery and drawing-room. Puppa had never ceased to grumble about that traffic, and his grumbling was about more than the "all kinds of people" traipsing through his house. It was also improper for the wife of a decent man to be carrying on a trade, but, alas, he couldn't make ends meet without the money brought in by that trade.

Mumma would not hear of moving the machine into Roy's room, for that would have been too much like saying out loud, *My twelve-year-old son, my sweet lagniappe child, no longer lives here. He has turned his back on us...*

~

One thing that had been settled by Mumma's fall was that there would have to be someone in the house all day with her while Gwynneth and Viola were at work. Mumma had instructed them to go to Pilgrim and talk with her god-daughter, Venus Polydore. Venus was a Mother of Queen Lottie's church, and she would find somebody to suit. Venus would send somebody.

Gwynneth planned to go up on Saturday, but first there was another battle to be fought. Roy had finally agreed to pay for help with taking care of Mumma; now they had to settle on the wage. Gwynneth tackled him in the gallery. Roy was only willing to pay the person $6.00 a month, because, he said, this woman was going to be living here, not paying rent, and eating tea-breakfast-and-dinner.

"What!" Gwynneth cried in disbelief. "Roy, that is slavery! You can't pay somebody *six dollars* after they work for a month! In this day and age? And who will be giving her tea-breakfast-and-dinner? Who going and give us money to feed her, you? Hah! We quicker see a lilac donkey coming down James Street. *We* will be paying for that – Mumma, Viola and me. So ketch youself!"

Roy was unmoved. Lounging on a chair in the gallery, he smoked his cigarette and knocked the ash over the bannister, right onto their pink, purple and white bougainvillea.

"That is the beauty of getting somebody from the country," he said. "You don't have to pay country-people much. They don't know about money. They grateful for whatever they get."

Gwynneth rolled her eyes upward. "Give me faith and patience," she sighed. "Roy. You forget your mother was a servant, too. You forget Mumma used to work in the whitepeople house from morning till night, with nothing to show for her labour but two-three shilling and the family leftovers? Eh? You know about that?"

Roy became agitated. He sat up and his head swivelled sharply, as though he had been stung. He shot a glance over his shoulder and into the road as if to make sure nobody had overheard, then turned to Gwynneth and hissed, "You ever see Mumma working in anybody house but ours? How you know she was a servant? You never see her doing servant work!" He was near breathing fire.

"Oh? So Mumma is a liar. Or she crazy. She used to siddown and make up stories about herself, just so. Your mumma was a domestic servant, Roy! More like a *slave*, Roy! Working in the whitepeople house from she was fourteen years old! You doan like to hear nothing bout that, eh? Well all that is what bring you to where you reach now, Mister – she been working herself to death ever since. And I going to go in right now and tell her how much you willing to put out for somebody to mind her in her old age."

Gwynneth got up and started in through the drawing-room door.

"Hey!" Roy stopped her. "Where you going, man? Why you must bring Mumma into this? You just want to upset the old lady. I will pay eight dollars and not a cent more."

"Ten dollars or I am going to Mumma, and ten dollars is still taking advantage."

"Gwynneth, where am I going to find ten dollars every month? You want me to take my children out of school?"

70

"No. I just want you to remember that the reason why you can send your children to high school today is that your mother work her fingers to the bone to send *you* to the bakra people school. You just never forget, you little piece of nastiness, that you went to Ascension so you could have a good, paying job today because that lady in there, that old lady take night and make day, sewing people clothes to meet *your* school fees and board *your* ungrateful little tail in town. Never forget it, *salaud*!"

Gwynneth by now was bending over him, glaring into his face. Then she straightened up and stepped back into the doorway, one foot inside the drawing-room. "So now, let me hear what I am going to tell her."

Roy crushed his cigarette to death on the bannister, snatched his hat and stood up: "Yes, Miss Holier-Than-Thou. Ten dollars it will be, Miss Paragon-of-Virtue, always on a high horse preaching right from wrong. Hah! What you know about right and wrong? If you knew right from wrong you would still be in your good paying job, too. But what you sow you reap! No matter – I will be the bobolee. I will take the licks for your mistake."

As he stormed down the walk to the gate, Gwynneth stood in the gallery with a half-smile playing across her face. She spoke, whether he could hear her or not: "Yes, Roy. You can keep on saying that until they put me in my grave and cover me up. My conscience is clear. One day, when you grow up, you will see some things in a different light."

6

But now Mumma's church was against the law.

Gwynneth had not been to Pilgrim for some time, not since Mumma stopped going, a year or so before this war. Only death or dire infirmity could stop Mumma. For the last months of her regular visits to Pilgrim, when she was still able to move around without too much trouble, Gwynneth would go with her whenever she could, and come back on the evening train. This service, Mumma made it clear, was not appreciated. But when the cataracts outstripped the arthritis in the race to tie her foot, Mumma's resistance weakened.

Grudgingly at first, she allowed somebody to accompany her on her voyages to Pilgrim and fetch her home again on a day appointed by her. They took turns. Gwynneth would make the journey by train, or, when Ollie was available, he and Viola would take a cool, unhurried drive in the lumbering old jalopy to get her to Pilgrim or bring her back. Up till that time, Mumma didn't want anybody following her around, because she was neither a little child nor a foolish old woman. "*Mwen vyé*," Mumma would inform them. "I old. But I ain dotish yet."

To throw off any willing escorts, she would spend days secretly gathering her bits and pieces and storing them out of sight: candles, olive oil and incense for the church; a little vest, a panty or two and maybe some sweeties for her brother's grands; some pone or two Guinness for her *makoumè* Madlain, Venus's mother.

Then one morning bright and early she would be dressed, head firmly tied, bags in hand and battered suitcase on her head, stepping out the door before Gwynneth or Viola could spin round. "*Mwen ka pati.* I gone. You see me when you see me."

It was no use arguing with Mumma; and she was certainly not going to stand up and argue with them, to end up missing her train. They could do no more than make sure somebody followed her to the station, although she made it clear that she wanted no tail behind her.

Mumma would be gone for days, and their worry was not so much the journey. The spirits went with her, she reminded them, and indeed at every turn there were spirits, mostly in human form, to lift her load, for she never went empty-handed; to take her across the Kings Port terminus to the Southern Line platform and settle her and her bundles on the train; to help her off the train at Wellington Junction and onto the San Pedro train; wake her up just before Clancy Halt if she happened to fall asleep on the train; follow her from the Halt to the corner where she caught the bus; and wait with her at Pilgrim bus stop while she commandeered a passing child and told him to run up by Mr Albert and tell them to send somebody to meet her.

The spirits even produced smelling-salts and fanned her face when one time a bad-feel came over her somewhere between Morne Rouge and Araujo. For sure, Mumma on her journey to Pilgrim was safe in the hands of her spirits. What Gwynneth and Viola worried about when Mumma went to Pilgrim was the ordinance. Mumma went to Pilgrim to go to her church, but now Mumma's church was against the law.

It had not been entirely unexpected. In this colony, David used to say, there was an ordinance against everything blackpeople did that had not been taught to them by the whitepeople – ordinance against the skin drum; ordinance against Kamboulay; ordinance against what they thought obeah was… He didn't live to see the ordinance against calypso, the "Theatres and Dance Hall Ordinance" that sought to outlaw not only smutty calypsos, but also calypsos that dared to criticise the actions of the high and mighty. It was what inspired Lord Messenger's composition "Gestapo in the Place":

> *Two ugly police come in the tent*
> *Walk in just so, ain pay one cent.*
> *Sweet kaiso singing*
> *But them only writing*
> *Cock up on the front bench, right in you face.*
> *Watch out, my brother, Gestapo in the place*
> *And somebody getting court case.*

For the Shouters it had been only a matter of time. Towards the end of the First World War their ordinance had come. Gwynneth's heart filled up with bile again as she thought of Father McVorran that Sunday morning at Mass, his face gleaming with their victory. That was when she should have left his church. Mumma had more guts than she. Nothing could make Mumma come to Mass after that Sunday morning. St Anthony's would never see her in life again. Puppa could fret and fume till Kingdom come; Mumma was finished with them.

Father McVorran was triumphantly waving the newspaper with the report on the Shouter Baptist Prohibition Ordinance, passed in the Legislative Council the week before. "The powers of darkness have been conquered!" he gloated. "We shall yet rid this land of savagery. If there be any of you here with one foot in this church and the other in that heathen camp, be warned! You are first and foremost breaking God's law; but now you will also be breaking the law of the land. Before you burn in hell, you will rot in His Majesty's Royal Prison."

And as he read out parts of the ordinance, Gwynneth could swear that he smacked his lips.

This was an ordinance to "render illegal indulgence in the practices of the body known as the Shouters"; but the body known as the Shouters might not have noticed. The authorities could just as well have issued a decree commanding: "Shouters! Increase and multiply!" for their numbers seemed to be growing. All over the colony Shouters were being arrested by the vanload, beaten, hauled before the courts, slapped with fines or thrown in prison for holding service or simply for wearing their colours.

Ollie related how a police friend of his had come to him for advice after an experience that had left him quite disturbed. He was one of a party of policemen that raided a Shouter church on the outskirts of Mundo Nuevo. The people were defiant and refused to disperse, so the sergeant ordered that the whole group be carted off to the police station.

All night, some in the cells, some on the benches in the front room, some leaning against the walls, they had kept up a steady sound that could not exactly be called singing, for their mouths were tightly closed. It was a low, haunting music that came from some drum they carried deep in their bellies. It hung in every corner of the compound. The policemen on night duty were rattled, but they could do nothing but bark at them to be quiet. By morning they were glad to let them go. On the night of that very same day, the group went back to their church and held service again.

They had to be raided again, and clearly this time the church would have to be broken down. But when the raiding party got to the church, Ollie's friend felt an irresistible urge, not to burst in and arrest the people, but to stretch his arms across the door-mouth and guard them against intruders. Something seemed to be holding him by the ankles, he said, preventing him from going in, until his police colleagues behind him rushed the door, catapulting him inside. "You think they put something on me?" he asked Ollie, anxiously.

Ollie roared with laughter, and then told him, with a straight face, that he had got The Call, and this meant that he had to join the Shouters and be baptised in their way.

"Ollie, man, talk serious nah, man. You like to make too much damn joke, man. I come to you with this thing because you is a half-a-priest and you could tell me what prayers to say, or if I have to make a lil novena or something, to beat back whatever obeah it is they put on me..."

One never knew exactly how much of an Ollie-story to believe, but Ollie swore blind that his police friend was now a fervent Shouter, in secret.

Everywhere Shouters were being hounded from pillar to post. Yet Mumma, and Madlain, and the whole band of Mother Queen Lottie's spiritual children were flying in the face of the ordinance, keeping up their church year in, year out. Only, they had stopped holding service at the back of Queen's house, and moved their church up the hill to where the bush was thickest, and where they could look down and see police coming before they were seen.

Better take in front before in front take you. Many a little church that Shouter congregations had built, mixing clayey earth and grass with their own hands and feet to make the tapia walls, had been smashed to the ground by the police. The members would pick through the rubble, gathering what they could – their bell, the scattered strands of their cocoyea broom, their candles spotted with grit – anything that was not too broken or too defiled to use again. They would carry whatever they salvaged up into the steepest, rockiest places and build again between trees that closed in to cover them.

Ordinance or no ordinance, Mumma would put on her clothes and tie her head, twice round and then the knot to the fore. This head-tie alone was reason enough for her to be picked up and carted away in the Black Maria. (In the midst of all their anxiety, Gwynneth and Viola allowed themselves some comic relief by picturing the possible scene of two or more hefty police officers trying to get Mumma into their van.)

Puppa would be beside himself with rage and apprehension as she set off down the road with a calm face and fearless stride, heading for Pilgrim, leaving them to wonder what police station, courthouse, jail or hospital they might have to go and take her out of in the next few hours or days. That danger was past, because Mumma could no longer ups and travel to Pilgrim whenever the Spirit moved her. Now, however, from time to time, Pilgrim would come to Mumma.

The day the first detachment of The Lion of Judah Mystical Tabernacle arrived at the front gate, Viola was frightened out of her wits. She stood staring at them as though she had never seen such a sight before – women in white with sashes of yellow, red, blue, or green, their heads swathed in the same colours or in white, accompanied by men who carried suspicious-looking parcels. It was Gwynneth who marched pointedly down the walk and let them in.

They filled up Mumma's room (but there were only seven of them, really – Mother Polydore and her daughter Lystra, Mumma's brother Shepherd Albert, Mother Elaine, Teacher Humfrey, Leader Gareth and Sister Edna). Viola sat in the gallery peering up and down the road, so nervous she could hardly breathe. When they started to raise a hymn, she flew up and shot inside, pulling in the front door after her. Mumma's bedroom door, the one to the gallery, was already tightly closed, but the sound was bursting through, and the whole house seemed to be rocking. Viola rushed to the back door to close the top half, then darted around closing windows and slapping the jalousies shut.

All of this sent Gwynneth into a rage. "Open the damn windows!" she exploded. "Open the door! Let them hear! If they want to come inside people bedroom and arrest them for singing hymns, let them come! They going have to step over me!"

This made Viola even more nervous, because she knew that Gwynneth meant every word. In one moment, a year after the end of the first war, Gwynneth had lost all fear of police, principalities and powers – if indeed she had ever feared them. Viola knew that her sister was quite ready, any day, for the whole of His Majesty King George's royal police to march over her dead body. They had already done their worst. They had robbed her of her darling David.

Now Gwynneth stood ever ready to take on the whole cabal, from the constabulary to the governor and the entire colonial government (especially the stooges, the one-or-two sons of black mothers who sat on the Legislative Council in cahoots with them), right up the ladder to King George upon his throne. *Lord, put a hand…*

～

Still today, with Puppa dead going on fifteen years and she a grown woman with a path of grey through her hair, sitting on the train to Pilgrim felt like tiptoeing into the kitchen to steal condensed milk; gathering under the house to play some secret game; or wading into a cool, dark, forbidden pool at a river-bend shaded by branches thick with leaves – bamboo, wild palm, immortelle.

If she listened, she could still hear Puppa's angry voice in the raging sound under the train, travelling part of the way with them – Mumma and her two little girls – until it began to fade away towards Araujo. Then Gwynneth and Viola could begin to get excited at the prospect of arriving in Pilgrim, and Gang-Gang calling out raucously the moment she set eyes on them down in the gap, and how she would run down and try to hug-up the two of them at the same time, kissing them again and again. Gang-Gang never got tired of them, and was never happier than when she had all her grandpickney around her – Lyris, Cutty, Gracelyn, Gwynneth, Viola and Uncle Cecil's two boys, Wilfred and Dan.

But Gang-Gang could be quite stern, too, and all she had to do was open her eyes big at a child who had committed a misdemeanour or seemed to be contemplating one. This might be followed up with a saying to suit the misdemeanour. After parting a fight, for example, she would admonish: "You hand da fou wash you face, and write you name, na fou lash nabaddy." And there the matter would end. Just knowing that you had vexed Gang-Gang's spirit was chastisement enough.

Some of Gang-Gang's aphorisms were entirely of her own creation, as Gwynneth came to understand, for they were never heard of or used by anybody else, except Mumma, sayings such as: "You cyaan make sweetbread outa sand", or "*Zanndoli sé zanndoli, épi kwab sé kwab*" ("Lizard is lizard, and crab is crab").

~

When Puppa got his first transfer, to Morain R.C. School, he breathed a large sigh of relief, thinking that they could now shake the dust of Pilgrim off their feet forever. This was not to be. For the rest of his life he would carry on a futile struggle against Estelle going back and forth between wherever they were living, and Pilgrim, the place of darkness. Were it not for his fear of the powers lurking in that very darkness, powers that were Estelle's familiars, he would have made quick work of her obstinacy (or so he dreamed) with the leather belt he wore on his shoulder in school.

In those days, Mumma always made sure to announce about a week in advance that she was going to Pilgrim, and taking Gwynneth and Viola too-besides. This was to allow Puppa to object, to lecture, to rant, to put his foot down as firmly as he could ("I know you are going down there for obeah! You had better not bring any of that into my house!"), and then to grumble threateningly for a day or two before Mumma made up her bundles, dressed her little girls and herself, and set out for the train station. "*Nou ka pati.* We gone."

On the train, far from Puppa's ears, the three of them prattled away in Patois, to their hearts' content. In Pilgrim they climbed mango trees, played down in the cocoa and bathed in the river with cousins whom Puppa did not wish them to know; and with their cousins and Gang-Gang and Mumma and Tantie Grace and Uncle Albert, and sometimes Papa Georgie or Uncle Cecil, they went to sing and shout, to clap and stamp and shake in the little church behind Mother Queen Lottie's house, breathing in the smell of camphor and a clean perfume that sprinkled the air, and the bell rejoicing and conch-shell hooting *Hooray*.

Puppa's motto was: "Look up, not down", and going back to Pilgrim was among the things that came under "looking down". For him, the village called Pilgrim would forever be a place of darkness, the wilderness into which the young Joseph Cuffie was sent to teach – was banished – a year after he attained his hard-earned First Class Schoolmasters' Certificate.

One of Gwynneth's deepest regrets was that she had learnt too late the full story of her father's life. Mumma's life was an open book; all the stories of her growing up that she had told Gwynneth and Viola were part of their growing up. Puppa, on the other hand, never spoke about when he was a little boy. All they knew was that he was born in town and had grown up in town. They got nothing more out of him by asking; and Mumma would give only the skimpiest of answers, or she would plead ignorance, if they cornered her with questions about him.

Mumma never let on how much she knew, not until Gwynneth and Viola were in their late thirties and their father was dying. They learned, then, that she knew everything about him. He had bared his soul to her in the early days of their friending, and, for the rest of his life, would now and then confide in her.

~

Joseph Cuffie was not given to idle, wasteful conversation, indeed was not overly given to conversation. He preferred thinking. But he did speak to his children. He did his duty by his children – admonished them; preached to them about walking the straight and narrow; told his son what was expected of him; told the girls what was expected of them; commented on his children's school-work and sought to remedy the weaknesses therein.

Much of his thinking he did while sitting in the Morris chair that occupied the corner between his bedroom door and the front door. There he would sit and mull things over. This chair gave him a commanding view of the drawing-room and dining-room, part of the pantry, and the passageway that led to the back door. What he enjoyed the most was contemplating his progress in life, reflecting on the things that, by the grace of God, he had been able to achieve. This property had come such a long way since 1900 when he first visited the parcel of land, a corner plot, that was Lot #18, Farfan Road!

He had managed, at last, to build the room for Roy. The day after his son was born, Joseph had started buying bricks and storing them under the house. Then sheets of galvanise. By Roy's third birthday he was collecting bags of cement. The room was finished just before Roy started primary school, but Roy would stay in the old children's room for the time being. Except for Estelle's sewing, Roy became master of that room, but nothing could dissuade him from leaving it at night to go and curl up in the bed with Gwynneth and Viola in the new room. (Joseph disapproved, but did not win the battle, for the boy's mother and sisters could see no harm in this conduct.)

The two extensions to the house, Roy's room and then Gwynneth's, gave him such an appearance of rising – *four* bedrooms! Only whitepeople had more than two bedrooms. He had already achieved, some years earlier, the major triumph of putting in the WC. He couldn't afford it at the time the house was built. He had drawn it into the house plan, but the stall remained empty, just collecting clutter – boxes, yellowing newspapers, bags of old clothes, bottles – until he was able to have the soak-away made, and the plumbing installed, a very expensive undertaking. It had set him back considerably, but it was worth it. Now his family would know better than the latrine, and his would be the only house, for what could be miles around, with an indoor flushing WC.

And then, to crown it all, electricity! The Electric Light and Power Company, that for years had been making its way at a slow crawl along the Eastern Main Road from Kings Port, had finally reached Turagua. Of course, his was one of only a few households in Turagua that could benefit immediately from the advent of electricity.

If the back door was open, he could see some of the yard from his Morris chair, and the beginning of the part of the property that remained forested. He had no intention of clearing it, either, for it served as a bulwark against whatever might come to pass north of his domain. In 1900, there were few neighbours, and they were all a good distance away, except for a ramshackle eyesore to the east of his property. Once he came into possession of his deed, and had cleared his house spot, he lost no time in putting up a barbed wire fence along that side, to indicate to the inhabitants of the hovel that he and his family would not be making common cause with them.

The cost of enclosing the whole parcel of land was beyond his means, but he hoped to be able to at least fence the house spot on three sides, with the forest – his piece of the forest – as protection to the north. Years later, having already fortified the eastern boundary with barbed wire, he fenced the front and western sides of his yard with chicken wire, although by then Estelle had grown a healthy hibiscus hedge along the front of the property.

The rickety board house that stood, or leaned, in the adjoining lot continued to be a grouse. It was too close for his comfort. The occupants, a clearly uneducated old man and a woman, were not the kind of people he had imagined having as neighbours in the stage of his life when he could settle into his own home. That was the second fly in the ointment. The first was not being able to get a property in town, or nearer to town; but, he had made the best of it. He had built up an impressive home.

Next he planned to build a shed in the backyard, for potted plants, maybe, which would make it a "greenhouse" – another thing that would raise his nose, for common Creole people didn't even know what a greenhouse was. Or, the shed could be for his wife and daughters to do the household laundry in modest privacy.

Looking into the future, Joseph could see a shiny car parked in that shed, his son's car, for the boy would have finished high school and moved up into a big job in the civil service. Roy would be living in the house with his wife and children, his sisters having married well and left the family home. And if, by the grace of God, Roy's old father and mother were still alive at that point, well, there were *four* bedrooms, after all. Such good fortune! It almost made up for the loss he felt at not being able to afford a home in town, and having to make do with Turagua, a good forty minutes' train journey away. But, driving his own car, Roy would get to town in half that time.

7
"I am Joseph Cuffie, a certificated schoolmaster."

Pilgrim R.C. School seemed to Joseph a cruel reward for his long and determined climb up the ladder of exams. He had spent most of his life up till then tackling one exam after the other, failing sometimes and trying again. In the end he had passed every exam he met in his way, all at Holy Family Boys' R.C. School, first as a pupil, then as a pupil teacher. The most difficult part of the climb had been his primary school grade exams.

For one thing, he was half-hungry nearly all the time. Also, it was not so easy to do as the teacher said: "When you go home, take up your book again." Home was on Alice Street, in Bourg Ravine, that part of Kings Port known unofficially, and unkindly, as *Chou Ravine*, meaning "ravine-backside". Every day, in the late afternoon, he sat with his reading-book on the doorstep of his family's barrack-room, to catch the last light of the sun. But this was like sitting in the market on a Saturday morning, or down on the wharf when there was a ship out in the harbour off-loading.

Sitting on the doorstep meant sitting in the yard, and this was a yard of twelve families. Each of these families lived in a room just like his, but they never all went inside until it was time to sleep. The rooms were small and stuffy and there were too many people to go into each. There were two rows of rooms facing each other across the narrow yard. Neighbours were coming and going around him all the time. On evenings, the yard was full of talking, shouting, boisterous laughter, singing, whistling, and sometimes loud quarrelling, cursing and fights between neighbour and neighbour, or between man and woman, and the bawling of beaten children.

At the pump, neighbours would be filling pans and pails, washing clothes, bathing little children. The drain running down the middle of the yard, passing right in front of his door, often gave up foul smells, not to speak of the latrines down at the end of the yard where, on mornings, he, Bella and Theodore, by turns, had to go and empty their family's near-to-overflowing po-chamb.

Some people would be cooking in the yard, but on many an evening there was no supper in sight for Joseph and his siblings, and seldom would a yard neighbour take pity on them. Other children in the yard didn't go hungry just because their adults were late coming home from work that evening, or sometimes had nothing to give them to eat. There would always be somebody willing to offer a wedge of roast-bake or two-three pot-spoons of rice, or to put some more water in the pot to stretch the soup or the porridge so a neighbour's children could get something in their bellies. Not Miss Delphine's children.

Joseph knew that their neighbours referred to his mother as "Madame Poor-Great", because she would never join the mêlée in the yard and would rather die than let any of them know that her family was in need of anything. She did not want these people thinking that she was the same as them. Miss Delphine was a shabeen woman who had not managed to pass her colour on to her children; they had all turned out as black as sin, and so she taught them: "More you black and knotty-head, more you must stay far from black, knotty-head people. No friend-friend with old-nigga."

Every last one of her children was born red-skinned like herself, but Delphine knew full well that this meant nothing. The blackest of parents could give birth to a red-skinned baby, but that baby could turn black before its navel-string dried up and fell off. Yet she dared to entertain the hope, with each birth, that this baby's skin would not turn. Anxiously she would examine the tiny ears, only to find a darkness around their edges that predicted the child's inescapable shade of skin.

There, hope was dashed, but still she thought she could do something about the nose. Each of Delphine's babies endured a daily pinching and kneading and pulling at its nose, meant to raise the flat, sprawling offence to Delphine's eyes into a "straight" nose. As for the knotty-head, the *chivé tak-tak*, the less said and the less grieved over that, the better, Delphine reasoned. There was no cure. The cap of hair that lay sleek and genteel on the child's head at birth would soon rise up and turn into a near-impenetrable bush, like the jungle in Africa. She couldn't understand it. Why was she being punished? She was a good person. A good mother and a hardworking woman. A God-fearing person. She no kill no priest.

As Joseph sat on the doorstep trying to concentrate on the words in his reading-book, he had to be constantly on the lookout for Scally, his tormentor.

Scally was a young man from another barrack-yard further down Alice Street who thought it was the greatest fun to sneak up on Joseph and snatch his book from him. Whenever Joseph saw him in the yard he would hurriedly close the book, put it on the step and sit on it. But if he wasn't lucky enough to see Scally first, then suddenly his book was gone and Scally would be running all over the yard or into the street holding it in the air and laughing, or threatening to throw it in the latrine. Mr Felix, the old man who parted fights among the yard's children, turned a blind eye, and some of the other adults looked on without a word.

The torture only came to an end when one afternoon Joseph's mother suddenly appeared with her half-laden tray on her head, her large body filling the entrance to the yard. She set down her tray, picked up a piece of wood from a broken cartwheel, and stood aside quietly watching while Joseph ran after Scally in a zig-zag line all over the yard, desperately pleading and crying for his book.

"*Mwen ké jété i nan latrin-la!*" Scally was chanting, "Me go throw am na latrine! Me go throw am na latrine!"

"*Epi mwen ké pousé tèt-ou nan latrin-la!* And me go shove you head na latrine!" came the voice of Miss Delphine, now bent over Scally's body which was writhing fearfully, face down on the ground. She had tripped him with her foot as he headed, chuckling, out of the yard, and now she kept him pinned to the ground by holding one of his arms twisted behind his back. Miss Delphine near beat the tripe out of Scally with the piece of cartwheel, all the while chastising him at the top of her voice: "You little nastiness! Get you black ugly tail outa this yard! If me see you inside here again, me go break you two hand and you two foot, *salaud!* You jealous the boy just because he da learn Book? Because he want be somebaddy? And you just want be one nasty lil stray-way ragamuffin nigga!"

Joseph would never forget that day, although, as a good Catholic, he blushed to remember some of the words his mother used on Scally,

While Joseph sat and struggled with his reading-lesson, his brothers and sisters would be playing noisily with the other children of the barrack-yard, rolling hoops, pitching marbles or rattling sticks along the cobblestones set into the dirt for people to step over the mud in rainy season. Some of these children were also enrolled in school (including one of Joseph's brothers, Theodore), but they just didn't bother with this take-up-your-book business.

Usually, at this time of day, Joseph's mother would still be out walking the streets of the town, or the Esplanade, with her marchand tray on her head. If darkness fell and she had not come back, it meant she had not sold enough sweets for the day. She would then be up on the pitch walk around the Savannah, hoping that some of the better-fed residents of the town, out for their after-dinner stroll, might fancy a piece of *halé-filé* or toolum to sweeten their mouths.

It would then be up to Joseph to get his brothers and sisters inside. If his mother came home after dark, foot-weary and bringing only a handful of coins tied into her kerchief, to find them still cavorting about the yard, the strap would fly. Worse if she had to send him to look for any of them dreevaying down by the sea wall, where they might have gone to watch the spectacle of kobo feasting on the newest dead dog brought down by the ravine in heavy rain. The games in the street afterwards might be so sweet that they and their playmates forgot all about their curfews.

On such evenings the room would be racked by the sound of blows and a chorus of bawling that only provoked more blows, most of them falling on Joseph, for he was the eldest.

Every evening he had to see to it that they washed their feet at the pump before they came in. He would go in and light the flambeau, then look in the safe to see what there was of bread, biscuits, sugar, or even old, half-melted sweets too out-of-shape to sell. They would mix sugar-water and try to fill up their bellies.

85

Then they spread out the pissy bedding on the floor and settled in for the night. By the jumping fire of the flambeau Joseph would take up his book once more. But with his brothers and sisters jostling each other, telling jokes and stories, vying to produce the longest belch or the loudest fart, accusing each other of surreptitious farting, and just refusing to be still, taking up his book was of little use.

Late one night their mother had not yet come home and they were all very hungry, for they had not eaten since morning. The two youngest ones began to cry with bellyache, but there was nothing to eat. Joseph could only offer them cup after cup of water. He couldn't make sugar-water because there was no sugar. The crying became louder and louder, until Miss Serrette, who couldn't help hearing them through the partition, came over to find out what the matter was, went back to her room and returned with a rum bottle full of thin flour-pap.

They let the youngest ones drink first, and then Bella, Theodore and Joseph each got a mouthful or two from what was left. Their mother arrived just when Joseph was draining the bottle, his face upturned with the bottle upside down on his mouth as he sucked out the last dregs of flour-pap. The tray was still on her head; one hand was balancing it. "Wha that you da drink?" she asked, her eyes open big. "Where you get that?"

Joseph, Bella and Theodore stood frozen, mute. The little ones answered. Miss Delphine's face turned grim. The strap was hanging on its nail by the window, too far from her hand; but the mortar and pestle were right next to the table. Swiftly Miss Delphine lifted the tray off her head, set it down on the table and in the same movement reached for the pestle. She grabbed it with such fury that the mortar tipped over, hit the floor with a thud and rolled in an arc, away from her.

She beat Joseph with the pestle until he, too, rolled on the floor, curled up like a congoree, his hands protecting his head. All the while she harangued them in a vehement whisper – a hiss – for, drunk or sober, she didn't want any kangkalang with Miss Serrette. "*Zot vlé fè mwen hont?* Ayou want make me shame? Ayou want bring shame pan my head? Ayou want them say Delphine cyaan feed she pickney-them? Eh? Me look like beggar? Eh? Me no tell ayou never eat nutten from them nasty, poor-ass old-nigga round here?"

When she was done, one of Joseph's thumbs was broken, swelling rapidly, and his whole body hurt. The next morning he was roasting with fever and couldn't go to school for days.

Joseph was an acolyte at Holy Family Church, right next to his school. He helped clean the church two evenings in the week, and served at Mass every Sunday. He loved just being in the church, in the heady ambience of its high vaulted roof, muted sunlight streaming through the many-coloured window panes that surrounded you with Bible scenes, pictures from a world so far away in time and place it could be Heaven; beautifully carved pews; the soft smell of incense diffused in the air; lit candles; the organ's throaty croon... And the high point: the Ave Maria sung by Daphne Matamoro – "Lady Daphne" as she called herself.

This woman was a very black and raucous chantwelle who led the lavway for a Kamboulay street band. Lady Daphne was a parishioner of Holy Family Church, and also, it was fairly well known, a Shango-worshipper. The church was in a terrible bind. At Mass, her beautiful singing voice soared over everybody else's, even the combined voices of the choir. She sang the Spirit straight into people's hearts. Still, they couldn't very well let her into the choir – she did not belong there. The members of Holy Family Church choir were all decent and upstanding white and brown Christian people.

In order that the congregation might enjoy the benefit of her inspiring voice, therefore, every now and then Daphne would be called upon to sing a hymn, solo. Not from the altar, for then there would surely be consequences. Something might catch fire. But she didn't need to stand at the altar. She could sing anywhere in the church and fill it with her voice.

For Joseph, hearing Lady Daphne sing the Ave Maria was an indescribable pleasure. Although she was very black, with big tottots and bamsie sticking out rudely before and behind – touching off impious thoughts – if you listened to her heavenly singing with your eyes closed, you could imagine this jamet as an alabaster saint, worthy to be standing among the others in the alcoves of the church in their sheer robes of alabaster – no part of their bodies sticking out.

One evening, Father Francois came into the church from the vestry as Joseph was wiping down the pews, and called him into his office. Joseph was apprehensive, wondering whether he had in some way given offence to the church.

"Joseph," Father Francois began. "Last Sunday, on the altar, I noticed you were barefoot?"

He had forgotten about the shoes, or the lack thereof. At Sunday Mass he had hoped no one would notice that he was barefoot, as his cassock, given to him by the church, was not exactly his size. The hem of it brushed the ground, so his feet were not supposed to be visible. Father Francois tried to reassure him: "Don't look so worried. We just want to see how we can help you. What happened to your shoes?"

"My shoe bust up, Father."

"Are you doing well in school? You know, do you not, that schooling is what will take you out of poverty?"

Father questioned him about school, and he answered with honesty, telling him how difficult it had been. He had failed the Standard 1 and Standard 4 exams, and therefore spent two years in each of those classes, not getting out of Standard 4 until he was almost fifteen.

"So now you are in Standard 5, and fifteen years old?"

Joseph hung his head. "Yes, Father, but I am working hard, and my teacher told me I will succeed."

"Good. Do you think you would want to be a pupil teacher and train to become a schoolmaster?"

Joseph, not sure how to receive this, looked at Father and answered cautiously, "Yes, Father?"

"I will speak with your headmaster. You are a hardworking young man, and you give unstintingly of yourself without asking anything in return. God will surely bless you."

The priest then wrote out something on a sheet of paper, put it into an envelope and handed it to Joseph, saying, "Go over to the girls' school office and give this to Sister Antoinette. She will find a pair of shoes for you."

Father Francois helped Joseph through his remaining two terms in Standard 5, lending him books to read so that he could gain mastery of English, and coaching him in arithmetic, which was not Joseph's strong suit. Father even brought boiled eggs from the presbytery kitchen and called him into his office to eat them, so that his brain could be nourished. Joseph passed his Standard 5 end-of-year exam and was taken on as a pupil teacher in the school.

There began a new ordeal of exams. Joseph's daily round became quite burdensome. After the day's work of teaching hard-head children, he was himself obliged to take an hour and a half of instruction given by the schoolmaster charged with training pupil teachers. Then he would go over to the church, taking his instruction materials with him, so that he could sit and study in the peace and quiet of the vestry. However, before he could sit down to the cruel mass of homework set by the instructor, especially on the days when he had cleaning duty, the evening was already far advanced and, more often than not, Joseph was tired. Father Francois tried to relieve him of cleaning duty, but Joseph chose to hold on to one of his two days of cleaning the church.

Now he was bringing home a small salary every month. Theodore, who now had to see about the younger children on evenings, had abandoned school and was hiring out his services to offices and shops around the town, penny an errand. Hunger could now be kept at bay; and within his first year as a pupil teacher, Joseph was able to buy new shoes and have the tailor make him two different suits of good clothes. He began to dream of moving out of Bourg Ravine.

At the end of his second year of training, Joseph passed the exam for his Third Class certificate. This earned him an increment on his salary. He did some calculations and had to accept, with great disappointment, that the salary would still not enable him to leave Bourg Ravine.

Joseph was put on the church's Sunday morning patrol. One of the acolytes who usually performed that duty was being given another responsibility. Part of Joseph's work, now, would be to help keep the front pews clear in the period before the start of eight o'clock Mass. Joseph applied himself conscientiously to ejecting any black riff-raff who would make so bold as to stray into this area and seat themselves. After all, these pews belonged to the better class of people; they had paid their money for them.

He also combed the pews behind, where the common people sat. There he sought out and rebuked young black women who were improperly dressed, flaunting flesh, their upper arms or even their shoulders exposed. "Young woman!" he would admonish. "Cover yourself! This is the house of God!"

Sometimes the young girls embarrassed and unsettled him with saucy responses. One of them had positioned herself, he was certain, at the end of the pew so that when he paused to scrutinise that row, she could whisper, right into his ear, "Well, *Doudou*, Lil Sweetman, take off you gown and gimme fou cover with, *non!*"

There were times when he spotted women of high colour or class who had to be reprimanded for their manner of dress; but then he would call Father Francois to do the necessary. He had to call on the priest also if the black offenders were women over a certain age. Joseph felt quite unable to scold such women; it would be like disrespecting your mother or your grandmother.

The front section of the church remained empty until one minute to eight o'clock, when suddenly the owners of those pews would materialise, splendidly attired, and take their seats. Their finery was a sight to behold. Understandably, they had no desire to find themselves caught in between the kind of people crowding in through the doors and encumbering the aisles for an hour or so before Mass.

When Joseph passed his Second Class certificate exam, he was ecstatic, for the increment that came with this promotion was what he needed in order to make the move. Now he could get out of Alice Street, out of the barrack-yard, and into a room of his own in a decent part of the town.

That Saturday morning Joseph got up early and bathed and bathed, scrubbing his skin with a stiff new torchon. Miss Delphine, proud of his rising, made cocoa-tea for him with powder that came in a tin from England, and laid out two airy hops-bread bought from the bakery. Not for this son the greasy chocolate-tea made from beans coming straight off a tree somewhere in the Cayerian bush, nor the heavy, belly-full roast-bake, both of which his siblings were still being raised on.

He dressed himself carefully, and gave his shoes a final rub with the cloth. Then he fitted his hat onto his head and stepped out of his mother's door. He picked his way across the cobblestones and mud, and when he was out of the yard, stamped each foot in turn and looked under it to make sure that it was clean, as if the trace outside the yard wasn't a worse mess of sticky mud and stones.

He took to the beaten track that ran alongside the ravine wall, going north. Soon he was making his way along the edge of LaCour Danglade. On the other side of the ravine, it was still the swamp, its odours rising with the sun. The swamp was the next-door neighbour of both Bourg Ravine and LaCour Danglade, and Joseph had named it "The Slough of Despond", after Father Francois lent him *The Pilgrim's Progress*.

Old Man Felix used to lecture the yard's children on the topic of Ambition, whenever he got an opportunity. "See them lilly shoebox house over there?" he would say, pointing at LaCour Danglade. "Awee over here could think we better off than them, and sarry for them because them da live na one shanty town, with house make outa rotten-wood and cardboard and dirt and old rusty piece-a galvanise fou wall and roof. But same way, somebaddy over there could throw word for awee over here, and say, 'Me no have no landlord fou come pound-down the door when month-end, and throw me family things out na road if me no have the rent money. Da me self whay build this house, with me own two hand. Me da *owner*.'

"So, no sarry fou them. Sorry fou ayou self if lilly nigga pickney whay da live na Bourg Ravine and LaCour Danglade no go na school and study Book. When ayou come big man and woman whay cyaan read one word, neither write ayou own name on a paper, then ayou, and ayou pickney, go never come outa barrack-yard and shanty town. Ayou go suck salt in this land."

Mr Felix was dead and gone, but as Joseph plodded north-wards, he thought how the old man would have approved of him.

The once scrawny youngboy Joseph Cuffie, son of Madame Poor-Great Miss Delphine, Joseph Cuffie, now 19 years old, armed with his Second Class Schoolmaster's certificate, was walking away from the barrack-yard to go and meet his better future. Mr Felix would have held him up as a model, a pattern, an example for the young boys to follow.

Joseph had already walked about half a mile, still following the course of the ravine, but he was not on any dirt track, now. He was walking on an embankment beside the ravine, with a paved roadway and fine balustrade. No swamp here. He was on Creighton Street, which would stick to the ravine embankment for the next half mile or so.

The bed of the ravine was also paved, thanks to a governor, Mr Felix said, who had ruled Cayeri about a hundred years before. Joseph and the other children of the barrack-yard knew that the ravine was really the bottom piece of Shadybrook River. They learned from Mr Felix that the river used to run down right through the centre of the town, until the governor ups and moved it over to the east. That was how it came to run, instead, like a fence along that side of Kings Port.

Joseph thought of how, as a boy, he would walk in a grappe of children along the bed of the ravine, trekking up into the hills to pick mango. That was in dry season, so there would be only a thin stream of water in the ravine. Sometimes they went up into Morne Cabrite, and at other times they would venture further north, all the way up behind Kings Port, through Brierly, Primrose Hill, and even to Shadybrook where the ravine came from.

He shuddered now at the thought of having walked so heedlessly, nay, so cheerily, down inside that nasty ravine time and time again. He continued along Creighton Street, but abandoned that route just before the ravine veered slightly eastwards, towards Morne Cabrite, taking the street with it. He crossed the next bridge over the ravine, to enter King George Street. The idea of looking for a room to rent in Morne Cabrite did not appeal to him. That place, which Mr Felix and many of his generation still called "Freetown" did not befit his new status as a certificated schoolmaster.

Mr Felix used to fill them up with tales of Freetown as a place where people liberated from slavery had built a new life with their own two hands on the green hillsides, tending their bounteous gardens and minding their goats, in contented peace. Delphine used to say to Joseph, "You wotless father bin da look fou buy piece-a thief-land, up inside that bush, from another nigga more wotless than he."

Morne Cabrite was a law unto itself, its brazen little dwellings sprouting all over the hillsides, *vaykivay*. You could almost call them "cottages", he mused, those that you could see from this distance. Many were hidden or half-hidden by bushy trees. The inhabitants made their way about Morne Cabrite on narrow, twisting lanes that were more like goat-tracks, or the paths of crazy-ants, than the streets of a town. There was no chance of his finding a suitable room there to rent, even if he had been so inclined. Most of the houses were so small that any room within those walls had to be smaller than the room that had housed him, his mother, and his four brothers and sisters. No, he would begin his quest in Kings Port proper, where a higher class of people lived. Better houses. Respectable citizens.

Joseph walked the length and breadth of Hillview and Maytown, calling at the gate of every house that seemed large enough to have a spare room for rent. He would first greet the house: "Good morning!" Some houses did not answer, and he would move on. If somebody did appear, he would introduce himself: "I am Joseph Cuffie, a certificated schoolmaster. I am seeking a room to rent."

At some of the houses, the occupants, or their domestic servants, perhaps, steupsed at him through the jalousies and disappeared back into the house. His heart quickened when he came before a house that had a sign displayed: "Room for rent". A man came out into the gallery and Joseph launched into his self-introduction, at the end of which the man looked him up and down and waved him away.

He took to calling out his credentials to each house, before anybody appeared, and often nobody did. Soon the possibilities of Hillview and Maytown had been exhausted, and now he was at the Savannah. The sun had meanwhile climbed quite high in the sky. He sought out a bench under a tree and sat for a while to rest and to ponder his next move. He decided against going further west, to Belair, Windsor, and other places where the houses were bigger, and the people whiter, so that he was likely to be treated with even more disdain. He chose to head northward, forgetting, for the moment, that the only difference between the people in the west and those in the north was that one set lived on flat land and the other on a mountainside.

Joseph trudged doggedly across the wide expanse of green, came out of the Savannah, and walked some more, until he found himself in Brierly. Just when the sun was at its highest in the sky, what should greet him but a sign saying "Room for rent" on the gate of a large house. Throwing all misgiving to the winds, Joseph shook the little tinkling bell attached to the gatepost. An elderly high-colour lady came out and stood at the top of the gallery steps.

"Yes?" she asked.

He rolled out his introduction. Halfway through it, he realised that in his nervous haste, he had forgotten to say "Good morning". Too late, he thought. Go brave. Not a time for faintheartedness.

"Where are you from?" the lady asked.

His heart sank; he had left home without a plan for getting over this hurdle. His mother had instructed him to tell people "Morne Cabrite" if they posed that question. She had a *makoumè* up there whose address he could use. But Joseph Cuffie could not practise deceit – he was an acolyte of the Catholic church. "Bourg Ravine, and I am an acolyte at Holy Family church. I also teach at Holy Family R.C. School," Joseph rattled off.

She let him into the gallery. It turned out that she, and more so her children, who all lived elsewhere, wanted someone to be on the premises at night, as she lived alone. "You don't have to *do* anything but be here in the night. We're looking for someone who will be a night-watchman – just by being here – as well as a tenant. That's why the rent is so low."

Joseph felt that he could not have wished for a happier ending to his journey, in the hot-sun, from the bottom to almost the top of Kings Port. He was far, far, from the ravine's backside disgorging dirtiness from the town. His gratitude knew no bounds – never mind his room, in the yard at the back of the house, used to be the horse's stable.

After two more years of relentless work – teaching hard-head children, submitting himself to instruction, studying, and sitting exams – Joseph had conquered the exam of exams and attained his First Class certificate. Now he was a full-fledged, respectable schoolmaster, with the attendant salary. The barrack-yard was behind him forever. He had fought his way out. His children, and all his generations after him, would never look back. Alice Street – the stench of rubbish rotting in the swamp; sugar-water for supper; and sleeping head-and-toe on pissy bedding under the table – would be his secret alone. But a teacher, and especially a teacher of the Roman Catholic family of schools, was pledged to go wherever he was called upon to serve. And he was called to Pilgrim.

Bush. And shrieking birds. And ignorant Creole people. Just when he had reached, he thought, a pinnacle, he felt as though he was plunging back into the pit.

What was he to do with these children? Some of them shocked him and made him uneasy because they were ghosts of his own wretched childhood, only more ragged, only sleepier than the boy Joseph, and really not too interested in anything that was going on in the schoolroom. Though they all seemed to understand well enough when he spoke to them in English, most of them would speak nothing but Patois. He had long put that uncouth tongue away and used it only when he had to address illiterate folk who knew no better. Nothing in his years of exam-taking had prepared him for this.

Before the year was out he suffered another great setback. Because he had been so occupied with his studies, and because he had tried to be a worthy Catholic, Joseph had not let his eyes or his thoughts wander too often to the opposite sex. He knew, though, how his wife was going to be. She was going to be something like all the women in *My Book of Catholic Saints*, given to him by Father Francois – the only book he had owned in his youth besides his reading-book for each grade.

Now in this godforsaken place called Pilgrim, he found himself in venial sin with a young woman who was nothing like a Catholic saint, and he was obliged to marry her. Saint Mary, Saint Ann, Saint Theresa, Saint Rose, Saint Philomena – Estelle bore no resemblance whatsoever to any of these beings, and they, from their saintly abode on high, must surely be blushing with shame for him.

Joseph had not pictured for himself a wife whose schooling had ended at Standard 3, was quite content to speak in Patois, and, most bitter blow of all, was not, in her heart of hearts, a Catholic. Estelle's family, it dawned on him too late, were of that heathen host, the Disobedient Baptists, whom the people called "Shouters" because of their abominable noise.

Their noise was not the worst part. They, as well as others who called themselves by different names, were people who had never been entirely cleansed of the demons of Africa, the place from which their ancestors had come, but so long ago! Why could his people not shake off the darkness of their past? Now he, who all his life had cleaved to the other side of the street, quickening his step and mentally crossing himself whenever errands for his mother took him past the evil Shango-yard in Bourg Ravine, would be yoked forever to such a person!

Estelle had attended Pilgrim R.C. School, had been christened, catechised, and confirmed, along with some of her schoolmates whose parents saw no disadvantage in letting their children tap into the power of the Catholic church in addition to that of their own faith. From time to time she went to Mass at St Dominic's, over in Clancy, where Joseph went every Sunday. More than once Joseph made up his mind to go and confess to Father O'Callaghan, and then seek an annulment of the marriage. This plan he abandoned, however, when he read in the *The Catholic Herald* of a teacher dismissed from his post in a Catholic school because he had been seen looking on at a Shouter prayer meeting held on a street corner.

It was a temptation Joseph himself had fought. To walk straight past a Shouter service was near impossible. You had to cross yourself (mentally, of course – not for them to see, for you could never tell what might happen to you) and finger the rosary in your pocket as you made your way past them. Everyone knew that their behaviour was ridiculous and contemptible and far beyond the bounds of decorum. Yet there was something about their singing, shouting, hand-clapping, stamping, dancing, and the bell that rang out at the height of their ecstasy... Better to hurry past.

Nor had Joseph pictured for himself a wife who would insist on carrying on a paid occupation of her own. Estelle knew how to sew. She had learned how to make every conceivable kind of garment, and she was an excellent seamstress. Joseph did not want his wife taking in sewing. The wives of respectable men did not work for others, like barrack-yard women. He quarrelled and fussed, but it was no use. As with her spiritual life, he was forced to turn a blind eye (though, of course, he had to keep up the fussing and quarrelling, for that was his duty).

And in later years he was thankful for Estelle's industriousness. On a schoolmaster's salary alone they would never have been able to lease the parcel of Crown land in Turagua and build the family home. Above all, he would never have been able to take the giant step of putting his son into the hallowed College of the Ascension. The Catholic Church had generously offered the boy a place and awarded him a partial scholarship, in recognition of his father's service to the Church. But in order for them to take up the offer and keep Roy at the college for the full five years, Estelle would pedal her sewing machine day and night. When at last Roy had finished high school and gone out to work in the Civil Service, Estelle's eyesight would never be the same again.

8
Everything is for a good. No bad doan happen.

A thick, high ixora hedge stood along the front of the yard, dark green bush holding out its bouquets of little blood-red flowers. Behind the hedge the family's prayer flags, of green, white, saffron and blue, rose into the air on tall bamboo poles. Just inside the gap, to one side, was a small fig patch – a banana stool with leaves broad and healthy, some tall and straight and waving skywards, others genuflecting in the breeze. Even though it was set on top of a mound of earth and protected by its own hedge of ixora and cactus, nobody could glance at it and accuse it of being anything but a fig patch. But Gwynneth knew that down between the stalks, and also buried in the earth mound, were offerings to a guardian spirit.

Venus was sitting in her gallery with a child on her lap, rubbing his skin, and did not seem the least bit surprised to see Gwynneth appear in the gap. She got up, and with the child clamped around her hip, unwired the gallery gate, came down the three or four steps, and set off to meet Gwynneth who was already on her way up the path, followed by Mr Brathwaite's two youngsters lugging most of her bags.

The yard was swept clean; there were still fine furrows on the ground, made by the cocoyea broom. Gwynneth walked up the path between beds of gladioli, zinnias, old-maid, and the frilly orange marigolds that Viola as a child called "church-flowers". The two girls used to walk about their grandparents' yard with Mumma as she gathered flowers and leafy stems to be placed in calabashes and lotas around the centre-pole of Queen's church; and when the stems of the marigold were cut, or its petals crushed, a powerful scent filled your nostrils and your head…

Before Gwynneth could open her mouth, Venus said gravely, "Something happen to Nenn Estelle. Is only this child prevent me from coming down there day-before-yesterday. How she feeling?" And then she was calling out to her husband, who was nowhere in sight, "Polydore! Poly! Aint I di tell you something happen to my Nennen? Aint I tell you so? Look Gwynneth come."

From behind the trees off to the side of the house his voice floated to them in answer, mixed with the barking of dogs. Gwynneth was settling into the gallery chair when Monica appeared around a corner of the house. She greeted Gwynneth warmly and took her bags inside. (On Mumma's instruction, Gwynneth had journeyed to Pilgrim bearing multiple packages which contained some of whatever they could find that was most scarce in the war and that they could afford – rice, flour, and sweet-soap – as well as the usual candles, incense, kananga water and olive oil for the church.)

As Gwynneth explained what she had come for, Venus nodded slowly, knowingly. She told Gwynneth about a dream she had had some nights before. In the dream, somebody was telling her to go outside and pick three different kinds of bush to make a poultice. When she asked who the poultice was for, the person answered: "*Ou ké wè*. You go see."

She knew as soon as she woke up that it was her godmother's voice she had heard. Venus now had the sudden feeling of a knot unravelling. *Everything is for a good. No bad doan happen.* She would send her younger daughter. That was the next best thing to going herself, and besides… The girl was friending with a wotless man over in Clancy, and Venus had prayed for something to come between them. This, she knew, was the answer to her prayers.

Elford LeFranc was a gambler and a ne'er-do-well, always in a rumshop. When he was sober he played the clarinet and sang with the Moonlighters Orchestra, the most popular dance band for miles around, famous even in San Pedro. At Carnival time he sang in a calypso tent in Kings Port, and it was said that he got more encores than any other calypsonian in that tent. He was also an excellent joiner, much sought after and well paid.

But the man was wotless. Whatever he was paid, he would gamble it away, drink it away, or dress himself up like a saga-boy, in flashy clothes, hats, gold chains and rings. Certainly, it was said, no chile-mother of his ever saw the colour of that money. LeFranc (also known as "Sugars") had something like five or six children already, scattered all about in Clancy, Beauregard and here in Pilgrim. So people said. LeFranc himself wasn't too sure.

Venus did not tell Gwynneth about LeFranc, because Gwynneth might think she was palming off trouble on her. More than that, she didn't want Gwynneth to think that Monica was a flighty girl. No. Monica was a very sensible girl who had shown very early that she knew her own mind. That was why nobody could understand this thing – what could be pulling a sensible girl like Monica to a locho like LeFranc?

Monica was not a little child, either. She was 22 years old. She had ambition. She was the proud holder of a Primary School Leaving Certificate – not many girls in Pilgrim reached that far. And now the post mistress was showing Monica a little book-keeping as she helped with selling stamps and stationery; addressing envelopes or even writing letters for people who had not spent much time in school; and keeping the place tidy. Miss Carrington operated Pilgrim's post office out of a front room of her house. Monica was looking to get a job in a store in Kings Port, so she could save up enough money to go to commercial school, and maybe even go Away after the war.

Venus's spirit soared. "*Bondjé bon.* God is good. 'My soul doth magnify the Lord,'" she sang in her heart, "'and my spirit hath rejoiced…'"

They talked it over. Gwynneth was concerned that Venus would no longer have the help that Monica gave her in the house. Venus assured her that neither Cyrus nor Malcolm had finny-hand, and were no less help in the house than Monica, because Venus wasn feeding no boy-chirren who couldn even boil water to save they life. So it was agreed. Now they had to ask Monica.

Venus started to set the child down, saying to him, "Go and call you Tantie Monica."

Before his feet could touch the floor he had begun to shriek, "Tattie Mokka! Tattie Mokka!"

He was as naked as he was born, except for the guard of beads around his chubby wrist.

"Go and stand up by the back door and call she, Clydie," Venus coaxed. "She down in the kitchen."

As he teetered through the house, still shrieking, "Tattie

Mokka!" Venus leaned towards Gwynneth and said, in a conspiratorial voice, "You going ask she, eh, Gwynnie? She quicker say yes if you ask."

Monica came around the corner of the house again, and into the gallery, drying her hands on her skirt. Clydie was back on his grandmother's lap. Gwynneth put the idea to Monica, whereupon Monica flared her nostrils and swiftly cut her eye at her mother. Venus stared studiously ahead of her, then looked down and became very absorbed in applying an additional coat of coconut oil to Clydie's leg.

But Monica broke into a grin and said, "Yes, Tan Gwynnie."

She shot another glance at her mother, a look that seemed to say, "You think you win, but is me that win."

Gwynneth sensed that some kind of battle was going on, so now it was her turn to make a studious face and stare out at the vegetation in the yard. She could also see that Monica was a young woman *good for herself*, and she approved. They would get along well.

"You will take some soursop juice, Tante?" Monica offered. "And I nearly finish cook."

"You go taste how she hand sweet," said Venus, beaming.

Before long Polydore came clomping into view in mud-caked boots, carrying a bucket of produce. He tipped his cap. "Long time no see, Gwynneth. Look we bring some provision for you. The dasheen cooking good."

With him was another child – an older version of Clydie – as well as two dogs who sniffed the air and growled enquiringly. Polydore barked at them, "Allyou go and lie down!"

The boy was carrying a hand of plantain.

"Eh-eh! This is Sylvan?" Gwynneth asked, suddenly recognising the boy as Lystra's child, who was five or six years old the last time she was in Pilgrim...

~

Everything turn old-mas, Mumma had related, when they found out that Lystra was making baby, because she was only sixteen at the time. For two whole days Polydore didn't go to his garden. Instead, he disappeared down behind the pig-pen for hours on end and all you could hear was the sound of cutlass sharpening.

On the second evening, Polydore came up from behind the pig-pen with the cutlass. Its edge was a strip one full inch in width, filed until it was shining white, like silver. He handed over the cutlass to Venus, telling her to hide it or he would go and look for the chile-father and chop him up fine fine; and if he didn't, one of Lystra's brothers would.

For days Venus had prayed loudly and loudly chastised Lystra. Madlain left her house and marched down the road to chastise all of them. Even after everybody had simmered down, Polydore still wouldn't speak to Lystra, nor would he look at the baby for well-nigh the first year of its life, making sure to be out in the garden, or down in the cocoa, or tending his animals, as long as Sylvan was awake.

~

"You getting big, man," Gwynneth said to Sylvan. "How are you?"

Sylvan squirmed and flashed his wide, square front teeth: "Well, thanks."

"Well thanks who? Well thanks Tantie Gwynneth!" Venus admonished, opening her eyes wide to look at him sternly. The boy, still grinning, repeated pleasantly after her, "Well, thanks, Tantie Gwynneth."

"How you expect the boy to remember me, Venus? Look how long it is since last I come here," Gwynneth said.

Polydore was sitting on the steps with pipe in mouth, fishing in his pockets for tobacco and matches. He stopped to pat the space he had left beside him, and there Sylvan sat down, resting his head against Polydore's arm.

"Poly!" Venus dropped her voice. "You going and smoke you pipe in the child face?"

Polydore put away the packet of tobacco and box of matches, but kept the empty pipe sticking out of his mouth. He tweaked Sylvan's nose, put an arm around him and squeezed him.

"And what about Lystra?" Gwynneth asked.

"She living in Beauregard with Clydie father. And she working, so Clydie staying here till when he could go to school." And, as if somebody had posed a question, Venus added (with some ferocity, Gwynneth thought), "Sylvan not going nowhere. He belong to he Papa and he Gang-Gang," (pointing to her husband and then herself).

Sylvan turned his eyes to his grandmother and gave another shy, big-toothed grin.

Gwynneth consented to lie down for a while before lunch. She did feel a little buffeted by the long train journey, and she still had to go up the road and see Uncle Albert and the family, then Tan Madlain, and further yet up the road to pay her respects to Mother Queen Lottie. She settled gratefully onto the big bed that filled up most of the room. In one corner a candle burned steadily, set in a soup-plate of water on the floor.

She drowsed, wondering whether Mumma would ever see Pilgrim again. Mumma certainly couldn't endure the train journey any more. *Maybe after the war, when they lift the gas rationing, we could get Ollie to drive Mumma and me to Pilgrim... Leave us there for a few days... Come back for us...* So much water under the bridge. It was some twenty years since the last time Gwynneth had slept in Pilgrim. It was in Pilgrim that she had begun to take up her life again... So much water under the bridge...

~

It was when Tantie Grace died, on the day before Old Year's, just one month after David, and the last thing Gwynneth wanted at that time was to be in another funeral. She had sat through David's funeral service barely seeing or hearing, with Sylvia and Ainsley pressed close on either side of her. She could remember nothing of the proceedings, nothing but the awful, leaden weight in her chest, and Sylvia and Ainsley propping her up.

But Mumma was coaxing her to go to Pilgrim with her for Tantie Grace's funeral. Mumma was at her wits' end. Gwynneth knew that her mother didn't want to leave her, even for one day, at the mercy of Puppa. And Mumma wouldn't want to go for only a day or two, either, just for the funeral. That was unheard of. Mumma had sat in Gwynneth's bedroom with her, night after night, while Puppa paced the floor between the front door and the back bedrooms and ranted about this black mark against his good name.

And (pounding on the dining-table), what about Roy? How was the boy to get a government job now? After they had worked so hard to send him to the college, three more years for him to sit his exam and leave school, what was to become of him now? Why must he pay for other people's misdeeds? Some people thought only of themselves, but he hoped they had seen how freethinkers and rebels and those who engaged in sedition always got their just deserts. "Police on my doorstep! Police in my house! This is what I have come to...?"

And his voice would trail off into a helpless spluttering and choking.

"Come go, *Doudou*. Come let Queen attend to you."

Gwynneth didn't have much will of her own in that time. From the end of November 1919 to early January 1920, when she and Mumma went to Pilgrim for Tantie Grace's funeral, she had lain curled up in her bed day in, day out, dry-eyed, motionless, not sleeping, only dozing off and waking up, dozing off and waking up. Through that time of dulled senses, it was Mumma who bathed her, somehow got food into her mouth, sang hymns and prayed at her bedside.

Gwynneth was distantly aware of other people coming to see her. Day and night were the same to her, but Mumma told her that they came mainly during the work day, so as to avoid Puppa. Those who could only come after work or on weekends were stoutly escorted in by Mumma, past his glowering at the front door.

Miss Amy, next door, was a great help to Mumma in that time. She came over on weekdays to lend Mumma a hand wherever needed, from hanging out clothes to sitting with Gwynneth when Mumma couldn't because she had to cook or go to the shop. The children, too, would come over, as soon as they got home from school, to see what they could do for Miss Estelle or for Tantie Gwynneth in the brief hour or so before Puppa came home. It was about a year since Miss Amy's husband, Mr Hugh, had died and Miss Amy's great-nephew and great-niece, Louis and Marjorie, had come from Petit Curacaye to live with her.

The children's father had been taking care of them since their mother's death when Louis was four and Marjorie was two years old. After Mr Hugh died, Miss Amy suggested to their father that one or both of them come and stay with her. By then they had almost finished primary school. Louis was about to enter Standard 6, and Marjorie, Standard 4. Their father pondered over Miss Amy's proposal and agreed. Apart from keeping his old aunt company, he saw their going to live with Tantie Amy as offering better opportunities for the children, at this juncture, than living in Petit Curacaye. In Turagua they would be closer to town, and trade schools, and, later on, better job prospects – better than picking cocoa or cutting cane for a pittance.

At the time, Louis was 14 and Marjorie 12. As young as they were, they quickly caught on that even though Miss Estelle, and Tantie Gwynnie, and Tantie Vie were very nice to them, Mr Cuffie and the boy wanted no truck with them. The children, therefore, never came over when Puppa was home. When they visited Gwynneth in her time of trouble, they would keep an ear out for Puppa's arrival. Mumma related, with some amusement, how, at the sound of the front gate opening, the two of them would abandon Gwynneth, rush out through the back door and scamper to the fence, where they squeezed themselves through the barbed wire, sometimes getting scratched in their haste.

Miss Amy's exit was no less urgent, but she no longer had the agility, nor the size of body required for climbing through barbed wire fences. When she heard Puppa arrive at the front gate, she would wait until he had wheeled his bicycle to the back of the house, and then she would leave through the front door. Mumma spoke of how briskly Miss Amy would make her way down the walk to the gate, and how pointedly she would slow down once she was out on the government road, heading, at her leisure, for her own front gate.

The one person who was not in the least put off by Puppa standing in the door, bent on making all visitors uncomfortable, was Ainsley. He would linger awhile in the gallery, holding a cheery, mostly one-sided conversation with Puppa before he stepped indoors at Mumma's bidding. Puppa took to retreating into his bedroom whenever Ainsley appeared, and, from behind the closed door, delivering his harangue about rebels and other miscreants.

In Gwynneth's room, Ainsley would hold another one-sided conversation: bringing her greetings from Moun Demmeh people

– those too unnerved by Puppa's hostility to come back after one visit; telling her that as soon as she was ready to get up again, he would take her to the beach, to lunch at Capitan's, to the calypso tents that would be heating up in a matter of weeks, when the Carnival season began; inviting her to come and spend some time at his home where she could get some peace and clear her head; regaling her with the latest exploits of Madame, the cat that had moved in with him and Pelham. Ainsley had come home from work one evening to find this haughty cat perched on top the bookshelf, preening herself, only stopping briefly to watch him cut-eye as if to say, *Who you?*

Gwynneth had no memory of either agreeing or refusing to go to Tantie Grace's funeral. Mumma packed clothes for her, got her ready, and led her out of the house. Uncle Albert's grandchildren came to meet them at Pilgrim bus stop, and toted the bags, boxes and Mumma's suitcase on their heads, like a file of bachac ants.

A large tent of bamboo and coconut branches had already been put up. It filled the yard on one side of Uncle Albert's house. Gwynneth and her uncle held each other in a long hug that needed no words; then her cousins Lyris and Cutty, each holding an arm, guided her solicitously up the front steps. Gracelyn was yet to come in from Venezuela, and they had held back the funeral, waiting for her.

From that first evening, Gwynneth was drafted into the army of women out in the kitchen, working by flambeau light to turn out pots of peas-and-rice and oildown, and gallons of coffee, and talking, singing hymns, teasing, telling jokes that sounded even more salacious for being told in Patois, bursting into scandalous laughter, or sampling the babash placed in their custody so the village *soulards* wouldn't empty all the stocks before the wake was over. Every now and then the kitchen would fall into a silence weighted down with thoughts of the departed, until somebody broke into one sankey or another:

> *When Jesus call me*
> *I will answer*
> *I will answer to my name…*

For hours each night until the funeral, Gwynneth walked to and fro between the kitchen and the tent, serving coffee, rum, biscuits or whatever they sent her out with, as tamboo bamboo thumped the earth and people beat kwa-kwa, danced the bongo, sang, chatted, played cards... During the day, Pilgrim people in a steady stream came by to deposit a bunch of green-fig; a bag of yam or dasheen; a basin of chicken, already seasoned; buljol; zaboka; a bottle of puncheon rum; ground coffee...

They didn't make her go to the graveside.

By now it had become clear that Mumma had no intention of going back home until such time as she saw fit. Tantie Grace's Nine Nights service was held in the drawing-room, with more people in the gallery and outside under the tent. In the middle of the hymn "Through All the Changing Scenes of Life", Gwynneth dropped to the floor in a blubbering heap, and (as Mumma added to Gwynneth's recollection afterwards), beat the floor and shrieked before going limp and perfectly silent again. (Mumma informed her as well, long afterwards, that the date of Tantie Grace's Nine Nights was also David's Forty Days.)

When she opened her eyes she was in the bed. Mumma and Mother Elaine were leaning over her, one fanning her and the other sapping her forehead with bay rum. Their two faces, lit by the candle on the floor, showed no anxiety. They looked calm; Gwynneth thought that they even looked satisfied.

They wouldn't hear her if she spoke, because the sound of singing and clapping and praying and speaking in tongues flooded the bedroom from the other side of the partition and surrounded her. She gestured to Mumma and Mother Elaine, and had to speak right into Mumma's ear to let them know that it was all right to leave her. Then she fell into a sleep such as she had not slept for what seemed an age. In the depths of this sleep, David came to her for the first time since his death.

He was grinning from ear to ear, as usual, and as usual peering intently into her eyes, daring her to keep a straight face. The little girl he held by the hand was in school uniform, and sometimes she was a little boy. In fact, you could not in any moment be sure whether the child was girl or boy, for the girl could be wearing khaki school pants or the boy's hair could be in cane-row.

107

Sometimes the child was Roy in his new little school uniform. Mumma had never taken so long to cut out and sew anything.

Tender, sweet-faced Roy, only the other day toddling about naked (when Puppa was not at home), helping "Titta and Lolola" to water the plants, for which he had his own little condensed milk tin with nail holes. Then there was five-year-old Roy, still joyful, still whole, handed over to Puppa, going off with Puppa that morning, to ABC class in Puppa's school.

Then David was nudging the child forward while he himself disappeared and reappeared again and again, as though the already dim light had started to flash on and off to the rhythm of a strong singing that she realised had been there all along from the beginning. In the end, there was only the child, with flowers in its hand, looking up at her and grinning cheekily. David had disappeared and, like the Cheshire cat in *Alice in Wonderland*, he had left his smile behind.

The next day they unplaited her hair and Queen bathed her, rubbing her skin with leaves and petals that sweetened the water. Queen rubbed olive oil into the centre of Gwynneth's scalp, the palms of her hands and the soles of her feet. She passed the cocoyea broom from her head to her feet, sweeping down each side of her body. She took hold of Gwynneth's hands, lifted them up, and braced her firmly, vigorously crossing and uncrossing her arms. Then she spun her around, and all the while Mumma and Lyris and Mother Elaine, and some other women whose faces she could not now remember, singing and offering prayers.

When one evening, of her own accord, Gwynneth helped herself to some roast breadfruit and akra, taking up little pieces one by one and pecking at them hesitantly until the plate was empty, Mumma declared to Uncle Albert, her face shining with joy, but ruefulness in her voice: "Well, boy, Free-Paper burn. I better go home before my husband put me out." And she made a brief sound that was somewhere between a giggle and a snort.

9
"Bondjé, Tan Gwynnie, police take Lennox!"

Gwynneth was happy with the outcome of her mission to find a helper for Mumma. She was escorted to the Pilgrim bus stop by Monica, Cyrus, Malcolm and Sylvan. They carried her bags, now bulging with the ground provision and green-fig from Polydore's garden, and huge navel oranges from Uncle Albert. She was grateful to Venus for suggesting Monica, and to Monica for so readily consenting. Neither Gwynneth nor Mumma had thought of Monica – or perhaps Mumma had? Mumma didn't always reveal what was in her mind. Gwynneth was sure, however, that her mother would be more than comfortable with Monica.

On the train home, her thoughts returned again and again to her visit with Mother Queen Lottie, who had greeted her ceremonially to begin with, locking upraised hands with hers as the two of them pressed cheek against cheek, left and right.

Queen was just into her eighties and still strong on her feet.

"Watch at Lottie," Mumma used to say. "A good ten years older than me, but long after I done dead and bury, she go still be up and about like a young-girl. Woman with no husband does last longer."

Her eyes were bright and clear in a face that had shrunk considerably since the last time Gwynneth had seen her. She pinched Gwynneth's cheeks, remarking, "Girl, you looking tired and down. You ain get over you teacher-boy yet?"

Queen's memory, Gwynneth thought, had clearly skipped back two decades and lodged itself there. "But you see me since then, Mother. I know is a while I ain come to Pilgrim, but before that I was coming with Mumma all the time."

"I know. I know. But you never look so, like you have all the cares of the whole world on you back."

She took Gwynneth's hands in hers again and clapped them together as she sang:

Weeping may endure for a night
Joy cometh in the morning.

She stopped and announced, "When you get your child, *Doudou*, that go be your joy."

A response formed in Gwynneth's head: *What child, Mother Queen? I am fifty-two years old.* But she did not speak it. Instead, she joked, "Another one, Queen? I have nearly forty children already."

"I know. I know you have you schoolchildren, and you love them, doan mind they wearing you out."

Gwynneth rued her own presumptuous notion of this woman's mind wandering off and getting lost in the past. Queen was right there, in the present and most alert. "But I doan mean them," she continued. "I telling you bout the new little child that coming to bless you. Wait you see. This one going to born and raise right in your hand."

She grinned, cocking her head to one side. "You think I old and dotish, aint? You think I talking dotishness. Wait you see."

Now on the train Gwynneth smiled at Queen's mysterious prophecy and mumbled to herself, "Right now, Queen, getting Monica to come and help us take care of Mumma is joy enough for me. That is what will lift the cares of the world off me."

Of course, a child in the house would be a wonderful thing. She had often enough toyed with the idea of bringing home a little boy or girl from St Hilda's Orphanage, and just as often banished the thought. Somebody who could barely feed and clothe herself would be crazy to take in a child, although so many people who had next to nothing didn't let that stop them. One of Earline's children – you couldn't tell which if you were a complete stranger – had become Earline's when she went to the country to visit family, did not like how this little girl in the house was being treated, and without another thought returned to Turagua with the child in tow. Deleena fitted in contentedly between Earline's second and third.

All of Earline's children went to school barefoot, but that was not a matter of great concern to them. They were not the odd ones out. Those of their classmates who did come to school in shoes promptly took them off upon arrival each morning and placed them under the desk, so that they, too, could gallop about at recess and sit in class with their "ten commandments on the ground". Earline's children went to church in an assortment of alpagats, lily-whitened washicong, and the not-so-badly-scuffed dress shoes of other children, bought for pennies at St Hilda's church jumble sale.

Earline kept body and soul together by cooking and selling black-pudding, akra-and-float, corn soup, roast-corn and boil-corn, standing for hours behind her coal-pot under the eaves of Aleong's shop. Her children's father, Milton (technically stepfather to the first two), was a casual worker, mostly out of work. He did an excellent job, though, of looking after the children, garden and house, and he often manned the coal-pot (he had the sweetest of sweet-hand) in front of the shop.

Gwynneth snapped out of her thoughts. The train was pulling out of St Paul station, and Turagua was the next stop. She started to rearrange her bags around her. They were much heavier than when she set out from home that morning. Now she wondered who was coming to meet her at the station, and thought what a welcome sight Ollie's ramshackle motorcar would be, a junk heap squatting patiently on Railway Road.

But there was no one waiting for her when the train pulled in, neither Ollie, nor Viola, nor Marjorie, nor Lennox, nor Marjorie's gentleman, Philbert. Before she could climb down the carriage steps, a boarding passenger took her bags from her and set them down on the platform. Then he held her hand to help her off the train.

"Bless you, son," Gwynneth said.

She made her way towards the railway hut, walking alongside the train as it eased out of the station. When the last carriage had trundled past her, she could look across into the savannah. It was almost seven o'clock, but there were still some boys playing football. She would sit and wait, and if they finished their game before anybody turned up to meet her, one or two of them would help her home with the bags. No sooner had she settled herself on the bench, however, than she heard the sound of scurrying feet, shoes clacking rapidly on the pitch beside the hut, and a breathless Marjorie appeared before her.

Gwynneth chuckled. "Slow down, girl. You done miss the train already. It gone."

Marjorie was so excitable and alarmist for a big woman. Gwynneth was always telling her that she would give herself a stroke one day. But when Marjorie stumbled into the hut and Gwynneth saw the expression on her face, she knew that something serious had happened. She shot up off the bench and asked in a whisper, "Mumma?"

Marjorie shook her head, and for a moment could not get her words out. "Lennox!" she sputtered. "*Bondjé*, Tan Gwynnie, police take Lennox!"

"What!"

"They hold he and some other boys that was beating iron in the road. Up by Baba Nate land. Is a little boy from up there come and tell me. Mr Ollie down in the station."

Gwynneth felt a stab of guilt and anger. Phillip's band! Lennox was in Phillip's iron band! And Marjorie didn't know, very likely because Lennox wished to spare her, and himself, the fit of panic she might have suffered. But she, Gwynneth, would have known, had she kept her promise to go and hear the band.

"Come. Let's tote these things home and get down in that police station," she said, her face grim.

"No, Tan Gwynnie. Mr Ollie say we must go home and stay. He go talk to the police."

Gwynneth relented, but only because she was quite tired – in no condition, at this point, to do battle with the police force. Ollie was the best bet. There was almost no place Ollie could go where somebody didn't know him. And among those who didn't know him, his light skin and his motorcar, old-junk or not, were always enough to make some black fool want to kowtow to him.

She couldn't tell who she felt more anger at – the police, or herself. She had let these boys down, miserably. But one thing she knew for sure. Nobody was going to mash up *this* iron band.

They had been home for almost an hour, and the waiting was too much. It didn't help that Marjorie wailed every few minutes, "Oh

God! What I going tell my brother? What he going to say? *Bondjé*, Louis going to kill me! Oh God!"

But it was when the wailing turned into, "I going to kill that child. So help me God, I going and kill him!" that Gwynneth snapped.

"Marjorie! Hush you mouth with that stupidness! You not going to do the boy nothing else but encourage him. The police wrong! Is them that wrong! Not Lennox and those other boys. They ain doing nothing wrong. The police have to leave them alone! Man, I going down in that station."

Gwynneth started to struggle out of the armchair.

Viola jumped in. "So nobody ain ready to eat, yet? So what I stand up in the kitchen for, whole evening, kneading flour and frying bake enough to feed the five thousand?"

When there was no answer, only two tense faces turning to stare blankly at her, she resorted to coaxing, "All right. What we need is a little appetiser. Marjorie, girl, help me with some glasses."

Viola went to the wagonette and took out a bottle of rum punch, while Marjorie got glasses from the kitchen.

Gwynneth raised her glass and said, with vehemence, "To the Turagua Iron Band!"

The other two looked doubtful, but raised their glasses all the same, and downed a first gulp of Mamzelle Vio's Most Dangerous Brew, as Ollie had branded it. The glumness soon lifted, but still the food was left waiting reproachfully on the table: fry-bake (flour so scarce that the bakes looked more like Holy Communion wafers); buljol; some kind of cassava dish that Viola had concocted; a decorative salad of zaboka slices scalloping the plate of tomato and cucumber and sweet-pepper from their garden; and soursop-leaf tea for a good night's sleep. Mumma had eaten much earlier, and they had not told her about Lennox. Places had been set at the table for Ollie and Lennox.

Then they heard the motorcar rattle and shudder to a stop at the front gate. Marjorie and Gwynneth rushed out to the gallery. There was Ollie's motorcar, but they thought they could see, through the hedge, the glint of another vehicle. Three figures were proceeding up the walk. Ollie, Lennox, and, bringing up the rear, Gaston Boniface, Barrister-at-Law. (Truth be known, and to his embarrassment, Gaston *Walter Raleigh* Boniface.)

In that moment, Gwynneth, like Marjorie, felt she was quite capable of killing somebody, and that somebody would be Ollie. She had suspected him and Viola of hatching a plot, from the moment word got around that Gaston's wife had packed her bags and gone back to England. (How the lady had put up with him for so long, Gwynneth couldn't fathom. Any woman who could live with Gaston for what would have been three whole years, deserved to be decorated with the Order of the British Empire). Viola was always trying to hitch up Gwynneth with some locho (not that Gaston fitted this description), with Ollie going along as her accomplice. Gwynneth often had to ask them, "All you see any sign on my forehead say 'Husband Wanted'?"

Lately, Gaston's name seemed to be cropping up in almost every conversation. Viola was going around humming sappy songs like "Into your Arms Again", and "Please Give Our Love a Second Chance". And this evening, thanks to the Turagua police, the conspiracy had gained ground.

Of course, Gaston was the person to call upon in this situation, of boys being detained by police for beating iron. This was a cause he would willingly take up. He had returned to Cayeri, with barrister-at-law papers and British wife, in the middle of the marches and strikes of '37, and had jumped right into getting protesters out of police station cells or defending them in court, *pro bono*. He was cited in an editorial of *The Kings Port Sentinel* as one of those over-educated rabble-rousers in the colony who should know better than to encourage the poor and unfortunate to bite the hand that fed them. Gaston's heart was in the right place, but, as Mumma would say, "Nobody ain make outa sweet-rice alone."

Marjorie had already catapulted herself down the steps, squealing, and Ollie stepped aside as she flung her arms around Lennox. She held onto him and practically lifted him up the steps – an entertaining sight, because Lennox seemed to be towering over her. Viola, left inside to cover down the food, now came out into the gallery. She pulled Lennox to her and hugged him, breathing "Thank God!" Then her eyes fell on Gaston, whereupon she let out a piercing shriek and clapped her hands like a little child.

Gwynneth stood stock still at the bannister, seized by one thought: Suppose Gaston had got it into his head that she, Gwynneth, had sent for him? She would have to disabuse him of any such misunderstanding.

10
"Allyou think I doan know is komplo allyou making?"

They had parted amicably, at least from her point of view. She liked him she had said, admired some things about him, and they'd had some good times together; but she was not interested in following him, or anybody else, to England, or anywhere else, for that matter. Never mind the guava season she was experiencing just then, she was quite content to stay right here, in this blessed place that she hoped she would live to call her own *country*, and not "the colony". His reaction had been less than amicable. Why couldn't she see reason? She was just too stubborn for words. "A lady stands behind her gentleman through thick and thin."

Usually, when he came up with lines like these, it made her want to giggle, but the occasion was not a good time to laugh at him. Once, in the early days, she had seriously wounded his feelings with her laugh. They were on a bus excursion to L'Anse Amandes with some friends of hers. In the course of the day, a tiff between Jerry and Sylvia became a full-blown altercation, and they had it out right there on the beach. It was after lunch, when everyone was either sitting on a fallen coconut trunk or sprawling somewhere among the almond trees, letting the food digest before they went back into the water.

Sylvia had bought a newspaper at the terminus in Kings Port. She now took it out of her bag and began to leaf through it. She stopped at an article about Marcus Garvey and observed aloud that the whitepeople were on his back again. Jerry put God out of his thoughts and snatched the paper from her, telling her to give politics a rest; they had come out to have a good time on the beach, not to study politics, and so on. Sylvia snatched the paper back and called Jerry an empty-headed moron who didn't give a fart what was going on in the world around him, etc.

Gaston commented afterwards, "What my old man would say to that is, 'A woman can't be in argument with her husband. The husband is above the wife. She is beneath her husband'."

And Gwynneth laughed riotously, thinking that he was making fun of his father. That was her first introduction to his peeved-and-deeply-hurt-but-taking-it-like-a-man face. Later on she discovered that Gaston did not know how to even begin to make himself a cup of tea, or slap two pieces of bread together into a sandwich; and the line to go with that was "Woman is man's helpmeet". He was visibly thrown when Gwynneth asked, "So who is woman's helpmeet?"

But he soon recovered enough to deliver a lecture to her. "Why would you want to upset the natural order of things? Men and women were clearly designed by Nature to perform different functions. There's no logical reason for men to do what is obviously women's work..."

There was no bad blood between them, as far as she was concerned; and he had rescued Lennox. She would be hospitable. He was still on the walk with Ollie, but while Viola warmly invited him in, Gwynneth was looking past the two of them, out into the road: "What about the other boys? They let go all of them?"

"Yep," Ollie replied. "We drop everybody home."

She did not have a clear view of Gaston until he was standing in the gallery, awkwardly holding out his right hand to her. He looked plumper than when he left, and there was some grey speckling in his hair. But all in all, the years had not been unkind to him. It was past eight o'clock, but Viola, officiating, sat them in the gallery for an appetiser and a profuse thank-you speech to Gaston. Gwynneth also thanked him, but if cut-eye coulda kill, by the end of the evening Viola and Ollie would have been lying dead on the floor.

Under strict instructions not to tell her anything about the day's events, Lennox had made a beeline for Mumma's room to say good night, and was still with her when he was called out to recount what, exactly, had happened that afternoon. It took some prodding, Lennox not being the most talkative of thirteen-year-old boys, nor keen on being the centre of attention, and more anxious, at this point, to address the rumbling in his stomach.

They pulled the story out of him, bit by bit. They had to keep their voices down, for though Mumma's hearing was going the way of her eyesight, it had been known to return from time to time, miraculously, just when somebody was saying something they would rather she did not hear.

It was as though the boys had been overpowered by the thrilling sound they were making and could no longer sit down in one place with it. They just had to come out and let it be heard. They spilled out from their spot, into the trace… *What spot – where?* Up in the land belonging to Phillip's family. Next thing they knew, they were tramping down San Miguel Road, beating a sweet rhythm, dancing and singing… *Singing what? Singing rudeness?* No. They were singing "Going Down Jordan". *How many boys?* Nine.

There was nobody else on the road, because there were not many houses up there, so the boys were heading down to the savannah, to entertain the people playing football and cricket or looking on. Some of the boys didn't even recognise the police van until it pulled up alongside them. Learie, Selwyn, and the two boys from the orphanage dived back into the bush, dropping whatever they had in their hands.

What it was allyou had in allyou hand? Everybody had a stick and something to beat on – a brake-hub, a hoe-blade, a paint-pan, a pitch-oil pan, a pot, a piece of bamboo, a gin bottle, a grater… *No knife? Ice pick? Cutlass?* No. *Allyou did thief anybody dustbin cover?* No. *Where allyou get the pot from?* Miss Ruth, Phillip's grandmother. They had got motorcar parts from Phillip's workplace, Mr Carl's mechanic shop. Phillip's uncle got the gin bottle for them.

And these orphanage boys, now – the orphanage know they taking part in an iron band? No. On Saturday afternoons the two boys crawled out through a hole in the fence at the back of their playing-field, to come and beat in Phillip's band.

By the time Phillip, Lennox, and the three other boys who had not fled, understood what was happening, they were being bundled into the Black Maria. The policemen were shouting at them and telling them they were going straight to jail. They were very frightened. *Allyou give the police any backchat?* No. *And when all of this happen? What time?* When they got to the station the clock there was saying twenty minutes past three.

"When last you get something to eat, Lennox?" Gwynneth asked.

"Lunch time, Tantie."

"All right," Gwynneth announced, abruptly getting up. "Time to let this boy eat."

At the table, Gaston was invited to serve himself first. Viola had obviously forgotten one thing about Gaston. So many years had passed since last they all sat around a table together, the rickety table at Catherine Street with its short leg resting on a book. Gwynneth looked at him out of the corner of her eye to see what would happen. She didn't lift a finger. She could not believe how accommodating to his foibles she had been in her younger years when she was quite intolerant of anything she saw as foolishness.

Gaston sat as though frozen, looking panicked as his eyes surveyed the table. Or was it panic? She couldn't really read the expression on his face. He looked overcome. His eyes blinked and his Adam's apple moved a little, like someone swallowing tears.

Viola handed him the cassava dish, still not remembering. He took the bowl from her and sat holding it clumsily suspended in mid-air until Ollie came to his rescue. Taking the bowl of cassava from him, Ollie set it down and took up Gaston's plate. Ollie went from dish to dish asking him: "Any of this for you? Say when. That's enough?"

Before this operation was over, Lennox, given the nod by Gwynneth, had already shovelled some of everything onto his own plate and devoured most of it.

~

On the occasions when Viola, Ollie and Gaston visited her at Catherine Street and they sat down together to eat, Gwynneth might choose to dish out Gaston's food. For one thing, Gaston was really quite inept at it, and couldn't get the food onto his plate without leaving trails of gravy, callaloo, soup or other matter on her one good tablecloth. But she accommodated him also because she did not wish to spoil the event by introducing any note of sourness. These gatherings were occasions of good cheer that she treasured. If it looked as though Gwynneth was not going to serve Gaston, Viola or Ollie would rush to his assistance as he set about the task with the most pitiful awkwardness.

Not even Roy, Mumma's sweet lagniappe child, and king of the roost in Puppa's eyes, was so handicapped, so pampered.

When Roy was little, he loved to be in the kitchen with Mumma, Viola and herself. It was his delight to be hoisted onto a chair placed before the sink, so he could "help" by washing the wares.

Of course, they first had to remove all breakable items from the sink, leaving only their most battered enamel cups and plates, an aluminium tumbler or two, and cutlery minus sharp knives. They also had to take off his jersey or merino beforehand, as the best part of washing wares was playing in water. He would stand on the chair and "wash" until he was taken down (sometimes forcibly, so there might be a little kicking and screaming), at the point when he, the chair, and the kitchen floor were sufficiently drenched.

But well before Roy reached high school age, he was washing wares with efficiency and dispatch. He could wash and iron his school uniform. On weekends he cleaned his room and swept the gallery, drawing-room and dining-room. He could do simple cooking – fry or scramble an egg, and make porridge. When he started high school he was just beginning to learn how to make some of the foods that he liked the most – pelau with pigeon peas, roast-bake and smoke-herring, pumpkin fritters, and stewed guava. Puppa was not impressed and accused them of trying to make the boy into a mamapoule. Mumma's retort was that no woman would ever make her son eat dry biscuit because she have licen to turn down the pot whenever she vex with him.

Gaston, on the other hand, as well as his two brothers and his father, had a pair of ready nursemaids in his mother and his sister. The sons and their father were called to the table and had their food dished out by the girl and her mother. The men ate and drank, and when they were full they pushed back their chairs and took their leave, while the nursemaids cleared the table and disappeared into the kitchen to wash the dishes. The girl and her mother also gathered up the men's clothes from wherever they left them, washed and ironed them, polished their shoes, made their beds.

Some of this Gwynneth had seen for herself when Gaston invited her home to meet his family. Other details of Life at the Boniface Home she learned about whenever Gaston found it necessary, or saw a good opportunity, to ply her with such information – all part of his effort to instruct her in the duties of man's helpmeet and the rules of proper deportment for a lady.

Lower your voice – you're too loud. / That scandalous laugh! / You always have too much to say. A lady knows when to hold back, so as not to put her gentleman in the shade. / You can speak better than that. You went to school and learned proper English. / You really find that dress appropriate? One could think you were just going to the market. / That place is a rumshop, and a rumshop is not a place for a lady. I don't care how many rumshops you've been into, or with whom. There are just some places where ladies don't belong.

Quarrels would break out, after which they would go their separate ways and not see each other for days, or weeks, and in one instance almost three months. Gwynneth swore each time to cut him out of her life, forever, but then, there he would be again, like a bad habit.

~

Gwynneth released Lennox as soon as he had finished eating, and he went home to his bed. Marjorie helped clear the table, swept the floor around it, and then excused herself. Philbert was visiting and had already been waiting for a while. She had some bone or the other to pick with him, and Gwynneth reminded her: "Marjorie, doan start no fight over there, now. Whatever it is you have to settle, allyou know not to cuss-out one another for the child to hear. You and Philbert settle allyou business without no kangkalang. Doan show Lennox no bad example. Is a miracle he could be such a peaceful youngboy when he grow with a wrango like you."

Marjorie chuckled in agreement.

Meanwhile Viola and Ollie were not going to let Gaston melt back into the night just like that. The four of them went out to the gallery again where they finished the bottle of rum punch and also knocked back a straight-rum or two as they talked over the events of that afternoon. Ollie told them how he had arrived at the police station to find the boys' family members in a huddle of strident fury outside the building. Most audible were the voices of Marjorie and some of the other women. Passers-by were stopping to stare. Ollie suggested they move down the road a bit to talk.

He learned that the family members had already been inside, but the officer on duty had barely looked at any of them. As each of them arrived and enquired after a detained boy, the officer had waved them away and told them to wait. They sat on the benches until they began to wonder what it was they were waiting for. Other people had since come to the desk, and the officer had spoken with each of them. One or two had gone back out, and some were now sitting, like themselves, except that these people seemed to know what they were waiting for.

Then something flew up into Marjorie's head. Without any warning she sprang up from the bench, rushed to the desk and started telling off the policeman.

She was immediately joined by the other women, as though they had only been waiting for the signal. By turns they were leaning over his desk to scold him and wag a finger in his face; stepping back in a dance of contempt; swivelling to address all the benches on the topic of big hardback police advantaging people chirren. When the officer got up with a loud scraping of his chair and backed his way into the interior, the three men in the group, certain they were all going to end up in the cells that evening, leapt into action and hustled Marjorie and her accomplices outside.

Phillip's uncle was part of the little gathering on the roadside. He explained to Ollie that his family allowed and encouraged the boys to make their music up in the old palay on what was once Phillip's great-grandfather's compound. This was further up the hillside, behind Phillip's family home. Nobody knew that the boys had gone off the land, because they had used the side trace leading out onto the public road, rather than come down through the yard. Nobody knew that the police had taken them, until two of the boys who got away broke through the bush and appeared in the yard.

The group decided to let Ollie tackle the police on their behalf, and Marjorie left at that point; she would have to go and meet Gwynneth, and the train was due in at a quarter to seven.

When the man at the desk saw the group coming in again, he held his hand up and ordered: "Leave those women outside!"

Ollie strode on towards him, saying: "Nah, man, Constable. How we go leave the ladies outside?"

The others, including the ladies, sat down on the benches once more. Ollie rapped a playful rhythm on the desk and asked to see the sergeant.

"You know what the sergeant tell me? That man bend forward and lower he voice: 'Mr Oliviera, doan stick out you neck for no black-hen chicken, you know. They ain worth it. Blackpeople chirren will drag you down with them.' So I had to ask he what colour he is, and if we could say that about *he* chirren. He just look confuse, and ain bother to answer.

"Then I ask him what is the charge laid against these boys, and he look more confuse. He glance at the next officer and ain get no help from he. Then he say 'Disturbing the peace'. So I ask him 'Who peace, for heaven's sake? Up in that bush, officer? Disturbing the douen and the soucouyan and the lagahou-and-them peace?'"

The company in the gallery laughed heartily.

"By the time Gaston reach, they was starting to change they mouth. Let Gaston tell you."

Gaston had not spoken more than a sentence at a time all evening, and for the most part only when spoken to. He had a nervous air about him, as though he felt he was under inspection and needed to mind his Ps and Qs. At first he had clung to the King's English, but as the evening progressed, he seemed to feel more and more relaxed, and then, wonder of wonders, he slid into the language of the company, moving between the King's English and Creole. It was a voice she had rarely ever heard him use.

However, now that Ollie had thrown him into the limelight, he looked just as uncomfortable as Lennox did at first, when earlier in the evening he was put up for cross-examination. Gaston cleared his throat and opted for his lawyer-voice. "'Regulation 22', the sergeant said to me. Now, they know very well that Regulation 22 is about processions of over 20 persons. Nine people going down the road is not an offence. This was just plain persecution. In the end they had to release them without any charges. The police here are just following the authorities in town – branding all the young men involved in this music as delinquents. Most of them are not, and all of them, including the badjohn ones, are really inventors. We should be proud of them."

Eventually Gaston got up to leave. Ollie also got up, but Gwynneth detained him with a menacing look. As soon as Gaston was out of earshot, she made Ollie and Viola sit down. First she reproached them for the conspiracy they had woven around her

123

with regard to Gaston. "Allyou think I doan know is komplo allyou making?"

Ollie and Viola opened their eyes wide and overacted their innocence, but when they looked at each other, the laughter they were holding down broke loose. Gwynneth ignored them and moved on to the next item on her agenda. She announced her plan for protecting and helping to build up Phillip's iron band. She informed Ollie that he was the patron of this band. The patron agreed to drive her around the next day, after lunch, to visit the homes of the band members. Lennox would be their informant – they would get the boys' names and addresses from him in case Ollie couldn't remember where he and Gaston had dropped people off in the dark.

The next day, Sunday, Gwynneth started her mission by speaking with Reverend Fields after morning service. As well as being the parish priest, he was the warden of St Hilda's Orphanage. She asked him to give his blessing to the iron band project; to give official permission to the two boys who for months had been running away to Phillip's yard to play in the band; and to tell the orphanage staff not to beat them for having run away. Gwynneth didn't think the Reverend needed to know about the hole in the fence behind the playing-field that they squeezed themselves through to get out. She had promised Lennox not to tell. Now they would be walking out through the front gate to come and practise.

Reverend Fields had always found it difficult to refuse any request of Gwynneth's, because, he said, she was one of those women without whose labour the Church would not be still standing. It had reached Gwynneth's ears that Valda Pierre was displeased at how much he indulged her, for example his agreeing to remove what Gwynneth called "belligerent" hymns from the order of service whenever she stood in for the organist, and giving her licence to choose other hymns to replace them. In Mrs Pierre's opinion, Gwynneth had this priest wrapped around her little finger.

Nice Englishman, with brown hair, greenish eyes, straight nose, and freckles… but what the poor fellow didn't know, Mrs Pierre lamented, was that the hypocrite didn't like whitepeople.

He had not yet come to Cayeri (indeed, he would have been just a boy) when twenty years ago Gwynneth and the rest of her cabal were busy with their wicked komplo. Gwynneth was among the miscreants bent on pushing all whitepeople out of the colony. Now the brazen Jezebel was currying favour with Reverend Fields. Valda Pierre was certain that Gwynneth had designs on the Reverend – looking to rob the cradle – and she wanted to warn him to be careful, or tongues would start wagging.

After lunch, Gwynneth and Ollie, accompanied by Lennox, went to see Phillip's family first, before going to the other homes. They called out "Good afternoon!" as they walked up the slowly rising path that had been cut through steeper ground. Up ahead of them were two houses, Ruth Benoit's and her son Melville's.

Phillip's family, especially his Uncle Chester, received with enthusiasm Gwynneth's proposal to adopt the iron band. It was agreed that she would come back in two weeks, to hear the band play and sit down a little longer with the family. Gwynneth apologised, again, for not keeping the promise she had made to Phillip about two months earlier. "Nothing doan happen before the time," Phillip's grandmother replied.

There were other people who, like Marjorie, had not been aware of what their boys were doing on Saturday afternoons. Two families had to be persuaded that the making of this new music was not the road to hell and damnation, and that what their sons were involved in was a worthwhile pursuit, just as important as cricket, which was what they thought their boys had been doing.

Even the most sceptical of parents warmed to the idea; after all, if Teacher Gwynneth could have such a high opinion of this thing … They were especially heartened when she used the word "educational". And everybody found it a sweet rebuke to the police that the band now had on its side a Father-priest, a Potoguee businessman, and Teacher Gwynneth. Furthermore, if the police ever interfered with their children again, there was a good lawyer standing by, ready to defend them.

On Monday evening, Ollie brought a message for Gwynneth. First he stepped away from her and stood in a comic pose of readiness to run, with his hands held up to protect his head should she pelt something at him. From that safe distance he rattled off "Gaston-send-to-say-he-want-to-see-you-to-clear-up-some-thing," and removed himself even further out of harm's way, pretending to sprint towards the door while throwing back glances of mock terror at her.

Ollie was such a clown. Gwynneth had to laugh, in spite of herself. Then she glared at him and snarled: "*He* want to clear up something? Good. I have something to clear up, too: I want him to know is *you* send for him Saturday, not me!"

By this time Ollie had dropped to the floor and, crawling on his belly and elbows in combat style, was trying to take cover under the little centre-table. Fitting oneself under this table was a manoeuvre difficult enough for a well-fed child (Gwynneth and Viola used it for hide-and seek when they were little), and quite impossible for someone the size of Ollie. When he stopped struggling, his head and shoulders seemed to be stuck among the table-legs and the rest of his corpulent mass was left stranded in plain sight. It was just too funny for Gwynneth to keep up her vexation. Everyone was laughing helplessly.

Gwynneth agreed to see Gaston, but it would have to be after Monica was settled in. She was due to arrive in a week's time, the following Monday.

They had to pull out Gwynneth's old canvas cot from under the house, dust it off, scrub it down, leave it in the sun to dry, and then put it in Mumma's room for Monica to sleep on until better could be done. Dog-in-the-manger Roy flatly refused to let them install her in his vacant room – never mind it had been standing empty for years. Nor would he let them take out his bed and put it in Mumma's room for Monica. They knew the likelihood was that he would say No, but they still lived in hope that he would one day turn back into a reasonable human being. Between Puppa's handling of him, and his time at Ascension College, Roy had grown into one insufferable ass.

They were fixing up the room for Monica's arrival, chattering and giggling like schoolgirls, now and then laughing out scandalously, Mumma the loudest. For the past fourteen years and some months Mumma's bed had sat regally in the very middle of the room, and now they would have to shift it to make space for the cot. They had helped Mumma into an armchair from where she supervised the operation.

So as not to scrape Mumma's floorboards, which in her able-bodied years she had polished with great pride, Gwynneth, Viola and Marjorie lifted the bed an inch or two off the floor and were making their way towards the wall with it, when Gwynneth wickedly asked: "I wonder who put this bed in the middle of the room, boy?"

And Viola sang, "O-o say, can you see / By the dawn's early light…"

Whenever the story of the bed came up, and they took to teasing Mumma about the komplo she had made with the joiner and the mattress-man, and how she had worked through the night to throw out her husband, Mumma would be sure to make a displeased face and scold them: "Allyou too damn faas. Stop talking me and my husband business." And then she would join heartily in the general amusement.

That day she was in ripping form. Mumma had arthritis, a bad knee, cataracts, high blood pressure and partial deafness, but nothing wrong with the mouth. "Who put the bed?" she shot at them. "Is you *mother* put it! *Sé mama-ou ki mété i.*"

The bed slipped out of their hands and hit the floor, but they didn't hear the thud, what with the raucous burst of laughter. "Oooo!" they squealed. "Mumma! You cursing! Watch you mouth, you old cuss-bird!"

They flopped down on the bed, thumped the mattress, held their bellies, gasped for air… and over it all, Mumma's toothless cackle. It was enough to raise Puppa raging out of his grave.

Viola took them back to the night of Puppa's Forty Days prayers, when she was awakened by a loud metallic crash coming from the other side of her bedroom wall. She thought it was still night, because it seemed to her that the people had only just left and she had barely got into her bed and fallen asleep. She flew up and rushed into the front bedroom. The light was on and she had to blink for a few moments before she could grasp what she was seeing.

There was a lot of bare wall. No bed. The big-bed was gone.

Puppa's grand, impressive tall-post bed was not there. The neat pile of metal forming on the floor was the posts and other parts of the bed-frame, and the woodpile was the laths. The mattress was nowhere to be seen.

"Mumma! What you doing?"

Mumma steupsed with irritation and went on stacking bed parts. "Child, go to work, *non*. Go and do the people work."

Viola rolled her eyes heavenwards. As she headed towards Gwynneth's room to alert her, she saw that the top half of the back door was open, making a square of grey-pink fore-day morning light. From the passageway she could see part of the backyard, where something lying on the ground caught her eye, something like a dishcloth. She soon realised that it was a corner of the mattress she was looking at. Viola opened the lower half of the door and went down the steps into the yard. The mattress for Puppa's tall-post bed was sprawled over the spot where on Saturdays they burned the week's rubbish.

Before Viola left for work or Gwynneth's schoolchildren started to arrive (she had only a few of them at the time), the mattress had turned into a delicate pile of coconut fibre ash. When Viola got home from work, she met a neat three-quarter bed installed plunk in the middle of what was now Mumma's room. It was made of new, pleasant-scented cyp. After Puppa's Nine Nights prayers, Mumma had hired a joiner to make this bed, unbeknown to Gwynneth and Viola. She had also engaged someone to make her a mattress. Mumma's brand new bed and mattress were both delivered on the day after Puppa's Forty Days.

Puppa would have vehemently objected and refused to allow any Shouter Nine Nights or Forty Days simmy-dimmy to be carried on his house, since it was all superstition and dabbling in the occult; but how would he have any more power over Mumma in death than in life? They laid the remains of the big-bed under the house, for posterity.

11

"Well, girl, this is Morne Cabrite."

To give Puppa his due, and contrary to what a few bad-tongue women whispered to others at the time, he never put Gwynneth out. Barely a week after she and Mumma came home from Tantie Grace's funeral, Gwynneth was ready to take up Ainsley's invitation. Pilgrim had brought her back into the land of the living, but Ainsley feared that Puppa's daily ranting at her about sedition and treason and rebellion would be enough to return her to the state of the living dead. It was when Gwynneth realised that Puppa's behaviour was distressing Mumma and Viola more than herself that she began to consider leaving home. She had shut off her ears and her heart to Puppa, and that, Ainsley pointed out, was another gateway to the land of the living dead.

Ainsley had been suggesting all along that she come and stay with him and Pelham until she could either go back home or find a place to live. Gwynneth knew that she would also have to find work. She had already been officially informed of her dismissal from the government teaching service, but the question of how she was going to make a living was one little grinning demon that, for the moment, she kept locked in a cage with iron bars, pushed to the back of her mind.

"The first thing you have to do is get away from him, Gwynneth," Ainsley said in a grave voice, his forehead creased with worry. "This is not healthy. You not going to catch youself – not with him barking round you like that all the time. That could send anybody in the madhouse."

Mumma agreed. "Just come outa he sight little bit, *Doudou*, and he go cool down. Wait you see how he boil down like bhaji. Then you could come back home."

Ainsley suggested that she take a few days to decide. He came back on the Friday evening after work, and she had packed her bags. They knew that Puppa was watching them bring the bags outside – the gallery side-door which led into the front bedroom was ajar. When they reached the gate to the road she was aware of him standing ominously in the front door. She was sorely tempted to turn and say to him (and the thought made her almost giggle, heavy as her heart was in that time): *Yes, Sir. I'm off to live in sin. And not with one man, nuh! Two! How you like that?* Of course she couldn't say it. He might have had a stroke there and then.

In time, she did cause Puppa to take bed, but that was some years down the road.

On her first morning at Ainsley's, she was up very early. Her sleeping was still not back to normal. For weeks she had been catnapping fitfully at night, and even if she managed to fall into a deeper sleep, she could be jolted awake fore-day morning by Puppa's voice, whenever he felt he had to get in some ranting before going off to work. She had forgotten what it was to have a full night's rest.

Ainsley found her peering out through the jalousies. They had arrived at his house after nightfall and now, in the morning light, she was getting her first clear view of the neighbourhood. The houses on all sides were so close, elbowing each other for breathing space. And when the people walking past in the street spoke to each other, they might as well have been in Ainsley's chinky little gallery with its steps that seemed to lead directly onto the public roadway. She had never understood Puppa's craving for a home in town and a posting at a town school. Puppa often complained that he had been sent to teach in one cow-pen after another, in some of the most benighted parts of the colony, and that when he was finally able to lease some Crown land for a home, the closest to Kings Port he could get was Turagua.

"Well, girl, this is Morne Cabrite. Not as green and wholesome as your part of the world, eh?" Ainsley commented. "But I hope you will be comfortable. Me, I born and grow right here. They go have to smoke me out."

He had inherited the family home by default, his siblings having all "gone for higher" as he called it – Canada, England; there was even one sister in France, reputed to be singing in Parisian nightclubs.

Gwynneth mustered a wan smile. "Yes, Ainsley. I'm comfortable. Thank you for your hospitality. You are a generous, generous friend." She hugged him.

"At your service, Ma'am," Ainsley said, with a deep bow and sweep of the arm. "You going and take a good rest here. Sleep. Read. If you doan find nutten interesting on our bookshelf, we could go down in the library. Some days you could go up by the Savannah and walk round the pitch, or just sit down on a bench and watch the hills. Is not long again before poui start to come in. Man, when that ready to cover the ground and take over the hills, that is a sight could make a body forget all ugliness. And any problem you might have here in the day, just go by Ma Quamina – the blue house up there. She will look out for you."

He pointed to the incline further up, where, between houses of uneven planks, dingy concrete, or bare red brick oozing hardened mortar at the seams, there sat a well-kept little board house, painted blue. "We go introduce you before the weekend done," he promised. "Ma Q is my nennen – *makoumè* to my mother, God rest her soul."

Pelham loved to clean and fuss about how the place looked; Ainsley was a kitchen jumbie. For the whole of that first weekend they waited on her hand and foot, no matter how much she protested that she was perfectly able to help with the housework. When she picked up a broom, Pelham gently relieved her of it. She had to practically fight them in order to get to the kitchen sink and wash the wares. During the week, while they were at work, she took to sweeping, needlessly; the floor was as always as clean as a whistle. But by the end of the week she had hit upon a way to make herself useful.

On the weekend she had seen them haul their clothes down from the lines in the little two-by-four yard and dump them in a cocoa basket just inside the back door. On weekday mornings they each dug something out of the basket to wear to work and dashed the iron over it. Gwynneth quietly observed this routine all week. Clearly neither of them was crazy about ironing – just like her. She often wore her clothes unironed, if they didn't look too obviously rough-dry. She would hang them in her wardrobe straight off the clothesline and hope that any stubborn wrinkles would smooth themselves out in the wearing. If some garment was so shamefully rumpled that it was not likely to get past Mumma or Viola, then it would get a lick and a promise with the iron; but she was no ironer. She would rather cut down an acre of bush taller than herself, or clean the streets of Kings Port on Ash Wednesday morning than iron one bodice.

Gwynneth enjoyed attacking a mess. She relished every moment she could spend getting rid of muck and clutter; weeding and cutting down bush; throwing away, burning; dusting, wiping and washing down, until the dirty and the unkempt were left lightened, ordered, transformed by her labour. There was no chance of that here. Dirt didn't accumulate in this house and no weeds prospered in the little piece of yard. Much of the yard was but a concrete fringe, anyway, a raised paving around the base of the house, so clean you could eat off it. She and Pelham were birds of a feather.

She let the weekend pass, and on Monday morning, as soon as the coast was clear, she attacked the cocoa basket. After that the matter was settled. They protested at first, but then gratefully conceded the ironing to her. And ironing, she learned, could feel just like tackling a patch of bush that teemed with razor-grass, stinging-nettle, stones and ti-marie, and turning it into a bed of clean, combed soil ready for growing something.

She would sprinkle the pieces of clothing one by one and roll them into damp balls. Then, when she spread out a shirt on the table, a pair of sliders, or a handkerchief, and drove the iron over it, she was not only smoothing out roughness, she was mowing down her sorrow. Now and then a piece that she had just ironed to a crumpleless finish would get sprinkled again from her crying.

Gwynneth was convinced that the men took turns at staying awake to listen out for her in the night. It was in the wee hours, the stillest time of the night, when even Morne Cabrite had put on a pall of quiet, that the worst fits of sobbing would overtake her. If she did not succeed in muffling the sound with her pillow, one of the men would quickly appear in the bedroom door.

"Gwynneth? You want some tea?"

She would often decline, but then she found out that they had taken to boiling soursop leaf every night before they turned in, and leaving it in the pot so that it could be heated up for her if she needed it. She tried, one night, to tiptoe into the kitchen and heat up the tea for herself, but before long, Pelham was at her side, followed in a few minutes by Ainsley. Pelham took over the tea operation. He put out three cups, and they sat around the drawing-room, enveloped in a thoughtful silence as they sipped the tea.

Usually she would recover (or pretend to) and go back to bed. On some really bad nights, nothing could calm her, neither soursop-leaf tea, nor gentle words of solace, nor one of them holding her hand or massaging her shoulders. On such nights, one or both of them would plump her pillows, tuck her into her bed and sit with her in the room until she fell asleep, exhausted by crying. On a few occasions she was so distraught that Ainsley thought it best to lie beside her on the bed for the rest of the night.

Madame, the cat, kept her distance at first. She would sit on the sideboard, observing Gwynneth in silence, slowly narrowing her eyes to slits and then closing them completely as if to shut out the sight of this intruder. If she put out her hand to stroke her, Madame swiftly removed herself from the reach of the hand. Gwynneth loved cats but had never been able to have one at home because Puppa was dead set against them, found them haughty and scornful of human beings; a dog, now, knew its place...

From about half past four on evenings, Madame would take up her position on the bannister of the gallery, looking down the lane for Pelham, then starting up a quarrelsome meowing, mixed with purring, the minute he came around the bend. And even as he stepped into the gallery, scooped her up and slung her over his shoulder so that she rode triumphantly into the house atop this perch, she could be heard still quarrelling with him and purring contentedly at the same time.

Gwynneth remained *persona non grata* to Madame for weeks, until one day, still keeping a safe distance, she meowed as Gwynneth walked past her in the drawing room – one syllable and very faint, but unmistakably addressed to her. She felt so grateful. Days later, when the cat casually rubbed herself against her leg and kept on walking, not for a moment looking back, she was near ecstatic.

Then, one evening, as Gwynneth sat in the gallery with Ainsley and Pelham, Madame suddenly jumped onto her lap, sat, and then settled herself into a snug ball shape. Gwynneth froze, not wanting to discourage her, but not even the burst of laughter from the two men, amused at Gwynneth's uncomfortable statue pose and the shock on her face, could unseat the cat. Soon Gwynneth heard herself laughing out loud, too. It was a sound she had almost forgotten. Scandalous, Puppa called it. Not ladylike. The laugh of a jamet or a marchand woman in the fishmarket. Ainsley was so glad to hear it that he got up and kissed her.

From then on, wherever Gwynneth sat in the daytime, Madame installed herself on the nearest piece of furniture, or on her lap. When Madame chose to sleep on Gwynneth's bed, snuggled against her or curled into a tight ball at her feet, those were the nights when Gwynneth slept soundly. The cat's purring, her gentle breathing in sleep, her daintiness, her stillness and her every cat movement and cat pose – stretching, rolling from side to side to shadow-box with the front door curtain, washing her face, cleaning every inch of her fur right down to the tip of her tail, lounging luxuriously belly up – the cat's whole presence brought Gwynneth a soothing calm. She began to call her "Consuelo".

Carnival passed over Gwynneth that year. She heard sounds of Jouvay outside on Bedeau Lane before dawn – singing, shuffling feet, the beating of pitch-oil pans and tamboo bamboo, the blowing of whistles – but she put her head under the pillow. She tried to go back to sleep, but had to give way to the images barging into her head, of Jouvay in Ste Marguerite, where David brought out a little band every year. She had taken part in it up to what seemed like only a few months before, not a whole year.

She would just as soon have ignored her birthday, but on the Sunday before the day, Mumma and Viola appeared at Ainsley's front gate. Now Gwynneth understood why all morning there had been such a flurry and an urgency around the normal Sunday routine of Pelham going to the market and Ainsley rattling pots in the kitchen; why they set the table and just seemed to abandon it – covered it with an embroidered tablecloth she had not seen before, and retreated, one to the bathroom, the other to the yard to busy himself with some unspecified task. Then Pelham upbraiding an invisible Ainsley for leaving his sweaty jersey slung over a chair in the gallery, and Ainsley's voice ringing out from wherever he was, steupsing and telling Pelham where he could put the jersey... Ordinary, run-of-the-mill occurrences, but today wound up to an unusual pitch.

In the end, familiar voices outside. Two smartly-dressed ladies at the front gate, the younger one scowling, and both weighed down like packhorses. Mumma never could travel anywhere without a full cargo. She held a basket. Viola held a fat cloth bag in one hand and Mumma's suitcase in the other. Viola had drawn the line at Mumma walking the streets of Kings Port beside her with a suitcase on her head, so Mumma had set down the suitcase on the road, saying, "Well, you tote it."

They came bearing zaboka, mango, pigeon peas, green-fig, and other produce from the yard and up in the land, some of Gwynneth's clothes, and a birthday cake with a big 32 drawn in green icing on the top; and they all spent a happy, talkative afternoon together, with hardly any mention of Puppa.

Ma Quamina didn't look out only for Gwynneth. Ma Q was the Bedeau Lane sentry. On afternoons she settled herself on a chair in her little gallery, where she seemed to fill up the whole space, for not only was she large, but she also wore garments and head-ties that seemed to involve bales of cloth. She supervised the comings and goings on the street, and those who came and went greeted her in passing or stopped to talk with her. A few houses after hers, the sloping roadway turned into a flight of steps, climbing past more houses set close together on either side of it. Gwynneth speculated that passersby who stopped to chat with Ma Quamina on their way up the lane were grateful also to rest their legs before taking on this hill of steps.

Now and then a child racing past Ma Q would be stopped in his tracks by her peremptory "Haï!" Such children would have to step back and observe the required formalities – give her the time of day and answer questions about their diligence in school (those who were enrolled in school) and their family's wellbeing.

Gwynneth had been introduced to Ma Quamina on her first weekend in town, when she went with Pelham to take Sunday lunch to her. He allowed Gwynneth to carry the bottle of juice while he held the basket packed with love by Ainsley. As they trekked up the lane, Pelham told her that Ma Q was looking forward to meeting her, for she had heard about her and read in the papers about the march. Just before Ma Q's, he stopped, and stood looking proudly at her house. "How you like the colour?" he asked. "Is me and Ainsley paint up for she, you know, this Christmas just gone. Ainsley did want to paint it in one tasteless grey. I say 'Boy, that go look real washout!' Ainsley ain have no taste, eh. He could go and buy a shirt with he eye close. He ain care what he put on."

Pelham was shaking his head wryly, but with an indulgent grin on his face.

In the little gallery Ma Quamina stretched out her arms to Gwynneth: "Well look at this little piece-a girl, nuh! And you face Goliath, you one! Come, *Doudou*."

Gwynneth broke into a smile and giggled inwardly at being called a little piece-a girl at the age of nearly thirty-two. Ma Q braced her in the way that Mother Queen Lottie had done just weeks before – the day after Tantie Grace's Nine Nights. She sent Pelham indoors to fetch the olive oil, and with it she anointed Gwynneth's head, hands and feet.

"Brave child," she said, solemnly. "You going make a way. No power of darkness cyaan touch you."

~

The sight of children in school uniform walking along the lane threw Gwynneth back to St Paul Government School… Rishi Sankar would now be in his first term at Government College… She hoped he was settling in comfortably. He had won a College Exhibition in the year just past, the first such scholarship to come to the school. Government scholarships to high school had become slightly less pie-in-the-sky since their number had doubled to eight, and when one of the eight went to a pupil of St Paul's, the jubilation was unparalleled. In what would turn out to be her last days there, the school was still rejoicing and basking in Rishi Sankar's achievement, and showering Teacher Gwynneth with praise.

She thought of the new crop of pupils just coming to the end of their first term with her. They were Fourth Standard children, handed over in the Christmas term to the teacher of Standard 5, the college exhibition class, to begin preparing for the scholarship exam of the following year. She wondered what these children had been told about her sudden disappearance, and, who did they now have as their teacher? She hoped to God it wasn't Burris the Beater.

Mr Burris was the previous teacher of Standard 5, who had never got over the headmaster's decision to move him to the Sixth Standard class and give "his" class to Gwynneth. Fifth Standard was the most important class, and it was always entrusted to someone thought to be the best teacher in the school. Gwynneth would gladly have taught the post-primary children, but Burris and some others saw those classes, Standards 6 and 7, as a graveyard, and Standard 5 as the road to glory for the lucky teacher who could bring home the Holy Grail – a College Exhibition for their school.

Gwynneth had been teaching Standard 5 at St Paul's for six years. Every year, most of the children in her class did so well that they would have functioned with merit in high school, if only they could get into high school. Without scholarships, high school was beyond their reach. In the class that sat the exam in 1919, there were two exceptionally bright and hardworking pupils – Rishi Sankar and Brenda Skeete. However, these scholarships were still only for places at the two boys' colleges, Ascension and Prince Albert Edward ("Government College"), none for entry to a girls' high school. Brenda Skeete was not in the running.

Three years before Gwynneth joined the staff, Headley Burris had arrived fresh out of Training School, most impressed with himself, and confident that he would be the one to perform the miracle of an exhibition for St Paul's. Because trained certificated teachers were thin on the ground and, perhaps, because of the self-confidence this new teacher displayed, he was assigned to the exhibition class. No scholarships came to St Paul Government School during the tenure of Headley Burris, no matter how much energy he applied to beating knowledge into the children. Then, in Gwynneth's time, the near-impossible had happened.

Burris was mortified at Rishi's success. While the rest of the school celebrated, he wore a scowl, and avoided Gwynneth like the plague. He, however, still had a job today, whereas she… How was she going to earn her living, now?

~

Gwynneth announced to Ainsley one evening that she was going out the next day to look for work.

"Where?" he asked.

"Oh, the stores downtown…" she said, breezily.

"Gwynneth. What kind of store downtown – them narrow, stuffy lil hole-in-the-wall, cram to the ceiling with goods helter-skelter; thick dust; scraps of cloth and God-knows-what on the floor; no windows, just a front opening; piles of store-rubbish on the pavement outside, just before the door; and inside, the place jam-pack with loud customers shoving and bouncing one another? All that on top of the measly money they does pay store-clerks?"

"I could handle all of that," Gwynneth said, weakly, for her conviction was waning.

"You could handle going in to buy something and coming out right away. But you could never spend the whole day working in a place like that, Gwynneth. You would die. You are just like Pelham – you cyaan stand untidiness and disorder around you. As for the other kind of store that clean and orderly, spacious, no crowd – customers coming in one-one because only rich people can afford to buy there – those stores does only employ fair-skin girls, remember?"

"Well, I could do domestic work, clean offices…"

"Gwynneth. Why you want to let you talent and you training go to waste? The government can bar you from teaching in they schools, but they cyaan stop you teaching. You can be a private tutor."

"I thought about that, but I wouldn know where to start. And then, who going to trust me with they children after people have my name all-about?"

"When you ready to start, we go find out what steps to take. But give youself some more time. Doan rush it. What you went through is not something you could bounce back from right away. You cyaan put it away just so and move on like nutten. We want you to recover. You doan have to go back out to work yet, Teacher Gwynneth. Doan hurt you head." He patted the top of her head and rubbed her back, and she felt a little less anxious.

"And most of the people that calling your name, Miss Cuffie, is with love. They on your side."

The first time she went to the Savannah, it was the height of the dry season, or the depths. The grass was brown, and there were large patches of bare earth giving up clouds of dust that got into the eyes, noses and mouths of the unwary each time the wind barrelled in from the east. ("That is Oya," Mumma would have warned. "Doan cuss the wind. You cussing Mother Warrior Oya, and you doan want to get *she* vex!").

The poui had started to flower, but the trees were still mostly clothed in their leaves. A scattering of poui flowers on the parched ground barely caught the eye, trampled as they were and tinted with Savannah dust. Often Gwynneth would leave the dried-up Savannah and wander over into the Botanic Gardens, an area that was kept green and flourishing all through the year – the front yard, as it were, of the Governor's residence, Mille Fleurs.

But by early April, parts of the Savannah floor were overlaid by a soft blanket of petals, with poui floating down from trees that had become huge pompoms of nothing but pink or yellow, no green to speak of. Leaves had surrendered to flowers. Two miles or so to the north the tree cover of the hillsides was interrupted by more of these balls of colour cheekily drawing all attention to themselves. She sat on the bench and kept watch for a long time, as though that could keep the poui's bloom from stealing away, as it would in a matter of days.

Mumma turned up again one day, by herself, lugging parcels once more, including another bagful of Gwynneth's clothes. After she had offloaded the bowl of ochro-and-rice; the fish fried dry; pigeon peas, stewed, from the garden; and pepper-sauce made by Viola, Mumma went into her handbag and took out a document. She explained that the police had come to the house again, this time to deliver a summons, and she gave Gwynneth the paper.

Gwynneth read that she was being charged with having seditious literature in her possession and would have to appear in court in about three weeks' time. She was fully expecting an outcome like this, but had not prepared herself for it. And she had never stopped reliving the previous visit from the police. That was one of the moving-picture reels still turning behind her eyelids to drive sleep away…

~

It had seemed like mere hours, not two days and nights since they had shot him, for the smell of sulphur remained still lodged in her nostrils. The dogs were barking. The light was on, and Mumma, with the big-flowered housecoat in her hand, was hustling her out of the bed to go and sit in the drawing-room where Viola was already sitting, her coverlet wrapped around her. Then Mumma was calling the men in from the gallery where she had made them wait.

Viola watching them with a deadly cut-eye as they file in through the front door. Puppa so indignant that he can't find his voice, just following them through the house with his mouth open as they dip into every room, he in his sleeping-clothes – faded blue sliders and sagging merino. Mumma's loud, dramatic praying laced with hymns: *No goblin nor foul fiend / Can daunt his spirit…;* and, *Whom shall I fear? Whom shall I fear? / The Lord is my light and my salvation/ Whom shall I fear?…;* and, *Yea though I walk through death's dark vale / Yet will I fear no ill…;* and, *Move, Satan, move, lemme pass / I am on my way, safe and sanctified / Move, Satan, move, lemme pass…;* and, *The Lion of Judah / Shall break every chain / And give us the victory / Again and again.* Outside in the darkness the dogs keeping up a high-pitched, frantic barking. The policemen emerging from her room with armfuls of her books and papers.

As soon as they were gone, Puppa exploded with rage, but his words broke off into sounds like strangulation. Mumma gave him some breadfruit-leaf cooling to drink and persuaded him to lie down.

What Gwynneth was remembering now, with some alarm, was Mumma going through the house room by room, holding a calabash of water with flowers and a lighted candle in it, to sprinkle the water into all the corners and ring her bell, *while the policemen were still there!* At the time, Gwynneth was too numb, almost absent from her body, to recognise the danger of Mumma performing this rite when the house was crawling with police. Now, some three months later, it suddenly occurred to her.

"But Mumma," she said, looking amused. "That night the

police come to search the house, how they ain carry you down – you, you bell, you candle and you calabash? What happen, they stop arresting Shouters?"

"That set must-be did fraid obeah," Mumma replied, with a cackle.

Although she laughed with Mumma, Gwynneth felt her rage rising as she scrutinised the summons again. Who were they to tell her what she could read? But she quickly calmed herself and presented a nonchalant face to Mumma, not wanting to cause her any further worry.

"This ain so bad, Mumma," she tried to reassure her. "They coulda charge me for much worse."

Indeed, she could have been sitting in jail these past few months, as she had given them ample cause to arrest her on the spot, put her in a cell, and throw away the key. They had the power to do all of that, under one ordinance or another.

~

They had kept on shooting, but into the air now, after David dropped onto the grass verge. For what seemed like ages they stood firing, with their guns pointed at the sky, as though they were trying to extinguish the moon. People fled in panic from the gunfire and disappeared into the cane, very few of them aware of what had happened to him. She knelt to help him to his feet although she knew in her mind that this would not be possible. Blades of grass around him were sticky wet. She stood up and, waving crimson hands, railed at the police. One of them walked over to her and levelled his gun at her face. She did not flinch. She stood her ground and directed some choice words into the barrel of the gun. A white man in khaki yelled and the gun was lowered. This was the episode telegraphed around the colony by word of mouth even before the newspapers could put it out.

In the days following, the authorities swore that the Riot Act had been read and the people given time to disperse; but that was a barefaced lie.

1 2

There was a human being inside this stuffed shirt.

The summons threw Gwynneth back into a numb daze. That evening she ate very little, and did not have much to say at the table. Then she withdrew to the gallery, where she sat in darkness, absent-mindedly stroking the cat. Ainsley came out and sat quietly with her. Eventually she turned to the bannister and eased the document out from under a plant pot. "Look," she said.

Next morning Ainsley marched her across town to a lawyer's office. He offered to stay and wait with her.

"Nah, Ainsley," she protested. "I good. You done late for work already."

There were four clients ahead of her – three sitting in the waiting room, and another being interviewed by a clerk. Gwynneth sat down. When the clerk was finished with those clients, he beckoned Gwynneth over to his chaotic little desk that had books piled askew and papers hanging off the edges. The floor under him was strewn with yet more paper, bits of string, pencil shavings, and here and there a stray cent or farthing. The man was trussed up in jacket, waistcoat and tie, so that he and his desk together looked like something out of Dickens.

There was a form to be filled out. He asked whether he should fill it out for her or would she do it herself – a well-rehearsed polite formality for "Can you read and write?" She took the form and he gave her a notebook to press on. She went back to her seat and filled out the form. When she returned it and he began to check through it, he looked up, startled, and asked in an awed whisper: "Gwynneth Cuffie?"

She nodded, distinctly irritated by him. She didn't know whether it was the untidiness of his corner, or the mas he was playing in those clothes – a Jouvay morning parody of British gentry.

"From the Grand Chemin march?" he breathed, and she nodded again.

He stood up and put out his hand, "Miss Cuffie, first of all, accept my sympathy for the loss of your…" He was searching for the respectable word.

"Meh mistah," Gwynneth offered, mischievously, just to rattle him.

Her irritation was getting the better of her. He seemed to wince, and looked down at the form, then back at her again, with a confused expression on his face. It was as though he couldn't match the writing on the paper with what had come out of her mouth. Gwynneth was happy to have unsettled him. Now she could relent and be civil. "Thank you," she said. "That is very kind of you."

"I am so pleased to meet you," the clerk said. "I do admire your courage. If I can be of any assistance to you in this time… which must be a difficult time…"

Perhaps she did succeed in arranging her face into a kinder expression, for he suddenly plucked up his courage and asked, "Can I talk with you after you've seen Mr Belfon?"

Gwynneth agreed. Why not? Why be ungracious? There was a human being inside this stuffed shirt, extending human solidarity, and it was human solidarity that had been holding her together for the months just past.

"I could take my lunch break as soon as you come out of Mr Belfon's office," he was saying. "Then we could go to Alicia's Café. It's just two streets away – a quiet, reputable place. Would that suit you?"

Mr Belfon undertook to represent her in court. Mumma had brought some money with her for this purpose, which Gwynneth had reluctantly accepted, pledging to pay her back when she got a job.

Alicia's was an old wooden dwelling-house of deceased plantation owners, converted into a restaurant, pleasantly bedecked with bright tablecloths and curtains. The clerk took a table on the veranda, which ran around three sides of the building. He was well known to the staff; they greeted him cheerily as "Mr Gaston" and joked with him. The coffee smelt like Uncle Albert's. It was the smell that floated up from the kitchen into the house at Pilgrim, fore-day morning, when Gwynneth, Viola and their cousins would be just beginning to stir…

~

The children slept on the drawing-room floor. No child wanted to sleep inside on a bed when Gwynneth and Viola were there. They spread bedding on the floor – crocus bags and old clothes – and, sitting or sprawling on it, they talked, traded jokes, held belching and farting competitions, and giggled, for as long as their eyelids would hold up, or until an adult voice rang out from behind the partition, bidding them hush and go to sleep. On some nights somebody might suddenly want to go to the latrine, and had to be accompanied by all – a gleeful expedition out into the night, with one of the older ones carrying the lantern. Eventually they slept the sleep of children who had run about in the hot sun all day and then tried to stay up all night.

As they slowly came to life in the morning, the coffee smell wafted into their half-sleep, mingled with the voices of Uncle Albert, Papa Georgie, Gang-Gang Sarah, Tantie Grace, Mumma, and sometimes Uncle Cecil, whose house was further into the land. The bigpeople would be out on the back steps or down in the kitchen taking their morning coffee, grown and brewed by Uncle Albert.

Some days the whole band of children would go down into the cocoa with Uncle Albert and help pick coffee berries off bushes not too much taller than themselves, growing under the cocoa trees. They sucked the flesh off the ripest berries. It was their job to watch out for rain when coffee or cocoa beans were laid out to dry in the yard, spread on crocus bags. Though as children they were never allowed to drink any, the smell of Uncle Albert's coffee had remained forever bound up in what Gwynneth thought of as happiness…

~

Early in the conversation the clerk revealed to Gwynneth that he was a member of Forward. She gasped. This fellow was the last person in the world she would have associated with Forward. The group was considered so dangerous to the established order that between 1916 and 1918 the man presumed to be their ringleader, Neville Ogiste, had been several times detained and released, under wartime regulations, and eventually interned. He was never charged with anything specific, simply declared a threat to security in time of war. Forward was high on *The Kings Port Sentinel's* list of rabble-rousers, communists, subversive agents, saboteurs, moles, etc.

Gwynneth soon found herself confiding to the clerk that her main worry was finding work, that she didn't know where to start, and that, truth be told, she had been evading the matter. He told her, with much apology, that he knew from the newspaper about her abrupt dismissal, right after the march, from the government teaching service. "Have you considered private tutoring?" he asked.

"My friend has suggested it, but... I don't know... I have no place where I can tutor children."

"You don't need a place. You would go to their homes."

"With my reputation? People who don't know me would let me into their homes and put their children in my hands?"

He permitted himself a look of amused indulgence. "You sound as though you'd been convicted of grand larceny. They don't know you, so let them know you. I'm sure you have people who would give you glowing testimonials – Training School staff? The parish priest? The headmaster of the school you taught at? Furthermore, don't think that it's only children who need tutoring. There are many grown people in the Civil Service and other jobs who can't get promoted because they're having trouble passing some exam or the other, often because their English and their maths are not up to scratch. They would have use for private coaching."

Gwynneth was barely listening, now. A tiny point of light had come on in her head and was growing steadily as she thought of all the people who had come out to David's funeral because of her – didn't know him from Adam, many of them, but came to show their support, to hug her and offer help, all the people who had braved Puppa to visit her at home in the days following, or sent cards and letters...

Her mind working rapidly, she singled out Mr Seignoret, her headmaster at St Paul, where she had taught for seven years. He did have a very high opinion of her as a teacher. She thought of Reverend Moorley, the priest at St Hilda's Anglican Church to which she had defected, in 1917, from Father McVorran's church; and she knew she could ask Dr Carmody, the family's doctor for donkey's years. Three testimonials. She would write to these three people as soon as she got back to the house.

"Thank you, Mr Boniface!" She heard her own voice and wondered how much of her thinking she had spoken aloud.

Then the anxiety leapt up again to pull her down. "But what's the point of making plans when I could be in jail week after next?"

"Then I promise to visit you in jail." The indulgent smile had broadened. Then he took on an earnest look again. "First they have to find you guilty, at which point there will be the option of a fine. Don't worry – Mr Belfon is a very good lawyer. I doubt they'll get to put you in jail for a charge like this."

Before long, his lunch break was up and he had to go back to work. He offered to make some enquiries about tutoring. Then they could talk again. She agreed.

In the following week Mumma was back, fresh from Pilgrim where she had gone down on Mourning-Ground at the church for three days to fast and pray for guidance on Gwynneth's court case. She now went into one of the bags she was carrying and took out a dress, striped black and white. She held it up. The stripes met in V formation down the front and back. Mumma went into the bag again, took out two red cloths and laid them beside the dress.

"This is what I get on the Mourning-Ground," she announced. "Eshu colours. Just how I see it, so I make it. This is what you have to put on to go in the courthouse." Taking up one of the cloths, she said, "This is a sash for you waist. And this next piece... Now, I know you doan like how you does look in head-tie, but they show me this on you head. It come like you get mourning-bands. You could put on a hat over it."

And she opened another bag from which she drew three hats – two of Gwynneth's and one of Viola's, for her to choose. Mumma made her try on the dress in her presence, so that if there were alterations to be made, she could take it back and fix it in time for the court case. The dress was quite stylish, and Gwynneth counted herself lucky, for the spirits were not constrained by the rules of worldly fashion. The clothes they instructed people to wear for particular purposes were not always in the most flattering of designs. Spiritual clothes sometimes came in an unusual cut, or in colours that to the human eye were mismatched, or in some other unconventional mode...

One woman she knew had to have a dress made with the left side, from shoulder to hem, turned inside out – half the dress with raw seams exposed, and looking like a washed-out version of the other side; but that person only had to wear hers to church, where everybody was family or friend. Gwynneth would have to wear hers before a courthouse full of strangers, so she was grateful for the unremarkable style. The dress hung on her somewhat, showing how much weight she had lost. Mumma would have used her previous measurements, but Gwynneth didn't let her take it back for alterations. She promised that she would eat well in the coming days and put back on some size before the court case.

She met with Gaston again when she visited Mr Belfon a few days before the hearing. Gaston had two high school students for her. Their parents were clients of the law firm. She would tutor them in their homes. He also had lined up a man who wanted to get into the police force but had not yet conquered the basic English test that was part of screening for recruitment. He had already sat it twice and failed. The man was desperate. Gaston had suggested tutoring, and told him about Gwynneth. This man, however, lived in a tiny apartment with his wife and four children, where there was no table space available for anything as fanciful as private tutoring. The children did their school homework on a bed – the largest clear surface in the apartment.

Gwynneth agreed to tutor him when she moved into her own lodgings, where she would accommodate adult students in circumstances similar to his. She would not dream of asking Ainsley and Pelham to let her tutor in their home. She knew they would have no objection – indeed, they would encourage her to have students there, but she felt that she was already imposing on them enough.

The court case was over in a flash, or, more accurately, never happened. They had sat in the courtroom all morning, waiting. Mumma, Viola and Marjorie were there with her, and so were

Ainsley and some other people from Moun Demmeh – Joycelyn, Fitz, Kamal, Edwin, Raj, Sylvia, Muriel, Sunil and Kenrick.

Case after case unfolded before them: two women bringing up their respective chile-fathers for maintenance; a dispute over a piece of land in Beauséjour; an action against a hapless man who had borrowed money from a woman in a time when he had a job, had since been laid off, and could not pay her back... Mr Belfon hovered in the outside corridor, talking with other lawyers.

Then the officers of the court were loudly calling for Gwynneth Cuffie, and even though she stood up inside the courtroom, raising her hand, clearly visible to all present, the men went out into the corridor shouting her name. Next they called for the two policemen who were laying the charge, Constables Archer and Burke. Gwynneth and Mr Belfon were now on the stand, and the court criers were still yelling for the constables, but they gave up after a while. Constables Archer and Burke never materialised. The magistrate, in a fit of exasperation, dismissed the case and lambasted the absent policemen for wasting the time of the court, not doing their job, etc. Mr Belfon had a brief word with Gwynneth in the corridor, assuring her that she was free to leave.

Gwynneth's people filed out of the courtroom after Mumma, almost on tiptoe, as though they feared that if they were seen or heard, the magistrate would change his mind and proceed with the case. Once outside, they rushed to surround Gwynneth, beside themselves with joy, talking excitedly all at once, shaking her hand, hugging and kissing her. Gaston, on his lunch break, had arrived. He joined the commotion and took the liberty of a swift hug and a peck on her cheek.

Ainsley had taken the day off to go to court with Gwynneth, and had cooked some pots of food before they left that morning. He invited the little crowd around her to come and celebrate over lunch. Gwynneth was light-headed. It was the first time in months that she could just forget everything and enjoy herself. She chatted and laughed and caught up on everybody's news. The celebration did not break up until late afternoon when Mumma, Viola, Marjorie and others going out of town had to scamper down the lane and out to King George Street where they could catch the tramcar to the railway station.

By the next day the inevitable jokes about the police had begun to make the rounds. The two constables who had charged Gwynneth were illiterate, Town said. One story circulating was that when the evidence was taken out of the police station safe on the morning of the case, a senior officer checked the titles of the "prohibited" books: *Alice in Wonderland*, *Oliver Twist*, *Royal Readers Book 1*, and *Favourite Nursery Rhymes*. It was the higher-ups at the station who had prevented the two constables from going to court and making a laughing-stock of the whole police force, Town concluded.

Other rumour-bearers claimed that the policemen had fled in panic when they came to court and saw the defendant in her red head-tie, for they were certain that obeah was afoot. (When she woke up on the morning of the case, Gwynneth knew that she wasn going to wear no damn hat over the head-tie. She would put on her dress, tie up her head, and step out like Mumma, like Queen). The kindest rumour was that the two constables were sympathetic to Gwynneth and had arranged to be ill that morning – Constable Archer reporting a running-belly, and Constable Burke an attack of itching from a brush with *pwa-gaté* vine. Burke had scaled an overgrown wire fence as he pursued a fowl-thief through somebody's unkempt backyard.

As far as Mumma was concerned, there was one clear explanation for the policemen's absence: it was the work of Eshu.

1 3
Sew you mouth with a black-thread.

Mumma had announced, as they came out of the courthouse and started down the steps, her intention to offer a thanksgiving for Gwynneth's deliverance. Two weeks later Gwynneth set out for Pilgrim on an early morning train from Kings Port. Minutes into the journey she allowed herself to drift into reverie, back to thanksgivings in Pilgrim when she and Viola were little girls... the two of them enveloped in the crush of children standing in a close ring, an inner circle around the thanksgiving table, with the bigpeople behind, surrounding them.

The children's eyes would shine as they surveyed every inch of the table heaped with offerings of good things to eat and drink. They joined lustily in the singing, but could hardly wait for the prayers and the talking to be over, when Mother Queen would invite every child to take one thing off the table – a king orange, a coconut drop, a roast-corn. And then Queen would walk all the way around the table with a loaf of bread and a bowl of honey, and everybody would get to break off a piece of the bread, dip it in the honey and eat it. At the end of the thanksgiving, everybody, children first, would get a little brown-paper bag filled from the offerings on the table...

Mumma's thanksgiving was held in Uncle Albert's house. Gwynneth, no longer a carefree child, welcomed the prayers and the singing and the talking; they were a balm to her spirit. When the thanksgiver was called upon to speak, Mumma said she was giving thanks because her daughter had been through the valley of the shadow of death and had come through so victorious and so strong that she felt as if her daughter, although not baptised in the faith, had come up from Mourning-Ground.

Suddenly Mumma lurched sideways, momentarily balancing on one leg, and her arms flew up in her body's attempt to steady itself. Immediately, Queen picked up the bell and rang out a vigorous welcome to the unseen visitor. As Mumma teetered and swayed, Queen's nephew and two older women moved closer to her, ready to brace her if she should lose her balance completely. Somebody had raised a singing:

> *The Lion of Judah*
> *Shall break every chain*
> *And give us the victory*
> *Again and again.*

It was not long before a piercing shriek was heard from within the gathering, and two or three people began to hover protectively near Mother Elaine. All of these things seemed to happen in the same moment, certainly within no more than seconds. After giving out the one shriek, Mother Elaine had fallen silent, and was now standing stock still, with a grim look on her face, mouth clamped shut and eyes opened wide, staring with what seemed like accusation. A tall, strapping woman, she stood with her feet apart and firmly planted on the floor.

Then her eyes were travelling furtively around the room, darting from person to person, searching for someone, until they fastened on Gwynneth. Mother Elaine uprooted herself from her spot and marched with great resolve towards her. People cleared her path. Now she was standing before Gwynneth, and the expression on her face had softened. The drumming stopped and the singing became a low hum. It was a man's voice that came out of Mother Elaine's mouth. "Me grandpickney," the voice said, "me grandpickney whay bin da tan up and fight. No fraid. Me da watch pan you ebery day as Garramighty send. Them no touch one hair pan you head. You walk you road, pickney. Walk you road."

Mother Elaine held Gwynneth by the shoulders and leaned towards her to gently press her forehead against hers, once, twice, three times, as the church sang in hushed tones, with one drum joining in:

> *I must walk this pilgrim journey*
> *I must walk it by myself*

No one else can walk it for me
I must walk it by myself.

And as Mother Elaine, with the spirit still on her, released Gwynneth and went on a tour of the space, striding with the gait of a man through the drawing-room, out into the gallery, and back inside to the table, all the drums resumed with full force. Mumma was now sitting, dazed, with someone fanning her, while another person put back on her head-tie that had unravelled and fallen off. Queen stood behind Mother Elaine and held her tightly around the waist. Then Queen spun her around a few times and Mother Elaine seemed to come back to herself.

Gwynneth was quite used to spirits manifesting in the congregation and talking through persons present. Sometimes they addressed the whole gathering, and sometimes their message was for one person. But she had never before been singled out by a visiting spirit. It was momentous for her, but nothing out of the ordinary for those gathered there, and the service proceeded without a backward glance.

That night, settling into bed, Gwynneth asked Mumma about the spirit that had come on Mother Elaine. But Mumma had not been aware of that happening, so Gwynneth recounted the message brought by Mother Elaine.

Mumma perked up: "Eh-heh? Well, that is Kofi!"

"How you know is not Papa Georgie?"

"But you self, Gwynneth. Like you forgetting you Papa Georgie! He woulda talk to you in Patois, girl."

Papa Georgie had died when Gwynneth and Viola were eight and seven years old. Gwynneth fell silent, thinking of the grandfather she had never met, the legendary Kofi, who, as Mumma had told it, the police did lost away in jail one Kamboulay fore-day morning, back in the time when Carnival was Kamboulay. In the midst of the festivities Kofi had laid out a constable flat on the road with one butt when the constable tried to take away his drum. Two other constables came to the rescue of their colleague. They mashed up Kofi's drum and whisked him away before the scene could grow into a full riot.

Mumma had first related the story of Kofi to Gwynneth and Viola, unbeknown to Puppa, when they were ten and nine years old. Part of the story was what happened when Kofi went to Government House to proudly register the birth of his son, Joseph Kofi. Puppa's father couldn't read or write, but one thing he could do was spell out his own name. He could also recognise it when he saw it marked down on a paper. However, the lady sitting at the desk screwed up her face and said that K-O-F-I sounded like something out of the jungle, so she would write C-U-F-F-I-E, which sounded more civilised: "Joseph Cuffie".

As children, Gwynneth and Viola had never tired of hearing about Kofi, even though Mumma said there was not much for her to tell. She also said that they must not harass their father with questions about Kofi. Puppa was about four years old when the police put his father in jail. Mumma spared her daughters, while they were children, the fine details of Miss Delphine's commentaries, but truth be told, Puppa's mother washed her hands of this man who had so embarrassed her. Bad seed, Miss Delphine said Kofi was.

Lying next to Mumma on Uncle Albert's big-bed, inherited from Gang-Gang Sarah, Gwynneth asked drowsily, "Mumma, you sleeping?"

"No, not yet," Mumma answered.

"Then tell me again about Kofi, nuh?"

Between Gaston's tireless recruiting of students for tutoring, and parents spreading the word about how much their children's schoolwork had improved with Gwynneth's help, it was not long before she had built up a reasonable clientele and saved some money. By the end of August, going on eight months after she came to stay with Ainsley and Pelham, she was able to move into modest lodgings on Catherine Street.

Very modest lodgings, rundown, and the paint on the walls so faded that you couldn't tell what colour it used to be, but clean, unlike the two other places she had visited. At the first one you had to pick your way across the yard through discarded paper, cloth and empty cans, and then crunch rat droppings underfoot inside the house. At the second place, an overpowering latrine smell met you at the gate and, inside, the walls of the room were streaked and splattered with indeterminate dried substances. These had mostly turned into mould – dark green, grey or black – with here and there a flattened mosquito, set in a maroon stain of the blood it had sucked from a human. In each case, Gwynneth mused, some hidden landlord, living far from the scene, was raking in good rent money.

The room she got was really half of a house, the half that had once been somebody's drawing-cum-dining-room and gallery, but the gallery was shared; Gwynneth's part of the house and another tenant's room, Glenda's, both opened onto it. The other half of the house was formerly its two bedrooms, each now rented out to a different tenant – Glenda, the seamstress, in the front room, and at the back, a dock worker, Cedric. The two bedroom doors that once would have opened into Gwynneth's area were now nailed up, and the latticework along the top of the dividing wall sealed off with a strip of linoleum. Gwynneth had a back door, and so did Cedric, but Glenda had to come out into the gallery and walk around the house to get to the communal kitchen, washtub and jooking-board, bathroom, and latrine, all of which were out in the backyard.

Gwynneth's part was a rectangular space, unfurnished. She began a round of jumble sales and second-hand stores. She found a pair of curtained partition stands. They each had three panels and were hinged, so that they could be folded away. She would get Mumma to change out the cloth. She also bought, at bargain prices, a folding canvas cot; a table, the worse for wear; and four cane-bottomed chairs. Pelham knew someone who mended cane-work.

He and Ainsley strung up some wires across the back end of the room for her to hang her clothes on until arrangements could be made to bring her wardrobe, her cedarwood bookcase (Puppa's gift to her on her thirteenth birthday), and whatever else she needed, from Turagua. She would screen off that narrow strip of the room for her clothes and her cot. The rest of the room, the front portion, would be drawing-room, dining-room and classroom.

It would be the working students, the adults, who made the tutoring worthwhile. People whose childhood schooling had short-changed them. Many remembered school as more a place of punishment and fear than teaching and learning. Many were starting almost from scratch.

Someone sent an elderly man to her. He had never been to school. He wanted to be taught so that he could read his Bible and the newspaper for himself. His first son used to read for him, but that son had gone to the war and never returned. Killed by a bomb, they said, in Palestine. His other son lived out in Gran Cocal, and didn't get to town but once in a blue moon. This son was willing to pay someone to teach his father to read, because Mr Liverpool didn't want any strangers coming to his home to read to him.

Mr Liverpool whispered to Gwynneth that nobody but his children and their deceased mother knew that he was illiterate. He was certain the people at his church didn't know, for he held his hymn-book before him as he sang hymns he had learnt by heart since he was a child. He often took the lead with giving out the words of the hymn – speaking each line aloud, amidst the singing, to help those who could not read.

The day he read a whole newspaper article without Gwynneth's help, he was so overwhelmed that tears ran down his face. "God will bless you, Miss Gwynneth, for removing the scales from off my eyes. Miss Gwynn…"

His voice got sucked back into his throat. But when he could talk again, he made a vow to her. He would stand up before God and the congregation the following Sunday and confess that he had been guilty of deceit all these years. He would call upon all the illiterate people in the church, many of them young people with their whole life before them, to come forward and learn. For those who could not pay right away, he would get the church to advance Gwynneth's fees, and those members would pay back the church when they could. That was how Gwynneth found herself standing before the pews in Hope Revival Church every Friday evening, teaching a group of people to read and write. Members of the church had painted a square of plywood black and built a trestle to prop it on.

And, over the years, she received at her Catherine Street home a steady stream of adults anxious to become literate, but in private. This part of her work was a joy. Teaching workingpeople did not bring in grand sums of money, but it did make it easier to put up with the supercilious children of the well-to-do on whom she really depended for her livelihood.

She lived in the room at Catherine Street for fully five years before Puppa knew.

Popular history had it that this area was once a lush green plantation on the water's edge, belonging to a British peer known among the black population as "Lord Ramgoat". It was said that in his late years he cut up the land and willed a parcel to each of his outside women. The trace (later "street") that bounded each woman's parcel of land on the east he named after her: Catherine, Dolores, Caroline, Rosina, Grace, Suzette, and Alice.

Generations later, some self-appointed people's historians speculated that Alice must have been the black one (the others being malatta), seeing that she was given the piece where the Ravine ended, emptying all manner of dirtiness into the sea. Others countered that Alice was more likely the favourite one. They pointed out that in Lord Ramgoat's time, the Ravine would have been just a piece of the beautiful Shady Brook that ended in a cool, serene lagoon with trees around it, where one could bathe with delight, not the cesspool that now stank up the place.

Some claimed that there existed a painting of this idyllic scene, done by an Englishman visiting the colony in that era. They couldn't say exactly where this painting was to be found, and therefore many suspected that this was nothing but hearsay. Others reported that there was, indeed, such a picture hanging on a wall inside the governor's residence.

Mumma had come to town to visit Gwynneth at Ainsley's in the period when she was preparing to move to Catherine Street. When Gwynneth told her where she had found the room to rent, Mumma gasped and warned her that her father must not know. That was when Gwynneth heard, for the first time in all her then thirty-two and a half years, about Puppa's childhood in the Alice Street barrack-yard. Mumma begged Gwynneth not to tell Roy his father's secret.

Once when they were little – it was in the house at Morain,

with the green jalousies and bannisters – a man came into the yard, calling out "Good morning! Good morning!"

They were startled because he looked so much like Puppa. They peeped at the man from behind the front-door curtain while he and Puppa talked, standing up in the front yard. The two men spoke under their breath, so Gwynneth and Viola could not catch what they were talking about. They could only catch a word here and there, enough to know that the visitor was speaking in Patois. Puppa was speaking angrily, waving his arms and shaking his head, while the man seemed to be relating a story. When the man came to the end of the story and fell silent, Puppa's shoulders drooped and his head fell forward. For a long moment Puppa seemed to be inspecting his own feet.

The man didn't stay. As he made his way back to the road, across the yard of baked dirt, Puppa turned and walked heavily towards the house. As he approached the front door, he quickened his step and then brushed past Gwynneth and Viola without a word. He was almost stumbling in his haste to get into the bedroom and shut the door. Mumma came to the front door and stood for a while with Gwynneth and Viola, looking out at the man until he disappeared down the road.

They heard her remark to herself that Puppa could have let him sit down a little bit and offered him at least a cup of water before chasing him back out into that hot-sun. Then abruptly she pulled the two of them away from the door and pressed a warning finger on her mouth. Though they were bursting with questions, they knew better than to start the interrogation before the coast was clear. They waited until Puppa went out to the latrine. He took the newspaper with him, so they knew he would be out there for some time.

Then Mumma, under cross-examination, told them that the man looking like Puppa was their Uncle Theodore, Puppa's brother, but it was not something to go to Puppa with. He had come to tell Puppa that their mother had died. Yes, that would have been their grandmother, their other Gang-Gang, and no, Mumma didn't know why their father never took them to see her. Yes, Puppa had more brothers and sisters, so, true, Gwynneth and Viola had more uncles and aunts, but no, she did not know where they lived. Well, yes, they probably also had some more cousins besides the ones in Pilgrim, but they were not to ask their father anything about any of that. *Sew you mouth with a black-thread.* They never found out how, two months after Roy announced his marriage, Puppa came to know where Gwynneth was living. Catherine Street was not at the actual backside of the Ravine, being seven streets away from Alice. Yet to Puppa, with Roy's "dastardly elopement" still wedged like a boulder athwart his chest, this news was the ultimate defeat. It was only downhill after that. Joseph's own prophecy had now been fulfilled: his conviction that if any of his children was going to bring him down, Gwynneth would be the one.

14
This person was, to all intents and purposes, a whitelady.

From the beginning it had been clear to Gwynneth and Viola that there was very little between Roy and Helen but mutual using. Roy finished high school in 1922. He came home, but made it clear to Mumma and Viola that it was only to wait for his exam results. Gwynneth was living in town at the time, so it was Mumma and Viola whose ears were wearied by Roy's dreaming aloud, day in, day out, of leaving home and renting a place in town once he'd started to work.

That dream did not materialise all at once. His exam results were satisfactory. Armed with a Grade 2 Cambridge School Certificate, he did get his government job. But then he discovered that the cost of lodgings in any part of town where he would deign to live was more than his whole salary.

He had tried Windsor Park and Belair in the west, and then the areas that looked down on the city from up in the northern hills – Brierly, Primrose Hill, Shadybrook. Nothing there that he could afford. He followed the classified advertisements in the newspapers to various rooms offered for rent at a lower cost, some with boarding and all, in other parts of the town, but from all of these he recoiled with scorn. Living in between such people was out of the question. Some of these neighbourhoods he saw as nothing but glorified barrack-yards. And so the family had the dubious pleasure of Roy in residence for more than two years – until he took up with this girl.

Roy's first appointment was at Customs, in 1923. He took the train to and from work, still scouring Kings Port for a place to live. Then Mumma began to complain that Roy was sleeping out without a word to the family. The first time it happened, they went to their beds not knowing whether he was just out having a good time (unlikely on a week night) or lying in a canal with chop wounds about the body and pockets emptied. When they got up in the morning, he had still not come home, and they were ready to call the police.

And what would they tell the Police? That their son, a civil servant employed at the Customs and Excise Division of His Majesty's Colonial Government, might have run away from home? That short of going into Kings Port and searching through all the buildings down on the wharf, they wouldn't know where to start looking for him, because he had never given anybody at home any precise information about his job?

Mumma near worried herself to death that day. She had slept with one eye open, and got out of her bed at 4.00 a.m. to confirm that Roy had not come home. She lit a candle in his room, and sprinkled water to the four corners. During the day she rushed out into the gallery every time she heard a sound in the road. Roy turned up quite casually after work, in the evening, and Puppa greeted him with roaring, but that had no effect. Roy commented to Mumma and Viola that he was a big man, and could therefore come and go as he pleased.

"You? A big man? Ha!" Viola jeered. "First of all, under the law, nobody ain no big man or woman before they reach 21 years of age. But you, as long as you continue with that selfish, inconsiderate behaviour, you will never be a big man. Whether you reach 21, 71, or 91, you will still be a pissin-tail little boy."

Mumma had to part them.

The sleeping out became a regular occurrence, and eventually he was more often absent than at home. When pressed, he announced that he had started boarding in town. Mumma and Viola tried to find out where, but he brushed them off, saying only that it was in town. Puppa appeared only crestfallen; he seemed to have expended all his anger. He now spoke as though Roy was just going through a necessary man-rite, and when it was over, he would surely head back home to take up his inheritance: "Stop harassing the boy. Let him be. A young man must get a chance to smell himself."

It was just at the time of Puppa's retirement that Roy completed his disappearance. He didn't even turn up in mango season. Mango knocking dog, almost piling up on the ground, but no sign of Roy with box and bucket. In the period leading up to the retirement, Puppa had gone ahead with the building of the famous shed that was to be Roy's garage when the boy would have risen to the stage of owning a car. (Puppa now and then remarked, without reproach, that he himself might have bought a car, years aback, had he not been spending a hefty chunk of his salary on Roy's high school fees.)

He had been planning and talking about this shed since Roy was in primary school. The shed was built, Puppa retired, and still the shed harboured only drying clothes, sleeping dogs, Puppa's bicycle tied to a pole, the hoe and pitchfork lying on the ground, and cutlasses (three-canal, brushing-cutlass and poonya) piled into the old squeaky wheelbarrow.

After a while Roy began visiting the family from time to time, and on each occasion Puppa would insist on prodding him and joking about girlfriends: "How are the ladies in town?" / "Not one of them could manage to tie your foot yet?" / "No girlfriend, yet?" / "What, you left the lady outside? Don't be shy, man, bring her in, heh heh…"

Then, one Sunday afternoon, Roy did bring a lady home, and introduced her sheepishly as his wife. This person was, to all intents and purposes, a whitelady.

Neither Viola nor Mumma could remember Puppa saying one single word as the five of them sat around the drawing-room. Puppa sat dumbstruck in his Morris chair. The girl did not say very much, either. Indeed, she did not seem to be part of the gathering. She looked sulky and irritated – vexed, as though she had been dragged there against her will. Mumma and Viola asked questions and found out that they had been married in a warden's office, and that the girl (named Helen Salazar) worked at Empire Bank.

Puppa ranted after they had left. "You sign a piece of paper in the warden's office and that is you wedding? You doan even invite you parents? And we never see the girl parents – we doan know if she drop from the sky? That is not the way! That is not the way!"

Mumma, meanwhile, declared the girl pregnant.

Through devious investigations set in train by Viola and Ollie, a story came to light. It was alleged that Helen wanted no part of any wedding that would put their combined relatives, his and hers, on display before the other people whom she would be obliged to invite – her friends from Maria Regina Convent High School and her workmates at the bank. These all belonged to the respectable white and brown strata of the colony. So, the two of them had sneaked out of Kings Port to the warden's office in St Rose Ward. Too risky to go to the Registry in Kings Port. Government House was a busy place. They were sure to run into somebody there who would recognise Helen.

When Viola reported a comment that one of the informants had made to Ollie: "She ain want them see she mirasme mother; she all-colour, knotty-head sister and brother and-them; and she husband Congo family, black as coals," Mumma chose the charitable path.

As far as Mumma was concerned, somebody was bent on making Roy's wife look bad, telling malicious lies about the young lady. "People too damn mauvay-lang," she said, "running they mouth with nansi-story, just to make lakouray and kangkalang. If you cyaan say good, doan say bad."

Helen's mother was a dirt-poor Panyol from Venezuela, a domestic servant. Her children were, indeed, of assorted hues, for Ramona Salazar had supported herself and her family not by domestic work alone. Helen's skin was the fairest, and she had got straight hair, which some of the others hadn't, because their fathers were Creole. Her father was a whiteman. Ramona had been cleaner, cook and washerwoman to his family up until the madam noticed that the girl's waist was thickening and that for days she was too tired to get her work done by five o'clock. She would be in their house up till all seven and eight o'clock in the night, getting in their way.

Then one day, while rushing towards the back door to get out to the maid's and yard-boy's latrine, Ramona threw up on the kitchen floor. The madam fired her on the spot, and made her clean up the mess before she left. But the man would secretly pay maintenance for the child and even put her through Maria Regina Convent High School.

High school education, fair skin, and straight hair – Helen was in a front-counter bank job before you could say "Jack Robinson". She had hastened to move out of her mother's hovel of a home and into a room in a better part of town. That was where Roy had been overnighting off and on, and later "boarding". With their two salaries put together, they were able to move up into a small apartment on the lower edge of Brierly. Gwynneth and Viola were convinced that Helen had only settled for Roy, and that she actually held him in contempt. Her family history stood in the way of her landing a whiteboy, and next down the ladder would be a blackboy with education. Roy was such a person – an Ascension boy, no less.

Viola pronounced on the matter: "They would hire her and put her to the front of the bank, but none of them bakra boys was ever going married her and put her in house."

Helen had to marry Roy without delay because she couldn't hide the belly from Empire Bank for long. The minute the bank noticed, that would be the end of the bank job – high school education, fair skin and straight hair notwithstanding. And Roy? For him it was simply a matter of lifting himself by her colour.

The news of Roy's marriage – the manner of it, and Roy's obvious pulling away from the family – was too much for Puppa. He had retired just months before the visit of Roy and Helen, and to all appearances had been enjoying his retirement. He had started to grow cassava, tomatoes, beigan and sweet potato, and spent hours in his garden tending the plants. The day he reaped his first tomatoes he presented them to Mumma with blushing pride. Mumma said that the look on his face reminded her of Roy, when he was little, bringing his exercise book to show her that he had got all his sums right.

Puppa had also been spending a great deal of time at St Anthony's, where he had recently been ordained a deacon. He was preaching at some masses, visiting the poor of the parish, and accompanying Father Xavier to help him administer Holy Communion to bedridden parishioners. Mumma said she had never seen him so happy.

But then, in the days following the visit from Roy and Helen, Puppa seemed to be shutting down. He stopped talking, and on days when he spoke, it was to continue his tirades against Roy. He would sit in the drawing-room and mope for a large part of the day. Whenever he got up from his chair and went outside,

Mumma would breathe a sigh of relief, only to discover after a few days that it was not to his garden he was going. She went out to wash some clothes and found him sitting in the shed, staring straight ahead of him.

Puppa's garden was drying up. Viola and Mumma had to take on watering what was left of it. They began receiving solicitous visits from members of the church. Puppa had stopped going to meetings, had abandoned his deacon duties, and was even skipping Sunday mass. When the visitors came, he would retreat to his bedroom, so that Mumma would have to tell them that he was resting.

One day, late in the afternoon, Father Xavier himself came to see Puppa. The two of them had a long, quiet conversation, interrupted only by Viola from time to time bringing out a laden waiter, in the words of Mumma, "Trying to drunk the Father-priest."

After that evening Puppa seemed to shake himself out of his state. He returned to the church and also set about repairing his garden. He was still not himself, though, and Mumma was no less worried. He continued to spend too much time just sitting in the shed, doing nothing. His pressure was high and would not go down, and he was not sleeping well. Mumma and Viola would wake up in the night to find light from the drawing-room streaking into their bedrooms through the latticework along the top of the wall, and Puppa sitting in his armchair, muttering.

Roy had not materialised again since the visit to introduce Helen, and Mumma thought that getting Roy to come and see Puppa might help him recover. Viola and Ollie could surely find out where Roy was living. But Viola did not warm to the idea of going all the way to Kings Port to search for the spoilchild and beg him to come and look for his father and mother. Mumma then turned to Gwynneth. She made the journey to town herself in the hope of persuading Gwynneth to come and see Puppa. She told Gwynneth that it was safe to come because Puppa had lost his sting; he hardly even raised his voice any more; all the fire had gone out of him.

Before Puppa retired, Gwynneth had visited home from time to time. This started only after she was settled into her life in town, earning a living, and daily coming closer to making peace with David's fate. She used to come up to Turagua when she could assume that Puppa was at work, and spend a large part of the day with Mumma. There were a few times when it turned out he was at home, and on hearing her voice he promptly barricaded himself in his room until she left. On each of those occasions Gwynneth cut short her time with Mumma and returned to Catherine Street, her spirit troubled. Once Puppa retired, that was the end of her visiting home. She stayed away, except for the occasion of Miss Amy's death, which she couldn't just ignore.

Marjorie's brother, Louis, was working in town at the time, and he brought the news to her. Gwynneth went up to the wake that same evening, quite prepared to bed down on the floor of Miss Amy's house afterwards and travel back to town in the morning. But Ollie was at the wake that night, so he gave her a lift to Catherine Street on his way home.

Gwynneth came up again two days later for the funeral. She went straight to the church and, after the service, to Miss Amy's house, for the sake of Louis and Marjorie. This time it was broad daylight, and through the kitchen window she could see Puppa toiling in his garden. She thought, wickedly, of taking a casual walk in Miss Amy's backyard, just for him to see her, but decided to leave him in peace. She went back into the drawing-room and sat with Mumma and the other guests.

And now, months after Miss Amy's funeral, here was Mumma entreating her to go and visit him. Nothing Mumma said could convince Gwynneth to make that visit. It would not do any good. It would only unsettle him further, not to speak of herself.

Some time later, however, Viola reported that all on his own Puppa was making a mighty effort to dig himself out of the hole that Roy had thrown him into. His garden flourished, as he approached it with a new vigour ("with a vengeance" was how it looked to Mumma). He was once more spending a great deal of time at the church, on some days going to morning mass as well as vespers. He took on a new duty – he volunteered to teach religious knowledge at the two Government schools nearby, St Paul and Oropuna, and brought tales home to Mumma about the little heathens he had to contend with there. At home he was chatting a lot more, and with much less bile. For one thing, he had stopped fulminating against Roy.

Then one evening he came home, hung his hat on the rack and dropped himself heavily into his chair without a word to Mumma and Viola. His action reminded Viola of what Mumma used to say when any of her children sat down so hard: "Hm. If your ass was a egg, now?" This was also what Gang-Gang Sarah said to any grandpickney who sat down too hard on one of her prized cane-bottom chairs. Viola couldn't giggle at this now, not even in her mind, for the sight of Puppa was anything but amusing. He was slumped in the chair like a bag of stones, and he had a look on his face that they did not like. It gave Mumma a frightful premonition of doom. They spoke to him, inviting him to eat. He did not respond to anything they said.

Suddenly he came out of the long silence to announce, in the voice of an automaton: "I know where she gone to live."

Then he hauled himself up from the chair and lumbered into the bedroom. Mumma snapped out of a momentary daze and went in after him. The room was dark and he was on the bed, curled into a ball with his shoes and all his clothes on. He had not even taken the bicycle clips off his trouser legs. He refused, with a violent head-shake, to come out and take some food, or to have food brought in to him. Mumma took off his shoes, went back out to the kitchen and made some corn-meal porridge. He refused the cup of porridge and remained curled up with his back to her.

The next battle would be to get him to take his medicine, the collection of tablets, powders and tonic that the doctor had put him on for the pressure, the sugar, the glaucoma, the heartburn, the palpitations... After Mumma had argued with his back for some time, she announced that she would have to bring Dr Carmody, who would most likely put him in the hospital. At this he began to uncoil himself, slowly. Mumma was waiting with the cup of porridge. She reminded him of the doctor's orders – no medicine on an empty stomach. Scowling, he took some of the porridge, and then the medicine.

Mumma woke up the next morning to the sound of him raging at Gwynneth and Roy. His children had brought him down, he cried out, especially that Gwynneth, who had gone to live in

Bourg Ravine, of all places, the town's latrine-hole, just to spite him. She had dragged him and his family back into the cesspit. Did she know what a struggle it had been for him to climb out of that pit of despair so his generations after him could hold their heads up in the world?

They did not immediately send word to Gwynneth about this turn of events. Mumma and Viola grappled daily with getting Puppa to eat, to take his medicine, to go and sit in the gallery and breathe some fresh air for even a few minutes every day. He was getting more and more difficult. Some days he stored the tablets in his cheek and then spat them into the cup of water they held out for him to swallow them with. He ate less and less. He stayed in bed more and more, until he became, to all intents and purposes, bedridden, except that he made his way to the WC and the bathroom when he needed to. If they thought they were going to strip him and sponge him down, or make him use anything like a bedpan or a po-chamb, indignities that one had to stomach in the hospital, then they were mistaken.

The time came, however, when his dragging himself off the bed and groping his way through the house to the bathroom area began to be a painful sight. He was thin and weak and getting dizzy spells. Mumma tried to persuade him to at least take the tablet for the pressure, and on the days when he spat it out, she drew breadfruit-leaf tea and worked every ruse she could think of to make him swallow a spoonful or two.

As weak and wasted as he was, he still had the strength to rant about Gwynneth and Roy. His voice was now rasping, croaky, often fading away entirely; yet he could quarrel for what seemed like hours at a time. But when, as part of his daily raging, he began to curse his mother, Mumma instructed Viola and Ollie to go and bring Gwynneth home, even if they had to tie her up and lift her into the car.

Gwynneth agreed, this time, to come home and help take care of her father. When Mumma had travelled to town earlier on to make the same request, Gwynneth's unspoken answer was that Roy and Helen should go and look after Puppa, since they were responsible for the state he was in. This round, however, she was the culprit; it was the news of Catherine Street that had brought him to this pass. She had unwittingly stuck another knife into Puppa's heart, and therefore could not leave Mumma and Viola to struggle with nursing him back to health.

The Christmas school vacation was about to begin, and that was a period in which, as a rule, she did not tutor. For all the years that she lived in Kings Port, she had spent the week before Christmas doing just what she would have been doing at home in Turagua – cobwebbing, dusting, sweeping, scrubbing, polishing, varnishing. On Christmas Eve, she would put up new curtains in her Catherine Street room before going off to night service at the Anglican cathedral, and she spent every Christmas Day with Ainsley and Pelham.

The plan she made now was to go and stay in Turagua for as long as she was needed. When the new term began in January, she would travel into Kings Port on weekdays to continue tutoring children in the after-school hours. It would be just too much to go into town on Saturdays as well, to teach the adult students that she had at the time. She would explain that she was only abandoning them for a while. They would be sure to understand her situation. Her father was ill and she had to spend some time in Turagua, helping with his care. She would resume her life in town as soon as Puppa regained his health.

It soon became clear, however, that there would be no return to health. Gwynneth came home to meet an unrecognisable, shrunken form on the big-bed. Puppa did not seem to recognise her either, or pretended not to. Day after day, between periods of deathly silence and stillness, and often in his sleep, Puppa would speak deliriously, when all the griefs of his life came spilling out of him, drowning Gwynneth in a deep pool of sadness. *Why had Mumma never told them? Why had she helped him, all their lives, to hide his face from them? Hide his heart from them?*

15
Then, one evening, he just fell silent.

There was no Christmas celebration in the home that year. Viola had already ground the fruits, weeks before, and put them to soak in rum, so she made the black-cake all the same. And they couldn't very well leave the sorrel on the trees to rot, so they picked the ripest flowers and boiled them with cloves. But when they strained off the juice, they just poured it into gallon bottles and left it to stand until such time as somebody might feel to sweeten it. They did not bother to make puncha-crema, or ginger-beer, or pastelle.

Mumma had taken her Christmas curtain cloth on trust from Aboud since the beginning of September. Aboud was her itinerant pwatik from Syria, who went to the villages and lugged around a suitcase packed tight with cloth and haberdashery. Years before, she had bought the precious counterpane from him – salmon-coloured, and machine-embroidered with white thread – paying him a shilling every month until she owned it. He gave her comfortable terms of payment when necessary, and chatted good-naturedly with her, stretching to its limits what English he had.

Mumma's curtain cloth remained stashed away that year, as she had neither the time nor the inclination to make Christmas curtains. Yet, drunk or sober, war or pestilence, you couldn't let Christmas and, above all, New Year's Day, meet the old year's dirtiness in your home, or you would be doomed to live in dirtiness for the whole of the new year. Gwynneth and Viola did a heavy-hearted cleaning of the house and yard, nothing like the joyous, all-out onslaught of other years. And they took down the old, fading curtains that hung at the doors and windows, washed them and put them back up.

As for Christmas music, parang sides had always bypassed their house, for they knew they were not welcome there. Puppa saw parang as nothing but a noisy invasion of country bumpkins posing as musicians and singers, whose real intent was to get at your Christmas refreshments, especially your rum. But every year when the group from St Anthony's church choir came a-carolling, Puppa would warmly welcome them inside.

One night in the Christmas season that year, the sound of carollers could be heard coming up the road. Soon they stood singing at the gate. Mumma went out into the gallery and, recognising them as parishioners of St Anthony's, beckoned them in. As they filed up the front steps, still singing cheerily, all dressed in their Red Riding Hood capes over white clothes, Mumma opened the door that led from the gallery into the front bedroom, and invited them to go in.

Those who went in first stopped singing – abruptly – and stood mute beside Puppa's bed. Those coming right behind them were still in the gallery, and could not see into the bedroom yet, but realising that those inside had stopped singing, did the same. However, those on the tail of the line, standing now on the steps and out on the walk, were still singing at their lustiest. They had not heard the silence up ahead. When, finally, Mumma had got most of them into the bedroom, the whole group stood dumbstruck.

Mumma roused them and requested that they sing Puppa's favourite Christmas carol, "God Rest Ye, Merry Gentlemen", so they stood pressed together along one side and the foot of the big-bed and sang, their cheeriness considerably dampened. Puppa mustered a smile and waved weakly at them when they bade him goodbye.

Puppa's condition was neither worsening nor improving, and Dr Carmody said that it was quite possible for him to stay like that indefinitely. He was still making his own way to the WC and bathroom. They had to listen out for the thump on the bedroom floorboards that meant he had hoisted himself up, inched his way to the edge of the bed, and landed on his feet. As he shuffled and stumbled through the house, somebody had to stand nearby, preferably hidden, so as to be ready to save him from falling and injuring himself. Dr Carmody advised them, though, not to prevent him from making this trip, as painful as it was to watch. "This routine," he explained, "is important for Joseph. It helps him to hold onto some shred of independence and pride; it's the only exercise he's getting and it might well be what is keeping him alive."

Gwynneth began to plan for moving back home. She debated whether to continue tutoring schoolchildren in town for at least the first term of the year, which would mean travelling every day between Turagua and Kings Port, or make a clean break with her students before the reopening of school.

A vision was forming in her head. She was eyeing Puppa's shed, built for Roy who had no use for it. Perfect for a little school. A little school for little children, the five-year-olds refused by Turagua's primary schools because there was no room in their First Primer classes. Some of these left-out children would have been placed all the way over in St Paul, either at the Government school, if there was room, or with a lady over there who kept up a private school under her house. Some parents would have had to send their children to Oropuna, even further away.

Parents considered St Paul and Oropuna too far from home for their five-year-olds. Somebody had to take them there in the morning and fetch them back at the end of the school day. Otherwise, these infants would have to latch on to older children from Turagua and travel with them. Some five-year-olds were simply kept at home to wait for the next school year.

There used to be a little private school in Turagua that took up the left-out five-year-olds in the past, but the teacher, Miss Griffith, had closed her school after she got married. Rumour had it that the man put his foot down the day after the wedding, although he had assured her again and again, before they got married, that he didn't mind her carrying on with her school in the back room. It was *her* house and land, inherited from her parents, the women of the village noted, as they expressed the hope that Miss Griffith wasn so dotish as to have put his name on the deed. Was either dotishness or shame, they remarked with some contempt, why she didn just put his ass out and keep her school.

Gwynneth told Mumma about her idea to start a school in the shed, even though it properly belonged to Roy and Puppa.

"*Puppa* shed?" Mumma asked, with a hmph in her voice. "*Roy* shed? You know how much-a my money jumping up in that shed?

You think is two cents I put in that? Oh he want galvanise roof. Carat roof ain good enough for he boychild. Girl, you just go ahead and put it to good use, you hear? Doan fraid. I give you licen. I doan know what coulda make he think Roy coming back here to live."

There was really no reason now for her to be living in exile, in a two-by-four room in Kings Port, when in Turagua she had a home, a family and a lush green yard that seemed like the setting of a fairy tale compared to the few square feet of broken-up concrete paving that was the yard at Catherine Street. Yet, when she gave the landlord notice and started moving her belongings out, she felt a wrench at parting with her bachie. (The first time Gaston heard her refer to her room as a "bachie", he was horrified. "But...but...you are not a man!" he sputtered. By then she was learning to choose which of his irritating utterances were worthy of a fight to the finish, and which ones should just be left to fade into the surrounding air.)

Gwynneth sealed her return to Turagua by going to midnight service at St Hilda's on Old Year's night. The church was full, what with all the people whom Viola referred to as her fellow Nowhereans turning out for their annual visit. Viola would point out that everybody in her home belonged to a different religion, and hers was Nowhereanism. She was the happy heathen of the family. Nevertheless, she, like many other Nowhereans, shared with the *poto légliz* and the rest of the population the belief that it was a good thing for the start of the new year, at the very least, to find you in a church. Before this large congregation, Reverend Moorley acknowledged Gwynneth's presence and welcomed her back.

She continued tutoring in town for the duration of the new school term, while word went out in Turagua that Teacher Gwynneth would be receiving children in her private school after the Easter vacation. She had decided that she could not give up the work in town just yet, as converting the shed into a schoolroom was sure to swallow up all her savings. The shed was just four posts, a roof and a paved floor, but quite spacious for a garage, as though Puppa's vision for Roy included one of those sprawling American cars. (Yet, a few years down the road she would have to extend it a bit, for by then the shed was bursting at the seams with children.)

She sought to enclose the space without blocking out the

breeze from the east. She did not want to block out, either, the sight of shrubs and trees and sky just outside, or the bush to the back of the yard, or, off in the distance to the north-east, the crest of Mount San Miguel. She therefore put half-walls of tapia, as in a Shango palay, along three sides of the shed.

On the western side she put a higher wall, of wood, so that things could be pinned onto it for display, and for the blackboard. On the eastern side, where the breeze blew in but also the rain, she had a tarpaulin roll installed that could be dropped down in an eye-blink. (Eventually she had to make a roster for the task of letting down the tarpaulin, for at the first sight or sound of an oncoming shower, a whole grappe of children would rush to it, abandoning whatever they were supposed to be doing. Everybody wanted to undo the cord and make the tarpaulin dramatically unroll and drop down. That enthusiastic rush to help would often end in loud and sometimes physical contention.)

Gwynneth installed her rickety table and four chairs brought from Catherine Street, though she knew that cane-bottomed chairs and lively children were not a good combination. Mumma made some cushions with tapes for tying them onto the seats, to protect the cane-work. She also got her joiner to give Gwynneth easy terms for paying off the cost of building a long table and two long benches.

Puppa, meanwhile, had ceased to rail against Roy and Gwynneth. Now all his wrath was for his mother, Delphine. He accused her of deceiving him, somehow robbing him, leaving him with nothing. He mocked her voice: "You go reach far, Joseph. You go reach so far, people no go see how black you be. Them go take you for one decent, high-colour man. Learn you book good, son. Da you whay go raise Delphine nose. No make nabaddy know Kofi be you father. No self call that old-nigga name near me."

Then, bleating with anger, he would respond: "Reach far, you liard bitch? And where Joseph reach? Nowhere! Joseph he no worth one fart in a paper-bag. He no be nabaddy! And he no gat nabaddy! All he pickney-them bin turn them back pan he. Like how you bin turn you back pan my pa, my good, good pa. All me pickney-them da hate me. And me da hate meself, too, Ma. *Me da hate meself!* Joseph? Who he? Joseph he be one jumbie! One jumbie! Da you do that. Da you whay turn Joseph jumbie. And you throw way Kofi! My good, good pa whay use to lift me up and kiss me. And put me siddown pan he lap and talk to me nice, nice. Hear you: 'Learn you book, and forget Kofi.' Miss Delphine, you be one wicked, liard bitch."

It had always been the case that a little Creole (or, as he called it, "old-nigga English") would slip unbidden into Puppa's speech whenever he got into an uncontrollable rage. But then he would fight it off and strive in his ranting to stay on the straight and narrow that was the King's English. He had spent years trying to enforce English in his house and in his classroom, and to banish Creole. Now he seemed to have been overpowered by the long-ago Creole welling up from the past, the tongue that was an even farther cry from the King's English than the Creole of the day.

Often Puppa's rage subsided into sorrow. One evening they heard him ask, in a piteous little-boy voice, "Ma, which part jail dey? Eh Ma? Where jail dey? Come we go jail look for Pa, *non*? Eh Ma? Come we go find back my Pa?"

Roy's son Gordon was born in March, almost on Puppa's birthday. They tried to convey to Puppa that he now had a grandson, but he only stared. He was drifting further and further away from them. By early April he had become so weak that he stopped getting off the bed and going to the WC. When they found themselves having to wash soiled bedclothes in the morning and again in the evening, they tore up old bedding to pad him with. But he wouldn't let them. He was not too weak to blast them away.

"Nabaddy no go put no nappy pan me!" he roared. "Ayou take me fou baby?"

All they could do was spread the old bedding over the mackintosh to help protect the mattress, and even that he grumbled about.

Mumma had already taken to sleeping on Viola's bed, to avoid waking up in the morning drenched in pee. Early one morning she was jerked out of sleep by Viola poking her back and whispering, "Mumma! Wake up! Listen!"

They got up and tiptoed into the front bedroom.

Puppa was speaking in Patois! That, by itself, was a bad omen. The war that Puppa had waged on Patois for all of his adult life was even fiercer and more determined than his efforts at exterminating the enemy he called "old-nigga English". In his house his children were forbidden to speak Patois, that "uncouth tongue" (he couldn't do anything about Mumma), and as a schoolmaster he wielded his leather belt with zest on pupils who let a word of Patois slip out of their mouths.

Mumma and Viola stood gawking at him that fore-day morning, as though they were witnessing some eerie transfiguration. His speaking Patois was, by itself, unsettling enough. But as they put all the pieces together, they began to brace themselves. Puppa was no longer facing the wall, which had been his fixed position over the past week or so. He had turned around and was now looking and speaking into the air on the other side of the bed, as though somebody was standing there. He was speaking gently, peacefully, sometimes addressing Delphine, sometimes Kofi.

He spoke to them in a steady stream for a few more days, calmly, never resuming his rant, constantly moving between Patois and the long-ago English Creole. Then, one evening, he just fell silent.

16
And then there was Moun Demmeh

For the first few days after Monica moved in, Gwynneth and Viola would still spring out of their beds at the crack of dawn, Gwynneth to tidy Mumma's bedroom, Viola to make breakfast for her, and the two of them to help her bathe. But they would be stopped in their tracks when they came upon Mumma and Monica in the drawing-room, Mumma reclining on the couch in a crisp, clean housecoat, her hair freshly corn-rowed or fashioned stylishly into Upsweep, and Monica pegging an orange for her, or holding the cup while Mumma drank her Cream-of-Wheat.

Some mornings, at Mumma's request, Monica would take the centre table into the gallery for Mumma to have her breakfast out there. Afterwards Mumma would decide whether to go back in, or stay out there on the couch for a while, catching some breeze, answering the greetings of passers-by, enjoying what she could see of the flower-garden – the baskets of fern hanging from the eaves, and just outside, the bougainvillea, the croton… Sometimes when Monica left her and came back out to check on her, she would meet her taking a little doze.

Monica also took over reading the newspaper to Mumma, except that she made it a daily routine. Viola and Gwynneth had been reading the paper to her now and then since her sight worsened, but Monica sat and read to her every day, without fail. Mumma was most appreciative, and so were Gwynneth and Viola. Monica would first read out the headline of each article, and Mumma would decide whether she wanted to hear that article, or not. She gave a running commentary on the news that Monica read to her, as she did when they listened to the news on the radio, with much steupsing at the monkey-tricks in the Leg. Co., and at how Hitler and them Nazties bombing up London… (Nobody could persuade Mumma that this was not how to pronounce the name of Hitler's miscreant band.)

Gwynneth, on the other hand, didn't want to hear a word about they damn war. When the BBC came on at "O-two hours, Greenwich Mean Time", its voice fading in and out through the crackling combined with a sound like the whole Atlantic surging, she would steups and go to her room, or into the kitchen, or out to the gallery, while Viola insisted on listening.

Throughout Churchill's "fighting speeches" Gwynneth had steupsed and sung and made a clanging in the kitchen sink, letting the pots and plates and cutlery crash against each other, while Viola clapped and cheered at everything Churchill said. Gwynneth made no great distinction between Churchill and Hitler, nor, for that matter, Roosevelt and Hitler. "None of these gentlemen," she insisted, "would have any qualms about putting blackpeople, by the stroke of a pen, back into slavery tomorrow morning."

But, of course, she had to listen, sometimes. She had to know what they were up to. Like the news, last month, that Churchill had made a deal with Roosevelt to trade away some "British soil" in the West Indies, over the heads of the people living there. The Americans wanted to get land for military bases and, in exchange, the Americans were giving Britain some old, laid-up battleships. "Destroyers for Bases" they were calling this deal. Parts of Cayeri were included in the "British soil" selected for the bartering-block. Three choice pieces of Cayerian land were being handed over, two for air-force bases, and one for a naval base. The Americans had captured the green, rolling countryside around L'Anse Amandes beach to put a naval base! Without a by-your-leave to the people of Cayeri. Gwynneth was beside herself.

By Saturday morning it had sunk into her head that she did not have to jump up as soon as she opened her eyes. Sun streaming in through the jalousie slats and no need to get out of her bed! She could hear Monica moving about in the kitchen. Gwynneth could lie in bed for a while longer, listening to the sounds of house and yard.

She realised that what had woken her up was a commotion outdoors. One of the dogs was yelping blue murder. This usually meant that Miss V (alias Queen Victoria) was up on her hind legs, delivering some swift cat-slaps to the face of a dog, she advancing on it while it backed away, and the dog would be falling over itself before it turned and fled. Or, Miss V had merely looked at one of them too hard, in which case the high-pitched sound of terror would be either Bubulups or Mirasme apologising to Miss V for being such an offence to her sight, and begging not to be slapped for so displeasing her.

In years past, Mumma had a friend up Wilson Trace whom Gwynneth loved to visit because she had cats. Gwynneth's ambition, then, was one day to be just like Miss Alcindor, who seemed to have a cat looking out of every window of her house, one curled up on every chair of her drawing-room, and, often, one slung over her shoulder. Now, Gwynneth reflected that Miss V was as good as ten cats.

This company had no understanding of the laws of cat-and-dog relations. In one minute Miss V would turn into a shrieking wraith with her back and tail up, and fur sticking out like the bristles on a quenk, charging at the dogs, and they would run for their lives, screaming. Sometimes she jumped onto the back of a dog as it fled in terror, and she would ride the poor creature until she'd had her fill of teasing it. Then, in another moment, the three of them would be variously sprawled or curled up together on the mat at the bottom of the back steps, Miss V in the middle, with the two pot-hounds half on and half spilling off the edges because Miss V had to have plenty of space.

Gwynneth looked forward gratefully to spending more time outside with Miss V and the pot-hounds. Wherever in the yard she lingered – hanging clothes on the line; burning rubbish; sitting on the backyard bench or the one in the flower garden; sitting on the low peerha to attack the weeds in Mumma's garden with her hands, but using the poonya on warrior weeds like ti-marie and stinging-nettle – the three of them would appear from nowhere and flop down around her.

She looked forward to giving her room a thorough clean-out, especially tackling her dusty bookcase before the silverfish could eat their way through every page of every book she owned (and now she might even get to read a book once in a while). And she looked forward to going to the market again...

Lennox had been making market for them over the past year or so, and was now more savvy about it than either Gwynneth or

Viola ever was. He could handle the market like Mumma. Lennox could tell if the cassava was past; if the dasheen would cook good; if a vendor was trying to give him short weight. He had been going to the market with Mumma since he was two years old, when all the vendors knew him as "Ma Cuffie lil husband". They would drop a ripe-fig into his toy basket, a bunch of chennette, a little paper cone of chilibibi or channa. They would take the farthing he proudly held out and hand him back a different farthing as "change".

Now he strode through the market on tall legs, sometimes carrying two baskets, for when Marjorie couldn't go herself, he would make market for her as well. Mumma's special vendor, Etwaria, her pwatik of many years, looked out for him, sold him only the best of her goods, and gave him a generous lagniappe on whatever he bought, sending love and maybe a mammy-apple or two sapodillas for Mumma.

Gwynneth smiled at the thought that Lennox would now have to pilot her around the market when she started going again, maybe next Saturday. This weekend was already swallowed up – no rest for the wicked. Today she was due to have that talk with Gaston, and there was choir practice. Tomorrow was church, when she would have to play the organ for the morning service because Mr Jeremy had a bad cold; and the afternoon was for the visit to Phillip's band.

She thought, with unexpected teariness, of how readily David would have taken to this iron-beating wonder...

~

If an iron band had sprung up in Ste Marguerite, David would have found time to go out and support it, sooner rather than later, as busy as he was. Besides the work he took on outside of his job, he had his parents to look after – Lance and Laura St Bernard. David's mother had suffered a debilitating stroke, and his father, who tended to her during the day, was himself in need of care. Yet he would not allow David to bring in hired help. Mr St Bernard insisted that as long as he had breath, he would be the one to take care of his sweetheart Laura. Breath he had, David commented, but what was needed for the task was health and strength. His father had a bad back, gallstones and lapses of memory.

One Saturday in every month, David's brothers and sisters, with their spouses and offspring, would swoop down and take over the house and yard. They cooked and cleaned, lavishing the oldpeople with attention. The children, lively as fleas, would leave their grandparents worn out but in high spirits. (Gwynneth chuckled at the thought of Roy, Her Majesty Helen and their children spending a day like that with Mumma... No use trying to form a picture to go with that thought – it would only tire out her brain this early morning).

The rest of the time it was David who took care of his parents, with the neighbours keeping an eye and ear out towards the house while he was at work. David made breakfast and lunch in the morning before he went to work, and also left a thermos full of tea. Then he hid the matches so his father wouldn't get it into his head to undertake any cooking and in his forgetfulness burn down the house. Mr St Bernard had already burnt a pot beyond recognition, forgetting it was on the fire while he and his sweetheart took an afternoon nap. The burning smell was detected in time by Mr Clement next door, as he pulled up weeds in his backyard.

Twice a week David bundled up the household's laundry and Miss Edith's son would pick it up and take it home to his mother for washing, starching and ironing. That was the only hired help Mr St Bernard would agree to.

At Ste Marguerite Government School where David taught Standard Four, he was also the scoutmaster, rounding up his troop every Wednesday afternoon after class. He did guard duty two nights a week with the wartime Special Police, when he and some other men from his unit were transported in the jitney along bumpy canefield roads to go on patrol around the Usine Sainte Marguerite sugar works.

David was treasurer and main wicketkeeper for the Ste Marguerite Jubilee Cricket Club – a hopeless collection of mostly middle-aged men exhausted by a lifetime of estate work, some with bulging torsos that their colleagues called "dhal-belly", and some younger, fitter men of David's age who were former classmates of his at CMI school, the primary school run by the Canadian Mission to the Indians.

On occasion, the team was joined by Reverend Hubert, the

portly, red-cheeked Presbyterian missionary from Canada. The Reverend's team-mates referred to him behind his back as "Two-Leff-Foot", for his running was so clumsy that he often tripped and lay stretched out full length on the ground until they could stop laughing long enough to go and help him to his feet again. David called his team "The Lame and the Halt". Among them David was known as "Seetahal". Puzzled outsiders who had difficulty matching this decidedly African person with that name were informed with a shrug that "Seetahal" was his Indian name, given to him by his team-mates.

They hosted fête matches on their home ground – the village savannah – and on invitation also travelled to other villages to play cricket. The members of Ste Marguerite Jubilee Cricket Club had a rollicking time together and shed no tears over the many matches they didn't win. They were too busy. So much to do. In mango season the men would pick green mangoes just about to ripen from the trees on the edge of the savannah, and rustle up a big enamel basin of mango-chow with plenty shadon benni, garlic and bird-pepper. The chow became their cutters as they shared a petit-quart, man to man, each of them taking a swig straight from the bottle.

Every so often they would make a cook down by the river – curry duck, bhaji and rice – to which they sometimes invited family or girlfriends, but would not allow them to get hold of the pot-spoon, as much as the women tried to take over their operation. When they had finished cooking and everyone had been served, the men jumped into the river, advising the women that they were free to take over the dirty pots and plates, if they so wished. At Divali, and again at Eid, David had to make the rounds of his friends' homes and eat a little dhalpouri here, drink a little sawine there, and beg off seconds, because he had many other such commitments to keep before the day was over.

And then there was Moun Demmeh.

Nobody could remember just how the group had got started officially, or exactly when (1916? '15?), although in some meetings they seemed to spend an inordinate amount of time arguing about just that. David had grown up in a family that had hosted

181

earnest discussion on their veranda for as far back as he could remember. He was simply carrying on the tradition handed down by his parents, until somewhere along the way the gathering got to the stage of a scheduled monthly meeting, sometimes with minutes and-all. The people who gravitated to David's wide and breezy veranda were originally friends and acquaintances of his – classmates through CMI School and Government College; fellow students at Training School; colleagues in teaching at Ste Marguerite Government School.

Then came others, attracted by the opportunity to stretch their intellectual muscles, or to show them off. Certain of the townpeople in the gathering were also drawn by the idea of a Sunday afternoon expedition into some deep and exotic hinterland they called "the countryside", which for them meant anything beyond the old toll gate post on the eastern edge of Kings Port. (Ste Marguerite Road was a turn-off five miles from Kings Port along the Eastern Main Road, and David's home was barely two and a half miles south on Ste Marguerite Road.) By 1918, this "social and cultural society" was more like an ongoing conversation, often degenerating into altercation, among a bunch of mismatched bedfellows.

Some came because they wanted to agitate for a change in the content of education in Cayeri and suggested that this could begin with ceremonially throwing the *Royal Readers* into the sea at L'Anse Marron. Others present swore by the *Royal Readers*, on which they all had been educated and they had turned out fine, they thought.

For some, the burning issue was attaining self-government, with every Cayerian from the age of twenty-one having the right to vote. Others were deeply disturbed by this vision of canecutter and scavenger and-all having a finger in government.

There was a loud chorus of steupses, with somebody asking "Whose war?" when it was suggested that the meeting take up a collection to contribute to the war effort.

Some members of the group dreamed of Cayeri growing a literature of its own. Then there were those who argued that the responsibility of a Cayerian writer would be to show that the colony could throw up its own Shakespeare, Wordsworth or

Dickens. There was also the suggestion that Cayerian writers could look into "quaint local folklore and strange superstitions" that would make entertaining reading for Europeans and Americans. The last word on this topic came from someone who declared that the aim of Cayerian writers should be neither the reproduction of Dickens and company, nor the amusement of foreigners, but getting at the substance of life as lived in their own surroundings.

The larger cohort that kept pressing for the group to speak out about the starvation wages labourers and their families had to live on were dubbed "Bolsheviks" by others, who deemed such preoccupations too political.

The group had also to confront the ghost of racial discrimination. Some were adamant that it did not exist – not in this colony, not any more – and that blackpeople would one day have to stop seeing prejudice where none was intended. The rumours about colour prejudice in the planters' and merchants' recruitment for the war were just that – peevish rumours. Wasn't there a whole editorial in *The Kings Port Sentinel* debunking all this?

"Just read the editorial!" one of Johnstone's people insisted, with irritation. "What they are pointing out is that, and I quote, 'men of the more educated and discerning class of Cayerians, *white and black*' are able to see that there are shortcomings in the local authorities' recruitment effort. That's the reason why they are shying away from government's BWIR recruitment. You don't have to put race and colour into everything."

The rumours were much richer than the explanations put out by newspapers and government to take shame out of their eye. People had got wind of whiteboys refusing to enrol in the public contingent unless they were commissioned as officers.

"What Town say," David reported, "is that the reason white families – planters and merchants – setting up they own contingent is to rescue Cayerian whiteboys from the indignity of serving down in between niggers and coolies. The komplo is for their boys to bypass the public contingent and go up to England, into a British regiment, with the help of the Colonial Office in London."

"Some saying is just rumour, but I hear they only accepting white and fair-skin recruits. That ain hard to verify. We could go and find out," Rawle suggested. "Let's go up to the recruitment office and play we come to enlist."

The majority of those present endorsed the plan (others found it a childish prank) to test the rumour about the planters' and merchants' contingent. A few days later, Rawle, Sunil and David, who had graduated together from Government College, went to the planters' and merchants' recruitment office that had been set up in their alma mater. The three of them were now variously employed in the civil service, a law firm and the teaching profession. Among those ahead of them in the waiting area they recognised Charles "Charlo" Rostant, a whiteboy who used to play in the Ascension College football team, and later in the all-white-and-light-skinned Clover Football Club.

Charlo, having maintained a reputation for low or failing scores every term, in everything except football, had dropped out of school a year before he was due to sit the Cambridge School Certificate exam, declaring for all to hear that he didn't see the point of hurting his head with all that studying. After all, his father owned one of the biggest import firms in Cayeri and he could simply go and work there. He didn't need any certificate to get a job. This fine specimen of "the more educated and discerning" did, indeed, "work" from time to time at Julien D. Rostant and Co. Ltd., but spent more time boating and diving and holidaying on the offshore islands.

It was mainly whiteboys waiting. There was one other dark-skinned applicant besides David and friends. The rest were light-skinned Creole boys, more or less the same colour as the tan that Charlo had developed from hours spent on the beach and in an open boat at sea. Whiteboys were strutting out of the office at intervals of ten minutes or so, with proud smiles on their faces, or trying to look blasé about their success. Then the blackboy went in, looking very confident, almost strutting like the whiteboys – and in the blink of an eye was back out again, with a puzzled expression on his face. He stepped rapidly, almost scurried, towards the archway that led outside.

David and friends exchanged glances. More would-be recruits went in. All of the white ones came out thumbs up, but none of the off-white ones looked happy on their way out, no matter how close to white their skin colour was. When Charlo came out it was with his arms in the air, as though he had just scored the winning goal before a worshipful crowd. Then it was their turn. Rawle volunteered to go in first.

At the next Moun Demmeh meeting they related their experience to the rest of the group, and the diehards who didn't believe in colour prejudice either said the three of them were making it all up, or argued that since the planters and merchants were financing the contingent, they were well within their rights to pick and choose their recruits.

Rawle reported that the moment he darkened the door of the office, the recruiting officer looked up, made a sound of exasperation and with his pen drew an arc in the air towards him that signalled *Turn around*. The man used up no words. Rawle stayed in the doorway long enough to flash him a broad smile and say to him, "Good! Now we have the evidence."

Determined to make the blind see, somebody brought to the following month's meeting the two most recent issues of the magazine *Phaedrus*, put out by the literary and debating club of the same name. In the pages of this magazine a small war was being waged among members of Cayeri's literati, over an article by Anton da Silva. This gentleman argued that self-government would be a mistake in a colony made up of mainly Negroes and Indians, for the brains of these peoples were not large enough to do the kind of thinking that the responsibility of government would require. It would be like giving monkeys the right to vote.

In the latest issue of *Phaedrus*, da Silva's opinion was supported by a British botanist working with the government's Department of Agriculture, and two other members of the Phaedrus Literary and Debating Club. The opposing side in this war was a one-man army in the person of J. R. D. Phelps, a young intellectual who put up a sterling defence of the brains of black folk, with no one coming to his assistance.

Parts of the debate were read out to a hushed meeting of Moun Demmeh, and some took this hush as a sign that everyone was equally shocked at the statements made in those articles that supported da Silva. But then the first to comment was someone

185

who wholeheartedly endorsed da Silva's views. The collective response of most of the group to this speaker could not be deciphered – it was simply a noise, thick like a thousand very angry bees swooping down on some living thing that had disturbed them.

Those who agreed with da Silva were strongly outnumbered but still managed to get in enough words to feed an extended clash, until one of them announced into a lull in the bedlam: "Let the white man leave these shores and the black man will grow a tail again."

The meeting dissolved, for what could anyone say to a black man saying this?

There was little or no contention in the meeting of November 1919 as to whether they would get involved in what the Workers' League was planning, for by then Moun Demmeh was pretty much down to the "Bolshies". Strikes were erupting in different parts of the colony. Workers on cocoa and sugar estates, scavengers and dock workers had gone on strike against deplorable working conditions and wages that could not feed and clothe their families.

Moun Demmeh gave careful thought to what support they could offer the strikers, knowing full well that for those members of their group who worked for the government, joining any of the worker demonstrations could result in their joining the ranks of the unemployed, not only in solidarity, but in reality. Then they would be in no position to offer even the paltry material support they were contemplating – taking food to families whose breadwinners were on strike.

Some of the strikers on the Usine Sainte Marguerite sugarcane plantation were David's team-mates in the cricket club. Moun Demmeh decided to take food to them and to as many other families as they could muster the means to help. Members of the group collected vegetables from their kitchen gardens, or their friends' gardens, and pooled money for other foodstuff. They bought the food items and held a bagging session on the St Bernards' veranda, following which David took the group to the barracks, out on a fringe of the plantation. There they distributed the packages, each containing powdered milk, rice, cornmeal, split-peas, ground provision, green vegetables and oranges from the trees in David's backyard.

Gwynneth had been to the barracks with David before – at Divali; to the funeral of his friend's grandfather, and on some of the occasions when he took oranges for the children, to help ward off the perpetual runny noses. But some of the Moun Demmeh people had, up till then, only heard about the conditions under which the barrack-dwellers of the sugar estates lived. What they saw caused them to come away feeling quite depressed.

Gwynneth's contribution to Moun Demmeh's letter campaign in September had focused on the unrest in the colony, and the suffering that was the source of this unrest. Her letter was printed in *The Voice*. The clipping still lay in the stash under her bed.

20ᵗʰ September, 1919

The Editor

Dear Sir

As we approach the first anniversary of The Great War's end, it is clear that the joy and celebration witnessed on the eleventh of November, 1918, were ill-founded. Cayeri is still at war, and the enemy is hardship.

Prices are, today, more than double what they were at the beginning of the war, but workers continue to be paid the same pittance as before. How can a family be properly fed, not to mention clothed and sheltered, if its breadwinner earns 12 cents a day while a pound of rice costs 7 cents, and a tin of milk 13 cents? Imagine the plight of the unemployed, if many people who have work can yet do no better than to send their children to bed at night with only sugar-water in their bellies.

The health of those who labour is being jeopardised by harsh working conditions, but employers in Cayeri have little regard for the wellbeing of their labour force. Workers in "The Mother Country" have the right to form trade unions, and they enjoy the protection of labour laws. "The Mother Country" extends no such rights to her working sons and daughters here in Cayeri. We have no authority to bargain with our employers, no legal rights or protection as workers.

The colony is a boiling pot of hardship, resentment and protest.
Consider, in the current unrest, the pain of our soldiers
returning from the war with their hearts already full of grievances,
enough to make the pot boil over, only to be further slighted, cast
aside like spent shells by the authorities here in their homeland...

The Workers' League had been hosting meetings all over the colony to let returned soldiers of the British West India Regiment speak about their experiences in the war. Gwynneth, David, and some other members of Moun Demmeh went to one of these meetings. It was held in town, at the church hall of St Philomena Catholic Church, readily given over for the evening by the parish priest, Father Harrigan, who was also most present at the proceedings.

This priest was something of a renegade, famous for aiding and abetting causes frowned upon by the colonial authorities; but neither Government nor Catholic authorities seemed willing to censure Father Harrigan. It was rumoured, for instance, that shortly after the passage of the Shouter Prohibition Ordinance, he had journeyed up a craggy hill outside the town, negotiating riverbed and fallen tree-trunk, to visit a little Shouter Baptist church that had taken refuge up there. He took part in their service, singing with great gusto, clapping his hands and dancing; spoke words of comfort to the congregation and, surrounded by a ring of church members, was anointed by Mother Bernadette.

... These soldiers are men who insisted on leaving their homes to go and defend "The Mother Country" in faraway places, though it was clear to them even before they left Cayeri that they were not welcome. We must never forget that the British army did not want black soldiers among their troops, and would not allow black men to fight against white men, never mind those white men were the deadly enemies of the British.

Nor were black soldiers allowed to be officers; that rank was reserved for men of "unmixed European blood", said the British War Office.

Our black soldiers were mostly shunted to Egypt, and "served" in the Great War as menial labourers – latrine-cleaners, load-carriers, diggers, washers of dirty linen... They were paid less than the white soldiers, segregated into living arrangements of the lowest standards, and treated like dirt by officers as well as supposed comrades-in-arms from "The Mother Country".

Then they came home, not to be welcomed as heroes and thanked for their service, but to join the growing throngs of the destitute. Benefits owed to them have not been paid. Most of the men are unemployed and many have been reduced to abject poverty...

The Workers' League plan was, perhaps, grandiose. The dock workers' strike had boldly held out for almost a week already, and the strikers were organising a march from downtown Kings Port up to the governor's residence to present their grievances. The League collaborated with a group of returned soldiers to organise a supporting action which would bring people together from all over the island into one long march to Kings Port. They were calling out demobilised soldiers, sugar and cocoa workers, the unemployed, the destitute, and organisations as well as individual citizens sympathetic to the cause. Along the way, they would seek out people who slept under bridges, in playing-field pavilions, on city pavements and in The Square, to invite them into the march.

People coming from the north-east were going to set out from the pavilion at Los Bajos Savannah. Another contingent would start from the pavilion at Patna Settlement playing-field, in central Cayeri, which would also be the gathering-point for people from further south. The march coming from Los Bajos would proceed west along the Eastern Main Road, and the one from Patna Settlement, north along Grand Chemin.

The two marches would join up, before daybreak, in the savannah near Majouba Junction where Grand Chemin met the Eastern Main Road. There they would rest for a bit, and then, together, head for Kings Port. By 7.00 o'clock they would be in The Square, where they would sit on the benches and on the grass, under the marble gaze of Christopher Columbus, to rest once more and refresh themselves with biscuits and water. Then they would take part in a rally with the dock workers, city scavengers, square-dwellers, and supporters from the general public, and join them on the march from Christopher Columbus Square up to Mille Fleurs, the governor's residence.

This supporting action came to be known as "The Grand Chemin March" because of how it turned out; but in the planning it had been conceived as "The Hunger March to Mille Fleurs".

Moun Demmeh had taken the decision to travel to one of the two muster points of the march, although they could have joined it along the Eastern Main Road, or in town. On the evening before the march they took the train from Kings Port terminus and headed for Patna Settlement, lugging on board two five-gallon tins of biscuits. The Workers' League had put out a request for groups that could afford it to bring biscuits in bulk, which would serve as breakfast before the march set out, and as sustenance along the way.

People filtered into the pavilion all evening. Some had taken the last train up from the south. Some jumped off rickety trucks that had brought them to Patna Settlement from God-knows-where. Patna Estate workers walked to the playing-field, and groups of them arrived on donkey-carts. By 8.00 p.m. there was a sizeable gathering in the stands, and a buzz of lively conversation. Two Workers' League representatives stood at the front and spoke to the crowd, delivering words of welcome and encouragement, in addition to going over details of the agreed plan. Before 9 o'clock there was quiet, and everyone had secured a spot on which to stretch out or curl up and sleep, for the time of departure would be 3.00 a.m.

From 2.00 o'clock the marchers began to rouse each other. They took turns at using the standpipes and latrines at the back of the pavilion. Biscuits were distributed. They huddled for prayers, and addresses from some of the leaders present. David spoke to the gathering. Gwynneth remembered him stressing that they should stay in single file and stick to the edge of the road.

Just before 3.00 o'clock they stepped out onto Grand Chemin. In the cool night air and soft light from the moon they made their way, finding the single file to be not in tune with their mood, so that soon they were clumping into twos and threes. And though it was meant to be a silent march, nothing could suppress the low human murmur that blended with the rustling and whispering of the canefield alongside, and the crapaud and cigale cries…

~

By now the teariness had grown into a flood that Gwynneth could not dam. It took her by surprise, because her sorrow, if not her rage, had dulled considerably over the years, and her bouts of crying or sinking down into the dumps were now few and far between. Now there was more rage than sorrow in her tears. Grief had been kept at bay, not only by her own willpower, but by the work that crowded her life.

It was almost a year, now, since the memorial service held by David's family in November 1939 to mark the twentieth anniversary of his death. Gwynneth had agreed, with some apprehension, to read one of the Lessons at the service. She did not know for sure how well this would go, but the whole tenor of the service turned out to be so uplifting that she realised she was in no danger of dissolving into tears.

David's nieces and nephews, now all grown-up young men and women, were in charge of the proceedings. Some of them would have barely remembered the living Uncle David, but the two youngest each told an anecdote, handed down to them, from the legend of his life. In tow was a new generation of the family, some little great-nieces and great-nephews. One of them, a six-year-old boy, recited a poem dedicated to his great-uncle David.

Moun Demmeh folk shared with the congregation some of their memories of David. With the help of one of the nephews, a veteran of the Ste Marguerite Jubilee Cricket Club shuffled to the podium, where he spoke with fondness of his team-mate "Seetahal", and how much David had done for the community of Ste Marguerite. A contingent of representatives from the labour movement paid homage to David, hailing him as a martyr of the struggle for workers' rights, then belting out a thunderous union song in his honour:

Hold the fort, for we are coming
Union men be strong
Side by side we battle onward
Victory will come.

Gwynneth stood at the podium and read the Lesson with love and regret in her heart and not a quiver in her voice.

~

In early 1920, when Gwynneth finally came out of the cocoon she had wrapped herself in since David's death, and gone to stay with Ainsley and Pelham, she knew that she had to visit David's parents as a matter of priority. But she was holding it off. Ainsley had already been to see them more than once, and on one occasion she promised to go with him on his next visit. At the last moment, however, she begged off. "Maybe next time, Ainsley. I'll be of no use to them right now, for I'll just start crying. You can't comfort people with crying."

"I know, my dear. And they do understand that you not up to it yet."

Eventually she braced herself and went with Ainsley to the home. Although the couple were still distraught, and seemed more absent-minded than she knew them to be, they were very gracious to their visitors. They received Gwynneth and Ainsley on the veranda, the scene of all Moun Demmeh's discussions, squabbles, planning, eating and drinking, sometimes even dancing and singing – and David's calm presence. It was almost too much for Gwynneth, but she steered herself away from disaster. "How are your grandchildren?" she asked.

Light filled Mrs St Bernard's face, and Mr St Bernard smiled from ear to ear, even as he did a pantomime of perplexity, rolling his eyes and throwing his hands up. "Better than us, as usual," he said. "They are fine. Too fine. We can't keep up with them!"

Mrs St Bernard spoke with enthusiasm about the grandson who had won an exhibition in the 1919 batch, and had just entered Government College. She was reclining in a deckchair. She had never fully recovered from her stroke, and to Gwynneth she looked even frailer than the last time she had seen her, just a week before the Grand Chemin march. For that matter, Mr St Bernard had himself become quite frail in that short time.

Gwynneth recalled, now, that as frail as they were, Lance and Laura St Bernard had outlived their son by almost ten years, and died, within months of each other, in 1929.

~

She found herself sitting upright on the bed, letting out, once more, a flood of sorrow and rage; acknowledging that there was still too much rage in her; and vowing, once more, that her life would not be overshadowed by either rage or sorrow. This, she knew, David would have endorsed.

Then she was jolted out of reminiscence by the sound of Roy's voice in the drawing-room. It alarmed her. There was no telling what trouble he would bring; he was still quite incensed at having to hand over what he insisted was an outrageous cut from his salary for help with Mumma's care. The Saturday morning sousing in bed was over. She had to get up and see to it that Roy did not so offend Monica that she would want to pack her bags and leave immediately.

1 7
She forgot she was trying to get rid of him.

Roy's mission was to let the master be known to the servant, to let
the servant know just who would be forking out ten precious
dollars to pay her every month. He also wanted to see what
Gwynneth had dredged up from the depths of Pilgrim and
brought here to live off him – no doubt one of those fat, black, old
Shouter battle-axes who still gave him such a strange feeling of
unease, even as a grown man. He would have to be firm, though,
and let the battle-axe know who her boss was.

Ten dollars this woman would be gouging out of him, ten
dollars *every month*! And Gwynneth had ordered him to come up
and pay the woman two dollars and fifty cents because she had
arrived and started working one week before the end of September.
He cleared his throat loudly as he entered the gallery, paused before
the front-door curtain, and announced his arrival with an officious
"Good morning", in the voice he used as supervisor of a section in
the Department of Road Works and Bridge Repair. He then shifted
the curtain to one side and stepped forward to carry out his
inspection.

Monica was sweeping the floor around the dining-table. Roy
almost tripped on the doormat. This was no fat old battle-axe. This
was a shapely young craft, blacker than he would normally look at,
but face and body? Woi! This might, after all, be well worth his ten
dollars a month. Gwynneth had rushed out of her room at his
"Good morning". She was at the door of the dining-room just in
time to witness the look of pure lechery that crossed Roy's face, and
to hear Monica's polite but deadpan "Good morning, Sir" that did
not interrupt for one moment the flow of her sweeping.

Gaston was going to "drop by" at two o'clock.

"What he mean 'drop by'? You didn invite him to lunch?" Viola
asked, disappointed, for she had hoped he would take lunch with
them and then stay on. She was ready to use up their last dust of

ration-card flour to bake a cake for him so he could have tea at four o'clock, as he must have got accustomed to Up There. Gwynneth poured cold water on all these plans, assuring Viola that by four o'clock he would be long gone. As two o'clock approached, Viola asked her what she was going to wear. Undaunted by Gwynneth's response, which was not amicable, Viola offered to style her hair for her, rub a little rouge on her cheeks, and put some lipstick on her mouth. In response, Gwynneth limited herself to a deadly scowl. No point exploding at her dotish sister – she meant well.

Gwynneth had to figure out, though, how to ward off Viola and her matchmaking mission during Gaston's visit. She decided that they would not sit in the gallery or the drawing-room. She would first take him to see her schoolroom, for, in spite of everything, he was the one who had set her on the road of private teaching. It was rainy season, but the day had started off with petit-carême weather, and if this bright sun and strong breeze held out, they would go and sit on the backyard bench, out of the range of Viola's hearing. Viola, though, was sure to take the occasional peep at them through the back door while they were out there. If the weather changed to rain, so-help-her-God they would sit in the shed and have their talk, where Viola could neither see nor hear them.

The tour of the schoolroom was quick, although he seemed to be looking for ways to prolong it. He browsed at the children's storybook table, and with a broad smile on his face peered at each of their drawings plastered all around the three half-walls. He bent down in the infants' corner to chuckle over Gwynneth's home-made alphabet chart – from **Aa** for *agouti, ajoupa* and *alpagat*, to **Zz** for *zaboka, zanndoli* and *zicaque*.

"No more 'A for apple', eh?" he commented. "Nice!"

Then he looked up at the display on the high wall. Above the blackboard were three pictures, laid out in triangular formation. He recognised and nodded at Mahatma Gandhi and Marcus Garvey, but was puzzled at the head-tied woman placed above them, at the apex of the triangle. Gwynneth, standing at the door so as not to encourage the dawdling, informed him that it was her grandmother, Sarah, and then stepped out into the yard in order to hustle him along.

As soon as they sat down on the bench, the animals gravitated towards the spot and settled at her feet. Gaston eyed them with amusement. He asked Gwynneth, "Your aide-de-camp and body-guard detail, eh?" He bent towards them: "Fellas, I am quite harmless. Trust me. I not going to assassinate her, or kidnap her, or any such thing."

The dogs wagged their tails furiously, sucking up to him in the most undignified way. One of them went so far as to roll over for Gaston to scratch its belly. The other one peed for joy, barely missing his shoe. Miss V opened one eye a crack, shut it and resumed her nap.

Gwynneth had managed to hustle him past Viola by promising that they would soon come back inside for a drink. *Mistake,* she now thought. *That drink going to stretch out forever. He just too comfortable, ingratiating himself with the animals and lolling against the back rest of the bench, crossing his legs.*

"All right," she challenged. "What it is you want to clear up? Lemme hear, because I have something to clear up, too."

Immediately he straightened up, as if snapping to attention, and put on a sober face. "You do? Would you like to go first?"

"Yes. I just want you to know that hauling you over here the other day was Ollie's idea, not mine."

He seemed to slump. "I couldn dream it was you, Gwynneth," he said. "I know you spit me out forever." He looked so forlorn that she wished she had left well enough alone. "Ollie summon me to the Turagua police station. I didn know he was going to bring me by you afterwards. Of course, I didn protest!"

"All right. What it is you wanted to talk about?"

He cleared his throat and shifted on the seat. "Well…" He shifted again. "Regarding Saturday evening, at the table… Well, what you saw was misleading."

"And what did I see?"

He ignored her question. "All you didn do was steups out loud. But the steups was on your face. Pure irritation. Even contempt."

"Oh! You mean Ollie dishing out your food for you!" She chuckled. "Well, boy, what to tell you? My face doan know how to lie."

"But that wasn me!" There was some desperation in his voice.

"Nah. Was your ghost."

"I mean that's not how I am, now. Not the pampered, helpless Gaston."

"Hmph," she murmured.

"But that evening was just too much for me... Threw me right back to your place on Catherine Street, sitting around the table with all of you, so many years ago. Then to be jolted back into the present with you glaring at me, giving me that disapproving schoolteacher look, waiting to see what this hopeless case would do..."

"'Glaring'?" she protested. "Mister, I did not glare at you!"

"Well, whatever it was, I got so flustered that I seized up. It was both things, the teacher frowning at the bad boy, and the bad boy finding himself so unexpectedly reliving a scene from the happiest three years of his life. Anyway, I'm proud to announce that the bad boy has turned over a new leaf. He is now a fully domesticated boy."

"Hmph. And what would have brought about this miracle?"

"Well, I would love to tell you about my baptism of fire, but you say you have a meeting to go to this afternoon. Or was that just to get rid of me?"

Of course she had a meeting. There was choir practice. She had no intention of going to choir practice, but he didn't have to know everything. She had already sent her apologies to Mrs Knight, having agreed to stand in for Mr Jeremy at Sunday morning service. Go and play the organ Saturday afternoon for choir practice and then go back again Sunday morning to play for the service, like some *poto légliz*? Why she didn just move her bed into the church? Mrs Knight would have to play the organ herself – she was quite capable – and put an adult choir member to manage the frisky youngpeople. You cyaan fraid chirren.

Gaston's story turned out to be so entertaining that she forgot she was trying to get rid of him.

When he set out for England in 1923, he struck up a friendship with two other young men who boarded the ship at Barbados. One was a Bajan, and the other a Grenadian who had sailed to Bridgetown on a fishing-boat to meet the ship. Together they endured a week and a half of seasickness, bad food, rough waters, and scornful looks from some of the whitepeople on board. They were all three headed for London, and by the time they had lugged their trunks and suitcases onto the train at Southampton, they had decided that they would face London together.

They stayed at a Salvation Army hostel while they went looking for a place to live. They found affordable digs in a basement. One of the rooms was already occupied by a Jamaican who had arrived in London a week or two before. The four of them shared kitchen, bathroom, laundry-sink in the draughty space between bathroom and kitchen, and a sitting-room that they called "the ice-box". There was no heating in there, so it was never warm enough for sitting, even in summer. They used that room for storing milk, butter, leftovers and other perishable food. Their sitting-room was the kitchen, where they sat around a paraffin heater.

On Christmas Day they would take the paraffin heater, table and chairs from the kitchen and place them in the official sitting-room so they could eat their festive lunch in there and, over drinks, reminisce about the celebrations back home. It was at Christmas time that the homesickness would bite them the hardest. The room was decorated with all the cheery cards bringing the season's greetings from family and friends at home.

Gaston paused here to complain that Gwynneth had never sent him a Christmas card, nor written to him, the whole time he was up there, not once, even though he had written to her as soon as they moved into their digs, so she would know his address. He had written several letters to her over the first few months, and sent her a card that first Christmas.

In the early days of their life in London, the four housemates cooked separately. Gaston's "cooking" was mainly bread-and-cheese. His mother had also prepared him for life without nursemaids by teaching him how to boil eggs and shell them, and how to make a cup of cocoa with Fry's cocoa powder – "Until you can find a nice girl up there to cook for you."

There was one hitch. Sweetened condensed milk, though it came from England, was nowhere to be found there. It took him a few tries and plenty brown liquid down the sink before he could figure out how to make a satisfactory cup of cocoa using plain old cows' milk, Fry's cocoa powder, and sugar. Once or twice he splurged: he bought fish-and-chips on the way home from his job on the Underground so that he could have something other than cocoa with either bread-and-cheese or bread-and-boiled egg for supper.

Gradually it dawned on them that they were spending a small fortune, given their shoestring budgets, each of them putting sixpence into the gas meter every time they cooked. The same sixpence worth of gas would provide breakfast or dinner whether you were cooking for one or four persons. They decided on communal cooking, each of them, in turn, cooking for everybody.

By then, mercifully, Gaston had discovered bangers – sausages that could simply be put into a pot of water and boiled, like the eggs. It had been a major breakthrough for him, especially as no "nice girl" had as yet come forward to cook for him. When it was his turn to make breakfast, he served bread and boiled eggs, and when he made dinner, it was bangers and bread. Before long they were calling him "Banger-Man", "Bang-Bang", and "Bangs". Baje's repertoire was tinned baked beans with mashed potatoes; tinned sardines with potatoes boiled whole; and tinned sardines or baked beans with potatoes cut up and fried.

The Jamaican, Eldredge, could make mackerel run-down, but complained bitterly at having to use the tasteless thing known as "kippers" in place of smoked mackerel – the proper salt-kind for run-down – and finding coconut was like going on a treasure-hunt. He could also make rice-and-peas, but first you had to put the dried red-beans to burst, and that would use up too much gas. He resigned himself to using tinned beans, for they were already cooked, but he insisted that rice-and-peas just did not taste the same with tinned beans. And though he knew how to make escovitch fish, that food he could mostly only dream about, for even if he could find pimento peppers somewhere in London, the cost of them would break his pocket.

Among them it was only Francis, the Grenadian, who knew how to make almost any dish from his homeland. His grand-mother had taught him to cook. They all longed for the food of home. All pretended that Irish potato was not only breadfruit, but yam, cassava, eddoes and tannia, too. They never found anything that could masquerade as dasheen. Gaston and his housemates

199

would have given anything for a taste of their mothers' and grandmothers' hand. It was some consolation that after they hit upon rostering the cooking, they were able to enjoy what seemed like marvellous variety in their diet, notwithstanding their strapped circumstances.

They were all working and saving to study, so they had to make do on meagre funds. Baje worked as a dishwasher in a restaurant. Francis sorted mail in the post office, and Eldredge was a hospital wardsman. Gaston was a guard on the Underground. He manned a turnstile at Golders Green Tube Station, clipping tickets.

As time went on, they added new dishes to their menu, mainly by watching Francis cook. Gaston told Gwynneth about the first time he ventured beyond bangers and experimented with cooking corned beef, putting seasoning and-all. He chose an occasion when his turn to cook dinner fell on a Saturday evening. Eldredge and Francis were out, and Baje was still sleeping off the party he had gone to the night before at a house of West Indians in Brixton.

Gaston fully intended to dump the corned beef if it did not turn out well, and revert to the simplicity of bangers, so when he thought it was ready, he tasted it. His corned beef seemed quite edible! He covered the pot and sat reading the newspaper. It was not long before the others started to wander into the kitchen, Baje first, then Francis. As they settled around the paraffin heater, Gaston lit the stove to warm up the corned beef. Just then Eldredge walked in, heading straight for the stove. He lifted the pot-cover, peeped in and exclaimed, "A-a! Carn-beef!" and they burst into cheering, clapping and drumming on the table. Then a lavway developed, accompanied by the drumming. Eldredge was the chantwelle. He chanted a call and the others piped up with the refrain:

No more
Bang-Bang
Bye-Bye
Bang-Bang
We no want no
Bang-Bang...

And so on, to the beat of riotous drumming on the kitchen

table. Gwynneth's laugh rang out. "So now you have your chef's badge, right?"

"Oh, now I'm almost as good as my Grenadian friend. He tutored all of us. He got tired of bread and potatoes. So, meet the new Gaston. Not only can I cook. I can wash the dishes, pick up after myself, wash clothes, clean a whole house... And! Me can taak Joomaican, too! Me can cuss bad-word..."

Drawn, no doubt, by the sound of Gwynneth's laughter, Viola could now be seen making her way across the yard, bearing a waiter of drinks, and beaming.

Viola practically invited Gaston to go with Gwynneth on her visit to Phillip's band the next day, Sunday. After serving the drinks, she had hovered with the empty waiter in her hand, visibly gloating over what she thought she was seeing. Gwynneth, though irritated at the triumphant look on her sister's face, was feeling some obligation to get a chair from the schoolroom so that she could join them, but decided against it. Time to break up the tête-à-tête. But Viola had other plans. During their conversation Gaston asked after the boys who had been detained by the police, and Viola wasted no time.

"Oh, Gwynneth is going to visit them tomorrow afternoon," she piped up. "Why you doan come to Sunday lunch with us and then maybe you can drive her over there?"

The scowl on Gwynneth's face told Viola that she was going to hear about this piece of mischief afterwards, but Viola was not perturbed. She got up, collected her glasses and coasters onto her waiter, and sailed off with a merry "I gone."

Gaston tried to wipe the amusement off his face. "So am I allowed to take up Viola's invitation to Sunday lunch?"

Gwynneth was still scowling. "I can't prevent you. That is between you and Viola. And yes, you should visit the band. I'm sure those boys will be glad to see you."

The chill in her voice indicated to him that the day's welcome had come to an end.

18
Something other-worldly had got into them.

As they settled into the car, Gwynneth began to give Gaston directions to Phillip's home. But he reminded her that he knew the way, having been part of the convoy that had delivered the boys to their homes two weeks before. He drove now with a look on his face which might have meant only that he was pleased with himself for remembering the way, but Gwynneth read this look as smugness.

Phillip's Uncle Chester came down to the gap to welcome them. Chester shook Gaston's hand for what seemed like a full minute, thanking Gwynneth for bringing him. Before they got to the top of the path, Phillip's grandmother, mother and aunt had come out into the yard. They exclaimed with joy when they recognised "Mr Gaston". At the commotion, three children squatting on the ground at the side of Uncle Melville's house, playing with some objects, turned to look at the visitors, but soon returned their attention to their game.

The guests were first taken up the hill to hear Phillip's band. It seemed to Gwynneth that it was a good five minutes' hike up the track, which took them through thinned-out forest, before they spied the clearing up ahead. The boys, sitting on some tree-trunks arranged in a semicircle, caught sight of them, and shot up off their seats to rush towards the visitors. The track opened out into flattish ground enclosed by more forest. On the right was the palay, with tapia half-walls and a carat roof. Over to the left another path began, then promptly disappeared into the forest.

The boys also treated Gaston as a most pleasant surprise sprung upon them by Teacher Gwynneth. They had a chair for her, and there was some jostling over who would get to lead her to it, but Phillip took her hand, and the others stepped back to follow in a cluster as he ceremoniously escorted her across the yard. Two of them ran into the palay, brought out a rough-hewn stool, and, apologising for its dingy look, offered it to Gaston. A little argument ensued, with some boys protesting that they couldn't put Mr Gaston to sit down on that old stool, for it would dirty up his good pants. Phillip started down the track at breakneck speed to get another chair from the house, but Gaston called him back; he had already settled himself comfortably on a tree-trunk.

Chester stayed on his feet in order to share some history. This place had been the home and Shango-yard of his grandfather, Nathan Benoit – Baba Nate. Right under their feet was the spot on which Baba Nate's house once stood, and his tomb was just behind the palay. Baba Nate had lived on this compound with his wife and children, one of whom was Chester's father.

Baba Nate's third son, Knox, was the one designated by spiritual injunction to carry on the shrine after Baba Nate died, but that son turned out kind of wotless. A gambling spirit took possession of him, and he couldn't help himself. When somebody alerted the family that he was about to gamble away his father's land, the other children ganged up and put him out. As expected, he came to a bad end, which was the fate of many who failed to fulfil their spiritual calling. He went down the Main and lived there for years, until the news reached them that he was dead – stabbed by another gambler. Chester's father carried on the shrine until his death.

Baba Nate's house had long gone to dust, while the palay was still standing. From time to time they had to change out carat leaves on the roof, and leepay the walls and floor when their surfaces started cracking and shelling in parts, but the posts had thus far remained quite solid. Chester pointed to the path entering the bush on the other side of the clearing, and explained that it was a trace connecting Baba Nate's compound to San Miguel Road. His grandfather had made it zig-zag – to slow down unwelcome visitors.

The boys sat and listened politely, though the history was well known to them, but Gwynneth could see that they were bursting with restlessness. They couldn't wait to perform for their guests. As it turned out, the boys had their own surprise in store for them. Chester reminded them that they were to play no more than three numbers, because Teacher Gwynneth and Mr Gaston wanted to also spend some time with Tantie Ruth and the family. "And you know this is not the last time you going to see Teacher Gwynnie," he added.

Gwynneth learned that the band did not have a name. She asked the band members to introduce themselves.

Phillip and the lingay boy named Selwyn (but better known as "Stretch") were the eldest, both eighteen years old. Selwyn worked in a dry goods store in St Paul. He was previously a member of the ill-fated St Paul Syncopators and still had a hard, blue-black lump on his arm from the day the police beat them out of their meeting-place behind the pavilion. Selwyn announced vehemently that he was never going to stop beating iron. He was very disappointed at the St Paul band members for giving up so easily, and had been urging them to find a new meeting-place where they could start up the band again.

Learie was Phillip's neighbour, from lower down San Miguel Road. He was sixteen years old, and so was Irwin, the scratcher-man in Phillip's band. The youngest member of the band was Irwin's little brother, Lloydie, whom they called "Cutter-man". He was seven years old. Mercifully, he was not with them on the day of the police raid, or their mother, Miss Claudia, would have murdered Irwin (as she told Gwynneth when she visited the families after the raid).

The boys from the orphanage, Leroy and Trevor, were four-teen and fifteen years old. They used to hang around the orphan-age brass band's rehearsals and badly wanted to join, but couldn't.

"Why not?" Gwynneth asked.

The two boys smiled wryly and bent their heads. Phillip provided the answer: "For bad behaviour, Miss. But them doesn bring none of that here," and he turned his radiant smile on them.

Lennox, Randolph (alias "Phantom"), and Hollis were all thirteen years old, and of the three, only Lennox was in school.

Gwynneth asked whether they all had their parents' and guardians' permission to be there, and when they answered with a resounding "Yes, Miss!" the loudest voices were those of Leroy and Trevor.

Irwin added, "Because of you, Miss. My mother say, 'Allyou cyaan go wrong with Teacher Gwynneth'."

All preliminaries completed, the boys rushed into the palay

and emerged carrying objects that could suggest they had just raided the La Basse dump. Almost everything in their hands, Gwynneth reflected, was discarded material that might have been left lying at the side of the road to be picked up by the County Council rubbish cart. Most of the boys seated themselves on the semicircle of felled trees, with Gaston right in the middle of them, while Randolph and Lloydie stood with lengths of bamboo at the ready.

Randolph held a thick piece that was as tall as himself, clearly the boom. Lloydie held a much shorter and thinner piece, and had a stick in his hand to beat on it. Gwynneth recognised Lloydie's instrument to be the cutter. Lennox hugged an unidentifiable motorcar part. Phillip's instrument was an upside-down paint pan that he carried by means of marlin twine tied to it and strung around his neck.

They first played "Going Down Jordan". That meant singing the lavway while backing it up with an accompaniment of rhythm. Or rhythms, for Gwynneth noted that just like the two other bands she had heard at close quarters, the players were not all beating out the same rhythm pattern. Yet all their rhythms were synchronised into a rich, intricate sound, anchored by the strong boom beat. She reckoned that the boy holding up the brake hub from a motorcar wheel, and beating it steadily with a metal rod, was helping to keep the whole band in line with that underlying beat. "Just knocking old iron, making noise"? Nothing could be further from the truth.

What spirit had entered these boys – scattered all over Cayeri, it would seem, and quite untaught, as far as she could gather – what spirit had entered them and gifted them with this skill? Watching the ecstasy on their faces, and the way they seemed to be borne aloft by the sound they were making, one could be convinced that something other-worldly had got into them. It was like seeing people in Queen Lottie's church catch power, or Queen's youngpeople, gathered in her palay, animated and lit up with an unfathomable joy by their own chanting of praise-songs to Shango, Ogun, Oshun, Yemanja and the other deities.

At the end of the piece, the audience of three clapped and cheered wildly. The boys looked up from their instruments with a quizzical air. It was as though they had forgotten about their guests until the applause brought them back to earth. The players had become their own audience, completely possessed by their music. Phillip had to nudge the two boys on either side of him as he got up from his seat, and these two, in rising, nudged their neighbours. It was then that the others scrambled to their feet, and all bowed together.

As they sat down again, they began to exchange conspiratorial looks, and there was some whispering. Then they fell silent and all eyes turned to Phillip. The boy with the brake hub (Gwynneth noted that she would have to try harder at memorising all their names) knocked on it four times to launch them into their second number. Gwynneth didn't recognise the song they were singing, and the boys didn't seem to know the words, for what they sang as they beat on their instruments was "Bam-bee-day la-la-la / Bam-bay-O…" with the same gusto they had put into the first number. They sang two rounds of this piece. Then they stopped singing, and everyone stopped beating on their instrument, except Phillip.

It was some seconds before it dawned on Gwynneth that what Phillip was beating, solo, on the bottom of his paint tin, was the melody that the band had just been singing. The sound of Phillip's instrument had been drowned by the singing and drumming, but now it rang out – the paint tin was yielding different notes! Obviously this secret had been kept even from his Uncle Chester, for he looked as amazed as Gwynneth. Gaston got up and went to sit next to Phillip. For the rest of the performance he peered intently at the instrument and followed the movements of Phillip's hand. The number was closed off as it had started, with another round of wordless singing of the tune, accompanied by the full band.

Gaston rose to his feet, clapping, and so did Gwynneth and Chester. "Well, give yourselves a big round of applause!" Gwynneth said. The boys clapped and cheered.

Phillip related how it had come about. Two weeks earlier, on the day after the police raid, when Teacher Gwynneth came to his home and set a date to come and hear the band, Phillip got so

206

excited that as soon as she left, he ran up to the palay to start preparing. He knew that later on he would have to get the band members together for a good clean-up of the palay and the yard. However, the first thing would be to replace the instruments lost in the police raid the day before, and check on the condition of those they had.

He had already walked up San Miguel Road, early that Sunday morning, to search for the ones that some of the band members had thrown down in panic. The four boys who got away had dropped their instruments as they fled into the bush. Lennox, on seeing this, had dropped his, too, though he didn't yet fully understand what was happening.

Along the grass verge Phillip had come upon the gin bottle, and, to his great relief, Lennox's instrument, the gas tank, which was something of a trophy. Mr Carl had let Phillip take it home after they stripped a decrepit old Ford for whatever parts were still usable. The tank had some rust holes in it, so it was of no further use as a motorcar part, but, played with a metal rod, it had brought a glorious new sound into the band. The hoe-blade and the brake hub were lying in the drain, and, a few steps into the bush, there was Gang-Gang's pot, sitting upright as though somebody was about to make a cook under the trees. The gin bottle was cracked, but all the other instruments were in fine condition.

Most of the boys taken to the police station had their instruments in their hands, and these had been confiscated: Phillip's "new" paint pan that Uncle Melville had recently obtained for him because the old one had begun to look battered; the grater that Irwin used for scratcher; Hollis's pitch-oil pan; and the tamboo bamboo cutter that Randolph was playing that day because Lloydie was not with them. Those instruments they would have to bid goodbye, but Phillip had found all the abandoned ones.

They had not gone on the road with the boom, so that piece of bamboo was safely in its place inside the palay. For the time being they would have to borrow a cutter from Uncle Chester, and see how they could get their hands on another pitch-oil pan, gin bottle and scratcher. Phillip decided that the next time Uncle Chester and the other men were going up by the river to cut bamboo, he would go with them, to get a new cutter.

On that same Sunday afternoon, the day of Teacher Gwynneth's first visit, Phillip decided to start the preparation by taking out his old paint pan, which was not broken, just bumpy and dented. He had been beating on the base of this pan since he was in St Paul Syncopators, and the surface was now looking as though the pan had been through the war. He decided to try and fix it, for suppose he couldn't find another empty paint tin, in good enough condition, before Teacher Gwynneth's visit? He searched the ground until he found a fairly smooth stone, and tried to make the surface of his pan even again by pounding out the bumps. It was in doing so that he noticed something – every bump and dent that he hit seemed to give out a different sound.

He discovered, too, that as he pounded away at one of the bumps, hoping to flatten it, the sound of that spot was slowly changing. He stopped pounding, to give some thought to what had just happened. This same old paint tin, which at the beginning would make the same sound wherever on its base the stick landed, was now giving out different sounds! Maybe he just hadn't noticed it before, but the months of being pounded with a guava stick was, all along, not only making the metal uneven; it was also giving it different voices. Pounding the pan with the stone had now brought out those voices more loudly. And, just as important, more pounding could possibly change the sound of one spot into any sound he wanted.

He had heard rumours that one or two iron bands in town had found some way to make a few notes on their pans, but how, he didn't know. Now he did! Now he, too, had found a way to make musical notes on a pan! Good thing he hadn't thrown away his old paint pan! He was overjoyed. "Teacher Gwynneth, I just bawl out 'Woi!' and next thing I hear 'Voosh!' A whole flock of birds fly outa the black-sage over there and head up the hill!"

He went out into the yard and picked up another stone – a piece of slate – and used this to scratch a mark around each of the spots that gave out a distinguishable note. There were four such spots. He played on them for a while, just sounding them out. Two of them sounded almost the same, so he concentrated on the others, thinking he could make up a tune with these three notes. That, he realised, would take some time; after many attempts, he still had not come up with any tune that really pleased him. It was getting dark, so he decided to try again after work next day, and to keep the discovery a secret for the time being, in order to give Teacher Gwynneth and Uncle Chester a big surprise.

By Thursday evening he had settled on a tune, and when the band met as usual on Saturday afternoon, they were sworn to secrecy before they started work on learning to sing the tune, and beating out a rhythm to accompany it. They practised that Saturday and every afternoon during the week.

Gwynneth now asked Phillip to play the tune again, and she listened intently.

"Good work!" she said. "But we have a lot more work to do. The notes need cleaning up. For one thing, you should be getting the same sound anywhere you hit inside the area of that note. Now and then a different sound comes out. If you got the notes by pounding with a stone, then you might need to start using a hammer, instead. A stone is an uneven thing. It not going to make a level surface that will give you the same sound all over. Take a hammer and pound the whole area of each note until it start giving out one sound, only."

She paused to make sure they understood.

"Yes, Miss!" the boys answered in chorus.

"The other reason why you might have unwanted sounds in your note is spillover from what is around it on the pan. Like when white clothes get washed with coloured clothes, and the white clothes end up not so white again?"

The boys nodded their heads, with knowing murmurs.

"You may have to dent the metal around each note, to protect it, making something like a little canal that other sounds can't cross so easily. Just a dent – you don't want to cut the metal, so you have to use something dull. I can't tell you what, but I am sure you will come up with something. What you think of that?"

"Yes, Miss," Phillip said. "That making sense. Another thing, Miss. Same way how plenty beating on the pan is what make it get different notes, same way these notes going to change after a while, because I going to be beating on them some more, to play tunes. I have to find a way to keep the sound from changing."

Gaston spoke. "I was thinking the same thing. What about if you cover the tip of the stick with something soft, to make a kind of shock absorber, so the notes don't get damaged? You know what I mean?"

"Yes, Sir!" Phillip's face lit up. "Like how they does put rubber washers to protect engine parts. I working in a mechanic shop."

Gaston was taking his handkerchief out of his pocket. "Let's try this," he said. "Lend me the stick."

He tore off a strip of the handkerchief, wrapped it tightly around the end of the stick, and tied it. The boys were following the operation with keen interest. Phillip took the stick and played the notes with it. There was general agreement that on top of protecting the pan, the soft wrapping gave the notes a better sound.

The boys didn't get to play their third number, because it was time for the guests to go down to the house. Still, they had had a full afternoon; the visit had given them a great boost. In high spirits, and with a new sense of their own importance, they put away their instruments and tidied the place. Phillip took the chair and went down to help his mother with final preparations for the guests, while the other boys went out through the trace. Chester and the guests made their way down the track, with Gaston finding it necessary to hold Gwynneth by the elbow, because, he said, it was easier to fall on the way down a hill.

They sat in the drawing-room with Chester and Miss Ruth, talking over the afternoon's events, while Phillip and his mother, Lorna, served refreshments. Gaston asked Chester whether he thought tamboo bamboo would die.

"Most likely," Chester said. "The bamboo good, but my father say was only because they did ban the skin drum from the road that people make tamboo bamboo. That is when he father, Baba Nate, was a young man. Skin drum was still beating in Shango-feast, but for outside, for the road, people had was to find a new thing to make rhythm. I is a bamboo man. I is a bamboo man till I dead. But now the youngpeople making a new drum; and that is tomorrow drum – tamboo demmeh.

"Bamboo on the way out. It cyaan last. And what the young fellas and them making now, nobody cyaan stop them. The government could do what they want – ban it, throw them boys in jail, harass them. They cyaan stop them. They cyaan mash up this drum. This is tomorrow music. And doan hurt you head – them cyaan kill the skin drum, neither. We bring that quite from Africa, and the ancestors protecting it." He sang: "All the way from Africa-land…"

"But aint some of the iron bands still have bamboo in them, like Phillip band?" Gaston remarked. "Why you think tamboo bamboo cyaan last, not only in the iron bands, but as full tamboo bamboo bands? Why you think it will die out?"

"Well, tamboo bamboo still good for stickfighting, wake and function that people does keep in they house and yard. There the band standing up on one spot. But for the Canaval, bamboo is a obzocky thing to walk the road with. Bamboo band does move slow on the road – too slow for the youngpeople. Them ain have no patience. And then, too, bamboo is a thing does split after a time. It does mash up from the pounding on the road, so you have to wait for dark-night again, and go in the bush again to cut new bamboo. The youngpeople not going bother with all that, when they could do better."

Gaston probed further: "And let me ask you this, if I may. You could tell me to go to hell if you find I faas and out of place. What I want to know is why none of allyou ain carry on the shrine after you father."

Chester gave a wry chuckle. "When my father come and die, most of he children did done scatter to the four winds already. Phillip have a aunt in Canada, another one in the States, and a uncle in England. Knox dead in Venezuela. Was only me and my brother Melville leff back. And the two of we still here. The two of we is still Shango people. We love we Shango. We beating drum in Shango-feast since we small – sometime the drum bigger than we. Phillip, too. Phillip beating Shango drum from he was three years old.

"We still beating Shango drum, in other people shrine, as it have Shango all about. But to say either one of we could put on we grandfather and we father clothes – that is serious business. We talk it, Melville and me, and we agree that neither one of we ain have the belly for that. And the spirit and them ain like impostor. You have to know you place and know you work. The work we get is to make sure the palay ain fall down."

On the drive back, Gaston ventured: "Look, doan take this the wrong way, eh. Is not a plot to get back with you, as wonderful as that would be. But if you need any help with the band, just let Ollie get in touch with me."

"Thank you. That's very kind of you," Gwynneth said, and promptly fell back into her tired half-sleep. She heard him talking still, and struggled to listen.

"If I may, I would also like to talk some more with you, when you have the time. Again, no ulterior motive. I've shared with you something of my not exactly scintillating life in London, and it would be nice to catch up on how you've been doing. Seventeen years with no news from a friend is a long time."

No answer.

He pursued: "I take it you not going to throw me away entirely, and that you'll allow me to be some kind of friend to you?"

Met with continuing silence, he turned to swiftly glance at her. She was more awake, now, but he could see she was not inclined to engage in conversation.

"So, I could be you friend, Miss?"

No answer.

"Comrade?"

No answer.

"Caddie-boy?"

The brief giggle she let out was music to his ears.

19

Mrs Knight did not hesitate to write down "Iron band".

Next morning, Monday, Gwynneth woke up with a start, one word pulsing in her head: "*Harvest!*" What exactly was in the dream she couldn't remember, but the thought it had left in her head was that Mothers' Union Harvest Fair was still three weeks away – time enough!

She had followed Mumma's advice to let they make they Harvest for theyself, volunteering only to help with decorating beforehand, and to be on the cleaning gang afterwards. The church hall had to be prettied-up before the event, for, as much as they wished every year that the fair could be an entirely outdoor event, in the church calendar Harvest time fell in the Cayerian rainy season. Some years, the petit-carême dry spell held out all the way to Harvest, but one could not bank on this happening.

The stalls were usually set up inside, along the two sides of the hall, leaving the remaining floor space free for the tea tables, the rows of chairs in front of the stage, and the standing audience at the back of the hall. In uncertain weather, it would be foolhardy to put the stalls outdoors, for if there was a sudden shower of rain, it would be impossible to make a quick retreat indoors, given all the baggage of Harvest Fair stalls.

There were the games stalls – bran-tub, punch-board, pick-a-pan, hoopla and others; market stalls selling produce harvested by church members from their gardens – baskets and boxes and crocus bags full; the bottle stall for home-made preserves and drinks; the sweet-tooth stall, featuring confections out of Creole and Indian kitchens; and, in previous years, the cake stall. Mothers' Union was in some doubt as to whether they would have a cake stall that year. In the year before, 1939, Harvest Fair was just weeks after the war began, so the shortages had not yet hit home. But after a full year of wartime, people could no longer get enough flour to make their bread, roast-bake, fry-bake and dumpling in the quantities their own families were accustomed to – unless they could afford the black-market prices – so it was unlikely they could spare flour for cake to donate to the Fair.

Some years, the day of Harvest Fair had been so wet that the whole event was confined to the church hall, with some spillover into the church. On other occasions, however, depending on the weather forecast given out on the radio for the day, the tea tables could be set up on the lawn between church and hall, if the ground was dry enough. Even so, no matter what the weatherman promised, they had to keep an eye out for rain. At the very first sprinkle, a crew of young people would converge and in a jiffy move furniture and crockery indoors, where they would set up the tea operation in the middle of the hall.

Gwynneth had not taken much part in the planning and preparation thus far, so Valda Pierre and company were sure to grumble anew when they heard the suggestion she was about to bring, at this eleventh hour, that Phillip's band be part of the entertainment. However, she would just have to remind them that the majority had voted, at the July meeting, for an iron band to play at the fair.

She knew that Mothers' Union had entertainment lined up – performances by St Hilda's church choir, school choir and orphanage band; solo singers (one or two of them self-appointed, like Audrey Ferguson, who fancied herself a singer, against all evidence); Mr Jeremy's son who wrung soul-stirring airs out of the violin; and schoolchildren doing choral recitations – "O Mary, go and call the cattle home…" or "Not a drum was heard, not a funeral note/As his corpse to the rampart we hurried…" For many, the crowning entertainment was the impromptu "fashion parade". Anybody brazen enough could volunteer to go up and strut their Harvest outfit across the stage to the sound of the orphanage band, along with the cheers and hooting that came from the audience.

Mothers' Union didn't belong to Valda Pierre and her cronies. Mrs Knight was now the head of the Harvest Fair committee, and Gwynneth decided that she would go straight to her that very day. She would also get Lennox to take a message to Phillip, asking him to come and see her the following day, Tuesday, after work. Gwynneth got up now, to catch Lennox before he could leave for school. She went into Mumma's bedroom and called out to him through the side window.

Mrs Knight did not hesitate to write down "Iron band" on her entertainment list, and the next day Gwynneth put to Phillip the idea of the band playing at Harvest Fair. Phillip was ready to spring up off the chair and immediately take the news to the others. But Gwynneth wasn't finished. If the band members agreed to play at the fair, she wanted them to meet in her schoolroom at 3.00 o'clock on Saturday afternoon, to plan for the performance.

"And, very important," she said, "you-all have to agree on a name for your band – before the fair."

"Yes, Miss," Phillip answered, and then looked a little anxious. "Miss, we could bring Kelvin? He is the leader of St Paul Syncopators. He hear how you and Mr Gaston encouraging we band, and he want to start back them own. He say you talk to Syncopators in a christening in February."

Though she wondered whether she would be biting off more than she could chew (as usual), she didn't see how she could refuse. In for a penny, in for a pound. After all, the St Paul band was the one originally invited to play at the harvest fair. And maybe they could, still! Join up the two bands, perhaps... Nor did she see a way to escape inviting Gaston to the meeting. He had offered to help with the band, and she could certainly use that help. But she was hesitant...

~

There was no doubt that Gaston had a genuine interest in the fate of Cayerian culture. It had been as important to Forward as it was to Moun Demmeh, except that Gaston and his comrades had a curious blind spot when it came to language. Once, when Gaston had succeeded in roping her in to a Forward meeting, Gwynneth engaged them head on over the language issue, ignoring Gaston's disapproving glare, though she knew she would never hear the end of his vexation afterwards.

Forward acknowledged Patois as culture, largely because there existed a scholarly work that codified its grammar, showing that it was by no means "broken French", but a language in its own right. (Gwynneth owned a treasured copy of the book. Mercifully, it had escaped the clutches of the police raiders, since it was in a box stashed under her bed. She had tried to get Johnstone to read it, but he dismissed it when he found out from the back cover that the author was neither European nor American, but just a local man, and black, and that the book had been published locally, to boot. He handed it back to Gwynneth without opening it.)

Though they recognised Patois as a language, the Forward revolutionaries would have been at one with Johnstone when it came to the other everyday language of Cayerians. They took a dim view of it. That was nothing but broken English, they said, brought to Cayeri by small-island immigrants who had not had any schooling, or, at best, poor schooling. One day in the future, education would be made widely available in Cayeri, and that would solve the problem – broken English would disappear.

Gwynneth pointed out that what they were calling "broken English" was as much a language as Patois, for it was also Creole. "Patois is French Creole, and our other Cayerian language is English Creole. Time will tell," she ventured, "whether English Creole will really be wiped out by education. Some educated Cayerians, including myself, speak both the King's English *and* English Creole, and we have no intention of parting with our Creole, our mother tongue."

Afterwards, Gaston accused her of hogging the argument. He said that her eyes were flashing fire and she was browbeating his comrades, not giving them a chance to make their point. He thought that she was showing off. She did not think that she had hogged the discussion, but she had certainly started it. And, as it turned out, she had also shut it down, by asking and answering the question, "What is the language of calypso?"

By then she was losing patience with them, and so, yes, at this point she might not have left any room for them to get in an answer. "You defend and value calypso, aint?" she reminded them. "Well, the great majority of our calypsos are in Creole – some in French Creole and some in English Creole. The same is true of our proverbs. So you disapprove of those calypsos and proverbs that are in English Creole? I doubt it. Let's just recognise and take pride in our multilingual culture. Cayerians speak Patois, and English Creole, and some also speak the King's

English, not to mention those who speak Bhojpuri, Spanish, French, Cantonese, Portuguese, Arabic…"

They didn't seem to have any answer to this lecture, as they changed the subject. But for the rest of that meeting, whatever the topic, Gwynneth spoke in her everyday voice, which employed English Creole, Patois and the King's English. By the end of the meeting, Gaston was ready to burst with indignation…

~

Now, however, she could see that for Gaston there was no dispute regarding the value of this new phenomenon on the cultural front, the iron band. He was embracing it without reserve, and Gwynneth knew that he would be only too happy to play a part in nurturing it. It might be unfair to think he was offering help for no other reason than to curry favour with her. Just to make it clear, though, that the invitation was strictly about the band, she would not only send a message to Gaston via Ollie; she would also invite Ollie to the meeting, as patron of the band.

The whole of Phillip's band was in attendance at the Saturday meeting, all ten of them, and so was Kelvin, with three of his members. Gwynneth remembered Kelvin, from Garnet's christening, as an earnest young man with eyes framed by a tense frown. The schoolroom was charged with excitement. Ollie could only stay in the meeting for part of the time, as he had another appointment, but Gaston was most present throughout. Phillip announced the name of their band as "San Miguel Warahoons".

Gwynneth's eyebrows went up. "Good name," she said. "But tell me, boys, you didn't choose that name because you find it sounds badjohn-ish, like the names some of the bands in town are giving themselves – 'Raiders', 'Commandos', 'Rebel Breed' and such?"

The boys exchanged guilty looks.

"Aha!" Gwynneth continued. "Well, you need to know that Warahoons are not badjohns! But I hope you'll keep the name, for then you'll be naming yourselves after a peaceful, gentle people."

She waited for them to respond, but they just looked puzzled. "What you want to do," she asked them, "keep the name, or look for a real badjohn name?"

The boys turned to Phillip, who said, "Keep the name, Miss."

"Let's make sure your members are comfortable with that. Put up your hand if you want to stick with 'Warahoons'."

They all agreed on "San Miguel Warahoons".

The meeting discussed the situation of the St Paul band, and the possibility of their also playing at the fair. Kelvin had so far spoken to six members of his band, and all were eager to start up again; but the band had no home. The police had warned them not to come back to the pavilion again, or any part of the savannah, or they would be arrested for loitering.

"Is that so," Gaston remarked, drily. He turned to Gwynneth and asked her, "The St Paul savannah is private land? It belongs to a sports club, or something?"

Gwynneth assured him that St Paul savannah was a public space, under the jurisdiction of the County Council.

Gaston asked the boys, "All of you know St Paul savannah? Tell me if it's a place where fellas go to kick ball, or to play a match of cricket, or where anybody can go in the morning and run around for exercise, anytime they want, as long as nobody had it booked for some big event? That is St Paul savannah?"

There was a resounding "Yes, Sir!" which slid immediately into a babel of indignant commentary by the boys on the topic of police chasing people off a savannah that belonged to everybody. They calmed down and listened when they realised that Gaston had started to speak again.

"Well," he was saying, "I might have to visit the County Council *and* the St Paul police."

"And until we sort out this problem," Gwynneth said, "Phillip, can you ask your family permission for the St Paul band members to practise up in your place, just for the fair? You would have to tell Kelvin and his members what they can and cannot do on that compound – let them know it is sacred ground." Phillip nodded.

Gaston had pointed out to Gwynneth, before the meeting, that since every one of these boys was under 21 years of age, it would be advisable to get their parents' or guardians' permission to perform at the fair. "Let's make this a serious, formal undertaking," he had said.

He now distributed copybook pages and pens, and asked the boys to copy off the blackboard the wording of a short note he had

218

put up. This was for their parents or guardians to sign. As expected, the copying was a formidable challenge for some, though the note was barely three lines:

> To whom it may concern: I hereby give my permission for my son / ward, named: .... to perform at St Hilda's Church Harvest Fair on October 19, 1940.

Most of the boys were done in a short time, but after ten minutes some were still either hunched over, labouring upon the paper, or staring hopelessly at the blackboard. Gwynneth knew that there would be some not up the task, so she and Gaston had a plan in place to spare those boys any embarrassment. Gaston sat at the teacher's table, and Gwynneth at the storybook table. All the boys were invited to come to one of the two tables to have their note inspected and get help where needed. One boy's page was blank – clean as a whistle. Kelvin's was incomprehensible – just a collection of squiggles and strokes. Three boys had copied part of the note, but had not yet finished; one of them had not got beyond the first two words.

Gwynneth and Gaston completed some boys' notes, or wrote whole notes for them, as necessary. They had thought they could give Kelvin a note for his other band members to copy from and take the copy to their parents. That, however, was clearly not a good idea. Before moving on with the meeting, Gwynneth enlisted the aid of Gaston, Phillip and Lennox in writing out ten copies of the note for Kelvin to distribute to his band members.

Already Gwynneth was trying to think how she could persuade those boys who were the worst off to let her help them improve their reading and writing, or, learn to read and write from scratch, as the case might be. One thing at a time, though. She would not broach that matter today. The boys' excitement had been dampened enough by this unexpected torture of reading and writing in the middle of a happy iron-band meeting.

They had to decide what band members would wear on the day. Gwynneth asked whether each of them had a long-sleeved white shirt. Some did. Lloydie had a short-sleeved white shirt for his school uniform. It was agreed that both bands would wear white shirts, and the boys would pin on a little ribbon to identify which of the two bands they belonged to. White shirts would be found for the three boys who had none. St Paul chose orange for their ribbon, and San Miguel, green. Gwynneth would see about the ribbons, with Viola's help.

They explored the idea of the two bands first playing one piece together in the concert, and then each band playing one piece separately. In the end, they decided that they would play only as a combined band.

When they realised that the event would be taking place inside the church hall, the boys were a little doubtful. They had assumed that they would be playing outdoors. They had never beaten iron closed into a building with concrete walls, and they were not sure that their music was suited to that kind of place. Phillip's band sometimes practised inside the palay, but that building was like a gallery, with walls that only went halfway to the roof, and those walls were made of tapia – mud and grass, not bricks and mortar. Kelvin reported that the only "inside" space Syncopators had ever played in was an excursion bus with wooden sides that were half walls, pretty much also like a gallery or a palay.

"But we could get rain on the day of the fair," Gwynneth pointed out.

"Miss, we could put up a lil joupa, like in Miss Bernice child christening, and take it down after," Kelvin offered. "We accustom to that."

Gwynneth liked the idea. A green ajoupa of freshly-cut bamboo and coconut branches in the churchyard would certainly add flair to the event. But she would have to bounce it off the harvest fair committee and the church management.

Meanwhile the bands would have to start rehearsing. It would be up to them to organise their rehearsals, and they should spend some time rehearsing every day for the next two weeks. Gwynneth made it clear that they would be performing for charity, as Mothers' Union had no money to pay them. "What you are getting is exposure," she said, "a chance to advertise your bands and build up a reputation, so that other people will hire you to play. Practise as much as you can. Kelvin, I want you to stay back after this meeting, just for about ten minutes, and talk with Mr

Gaston. Your friends can sit on the bench out there while they wait for you."

Gwynneth had chosen not to ask questions when she heard at Garnet's christening that two members of Kelvin's band were in trouble with the law, but now that she was taking on a measure of responsibility for these boys, she needed to know. She had asked Gaston to raise the matter with Kelvin after the meeting, and now she sat with them in the schoolroom. As it turned out, Kelvin himself was one of the two boys who had court cases pending.

The charges against Kelvin and the other boy, Ralph, had arisen from the same incident. They had got into an altercation with a group of boys who loafed on a street corner amusing themselves by taunting passers-by. As Kelvin and Ralph walked past them one evening, a voice rang out: "Look two *makoumè* man!" and the whole group laughed.

Kelvin responded with cursing, and they laughed again. Ralph picked up a handful of gravel and threw it in their faces, and there began a full-scale street battle, five against two. They fought for what seemed an eternity, as other boys appeared from nowhere to egg them on, shouting "Heave!" A man passing by on a bicycle pedalled as fast as he could to get to the police station, and the Black Maria appeared on the scene. Some boys tried to run off, but nobody escaped. They were all caught and taken to the police station, all charged with disorderly behaviour in a public place. One of the five reported to the police that Kelvin had used obscene language, and the other four bore witness. Kelvin therefore faced an additional charge.

Kelvin stopped talking and sat with a look on his face even more worried than the look he seemed to wear all the time. There was silence for a while.

"So, Kelvin," Gaston asked. "You and Ralph couldn just keep on walking, go your way, and ignore whatever those boys were saying to you?"

"Yes, Sir," Kelvin replied, in a small, sheepish voice.

"You get into plenty fights?"

"Not plenty, Sir."

"Police ever hold you before?"

"No!" Kelvin said, almost indignantly.

"And Ralph?"

"Neither, Sir.

"Well, Kelvin, you going have to learn self-control, eh? No more fights, you hear? Being a leader is a serious matter, man. You have to set example."

"Yes, Sir."

"Now, when is this court case, and your family getting a lawyer for you?"

"Next month, Sir. My family doan have no money for lawyer. Neither Ralph family, Sir."

"OK, so you looking to spend next-year Carnival in jail?"

A look of utter devastation passed over Kelvin's face.

"Doan worry," Gaston assured him. "I will go to court with you. But you will have to promise that this going to be the last time you see the inside of a courthouse, unless you plan to become a lawyer, or a judge. And you make sure and talk with Ralph about this hastiness. The incident didn have to end in fight. All you coulda just walk away. Learn to ignore provocation. Doan respond to idleness, man. You better than that."

"Yes, Sir."

"I have to get your parents' consent to represent you in court. They can come and see me in my office, or they can send a letter giving their consent. Let them know they don't have to pay me anything."

Gaston stood up. Kelvin shot up off the seat and shook Gaston's outstretched hand, saying, "Thanks, Sir. Thanks, Miss."

"Go and pull your band back together, Kelvin," Gaston said. "You are a pioneer. You know that? You have important work to do."

"Okay, Sir," Kelvin replied, smiling at last.

Gaston saw him to the door, and turned around, to find Gwynneth staring at him, speechless. He had a moment of anxiety, trying to think how he might have erred, but then she said, "Thanks, Sir!"

He grinned. "Let's hope this turns out okay."

"Well done, Gaston. You miss your calling, man. You have the gift – you should be working with youngpeople!"

"At your bidding, Miss!" Gaston responded.

They went over the afternoon's proceedings – the plan for the bands' performance at the fair; the court case; getting the use of the St Paul savannah for Kelvin's band. "But we should really help them find a better place than the savannah, you know," Gwynneth said. "I don't think…"

"So when we going to have that catch-up talk?" Gaston cut in. "Next Saturday? Lunch in town?"

"Well…" Gwynneth hedged. "I have choir practice that afternoon, you know. I missed choir practice entirely in September – both days. On the second Saturday of September I had to go to Pilgrim; and as for the fourth Saturday, well, that was your fault. Saturday coming is the next practice. I can't let down Mrs Knight three sessions in a row."

"What time does choir practice end?"

"About five o'clock."

"Well, they have nice food in town in the evening, too, you know. We could go to dinner at The Coal-Pot. What say you?"

"All right. I say okay," she replied.

There was no plausible excuse she could concoct on the spur of the moment, and anyway, she found that she was not averse to the idea of holding a conversation with him about things other than helping youths to organise (as necessary as that was), and away from Viola's hovering. She had to admit that he had become a very interesting, even intriguing figure – a would-be English gentleman who had gone to England and returned more Cayerian than before! Not to speak of his reported domestication. England had worked wonders for him. It had stripped him of layers of foolishness and brought him down to earth. She was beginning to look forward to "that catch-up talk".

20
"Which of us was the better helpmeet to the other?"

The Coal-Pot Creole Restaurant was still something of a novelty in town. By all appearances this was a posh establishment, made for the hoity-toity – red carpet from wall to wall; linen tablecloths and napkins; an assortment of heavy silver set around porcelain plates; and waiters in crisp white shirts. Yet this place was serving, of all things, Cayerian food!

Wasn Miss Mavis greasy hole-in-the-wall cook-shop, with cracking linoleum on the floor, drink-stained tables, chipped enamel plates, and some drowsy flies in residence. Wasn the coal-pot that Earline and Milton cooked on in front Aleong shop, nor the enterprise of any other pavement vendor offering Cayerian fare by the light of a smoky flambeau. Yet the menu featured callaloo, coo-coo, black-pudding, stewed pigeon peas, sancoche, akra, pelau, oildown, souse, ochro-rice, pound-plantain...

She asked after his father. "I know your mother died while you were away – I heard it on the death announcements – but how is he doing?"

"Hmm." Gaston frowned. "Incorrigible, stubborn old mule. He is well. Hale and hearty, because my poor mother devoted her life to looking after him. She may have died of exhaustion. He is healthy, but utterly helpless, which is not to say physically handicapped. On the contrary, he is remarkably able-bodied. He can't do anything for himself, because he simply does not know how. Still, he gives a lot of trouble to anybody my sister puts there to look after him.

"They not folding his clothes with due care; not fluffing up his pillows right; not making his tea to his taste – too much milk, not enough sugar, too hot, too cold... They setting out the food on his plate wrong – the salad musn't touch the meat, the gravy must wet the rice only so much and no more, because the rice mustn't be dry and it musn't be sappy... One woman, a week after Gloria hired her, took up his plate from the table, went into the kitchen and scraped all the food back into the various pots and bowls, washed the plate, and then walked off the job, with the parting words: 'Mister, you go have to dish out you food for youself'."

"*Bondjé!*" Gwynneth exclaimed, but she couldn't help thinking that this might easily have been a portrait of Gaston at his father's age, 76, were it not for what he called his "baptism of fire" in England. He seemed to read this thought on her face.

"Well, he gives me a glimpse of the future I escaped," he remarked. "There but for the grace of God…"

And she concurred, "Amen!"

There was more delving into the years before he left Cayeri than catching up on the seventeen years since. Gaston went back to their beach excursions, reliving the good times at Bounty Bay, Tucupita, Diamond Beach, L'Anse Marron, L'Anse Amandes… The very mention of L'Anse Amandes was like a stab to the heart. They interrupted their reminiscence to ponder on the imminent fate of that whole area, soon to become "Fort Roosevelt Naval Base".

"Hm," Gaston reflected. "The beach is sure to be off limits to us natives. 'Trespassers will be shot on sight.' As a boy scout I used to go camping in there, and hiking in the hills around. Already word is that they going to evict all the villagers living there, demolish they homes, and appropriate they land. Farming families and fishermen, providing food – all will be kicked off the land. Heaven knows whether any of us will ever be able to set foot inside there again – our generation or the ones to come. The lease is for ninety-nine years! We might as well saw off that corner of our property and send it to the US, let them attach it to Florida…"

Their conversation trailed off and they sat in a heavy silence for a while, until Gaston sought to dissipate the gloom. "When we become an independent country," he said, "one day, one day, congotay, we will right that and other wrongs. What we can't fix immediately must not overshadow our present. But speaking of the beach, let me tell you about me and what passes for 'beach' in England. Up there I missed sea-bathing so much that one summer I put God out of my thoughts and agree to go with some British friends to their famous Brighton Beach. Well, who send me? Was the height of summer, sun shining in the sky, so I run down to the water and throw myself in.

"Man, the scream I let out, people on the beach turn they head to see who drowning, that is, those people who wasn staring already at the black apparition. *Ice-water.* I throw myself in ice-water, and all around me, children in that freezing sea, comfortable, splashing and shrieking with happiness…"

Gwynneth appreciated the comic diversion. She turned to reminiscing about the "nonstop" dances they went to at Harmony Hall whenever Earl "Lennie" Lendore's band was playing there. Lennie's was their favourite dance band. Apart from the dances at Harmony Hall, now and then they would join with others to organise a Saturday night excursion to a place out of town where Lennie was playing that night. She also recalled with fondness the Workers' League rallies in The Square that they took part in. The rousing speeches. The thunder of voices chanting "Better pay, today!" and "Slavery dead and gone!" and the singing – now a hymn in Shouter Baptist rhythm, now a lavway of rebellion from the annals of calypso…

And the time when, to back the singing and chanting, somebody in the crowd was beating a skin drum, flouting the law, and police squeezed their way through the crowd to try and find the drummer, but people began to pass the drum from hand to hand, so that every now and then the sound would ring out from a different part of The Square. Then more police were sent to spread out in the crowd, but they never got their hands on the drum. Its voice was last heard from somewhere on the edge of the crowd, after which it was spirited away to safety, and the crowd went back to knocking small stones on bottles, beating kwa-kwa, clapping hands and stamping feet to accompany the singing and chanting.

Gwynneth and Gaston recalled the demands that Workers' League was making in those years – improved wages and working conditions; an eight-hour working day; old-age pension; the right to vote representatives into the Legislative Council… They reflected on the current state of affairs, and how long it had taken – nearly two decades of struggle exploding into 1937 – for any part of the demands of workingpeople to be heeded, and how much more change there was still to be forced out of the authorities.

"You only have to consider today's Leg. Co., for example," Gwynneth remarked, "to know that what was tossed our way for 'representative government' is still not even half a loaf."

A most impish look appeared on Gaston's face, and with an exaggerated clearing of the throat, he asked, "Ahem, Miss, you say 'representative government', Miss?"

She immediately caught on, and they burst into laughter. Good that he can laugh at that episode now, Gwynneth thought. Not so at the time of the meeting where she put in her two cents' worth on the topic. It seemed that whenever she went with Gaston to one of his Forward meetings, she was sure to end up creating some kind of ruction that brought on his peeved-face and an argument afterwards...

~

At her very first introduction to Forward, after months of Gaston trying to persuade her to go to a meeting with him, there was one moment that might have turned awkward, had she not decided to exercise her best manners. They had welcomed her warmly, bless their hearts, making speeches and cheering her "brave resistance on the night of the Grand Chemin march", and so on. Then, as they turned to the business of the meeting, the chairman, Victor Murray, had a brainwave:

"Wait a minute! Comrades, now we have a secretary!"

He seemed to be looking straight at Gwynneth, who blinked rapidly and looked behind, to the right, and to the left of her, to see who he was referring to.

"Miss Cuffie? Would you be so kind as to take the minutes?"

"All right," Gwynneth said. "I can take minutes, but I have no training in secretarial work, Comrade. I am a teacher."

He responded with what he clearly thought was flattery: "Oh, but you're a woman. That makes you a natural-born secretary!"

"No, it does not, but I will take the minutes of this meeting," she replied, adding, with the sweetest smile she could offer, "not because I am a woman, but because I went to school and learned to listen, précis and write, just like all of you here."

She refrained from looking at Gaston, for he would be cringing with apprehension, having learnt from bitter experience what kind of response Murray's comment was likely to draw from her.

Gaston thanked her afterwards for not completely biting off Murray's head, although she had scolded the man, in his own house. (Forward meetings were rotated among the members' homes, and he who hosted the meeting had also to chair it.) Gaston confessed, too, that he wanted to slide under the furniture when Murray made the foolish comment.

Then, at another Forward meeting she attended, there was that debate (or, in Gaston's eyes, just another scolding) about English Creole.

A third occasion, the one that Gaston was remembering now, was the meeting at Arthur Clarke's house, in 1922, when Forward discussed the just-released Royal Commission report on constitutional reform. This commission had been set up the year before to ponder on why the natives were acting up so fiercely in those years following the war – strikes, marches, riots, arson, and other disturbances – and to recommend what form of sop the colonial government could throw to them to make them behave.

From their investigations, the commission had determined that people in this colony were railing against Crown Colony rule, and were insisting, more raucously than ever before, that they should have a say in government. These inhabitants resented the fact that every last one of the 26 members of their Legislative Council was appointed from on high, so that those whose affairs they governed had no part to play in putting them there. Thus it was that in 1922 the Royal Commission proposed a reform of the Leg. Co., in order to quell the agitation for representative government. The Forward discussion shredded this "reform".

"Only seven seats, out of the twenty-six, little more than a quarter of the Leg. Co., to be elected? And elected by whom?" one of them was asking. "What kind of reform is this? To sit on the Leg. Co. you will still have to be someone owning valuable property, or making a lot of money, so no change there. The big change, the big reform, is that the governor will no longer appoint the whole Leg. Co. Some members will be voted in by citizens. *Some* citizens will now have the right to vote to put men in the Leg. Co. And *which* citizens will now have this right? Certainly not Tom, Dick and Harrilal! Because to vote you will also have to own big property, or be earning big income."

"Same old khaki pants," said another. "*Menm laka lòt-la. Menm bagay.* Who gets to sit in the Leg. Co.? Rich people. Who gets to vote for a representative in the Leg. Co.? Rich people – a handful of Cayerians. The great majority of the population will remain well outside of representative government..."

"Agreed. There will be just one or two coloured people sitting in the Leg. Co., as is the case at present, and the voters will also be mainly white people. The bulk of the population, the Creole and Indian underclass, will continue to be excluded from political power."

The irate discussion continued, and Gwynneth listened, quietly agreeing with all that was being said about this "reform" that preserved race and class inequality. They might have forgotten her, for when she finally ventured to speak, the sound of her voice seemed to startle them.

"When will women be allowed to sit on the Legislative Council?" she asked. "The 'reformed' constitution still bans women from sitting in government. To be a candidate for election to the Leg. Co., you have to be not only wealthy, but male. And no woman can be elected to the City Council, either. What do you think of that?"

Gwynneth's question fell dead into a freezing silence. Undaunted, she pressed on. "But, good news! It doesn't say no woman can *vote*! Some can! But, like the men, they must have big property or big income. And how many Cayerian women, do you think, white, Creole or Indian, own property to the value of $12,000.00, or earn $2,000.00 a year?

"And you notice, by the way, that for a woman to vote, she must not only have wealth, she will also have to be over 30 years of age, while the men will be able to vote from age 21? What, we retarded? Women take nine more years than men to reach maturity? At age 21 we are still children, and therefore cannot be trusted with voting? And just by the way, if either of the two sexes *does* develop later than the other, it's not the female. Those of you who are teachers, or who have adolescent children, might have noticed that girls tend to mature ahead of boys, and then the boys catch up at a certain point. There is no reason to withhold the right to vote from women for nine years of our adult life."

The silence held for a moment, then came a kindly chuckle or two, and a guffaw, not unlike Johnstone's, only milder, and someone said "Ah! A suffragette!"

"Oh, good," said Gwynneth. "You have been paying attention to the suffragettes, so you know that as a result of their struggle, the right of women to vote became law in America two years ago. That is to say, *white* women, of course.

"Those who opposed the suffragettes used arguments like 'Women are not fit to take part in government because they can't think logically like men.' Isn't that just like what the racists here and elsewhere have been saying to oppose the idea of Creoles and Indians getting the vote – that they don't have the mental capacity to be given such a responsibility? Think of Anton da Silva, and those who agreed with him."

They murmured, and some nodded. "To quote Mr da Silva," Gwynneth continued, "'if we are going to let Negroes and Indians vote, we might just as well also give apes and children the right to vote.' For the likes of da Silva, coloured people have their God-given station in life, which is not to rule, but to serve the master race. Well, those who opposed the suffragettes also used that argument. For them, a woman's God-given station is to serve her master – her husband – and his children, not get herself mixed up in public life."

She paused, to give others a chance to speak. But they were all just staring back at her, except for Gaston, who was looking everywhere else but at her. Nobody had anything more to say.

"All right," she conceded. "Maybe you haven't thought about this yet. Everything you've said is true, but then there is this other truth – this other inequality that is worth your attention. Maybe one day you'll put it on your agenda, for there will be no representative government until women are also represented. Sorry to interrupt your conversation, gentlemen. I will continue listening."

And she leaned back into the comfortable cushions of Arthur Clarke's Morris chair, with their neatly sewn covers. But the conversation had been scuttled beyond repair. Clarke suggested that they move on to the next item, and somewhere in the same stream of speech he said "Yvonne" so that seconds later his wife, invisible up till that moment, appeared with a tray of sandwiches, put it down on the centre-table and went back to being invisible.

Days later, Gaston handed Gwynneth (a little churlishly, she thought) a formal invitation from the group to be the guest speaker at their next meeting, or on a date to be set at her convenience. The letter was signed by the head of Forward, Neville Ogiste, who had not been present at the meeting in Clarke's house. The request was for her to speak on "Equality of the Sexes"…

~

"That turned out to be one of the best sessions ever, in the whole history of Forward," Gaston recalled.

"Oh, really? You never told me so!"

"Well, to tell you the truth, I remained a little pissed off after the discussion at Clarke's home, but all the Forward men had to admit that even that first round at Clarke's was quite an education for us. You have to understand that we just *did not know* this point of view. We had never had any exposure to such ideas. You really set us thinking, although nobody seemed willing to talk that day." He chuckled. "Maybe they were remembering…" His chuckle became a wicked laugh that broke up his sentence, "remembering how you did boof Murray… in he own house, when he try… he try to appoint you to the post of secretary…"

"I did *not* boof…"

"But nothing wrong with that. I find he deserve the boof – he look for that. I coulda see it coming, because, Miss, by that time I did done get my share of boof from you on the topic of Woman. I take my boof, do a little thinking, and learn something. Anyway, your session at Neville's house, when you got everybody talking, and nobody wanted the discussion to end – that was great. I was still a little pissed off, but at the same time, very proud, Miss."

"Well, thank you, Sir, for your kind compliment," Gwynneth said.

And what flashed into her mind was Gaston saying to her, on the way home from Neville Ogiste's house that evening in 1922, "How are you going to change the world if you don't share your thinking with others? People behave in particular ways because they just don't know better!"

He said it in a huffy way, but after some minutes of stony

silence he added, in a kindlier tone, "Why don't you go back to writing in the newspapers?"

He had pursued the idea, bringing it up every time he saw her thereafter, until she did write a letter, which appeared in *The Voice* in November 1922, about women being excluded from political power, except for that tiny percentage of the female population who were allowed to vote, and no women at all being allowed to sit in government. At that time she had not written to the press in three years, not since Moun Demmeh's last letter-writing campaign, and she acknowledged, now, that it was actually Gaston who had got her started again.

"Well, things have certainly begun to change," Gaston remarked. "I came back to Cayeri to find a lady ensconced in the Kings Port City Council!"

"Yes, and she didn get in there just so. Was one long contention: motion tabled in the City Council to amend the ordinance that debarred women from being elected to said Council; motion hotly debated; motion defeated. Motion tabled again and again, and defeated every time it was brought. That took up eight years, with most Council members, including some political 'revolutionaries', putting up strong opposition, and the good old *Kings Port Sentinel* joining in, running a campaign against women being let in as councillors.

"The amendment was passed, finally, in 1935; but when two female candidates came forward to run in the next election, one was disqualified, and the other, Olga Frederick, had her qualifications challenged in court. Miss Frederick won her court case, *and* the seat that she ran for."

Gaston clapped his hands together, noiselessly. "When we become an independent country," he said, "with equal political rights for all, we will support the candidacy of Gwynneth Cuffie for a seat in the sovereign parliament of Cayeri."

"Indeed. By which time the said Gwynneth Cuffie will be one hundred and one years old, cyaan remember where she put her teeth, and couldn care less if Good Friday fall on Ash Wednesday."

The last time they had sat together like this, in a restaurant, did not make a pleasant memory. It was a rendezvous, one week before he left for England, that had come to a premature end. She wondered whether it would be wise to bring that memory into the conversation. There was so much that was best left buried…

~

It was lunch time on a working day. She and Gaston were in La Marina restaurant, on the upper floor of a building on the Esplanade. They were sitting on the veranda enclosed by pretty wrought-iron railings and overlooking street and sea. What was that quarrel about? Gwynneth could not now remember. In those last days, when he was getting ready to travel, he was all nerves, on edge all the time, so it would not have taken much to start a quarrel. While they shot their wounding darts at each other, no one else in the restaurant was any the wiser, for they kept their voices low and their faces expressionless.

They had not yet ordered food, only drinks. They were still looking through the menu when the quarrel erupted. Eventually Gwynneth stopped making any retort, and, taking her time, finished off whatever it was she had been sipping. Then, still without a word, she got up, eased her chair neatly into its place under the table, and made for the indoor section of the restaurant, where the staircase to the ground floor was. She went down the steps and out to the street. There she turned left, walking briskly now. At James Street corner she got on the tramcar going north.

It was only twenty-five past twelve, and her session with the child in Primrose Hill was not till a quarter to three. She would get off at a stop around the Savannah, find a vendor selling akra-and-float, or bara-and-channa, and sit on a Savannah bench to eat. She could sit and watch Kings Port go by until two o'clock, then take a leisurely walk up to Primrose Hill. In that part of town the streets were lined with well-kept trees that would shade her on her way.

In the evening, he turned up at Catherine Street, glum, seething from the day's contretemps, but anxious to keep the peace. He wanted to spend as much time as he could with her every day until he got on the boat.

~

She decided, now, to remind him of the incident. No harm, she thought.

The mere mention of La Marina restaurant seemed to give him a little jolt, but he took the recollection in stride.

233

"*If* I remember that?" he responded. "Girl, you ain betting you use to treat me bad, nuh! But I didn care what you do to me."

He smiled wryly, and fell silent for a few moments, slowly shaking his head. "Lemme tell you how that same La Marina lash me with a tabanca again, in more recent times."

He hesitated. Then he spoke as though he were treading on eggs. One day, some months after his return to Cayeri, he went looking for a place where he could have lunch quickly. He had spent the whole morning in court, and needed to get back to the office as soon as possible, to see some clients. As he walked along the Esplanade, he looked into each restaurant to gauge the crowd and the time it would take to get lunch there.

When he got close to La Marina restaurant, he looked up to see if there was room on the veranda. "I saw a few empty tables, but then I also spotted… the love of my life, at a table for two, deep in conversation with a gentleman. Needless to say, I kept on walking, gathering speed. By the time I turned Mary Street corner I was almost running. Well, I forget about lunch that day. Was straight back to the office."

Gwynneth cocked her head to one side like a bird. "If is me you talking about," she said, "I doan know what to do with that report, Gaston. Life goes on. Your life continued, and so did mine."

"Yes, I know. Sorry to bring it up. I know it's not my business. I will tell you, though, I can't say my life continued. A huge part of my life is stuck somewhere back in 1923. Since then… but I suspect that you don't want to hear anything about my married life…"

"No I don't. Not my business."

"Okay. Lemme shut up about me. I making you uncomfortable. Let's go back to cheerier things. I'm grateful that you agreed to come out with me, and I won't spoil the occasion."

How to go back to cheerier things, Gwynneth thought, and what cheerier things, when there was obviously something weighing him down that he needed to say. She began to regret bringing up the story of their quarrel in La Marina, but if he had things to offload, he was going to, sooner or later. She should listen to him.

"You weren't planning to bad-talk your wife to me?" she cautioned. "I not going listen to that."

Gaston looked taken aback and hurt. "You really have such a low opinion of me? I not going to do that. It's the opposite – I want to bad-talk *me*."

"I don't find that any more appealing," she said, "but I listening."

"Well, as I said, I never moved on. *Mea culpa* – that wasn't fair to Ann, my wife. I realised, one day, that in my mind I was constantly comparing her with you, and deciding that she didn't measure up."

Gwynneth was startled. She continued listening to him with eyes wide open in alarm.

"Just as I always had the impression you were comparing me with David, and I didn make the grade, either."

"Hold up, Mister, hold up! What woulda make you think I was comparing you with David?"

"Oh, the way you talked about him."

"Talked about him? I never talked to you about David!"

"Clearly you forget, or, you didn realise it at the time. But, it was not a problem to me. I never objected. On the contrary, I was honoured to be the listening ear. I convinced myself that I was helping you get over the grief."

Gwynneth was flabbergasted. She had no recollection of ever speaking to him about David. If it was true, then she had suffered a most curious strain of amnesia! But surely he had no reason to make up such a story? Being with Gaston was no walk in a flower-garden, but she had always admitted to herself that during their time together he did everything in his power to help her pick her life up again and move on.

"You know," she said, "with all the lecture you lecture me, in those years, about 'Woman is Man's helpmeet', think about it – which of us was the better helpmeet to the other?" She reached across the table and took his hand. "Thank you, Gaston," and she raised her glass: "Cheers!"

As for her somehow coming between him and his wife – she, Gwynneth, in absentia, an ocean away from them – that part of Gaston's unburdening she could not entertain, not for even one second. If there was anything to be left buried, that would be it.

2 1
"Encore! Encore! We ain going home."

Weeks after St Hilda's Harvest Fair of 1940, people were still talking about it, from St Paul to Oropuna. Word had got around beforehand that there would be two iron bands playing. The word had spread with the help of Earline, and Janice, and Gemma, and Garnet's mother, Bernice. And Mrs Knight! All Mrs Knight didn do was take a bell and walk the road ringing it to call out people.

Gwynneth and the two bandleaders were invited to a meeting of the harvest fair committee a week before the fair. The ajoupa had been approved, so they now had to decide where to put it. The hall had two doors leading out onto the lawn, one at the midpoint along the wall. It was decided that the ajoupa would be put up outside this door so that the iron bands could be heard by everyone inside the hall, whether they were seated in front of the stage or at the tea tables, or standing at the back of the hall.

The tea tables were going to be set up inside, because it was no longer petit-carême weather. The sky had been overcast almost every morning for the past few days, and on some days there were showers. Mothers' Union was therefore planning for an indoor event. If, in spite of appearances, the weather turned out to be dry that afternoon, people could come outside to hear the iron bands play.

They worked out the order of performances. The tea service would begin at 3.30, announced by the orphanage band striking up, and this would also signal the start of the concert. That band would play three pieces, and the rest of the entertainment would follow. The climax of the entertainment would be the combined iron bands, also playing three pieces.

On the Wednesday before the fair, the boys trekked uphill from Baba Nate's compound to where the San Miguel River crossed his land, and they cut poles from the flourishing bamboo growing along the riverbank. They dragged them down the hill to the pile of coconut branches they had already collected and placed in the front yard of Phillip's home. A member of St Hilda's congregation who had a truck came and took the load to the churchyard.

The building of the joupa, scheduled for Thursday evening, would have to be supervised by Mr Scantlebury, St Hilda's cantankerous sexton, guardian of the church, its outbuildings and its grounds. This responsibility he took too literally. He seemed to think that anybody he did not recognise as a member of St Hilda's congregation was a danger to St Hilda's. Gwynneth and Mrs Knight were worried about how this supervision would go. Mr Scantlebury was known to have angered workmen (engaged by the church to repair or paint, or some other task) to the point where he and a plumber once came to blows and Mr Scantlebury narrowly escaped being brained by a spanner wrench.

Mrs Knight was quite willing to come out of her house and stick around for the entire building operation so she could place herself between Scantlebury and "Gwynneth's boys", but Gwynneth decided to call upon Gaston. On the appointed Thursday, therefore, Gaston came up to Turagua and sat on a bench in St Hilda's churchyard distracting Mr Scantlebury with conversation while the boys got on with building their joupa. Mrs Knight paid them a visit, introduced herself to Gaston, and, having conducted a brief interview with him, promptly enlisted him as part of her crew.

The day of the fair, Saturday, began with a grey sky, and the 8.00 o'clock weather forecast was of no earthly use: "Partly cloudy, with a chance of rain." At mid-morning, a light drizzle caused Gwynneth some anxiety. She found herself chanting, in her head, *Rain, rain / Go away / Come again another day...* Although arrangements had been made for the fair to be held indoors, rain could still be a real bother.

For one thing, it could affect attendance. Some people were not keen on leaving their houses in wet weather. Then you had to worry about the state of the lawn. Persistent showers, or just one heavy downpour, could leave the ground swampy and the crowd would not be able to spread out into that space, sit on the garden benches, or stand on the grass to chat. People would ban their children from running gleefully up and down the lawn as they loved to do, for that would get their good shoes muddy. Children would then be cooped up inside the hall, which was not much fun for them. But the worst thing was that a muddy lawn would prevent people from coming outdoors for the iron bands' performance.

Slowly, however, the grey, low-hanging clouds drifted away, leaving a clear, bright sky. Now, if only that weather could hold for the rest of the day. Gwynneth called upon all the good spirits, saints and forces of the universe to stay the rain.

She set out for St Hilda's just before one o'clock. She had promised to help Earline and Janice put the final touches to their market stall. As she approached the church she was taken aback by the large crowd, of mainly young people, already waiting outside the gate, for the fair was not due to start until two o'clock. Mrs Knight would have seen to it that Mr Scantlebury was occupied elsewhere, for there was a real danger he might shoo them away. She had also stationed at the entrance two hefty gatekeepers from Mothers' Union, Lenore and Octavia, two ladies not to be trifled with. They opened the gate for Gwynneth to pass, and swiftly closed it back, assuring the crowd that they would soon be let in.

The place was teeming with helpers. Gaston had arrived earlier, as per Mrs Knight's request. On his way there he had picked up two boxes from Viola. One was a shoe-box containing the ribbons for the boys. The larger box contained the things Viola had made for the sweet-tooth stall – pawpaw balls, guava cheese, pone, and kurmah.

She had made the sweets during the week, all except the kurmah. She wanted Dolly, Sookram's wife, to come and supervise her as she made it. Viola could very well make kurmah – and pholouri, and dhalpouri, and a whole lot of other Indian foods. But when it came to making them for public consumption, she saw herself as not qualified. If her kurmah was going to be sold at the harvest fair, then it had to be perfect, or bad-tongue people were sure to whisper behind they hand to one another, *Who fool she and tell she she could make kurmah? Why she ain leave the people thing alone?* Her reputation was at stake.

Dolly came over on Friday afternoon and the two of them stood in the kitchen and made kurmah. Then they sat down at the dining-table to cut up shop-paper and parcel off the kurmah into little packets. Out in the schoolroom Gwynneth could hear scandalous laughter coming from the house, the kind of mirth that went with smutty conversation. When asked about it afterwards, Viola would only say, with a twinkle in her eye, "That Dolly well good for sheself, *oui!*" as though she, Miss Viola Holy-Mary, had taken no part whatsoever in the talk.

After the fair, Gaston told Gwynneth that Mrs Knight had taken him around, introducing him to Mothers' Union as Gwynneth's friend, a lawyer, and a patron of the iron bands. He related, chuckling, how one of the ladies had introduced herself to him as the wife of Mr Arnold Pierre, the notary public; maybe Mr Boniface knew him? This lady had sought to detach him from Mrs Knight, offering him a tour of the church, a cup of tea, a glass of juice... but Mrs Knight informed her that she had work for Mr Boniface to do. Gwynneth reflected with satisfaction that being officially put in charge of the fair seemed to have brought out a side of Mrs Knight that Mothers' Union had not experienced before – and that everyone would henceforth have to reckon with.

When Gwynneth entered the church hall, Gaston was helping to push tea tables closer together, to make more space at the back for the standing audience, and simultaneously trying to be polite to Valda Pierre (dressed to kill, her hat like a basket of grapes on her head). She was intent on shadowing him, making it her business to "help" with every table or chair that he took hold of, while chatting his head off in her best hoity-toity voice, striving to mind her *th*s and *ing*s: "Like we'll be getting a good thurn-out, eh? Lovely! I only hope we can accommodate everybody ing the hall. Must be the iron bands athracting this athention. Oh, I cannot wait to hear those boys beathing those drums. Ah! Look Gwynneth reach. Gwynneth, my thear..."

Gwynneth my thear? So, suddenly "Gwynneth" is you bosom friend? Gwynneth steupsed to herself. She waved at Mrs Pierre but continued on her way to the eastern door where the joupa was. She stood in the doorway and looked out. A little gasp escaped her as the boys rose in unison from their seats and greeted her with bright smiles: "Good afternoon, Teacher Gwynneth!"

They looked so dashing! Gaston had placed chairs for them in the joupa, and some just in front of it, under the eaves of the building. He had invited them to sit until the fair started, when they could get up and walk around, visit the stalls and chat with people. He advised them not to make any sound on their instruments before it was their turn to perform. And so, there they were, splendid in their white shirts, each with the little ribbon on the left pocket. Viola had cut up the ribbon, folded and tacked each piece into a loop with two tails, and stuck a pin into it. Gaston had helped the boys to pin them on their shirts.

Gwynneth chatted with them for a bit and then went back indoors to help with the stall. Earline and Janice, assisted by their children, were in the process of decorating their market stall, profusely, with sweet-broom, many-coloured croton, bunches of bright red gri-gri, small palm branches, hibiscus flowers... Earline pointed Gwynneth to a chair: "Siddown, Miss G. Let them chirren work. We want you to cash for us, please, when we start to sell."

Normally, for the fair, the gate to the churchyard was opened just a crack at two o'clock. People would file in one at a time and the gatekeepers would direct them up the short path to the main door of the church hall where three more Mothers' Union ladies sat behind a table, two of them ready to collect the admission fee of 12 cents for children and a shilling for adults, and the third to sell tea tickets. On that afternoon, however, as two o'clock approached, it was clear that the one-at-a-time method of entry would not be practical, such was the crowd outside the gate.

For the tea service and concert to actually start at 3.30, with sufficient time before that for people to do a first round of browsing and patronising the stalls, admission would have to go a little faster. Mrs Knight took the suggestion coming from Mesdames Lenore and Octavia that they should open the gate a little wider and let people in two at a time. More than half an hour later the crowd that had built up outside was still streaming in through the gates.

While this was going on, Reverend Fields slipped quietly into the hall through the back door. Gwynneth noticed him out of the corner of her left eye. And immediately, out of the corner of her right eye she saw Valda Pierre unmoor herself from the spot she had taken up at the front door. The next thing Gwynneth knew, the blue-flowered dress, topped by the basket of grapes, had flashed past her, heading for the priest, who looked as though he would have liked to turn tail and run back out. Valda Pierre got hold of him by the elbow, searched the hall with her eyes and spotted Gaston standing at the side door where the joupa was. Valda Pierre began to navigate her captive between people, chairs and stage, to get him to Gaston.

All this time Gwynneth could see Valda Pierre's mouth working nineteen to the dozen, but she could not hear her above the noise of people steadily filling up the hall. She saw her getting the two men to shake hands, then nudging Reverend Fields out through the side door and down the two or three steps that led into the joupa.

Gwynneth was kept very busy in her cashier job, for the market stall was doing well. People were browsing and buying at all of the stalls. Mrs Knight arranged for Gwynneth's boys to be served juice and sweetbread in the joupa, after which they came into the bustling hall and walked around for a bit. They returned to their places well before the orphanage band struck up to start the concert. The church hall was packed. Those who couldn't fit inside were spilling out of the doors, with some standing outside along the walls, under the eaves. Gwynneth's boys mostly sat in the joupa and listened to the performances, while some of them got up and squeezed their way in through their side door to take in certain items, like the comical skit done by two church members, and the almost as comical fashion parade.

Phillip had told Gwynneth beforehand of his decision not to bring out the pan with the notes to this public event. It wasn't perfect yet. He wanted to do some more work on it, but there wasn't time. All his spare time was taken up with practising for Harvest, for which his Uncle Melville had got him yet another paint tin.

And now the MC was announcing "the long-awaited iron-band performance – presenting the St Paul Syncopators and the San Miguel Warahoons." (Gwynneth had tried hard to explain to a very puzzled Valda Pierre how come she had allowed the boys to call themselves "warahoons" when she had so unkindly criticised her for saying that word. No amount of explaining could clear up the puzzle for Mrs Pierre). Young people were pouring out of the building, already clapping and cheering. Some of the less young sat inside the hall to listen, but most people were moving outdoors. Gwynneth and Gaston got the boys to quickly turn their chairs around to face this excited audience forming on the lawn.

Meanwhile the MC had taken up his position at the front of the band, and was proudly briefing the audience: "What you seeing here, ladies and gentlemen, is two iron bands, one from St Paul, one from Turagua, that will be playing together as one, not warring, not pelting bottle and stone at one another. Give them a round of applause!"

The crowd obliged.

The iron band was scheduled to end the concert with three numbers. That was the plan. The boys had chosen the calypso "Keep Allyou War Over There", to be followed by "When the Saints Go Marching In" and "Going Down Jordan".

At first the crowd listened to the band in a disbelieving silence and stillness. But not for long. The whole space between the church hall and the church soon broke into the rollicking jump-up for which Harvest Fair 1940 would long be remembered – dancing, singing, clapping, cheering... In the middle of the second number, a light drizzle came down, and Gwynneth's heart sank. But the drizzle did not interrupt the proceedings for one moment. Indeed, people were holding their hands up in the air, palms upturned to catch the fine spray, and some were heard to call out, "Showers of blessing!" as they danced with even more excitement.

The drizzle did not last. The band ended their performance with "Going Down Jordan".

As planned, and as diligently rehearsed up at the palay, the St Paul boys stood up and took a bow, and in the same moment that they sat down, San Miguel rose and bowed. The crowd broke into cheering and the MC had to wait for it to die down before he could speak. From the page in his hand, he introduced Gwynneth as the "mother" of the bands, and Gaston and Ollie as their patrons. Ollie had arrived during the concert. The MC thanked Mothers' Union, whereupon Valda Pierre, having carefully positioned herself so as to be seen, took several deep bows. He thanked the St Hilda's Harvest Fair Committee, all the performers in the concert, all the persons who had donated items for sale, and so on, with the crowd applauding heartily...

And then, for Gwynneth, a flash of light. At the start of the concert, inside the building, she had got a glimpse of the MC on stage when she stepped out of the market stall for a brief moment. She thought he looked familiar. Nobody had introduced him to the audience, nor had he used up any time introducing himself; he had simply stepped on stage and got the concert going. Now that the proceedings had moved outdoors and she could see him at close quarters, she became even more convinced that this was a face she knew, but she could check afterwards.

"And now, ladies and gentlemen," the MC said, "let me introduce you to the person that work the hardest to make this beautiful afternoon – the head of St Hilda's Harvest Fair Committee, Mistress Cicely Knight!"

Mrs Knight was standing at the side of the ajoupa, holding a pencil in one hand, and a little bunch of papers in the other. She was startled by this announcement, which clearly wasn't on the paper she had handed him earlier. The MC went to her, took her by the arm, and walked her around to the front of the ajoupa. That was when it clicked. Just the way he held her arm. Just the way he leaned his head to peer at her.

This MC was Delbert George, the man Mrs Knight had recommended to Gwynneth when she needed someone to fix the side gate at home. The top hinge had rusted and broken into two pieces, and they had to fasten the gate to the post with a piece of wire until they could get it fixed. He came and inspected the problem, went and bought a new hinge, and repaired the gate. That was more than a year before this Harvest Fair, Gwynneth calculated, as the new war had not yet begun.

This was Delbert George who, people said, was more than odd-jobs-man to Mrs Knight. That talk had been going on for quite a while, but Mrs Knight had always held her head high and paid no attention. Everyone knew that Mr Knight had gone to Canada years before and, it seemed, just disappeared into Canada. The plan had been that he would settle in and then send for his wife, but after a few months and a few letters from him (so said the maccoes), Mr Knight moved from the address in Toronto at which he had been living, and Mrs Knight's letters to him started coming back to her marked "Return to sender" and "Not known at this address".

But even the maccoes had never been sure that the rumours about Mrs Knight and the odd-jobs-man were true. Some did not even know him, as he hailed from Oropuna. None of this prevented said maccoes from remarking on the age difference ("She could be his mother"); the difference in education ("You think he reach Third Standard?"); and his lack of a steady job ("She must be minding him").

During the fair, some might have been shoo-shooing to each other about the MC, but Gwynneth would have been too busy to notice. After this event, however, the shoo-shooers would surely be having a field day. Mrs Knight had brought her man out. *Bravo, Mrs Knight. Who want to talk, could talk, and who vex, lost,* Gwynneth crowed silently.

The MC wished everyone present a safe return to their homes, but the crowd did not budge. A low rumble gathered strength until it turned into chanting, "Encore! Encore! We ain going home."

The MC conferred with Gwynneth, and the band was happy to render "Going Down Jordan" again. While the band played, with the crowd belting out the words and dancing, looking every bit as though they were just settling into an all-night jump-up, swift consultations took place behind the scenes, involving Gwynneth, Mrs Knight and Gaston. At the end of the piece, as foreseen, the crowd stood their ground, but the MC had been briefed.

"Thank you, ladies and gentlemen," he announced. "Thank you for your appreciation. Thanks for encouraging these talented youngboys. We hope you will remember them and hire them when you looking for entertainment at your function – christening, wedding, birthday, excursion. Remember the San Miguel Warahoons from right here in Turagua, and the St Paul Syncopators from over in St Paul. Mothers' Union can help you get in touch with the two bands."

Valda Pierre nodded vigorously and smiled, standing close to the MC, as though she was the one who had made the whole event happen. Throughout the fair she had made sure to be constantly visible and audible, everywhere. The MC wrapped up his speech: "And now, in appreciation of your appreciation, we giving you lagniappe. The band will play, again, 'Keep Allyou War Over There'. Then we going into Last Lap – we marching home with Louis Armstrong and the saints."

In the same moment that the last beat was struck, Gaston and Ollie began pointedly moving in to help the boys pack up their instruments and carry them to the two motorcars.

As the crowd drained away, reluctantly, some still singing "Oh when the saints…" Gwynneth thought she could go in and help with cleaning up the church hall. But she was detained in the joupa by family members of the boys, who had looked on and listened in amazement to their performance, and now came to her, full of pride, to shake her hand and thank her for what she had done for their children.

When everyone seemed to have left the church compound except for helpers, Gwynneth made to get up off the chair and go inside. But then a woman was suddenly sitting next to her, a head-tied woman in voluminous clothes, like Ma Quamina. She appeared out of thin air, Gwynneth would swear afterwards, because the joupa was empty except for herself. Gwynneth would always think of Miss Verna as a spirit sent to her that evening. Miss Verna knew Reynold, one of the boys in the St Paul band. He was a neighbour's child, living two houses from her. Reynold was very kind to her, she said. He came over and cleaned up her yard from time to time, and ran errands for her. Through him she had heard about the band, and the police beating them out of the savannah, and the band shutting down as a result, since they had nowhere to meet.

She wanted to offer St Paul Syncopators the use of a shed on her land that was just there growing vine since her husband died. He was a carpenter and that was his workshop. But she had wanted to be sure that she wouldn't regret accommodating the boys, because she was hearing so much talk about badjohns in the iron bands. She had come to the fair especially to meet the boys and hear them play. She had visited the joupa before the concert began, and chatted with them. Now she knew that they were just youngboys, some with they mother milk still on they face, just human pickney, with good and bad in all of them. She knew it was an important work that they were doing, and that she had to help them.

Gwynneth wanted to pinch herself. She could be dreaming, as she was very tired and might well have dropped off for a moment. She had often experienced the unfolding of a whole dream scene in some tiny crack of time between sleep and wake, sometimes in the middle of a conversation with other people. Miss Verna had finished speaking and Gwynneth was still gaping at her. Gwynneth brought herself back. "*Bondjé*! Miss Verna!" she exclaimed, leaning over to throw her arms around her. "You are a godsend!"

They agreed that Gwynneth, with Kelvin, as the leader of the band, would go and visit her the following weekend.

22
Lennox brooded and Marjorie fussed.

As if Harvest Fair had not brought enough excitement to last for the rest of the year, two days later, on Monday afternoon, Marjorie flew over to Gwynneth and Viola with a crazed look on her face, more hysterical than they had ever seen her. She held out an airmail envelope to them. Gwynneth took it. She saw that the stamp was Canadian and the sender, Babsie. Over the years Babsie had written to Marjorie many times, to ask after Lennox, and Marjorie had not reacted with any panic, not to their knowledge, anyway. She would simply write back to say that Lennox was fine, and give a little news about him. *He has two teeth now. He is going to big-school now. He is in Cub Scouts now...*

True, Marjorie had resolutely ignored Babsie's requests for a photograph of Lennox, for she was afraid that if Babsie saw what a beautiful child he was, she would want to take him. Babsie appealed to Louis, for she knew that Marjorie had been sending photos of the child to him. Thus it was that from time to time, a photo of Lennox, sent by Marjorie from Turagua, Cayeri, to Louis in Birmingham, England, would reach Babsie in Toronto, Canada. That was up until Babsie got married.

Marjorie, having temporarily lost her tongue, motioned to Gwynneth that she should read the letter. Gwynneth read it aloud for Viola to hear. Babsie had written to say that she was coming home on a short visit and would like to see Lennox. She acknowledged that there wasn't enough time for a response from Marjorie to reach her before she left Canada, so her friend Claudette was going to come to Marjorie to find out when she could see him. The date of Babsie's arrival, given in the letter, was the date of Harvest Fair. Babsie was already home.

Marjorie had begun to breathe too fast. Gwynneth sat her down while Viola went to get a paper-bag, and after Marjorie had breathed into it for a while, she seemed to calm down. "You think she coming to take him?" she whispered.

247

"No, Marjorie. She can't take him. You know that. Louis has legal custody of Lennox."

Marjorie pondered over this for a moment, then asked, "But what Louis going to say?"

Gwynneth was losing patience. "What the *France* he could say? That Babsie mustn't see her child? Marjorie, pull youself together! Lennox is the one you have to think about right now. You going to confuse the boy with this panicking."

Lennox had never displayed much curiosity about his mother. They showed him pictures of her, but just like his deceased grandparents in Petit Curacaye, whom he knew only as two fading photographs, for him Babsie was not a real person. Nor were the boy and girl they said were his little brother and sister in Canada; they were imaginary children. From an early age Lennox had been told, bit by bit, as much of the story of himself as they thought he could grasp. What he knew, to begin with, was that when he was born, his father went and got him and brought him home. Later on, he understood that his father had taken him because his mother's family was going to give the baby to another family and send his mother to Canada.

He had grown up hearing the story of his arrival in Turagua, told as an epic adventure that thrilled him just as much every time he heard it. His father had come to the front gate, breathless and frantic, calling for Mumma. He was carrying this bundle that was more blanket than baby, and piece of the blanket trailing down to his knee, almost tripping him. Louis could not catch his breath, could not say anything but, "Miss Estelle! Miss Estelle!"

He had run all the way up the road, holding this most precious bundle to his chest. They said that Louis had been running since he got out of the taxi on the main road at Wilson Trace corner. He knew that Marjorie would be at work, so he didn't even bother to go to their house. He ran up the Cuffies' front walk and gallery steps and stood in the front door, gasping. Mumma came to the door and stretched out her arms for Louis to hand her the baby, just before he near collapsed on the gallery couch. But, tired as he was, he had to get up and hurry down to Aleong to buy a baby's bottle and a tin of Klim, as instructed by Mumma. When he got back they mixed some Klim and fed the baby, who promptly fell asleep.

When asked, they told Lennox that the reason Louis had been running was that the baby was getting hungry. (They did not think that Lennox needed to hear, just yet, about every piece of the kangkalang that attended his coming into the world). They said his mother had nursed him just before his father took him, but his little stomach was going to be empty again pretty soon. That may have been so, but the running was more to do with putting as much distance as possible, as quickly as possible, between the baby and its hoity-toity grandparents.

Truth be told, Louis had been running since he left the grand-parents' house in Plaisance, having snatched the baby from the grandmother. He had run from their house to the main road and jumped in a taxi. The passenger sitting next to him in the taxi eyed him with some contempt, and asked, "Where you going with baby in you hand, man? You wife leff you?" Louis only smiled at him.

~

After his apprenticeship at the Central Foundry, Louis had begun to set his sights on going to England to work. Somebody had advised him that with his training he could get a good job in a factory up there. But he realised that to accumulate the boat fare alone, he would have to work in Cayeri for perhaps a year. Louis went looking for a job in town and had to take what he could get.

It was on the train to Kings Port that he and Babsie met. She was nineteen years old, a clerk in the office of de Montbrun's, up Mary Street. He was twenty-two, a stevedore down on the docks. They got on the train to town every morning, he at Turagua, she at Plaisance. They agreed to always get into the third carriage, so they could find each other and sit together, morning and evening.

After work they took the 5.08 train from Kings Port. Sometimes he got off with her at Plaisance and walked her home – or almost, because he had to abandon her before her house came into full view. Her parents would each suffer a stroke if they found out about him. He walked her to a corner two streets from her home. There he stood and watched as she walked along the road. He did not leave until she had disappeared into her gateway.

Then he would go out to the main road and take a taxi, or he might walk part of the way home, for he was walking on air.

By then it had become obvious that the wages he earned on the port would not yield, in one year, the savings required for him to go to England. There was no guarantee that he would walk straight into a job when he got there, so he would need to have some money to tide him over, money for lodging, food, winter clothes, transportation, and God knows what else. He would have to work in Cayeri for another year, but now that did not seem like such a calamity. Babsie was his world, now. On some days they met up in town after work and went out together, Babsie alleging to her parents overtime at the office, or a girls' outing. He could not visit her home, but she lost no opportunity, spurned no subterfuge, to visit his.

Babsie was determined to get around her parents. If they found out about Louis, she said, they would interrogate her about who his parents were, what was his father's job, what was Louis's job. They would then pronounce him a nobody and forbid her to have anything to do with him. Quite a few friends and workmates of hers had been declared *persona non grata* by her parents because of where they lived, what shade of skin they had, or what kind of school they didn't go to.

Louis and Babsie began planning to get married and go to England together, and so they might have got a little careless; they might have thrown caution to the winds. Long story short, Babsie's mother noticed that her daughter was pregnant before Babsie could tell her. Mrs Hackett grilled Babsie about the child's father and was horrified. Not even the chance of a quick wedding to smooth things over, for Babsie had gone out of her way to find the lowest possible riff-raff for a boyfriend. Always contriving to shame her family.

Babsie's parents made her write a letter of resignation from her job. The next day they informed her that she was going to be kept indoors until the child was born; the child was going to be put up for adoption; and Babsie would then go up to her Aunt Ida in Toronto and further her education.

The parents allowed two or three of Babsie's friends of the right social pedigree to continue visiting her, with the understanding that her condition was to be kept a secret. One of these friends was Claudette, who let Louis know, without delay, of Babsie's cloistering and the plan to have Baby Riff-Raff adopted. Louis turned up at the Hacketts' home to introduce himself as the father of Babsie's child, and to let them know of his and Babsie's intention to marry. This news he delivered standing in the gallery. He was not allowed any further into the house, and Babsie was not allowed out onto the gallery.

"What child are you talking about?" Mrs Hackett asked, fixing a steely glare on him. "There is no child. You hear me? And if you go around claiming that our daughter is having a child by you, we will get the police to charge you with molestation. Now just leave our premises or we'll call the police right now."

Louis was so stunned that he walked out backwards. The next day he went and talked with Tantie Gwynneth. She advised him not to aggravate the situation by going to the Hacketts' home again. Since Babsie was not yet twenty-one, her mother and father still had parental rights over her. Louis and Babsie would just have to wait until she was twenty-one to carry out their plan. By then, of course, they might have sent Babsie off to Canada; but nobody knew what the future would bring, so they should not lose hope. Meanwhile, as soon as the child was born, Louis should go to the warden's office and register the birth himself, and then get a lawyer to file for custody.

Over the next five months of anguish for Babsie and Louis, Claudette was the go-between, delivering letters that the two of them wrote to each other. It was Claudette who brought the news, early one morning, that the child had been born during the night. Louis did not go to work that day. He registered his child, and then went straight to Babsie's home. Finding the lawyer was for after he'd attended to some business with the Hacketts that was not part of Gwynneth's advice.

He stood at the gate and politely called out to Mrs Hackett, once, twice, three times. It was clear that she was not going to answer, so he dropped the respectful approach and shouted to the household that he would get louder and let the whole neighbourhood know their business. In a flash, Mrs Hackett appeared in the gallery and beckoned to him. She let him into the drawing-room, closed the door and began to shower him with abuse.

"Louis?" Babsie called from somewhere in the house. "Louis! They're giving him away tonight! Somebody's coming for him. Don't let them take him!"

"Babsie!" Louis shouted back. "Doan worry youself. They cyaan take him." Then he said to Mrs Hackett, still speaking in a voice loud enough for Babsie to hear, "Madam, I come for my child." He flashed the registration paper at Mrs Hackett and threatened to go and report to the police that his child was being kidnapped.

"Nobody is taking any child..." Mrs Hackett began, but nearly jumped out of her skin at the sound of Babsie's voice right behind her.

"Here, Louis. Take him," Babsie said.

Mrs Hackett turned in anger and put her hands on Lennox, but before she could get a firm hold, Louis deftly intercepted, grabbed baby, blanket and all, and made a dash for the front door.

Mr and Mrs Hackett would have liked to put Babsie on a plane the next morning, but the arrangements were taking some time. In the period before she left they gave up trying to contain her, for she was determined to see her baby. She disappeared for hours to spend time with Lennox and Louis, no matter how frantic this made her parents. Lennox was almost six months old when, with a deep sigh of relief, they packed Babsie off to Canada, but not before she had dealt them a parting embarrassment.

Babsie bawled down the airport. Babsie put down a bawling that made the whole airport stop to watch – personnel behind the counter, passengers, family and friends of passengers, taxi drivers, guards, porters. Babsie related, to this sympathetic audience, the awful thing her cruel parents were doing to her. And her cruel parents were duly discomfited, what with people giving them cut-eye and some even throwing words.

Louis had got Marjorie to leave her job in St Paul and was paying her nearly half his monthly salary to take care of the baby. Louis's wage was meagre, but Marjorie's was pitiful. Half his salary was more than she was being paid by the restaurant for full time work. At this point in the story of Lennox Tantie Gwynnie often did some ranting. "If your Tantie Marjorie was a man," she'd say, "serving the same tables, washing the same dishes, and cleaning the same restaurant, they would a pay him more than she was getting. Just like how female teachers getting a lower salary than male teachers doing the same teaching."

Louis spent Lennox's first Christmas with him, and then left for England in January. Though Louis and Babsie continued to write to each other, the plan for them to meet up in England, settle there and send for Lennox became more and more of a pipe dream as time passed. Babsie was the first to get married, and about two years later, Louis announced his marriage, upon which Marjorie wrote to him to say that if *he* thought *she* was going to send Lennox up to him for any stepmother to treat him bad, that was a thought wasted. Marjorie agreed, however (because at the time it seemed a long way off), that when Lennox finished high school, he would go to England and study to be a doctor, or a lawyer, or – Tantie Gwynnie would add – whatever he wanted to be. Then he would come back home.

This agreement was made when Lennox was about five years old. It was a certainty he had come to take for granted. There were some of his schoolmates who lived under the same expectation – high school, and then off to England to study. Lennox was at Alleyne's, one of the private high schools that students at the College of the Ascension, and Prince Albert Edward College, and other such establishments, looked down their noses at. Its proper name was Academy of Excellence, but everybody called it "Alleyne's" after the retired schoolmaster who had founded it. Gwynneth was always singing the praises of schoolmasters like Alleyne, Foster and Blandin who, in their retirement from teaching, had set up high schools, creditable in their own right, and accessible to children of lesser means.

Of course, there were fees, and Lennox could only be at high school because Louis was paying his fees. Unlike Babsie, Louis was real. He was Lennox's provider and his pen pal. They wrote to each other all the time. In Lennox's early years, Gwynneth had encouraged Marjorie to send his drawings to his father, and Marjorie also wrote letters to Louis on Lennox's behalf, finding out from the child what he wanted to say. Marjorie would read Louis's letters aloud to his son, and she had never stopped supplying Louis with photos of Lennox as he grew.

The little sister in England also seemed to Lennox to be real enough, but not of major interest to him.

On the day Babsie's letter arrived, Gwynneth went over as soon as Lennox came home from school, to talk to him along with Marjorie. His eyes widened with alarm when they told him his mother was in Cayeri and wanted to see him.

"I doan want to go with her, Tantie Marjorie! You's my mother. I want to stay with you!"

Gwynneth sought to reassure him that Babsie was not coming to take him away, and in any case did not have any legal right to take him. She just wanted to see him, talk to him and know that he was happy. Lennox was not persuaded by any of this. He wanted Tantie Marjorie and Tantie Gwynneth to be present when he met with his mother.

"Yes, we'll be there. But what about if your Tantie Marjorie and I sit in for a short while with the two of you," Gwynneth proposed, "and then we leave you talk in privacy?"

(Marjorie was not in favour of this plan. She thought, but refrained from saying, that Babsie should not be left alone with Lennox.) Gwynneth assured Lennox that she and his Tantie Marjorie would be nearby all the time. Babsie's friend Claudette visited, and they arranged for Saturday afternoon.

Marjorie and Lennox were on tenterhooks all week. Lennox brooded and Marjorie fussed. But then the visit came and went, harmlessly. Babsie arrived with Claudette, driven by Claudette's husband. Marjorie went down the walk to meet them, while Gwynneth stood in the gallery with Lennox. When Babsie got out of the car and spotted Lennox, her two hands flew up to cover her mouth, and she stood staring at him as tears welled up in her eyes. Claudette came out of the car, and her husband waited while she went in with Babsie. They sat down in the drawing-room. Babsie was still a little overcome, so Lennox got up, strode over to her and asked whether she would like some juice. This was a big help, because Babsie laughed along with everybody else when Gwynneth, smiling broadly, said to Lennox, "A-a! So what about the rest of us? We ain have no mouth?"

Babsie requested water, and he brought her some, in a good

glass, with coaster and-all. Now that Babsie was more settled, Claudette excused herself and left to run errands. Marjorie and Gwynneth saw her off and sat down in the gallery. Marjorie remained perched on the edge of her seat, griping and fretting, as only muffled sounds of conversation were leaking out of the drawing-room. Lennox was not a boisterous child, and Babsie was not speaking any more loudly than he was. This made Marjorie suspicious, but she held her tongue.

After quite some time Lennox emerged, looking calm and cheerful. He announced that Babsie wanted to see Mumma. It was one of the weekends when Roy was in residence, so Gwynneth went over first, to let it be known that Mumma was having a visitor. Mumma was glad to see Babsie, and held a lively conversation with her.

When they went back over to his home, Lennox took Babsie on a tour of the yard, mainly to show her his garden. He picked some tomatoes to give to her. Then they went back inside and he took her to see his room. There he showed her his bookshelf, his school uniform, and the medals, prizes and certificates he had earned in school sports and the 4-H club. He brought forth some drawings he had done of landscapes: the view of the hills from his backyard; L'Anse Marron beach; a train pulling in to Turagua station; the palay with members of the iron band practising. Babsie asked if she could have one of the drawings, and chose the train.

Then they sat in the gallery where Marjorie served them soursop juice and coconut drops. Claudette came back for Babsie and found her and Lennox chatting as though they had known each other for all of Lennox's thirteen years.

23
Roy's project, however, was not going well.

They were seeing rather too much of Roy. Having done his inspection on the Saturday after Monica arrived, he returned on the following Tuesday evening, and Thursday evening, and again on Tuesday in the week after that. It had been agreed that Monica would have two weekends off in every month – the first and third – when she would be free to go home. They did not see him on those two weekends.

On the second weekend in October, Roy turned up in time for Sunday lunch. He did not join them at the table. Instead he went up into the land with a cardboard box which he filled up with zaboka and whatever else was bearing. He brought the box inside and placed it on the pantry table; then he peeped into the dining-room. They were still eating. He went into his room and came out later on to peep again. Roy was clearly hovering, waiting for them to get up from the table, and when they did, he sat down and ate alone. Only Mumma was interested enough to ask why, and his offhand answer did not shed any light. Having eaten, Roy announced that he was going to his room to take a nap.

Mumma seemed happy just to have her errant lagniappe child in the house more often, but Gwynneth and Viola knew what he was up to. They suspected that Mumma, too, could see right through him, though she said nothing to them. When, however, he arrived with Monica's pay at mid-morning on the fourth Saturday of October, settled in for the day, and slept over to Sunday, Mumma began to show concern. On Sunday morning when he emerged from his room, she asked him if he was leaving his wife and children in smart. He laughed it off and asked Mumma, "So I can't come and spend some time with my mother? I only have one mother, you know."

"Oho!" Mumma retorted. "So how much wife you have?"

After he'd had lunch, again by himself, Roy disappeared once more into his room. Later that afternoon, Mumma and Monica were in the drawing-room. They were both sitting on the couch, Mumma's neck supported by a pillow.

"You still going to school?" Mumma asked.

"You ain remember, Nenn Estelle?" Monica replied, patiently. "I pass my exam and get my school leaving paper."

Mumma pondered this for a bit, then asked, "So why you doing servant work?"

Monica stroked Mumma's hair and kissed her. "So you ain glad I come to see about you?"

"Yes, *Doudou*. But what about when you finish with me? You going and do servant work all you life?"

"No, Nennen. I saving my money so I could go to commercial school."

"Oho! Like Viola?" Mumma's face brightened, and she went on to relate, with much cackling, the events of the day her mother pulled her out of school.

In a more sombre tone, Estelle revealed to Monica that she would have liked to go back to school, even after the trouble with the teacher, and her mother going over there with her bell and her cocoyea broom to make them fart. A week or so after that incident, the Father-priest visited her family to let them know that the teacher who broke her fingers with his belt-buckle had been reprimanded, and that they were looking forward to Estelle coming back to school. Her parents, Sarah and George, entertained the Father-priest politely and when he got up to go, bade him farewell with many good wishes.

George had never been too keen on this schooling zaffaire that they were luring blackpeople children into. He simply did not trust it, like everything else that came from the whitepeople. He had sent the boys to school for as long as it took them to learn how to read, write and count. (He himself could not read or write, but he could very well count his little money, and nobody coulda bamboozle George Casimir.) He needed his sons on the land to help with the cocoa and coffee which brought in cash, and to work in the garden so the family would have food to eat as well as take to the market.

Sarah wanted more for her girl-pickney. She wanted Estelle to take in more schooling so she could become a nurse or a teacher. After the visit from the Father-priest, Sarah was inclined to give the school another chance, but George was convinced that schooling was a whitepeople komplo to thief the children spirit. Estelle was disappointed, but not willing to mount a rebellion against her family. Against the hateful Standard Three teacher, yes, she had rebelled by speaking only Patois and pretending not to understand English, which drove him into paroxysms of temper. She resigned herself to working at home with her family, in the house and on the land, instead of going to school. But Sarah could see that she was languishing.

At school Estelle had done well in needlework, and she loved to sew. She had made her own school uniform and church clothes, the curtains at Christmas time, dolly clothes, shirts for her brothers… Sarah decided to go and see Miss Dalrymple, a seamstress much admired for her sewing, who took in girls to help her with tasks like basting and hemming, taking out seams, sewing on buttons and fasteners, and some housework. In return, the girls learned her trade. Miss Dalrymple agreed to give Estelle a try-out, and was very pleased with her. Estelle, for her part, was happy to go to her house on three days in every week. It was with great fondness that Mumma recalled her time at Miss Dalrymple.

One of the people Miss Dalrymple sewed for was the estate owner's wife, Mistress Medford. On her regular visits to have clothes made, Mistress Medford seemed to be closely inspecting Miss Dalrymple's girls at work, and paying more and more attention to Estelle as time passed. After about a year and a half, Miss Dalrymple admitted to George and Sarah that there was nothing more she could teach Estelle about sewing, and testified to the estate owner's wife that the girl did not steal. Mistress Medford then approached Estelle's parents with the offer of a job for her.

The Medfords' cocoa estate lay at a little distance outside Beauregard, along Old San Pedro Road, and their family home (the Great-House, as people called it when Mumma was a girl) stood just short of two miles from Pilgrim Road corner. Close enough, George and Sarah decided, and they agreed that Estelle could take up the offer, if she was willing to.

At first her job in the Medfords' house was to look after their two boys, but when they reached the ages of ten and eleven, they were shipped off to boarding-school in England. Estelle then became

258

chief-cook-and-bottle-washer, at the age of seventeen, replacing the over-exhausted Wilma who was glad to go home to her little house and garden and her man and her grands. The Medfords now wanted Estelle to live in their servant quarters and go home on weekends, as Wilma had done, but George and Sarah bluntly refused. Estelle continued to leave for work every morning at five o'clock. She happily fell in with the band of estate workers making their way down Pilgrim Road on mornings at that hour to get to the Old Road. Along the Old Road, part of the band turned off about half a mile before Medford, into the plantation owned by Boucaud, and the rest continued on to Medford's.

On evenings, she set out for home as soon as she could put dinner on the Medfords' table. She would go back every morning and meet everything right there, with the skirt of the tablecloth turned up to cover the mess: plates with chewed-up bones; sticky cutlery and dessert bowls; nasty napkins; leftover food in open dishes overrun by crazy-ants; flies and bees hovering ... The mess was even worse before, when the Medford boys were there. In the last months of the year, when darkness fell early, Albert or Cecil would go and fetch her home. And at home on weekends, her family did not allow her to lift a finger.

Years later, when Estelle, a grown woman with husband and children, took her daughters to spend time in Pilgrim, she would sometimes get up from her bed fore-day morning and wait in the gallery to wish blessings on a new generation of estate workers trekking to work in the semi-darkness. Gwynneth or Viola, or both girls, might also wake up to stand beside her in the gallery and wave at them.

Gwynneth still carried in her head the sight of this almost ghostly phalanx of men and women passing swiftly before her. They moved in a close huddle, at a purposeful speed. Were it not for the swishing of their feet, one could think that they were moving without touching the ground. Some wore sapats, some were barefoot. Their heads were covered, some with old, battered felt or straw hats; others, men and women, had their heads tied with cloth. Everything about them looked grey.

They carried tools – a hoe over the shoulder, or a cutlass in the hand. They each held a cloth bag or a little cloth bundle tied in a knot. This was their breakfast, Gwynneth learned when she asked Mumma. Gwynneth could hear chatting inside their ranks, but could not catch what they were saying. They waved and answered Mumma's greeting, and in quick time they would be past the house, still in the tight huddle that seemed to brook no straggling.

~

Roy was awake. He had stepped out of his room, and was heading for the kitchen. He heard Mumma's voice coming from the drawing-room and thought nothing of it, until he caught the word "Medford". That stopped him in his tracks. He tiptoed across the pantry and stole a glance through the dining-room door to see who she was talking to. Then he pulled back and took up a position out of sight, to eavesdrop.

He was livid. Why was she revealing all of this information to the servant? He could hear Gwynneth and Viola chatting in the gallery, so he came out of hiding, strode indignantly past the dining-table and past Mumma and Monica, barely acknowledging them, to the gallery where he summoned his sisters: "A word with you two, please."

They didn't even bother to turn their heads in his direction. They were sitting on the gallery couch, facing the outdoors. Viola steupsed, and Gwynneth said to the air in front of her, "Well, talk nuh!"

Neither of the two moved a muscle.

Roy insisted, "In private, please!"

Viola replied, "A-a. Well we 'in private' right here. We home at us."

"Stop playing with me!" Roy hissed.

They were just beginning to enjoy provoking him, but Gwynneth suspected that he had overheard Mumma talking, and she knew that since his secondary school days Roy was liable to get worked up whenever there was mention of Mumma having been a servant. It would probably not be a good idea to rile him up any further, so Gwynneth got up with a long-drawn-out sigh and led the way down the front steps. They walked around the house to the backyard bench.

He began to sputter before Gwynneth and Viola could properly seat themselves on the bench, leaving him on his feet.

"So I am paying money for this girl to come here and sit down on her tail doing nothing, just liming?"

"Doan be an ass!" Gwynneth fumed. "Monica doing all the work we expect of her, and more! You should be happy that she willing to spend time sitting down with you mother, chatting with her, and even more important, listening to her. When last you spend five minutes chatting with Mumma? And when last her grandchildren spend even one minute chatting with they grandmother?"

As though Gwynneth had not spoken, Roy continued: "And what is this business of having the servant seated at the table with you? Why can't she eat in the pantry and one of you help Mumma handle her food?"

"What!" Gwynneth and Viola exclaimed at the same time. The two of them exchanged glances, understanding now why he chose to eat alone.

Gwynneth calmed herself. "Roy, you asking us to treat Monica the way the Medfords treated your mother? You want to hear more about you mother in Medford house?"

Roy turned abruptly and left them. He stamped up the back steps and into his room, shut the door and threw himself on the bed. But there was no way to shut out the sniggering of Ascension boys, including himself, behind the back of Anderson Mitchell, the free place boy...

~

It was one of the light-skinned Creole boys from a well-off family who whispered around the class that Mitchell's mother was a servant. He knew the house where she worked, in Brierly. The boys all agreed that their fathers did not think they would be paying good money out of their pockets to send their sons to school with the servants' children. Roy hastened to make it known to all who would hear that his father was a schoolmaster, and his mother did not work, for this he understood to be the rule for mothers in proper families.

What was Mitchell doing up there, in Ascension College? Clifford Hinds's father was a lawyer, but what was this other one doing there? It was so plain to see that Mitchell was out of place.

Government College was the place for boys like Mitchell. His hair – why didn't he keep it low? Such an abundance of *chivé tak-tak*, almost half an inch standing up on his head, was an affront to decent people's eyes. Some boys swore that he smelled of rancid coconut oil. He couldn't pronounce *th*. They made fun of his nose, calling him "Broadway", until in literature class they met Longfellow's poem beginning "Under a spreading chestnut tree" and renamed him "Chestnut".

There were only three dark-skinned boys in the class – Hinds, Mitchell, and himself – "like three black-pepper grains in the sugar," the maths teacher would joke, and have the whole class laughing with him. Hinds found a place among the five well-off Creole boys of lighter skin, every one of them bent on eventually finding a place among the white boys. Mitchell latched on to Roy, with the comment, "Well, pardner, we will have to stick to-gether!" and Roy accommodated him at first, for that was a daunting time.

In the early days, Roy had the distinct impression that the Creole-but-well-off boys were fleeing at his approach, and he was certain that the white boys, the bulk of his classmates, just looked straight through him, as though he were a ghost.

He had never come so close to such people. At his primary school there was one child from a poor-white family, but everyone knew that bakra-johnny did not count as real whitepeople. And there were any number of red-skinned Creole children who were of no greater worth, either, than anyone else. With no wealth or social standing to speak of, they were just red-niggers. The one-one whitepeople he knew were distant beings: Father McVorran, an incarnation of God; Mr Laurent, the Manager of Turagua Estate, and his family, who sat in their own front pew at St Anthony's church; and the overseer, who seldom ventured off the estate, but was sighted in the village now and then, like a character from myth, in khaki clothes and cork hat, riding on a horse...

The preparation Roy's father had given him for life at Ascension was: "This is whitepeople you will be going to school with, boy. I never had that chance. Don't go and show your worst colours up there, now. Learn from the whitepeople and better yourself."

When one of the whiteboys' cliques at Ascension adopted him, he was thrilled, even after he realised that they had taken him in to be their caddie-boy. Roy would go and stand in the long tuck-shop line with their money and the list of their orders. He did homework for some of them who couldn't cope with it or couldn't be bothered. He waited at the gate on mornings for clique members who rode to school, and he wheeled their bicycles to the shed for them so they could head straight for the clique's before-assembly huddle in which he had no part...

He did everything he could to shake off Mitchell. It soon became clear that Mitchell was by far the brightest student in the class, which was not surprising – he was in their school because he had won a college exhibition. Back in those days there were only four college exhibitions each year, given to the four boys who got the highest marks of all the children in Cayeri who had sat the exam. Mitchell was one of the four in that year's batch.

By the third week of the term, two whiteboy cliques were vying to recruit Mitchell so he could be their homework man. None of this affected in any way the sniggering behind Mitchell's back. He was still a tar-baby, a golliwog, an FPB (for Free Place Boy, or Free Place Blackamoor), the son of a servant. Roy joined in the sniggering and mauvay-lang at every opportunity, and lived every day in fear of somebody finding out that his own mother had once been a servant.

~

One afternoon Gwynneth looked out from the shed into the yard and saw Monica hanging out clothes. Among Mumma's nighties and housecoats and flannels and pillowcases strung up on the line, she spied two shirts of Roy's, flapping and waving in the breeze. She was enraged, but calmed herself and continued the reading lesson with her fidgety Standard Twos.

Usually if the afternoon was so hot and stuffy that it made the children restless, she would take them all outdoors. Under the shade of the mango doudouce tree one set would stand in a semicircle and finish their reading. Some would gather under the caïmite tree that stood on the edge of the bush, to recite their multiplication tables with the help of a Fourth Standard pupil. Another group might be sent around the yard to collect plants and put them in jam bottles with water for the next day's nature study lesson. When all of that had been

263

done satisfactorily, the rest of the afternoon would be for storytelling, cricket, rounders, ring-games, or music time – whatever they chose, as long as they had done their work.

But this afternoon she was in no mood. And there was a strong breeze blowing into the schoolroom, anyway, so it wasn't all that stuffy. After school was dismissed, she marched indoors with a grim face and barged into Roy's room, where her suspicion was confirmed; he had moved a stock of clothes into his old wardrobe and chest-of-drawers.

The next time he visited, which was not long after, she took him to task. He argued that he was paying Monica's salary, so what could be so wrong with her doing some washing for him.

"Roy, Monica is to wash for Mumma and Mumma only. Viola and I are washing our own clothes. Monica has enough to do looking after your mother. And what, you living here, now? Her Royal Highness put you out? If you doan stop giving Monica your dirty clothes to wash, I will send and tell Helen how you running behind a young-girl over here. Then, for sure, she going put you out. You have no shame."

Roy's project, however, was not going well. Monica had the most amazing ability to ignore him and his attention, even at such close quarters. Roy would sit in Puppa's chair, following her every move with his eyes as she cleaned the drawing-room and dining-room, and all the while the expression on her face would be that of a person completely absorbed in the work she was doing, or in her own thoughts. From time to time her silence would slide into absently talking to herself, or humming snatches of a hymn.

Roy would make muffled remarks to Monica when there was no one else in the room. Her answer could be heard from almost any part of the house: "Yes, Sir." "No, Sir." "No thanks, Sir." But try as they might, neither Gwynneth nor Viola could make out exactly what he was saying to her. All they could hear was the oily cajoling and flattery in his tone.

On one occasion, though, they did hear both tone and text. It was a Saturday afternoon and Monica was tidying the dining-room after lunch. After a period of murmuring under his breath and getting the usual blank responses from her, Roy suddenly blurted out, "Who do you think you are!"

Gwynneth and Viola were in the kitchen and both rushed to the door of the dining-room. Monica, who had been folding the tablecloth, now stood with it in her hands as she answered him: "I am Monica Polydore, Sir."

Gwynneth and Viola hurriedly backed away from the door and retreated into the kitchen with their hands over their mouths, stifling their amused wonderment.

Roy disappeared for a couple of weeks, resurfacing on Monica's next payday. On the fourth Saturday of every month thereafter he would arrive, bright and early, to bring Monica's pay, to see Mumma, to make sure he took his share of whatever fruits were in season, and to linger in the house until evening. He would also arrive unannounced from time to time on a weekday. His purpose, he said, was to see to it that he was getting his money's worth out of the servant.

Gaston was becoming a habit once more, as in the days of Catherine Street, when again and again they would quarrel and separate for a period of time, at the end of which he would turn up on her doorstep, and she could not find it in her heart to chase him away. Now Gwynneth knew that she was having a relapse, when she came home from church one Sunday, met his car parked by the gate, and thought nothing of it. As she entered the house, she heard his voice coming from the kitchen, wrapped in the sounds and aromas of Sunday-lunch cooking in progress.

He was trying to answer Viola in Patois, which he understood perfectly but spoke less well. His grandmother had spoken with him in Patois from his early childhood, much to the displeasure of his father, a displeasure which the father just had to swallow. In the long run, however, home and school had joined forces to beat the Patois out of him. Whenever he tried to use what was left of it, he had to fill in the blanks here and there with English words. Viola was patiently helping to restore his vocabulary.

Gaston was visiting unannounced (to Gwynneth, at any rate), had infiltrated the kitchen, and was obviously going to be most present at Sunday lunch. All with the complicity of her busybody sister, Madame Matchmaker. Only weeks before, Gwynneth would have been highly annoyed.

24

"Bless you, Papa Kofi. Look we Kamboulay still alive."

They went to Miss Verna's home on the Sunday afternoon – Gwynneth, Gaston, Kelvin and Reynold. She led them across the grassy area at the back of her house to where the shed stood, barely visible, as the bush was trying to reclaim the spot it occupied. Kelvin and Reynold immediately set about peeling away the covering of leafy vines draped over it. Miss Verna showed them where the door was, and they uprooted the tall weeds rising from the ground in front of it before they cleared off the vines that held it shut.

Kelvin and Reynold fought with the door and finally succeeded in wrenching it open. They all peered inside. The carpenter's workbench stood abandoned, with one or two stools and a low pile of planks stacked against one wall, all dirtied with small-creature droppings. When the boys stepped in, rows of bats hanging upside down from the rafters began detaching themselves and circulating blindly overhead. Lizards scurried in all directions, along the walls and between the weeds that pushed up through the floorboards.

It was agreed that the band members would come on Monday afternoon and first cutlass the whole of Miss Verna's yard, then fix up the shed. They would now be responsible for keeping her yard cut low, from the hedge at the front, right back to where the forested part of her land began, a little way behind the shed. They would also help with the chores that Reynold had been doing for her, and anything else she needed help with. There was to be no iron-beating in Miss Verna's ears after 9 o'clock in the night, and no rowdiness at any time whatsoever.

At the end of the visit, the two boys had already pulled up most of the weeds growing inside the shed, and Kelvin was still looking around the space as though it was all likely to disappear when he woke up. They couldn't have been happier. The two of them just beamed, wordlessly, at Miss Verna. Now, regarding the future of the band, the only thing left to furrow Kelvin's brow was the court case, coming up in just over a week.

The court put Kelvin, Ralph and the other set of boys each on a bond of good behaviour. Outside the courthouse, Gaston had a word with the family members of Kelvin and Ralph. He repeated what he had said in his previous conversation with them: "Support your boys in the work they are doing with their band. Don't listen to people who are trying to give every boy in an iron band a bad name. You know that your boys are not badjohns. What they are doing is good, constructive work that can keep them out of trouble. They are achieving great things and they will make you proud."

The parents had turned up at Gaston's office weeks before the court appearance, with bags and boxes containing fruits and vegetables, as well as bottles of preserves and home-made wines. This was a common occurrence in the lives of lawyers who did *pro bono* work where they saw the need, but Gaston was never any less touched by the gesture. He accepted the families' gifts graciously. What he received was much more than he could use or properly store, and he knew he would have to think up a list of people he could share it with.

St Paul Syncopators had cutlassed Miss Verna's yard, cleaned up the shed and installed their instruments. On the Saturday after the court case, in the presence of the whole band and invited guests – Gwynneth, Gaston and Phillip – Miss Verna blessed the new home of the band.

Late in November, Gwynneth, Gaston and Ollie visited Phillip's band. Reverend Fields had invited them to perform at the orphanage's Christmas concert, and they were preparing for that event. Phillip told the visitors that he would have liked to make a pan with notes to play the chorus of a Christmas carol at the concert. He had decided, however, that there was still more work to be done with just the idea of putting musical notes on a paint tin, before they could play tunes in public.

He had been working on weekday evenings to improve the old pan with the three notes on it, in order to develop more skill at the task. On some evenings his neighbour, Learie, joined him in this endeavour, and sometimes Phantom. They were eager to report on what they had achieved thus far. First, they showed off the pan-sticks. The boys had taken further Gaston's suggestion of a shock absorber. Phillip had got hold of the discarded inner tube of a bicycle tyre which he cut into strips. Now one end of each stick was tightly wrapped in rubber, as Gaston had demonstrated with cloth strips from his handkerchief.

The notes on Phillip's old paint tin were three little islands scattered on its base. Gwynneth had made two suggestions. One was to try sinking a "canal" around each note to prevent other sounds around it from leaking into it. The other was to even out the surface of each note, using a hammer, so that the sound would be the same all over that note. In making the dent around the first note, they had met with the very accident that she had cautioned against: the chisel they were using punctured the metal from time to time. This, however, would turn out to be a happy accident.

They managed to sink a groove around the second note without any puncturing, and then they worked on smoothing out its surface. When they struck these two notes, one after the other, the one with the accidental cuts around it seemed cleaner than the one with the intact canal. They speculated on whether a canal was what they needed, or a canal with cuts, or just cuts? Did they really have to make a canal? Wouldn't it be enough to just make some slight nicks around the note, with a smaller chisel? Learie came up with an idea. "You see all that pounding and cutting with the chisel? Them cuts go make the pan bust and mash-up quick. What about if we just take a nail and punch some lil holes around the note?"

This suggestion was put to the test on the third note. Now they sounded each of the three notes for their visitors to hear, and they agreed that the third solution was the best – just punching nail-holes around the note.

Phillip announced that after Christmas they were going to get a new pan and place more notes on it, in a more orderly way. "I was only pounding on this old pan to smooth out the bumpiness. Then, hearing these sounds, I just put a note wherever I hear a different sound; but on the new pan, we going and lay out notes side by side, in a ring around the edge. Then we go be using *two* sticks to play on the pan."

For the St Hilda's Orphanage Christmas function, they performed "Go Tell It on the Mountain"; a parang song, "*Alegria Alegria*"; and a syncopated version of "Hark, the Herald Angels Sing". They followed their usual rotine of beating out a rhythm to accompany the singing of each song. Not only did Phillip's band play at that event, for which they were paid a fee; Kelvin's band was hired to play at St Paul Government School's Christmas bazaar. Then, on Christmas morning, the bands created a sensation in Turagua and St Paul by coming out on the road, each parading from the band's home to the savannah and back – Warahoons to Turagua savannah and Syncopators to St Paul savannah – repeating the performances they had given at the Christmas functions, among other numbers. The police didn't bat an eyelid, not inclined, perhaps, to be the killjoy on a Christmas morning.

The boys were bursting with excitement at the approach of their first Carnival on the road. At the last Carnival, Kelvin's band was only months old, and Phillip's had not yet been formed. Now, Phillip's project to make a new pan with notes got further put off to after Carnival 1941. They would not need it for parading on the road. One pan playing a tune in a Carnival band would be drowned by the noise of tamboo bamboo, iron-beating, and a whole crowd singing as though bent on raising the dead. Both bands spent the two months between Christmas 1940 and Carnival 1941 perfecting rhythms for people to sing and chip along casually, or jump-up to.

On the morning of February 24, 1941, Carnival Monday, a Jouvay crowd gathered in semi-darkness at the bottom of San Miguel Road, waiting for the band to come down. A loud cheer went up at the first tinkle to be heard from the hill. There was even louder cheering, with clapping, when the band came into view. Some people went up to meet them. The crowd followed San Miguel Warahoons up and down the main road, from one end of Turagua to the other, with more and more people joining in all along the route. This continued until mid-morning. In St Paul, Kelvin's band also came out for Jouvay, to be followed, too, by a gleeful crowd.

Carnival in Turagua ended with Jouvay, but in St Paul, Carnival was always a full-blown affair, with bands coming out on both days: on the Monday morning for Jouvay; on Monday and Tuesday afternoon for pretty-mas and all the other kinds of costumed bands; and on Tuesday after dark until midnight, for Last Lap. When San Miguel Warahoons got on the train to St Paul on the afternoon of Carnival Monday, there was barely enough room for them and their instruments. The carriages were packed tight with Carnival peongs from further east, heading either for St Paul, or for the grander festivities in Kings Port. The buses were also arriving from the east already full, so that many Turaguans were walking to St Paul.

Warahoons and Syncopators had agreed to parade separately in St Paul for Carnival Monday and Tuesday, for two iron bands would be better than one. There were tambooo bamboo, brass and string bands, but no other iron bands. The more bands on the streets of St Paul for Carnival, the merrier, as people came not only from Oropuna and villages further east, but also from Plaisance and Canaan, some to play mas, some to watch mas, and others to chip or jump-up behind a band.

As it turned out, Phillip's new project got postponed again after Carnival 1941. For one thing, the band was getting more engagements – a birthday party here, a christening there, and the Turagua Stars football club retained them to play at their league matches, which sometimes meant travelling with them to another part of St Michael County. Now, Phillip did not have as much time to work on the new pan. The other thing, however, was that not all the members of Phillip's band shared his enthusiasm for making notes on a pan to play tunes – not beyond their excitement at his first tuned pan. It was the same with Kelvin's band. Kelvin himself was not averse to the idea, but he had not acted on it. The boys had been drawn to iron-beating by the headiness of rhythm, and better still, rhythm enhanced by the glorious tones that came from striking metal objects.

Phillip's Uncle Melville had obtained another five-gallon paint tin for him, but apart from cleaning it, which involved using turpentine to scrub off the film of hardening paint left on the inside, Phillip had not yet done any other work on it. This Gwynneth learned from probing Lennox about the pan-tuning. She sent a message to Phillip via Lennox, asking him to come and see her one day, after work.

It was early September, 1941. The two bands were due to make a guest appearance again at St Hilda's Harvest Fair, on the third Saturday of October. When Phillip came to see Gwynneth, he told her that his band had also been booked for some paid engagements over the Christmas season, and he wanted to put notes on his new pan to play the chorus of "Go Tell It on the Mountain". "Last year, for the Christmas songs, we still just beat the rhythm and sing to it. This Christmas, if is for one song at least, I want us come out with tune."

"Good going, Phillip. How many notes you need for that chorus?" Gwynneth asked.

"I doan know yet, Miss."

"Sing it lemme hear."

Phillip sang:

Go tell it on the mountain
Over the hills and everywhere
Go tell it on the mountain
That Jesus Christ is born.

"All right," Gwynneth said, getting up. "Let's go to the piano and find out how many notes you will need."

They found out that he would need five notes for the first line.

"And the third line is the same as the first – same words, same tune," Gwynneth pointed out. "Now, making five notes on the pan will take some time, and you'll have to add more notes for the second and fourth lines. What about tuning the pan, for now, to play just the first and the third lines, and the band can sing the other two? You could perform the chorus in this way at Harvest Fair, and then aim at adding the notes for the other two lines in time for the Christmas engagements. There you would be able to play the tune of the whole chorus."

Phillip was nodding vigorously. "Okay, Miss! Thanks, Miss!"

He brought the pan to Gwynneth in the second week of October and played the line for her. It was crude, yes, not all the notes quite as precise as they could be, some a little off-key, but it was a marvellous achievement. Gwynneth clapped and insisted on giving him a hug-up. There and then she put to him the idea that she had been turning over in her head for some time, but still needed to think through.

Gwynneth had recognised that some formal training in music could be useful to these young men as they forged ahead with their invention. If melody gained importance in this venture, as she felt it would, there were a few basic things they needed to know about. She could offer a weekly class to members of the two bands, where they would be introduced to the rudiments – notes, scales, key, harmonising, etc., as well as reading and notating music.

She felt, however, that some of the boys might not wish to be pressed into anything resembling school. She also chided herself for wanting to create a whole new weekly commitment to add to her workload, just when she had settled into an easier life with Monica joining the household. But now Phillip's enthusiasm and his diligence convinced her that she had to offer this help. It occurred to her that it was not necessary to set up a class. She could just incorporate Phillip into her piano lessons schedule, and the band members would benefit from what he learned. Phillip was thrilled, and eager to start.

Gwynneth wondered whether Kelvin would be as keen as Phillip. If he could also be exposed to the basic training, he, too, could pass it on to his band members, but as she and Gaston had discovered, Kelvin was, to all intents and purposes, illiterate. That would be a hindrance. She decided that Gaston would be the best person to go and speak with him, to let him know that Teacher Gwynneth was willing to help him with his reading and writing, and to give him music lessons, one thing at a time – the reading and writing first.

Gaston spoke with Kelvin and reported back that the young man had expressed one fear: he didn't want to be placed in a class of students who could already read and write. Once he was assured that Teacher Gwynneth was going to teach him by himself, he readily accepted the offer of help. He told Gaston that he had been taken out of school in Standard 2, when he was twelve years old in a class of mostly eight- and nine-year-old children, all more skilled and knowledgeable than him. One day his father went to the school to complain that the boy did not seem to be learning anything, and found out that he had not been going to school every day.

In the first place, Kelvin had not started school until he was six years old, going on seven, because when he was five, there was no room in ABC class at any of the primary schools in St Paul. Then, in his first year of school, he got whooping cough. He remained sickly after this illness, and his family kept him at home for a year. His granny was alive at the time, and she would not allow them to send him back to school until she considered he was strong enough. On his return to school he was placed, not in Second Primer, which he had missed entirely, but in the next class up, Introductory, where he floundered, so he was kept there for an extra year. He was also kept in the next class, Standard 1, for two years, and as a result he turned twelve in Standard 2.

That was when he got in with a side of boys from Standard 4 to Standard 6 (an age range he fitted into) who hated school as much as he did, and who had solved the problem by breaking *bish* two or three days a week. Their main hideout was down by the river. Sometimes they followed the river up into the mountainside to pick mango, pommerac, balata, mammy sepote and tonka bean, and feast on these as they sat out the school day under the trees. On some days they raided a backyard or two for fruit, on their way to the river. They bypassed cashew trees, for as juicy and tempting as the fruit looked, it was not something to eat in your school uniform. Cashew juice left indelible stains on your clothes.

At the river, some of the boys might catch crayfish or guppy, while others went and dug up wild yam, to make a cook. They roasted the food on a bed of large stones. They sometimes bathed in the river, carefully spreading their school clothes on nearby bushes before they waded into the water. If Curtis, the biggest boy, managed to smuggle out a poonya from his home, they would make their way over to the canefield that extended from Turagua almost to St Paul. With the other boys on the lookout for Turagua Estate constables, Mervyn would chop off some lengths of cane that they cut up afterwards and sucked down by the river.

"And so," Gaston concluded, "Kelvin, like some of his colleagues in *lékòl bish*, has never properly learned to read or write. But he is more than willing to learn now. I can sense that he won't waste this opportunity."

Kelvin and Phillip were busy with their bands' preparations for Christmas engagements, and in January, they would be going straight into preparations for Carnival 1942. There could be no thought of lessons – in literacy or in music – before March. Gwynneth also decided it would be best to stagger the starting dates of these two undertakings. She would first tutor Kelvin and bring him to a level of literacy that would allow him and Phillip to begin music lessons together.

The two bands paraded on the streets again on Christmas morning, 1941. Once more, neither Turagua nor St Paul police were moved to object, while in Kings Port the authorities were getting more serious about wartime restrictions. There, people also came out and celebrated Christmas in the Carnival style, but some were arrested by police. From New Year's Day, the two bands began preparing in earnest for Carnival 1942, and for the next six and a half weeks they rehearsed without flagging. Each of the two bands also worked on obtaining some kind of costuming that would allow its members to come out in uniform style.

St Paul Syncopators wanted to come out as a sailor band. However, when they calculated the cost of cloth for thirteen sailor costumes, not to speak of paying a tailor or seamstress to get them sewn, they settled for just getting sailor caps, and a few cans of baby-powder that some of their faithful followers would shower on spectators along the route. They named their Carnival band "The USS All Aboard".

San Miguel Warahoons spent a week or two collecting sturdy feathers, dyes, and old khaki pants to be cut into strips for head bands. Then they turned the palay into a mas camp where they worked feverishly on dyeing the feathers and attaching them to the strips of cloth, to produce some modest headdresses that would pass for black-Indian mas. On Carnival Sunday, they would grind charcoal to dust, mix it with coconut oil, and paint their faces on the Monday and Tuesday to go on the road. Syncopators and Warahoons were preparing with all their hearts.

Then came the crushing disappointment of Carnival 1942. They had been half expecting it, for they had heard rumours. Yet they were hoping against hope. All over Cayeri, people with Carnival in their blood were working day and night on their costumes and accoutrements to play mas – old-mas, pretty-mas, mud-mas, bat-mas, cow-mas, devil-mas, minstrel, wild-Indian, fancy-Indian, black-Indian, fancy-sailor, midnight robber, moko jumbie, Dame Lorraine, Pierrot Grenade, and more... Every mas-player gearing up for the Jouvay-to-Last-Lap bacchanal. Music bands and chantwelles practising their songs. Street vendors stocking up for the two days' worth of heavy sales.

Preparations for the Carnival were in full swing when the Governor, Sir Charles Robotham (to Cayerians, "Charlie No-Bottom") announced, just one week before said Carnival, that as a measure "necessary for the defence of the colony in time of war", there would be no Carnival. The boys were inconsolable. And a large part of the Cayerian population was outraged. The Governor could not be in his right mind. His words meant that for however long this damn war was likely to last, people would not be allowed to come out and celebrate on the streets as they were accustomed to, neither at Carnival, nor Discovery Day, nor Christmas, nor New Year's Day, nor any other occasion! The 1940 calypso "Keep Allyou War Over There" enjoyed a new surge of popularity.

Now the rumour was that in town, the badjohn bands – in Bourg Ravine, LaCour Danglade, Jericho, Morne Cabrite, and Rat Hole – were planning to come out for Carnival all the same, with sticks and stones concealed in their clothes to fight with police, and that the police were just waiting for them, hefting their batons and licking their chops. There was also talk of a British warship anchored out at sea, ready and waiting to offload a contingent of soldiers, armed to the teeth, who would overrun Kings Port and any other place where people dared to defy the ban.

Gwynneth did not wish to take these rumours too seriously, but along with the rumours, a lavway had sprung up in Kings Port and was making its way around the colony:

Is Charlie No-Bottom
Whay ban we Canaval.

Charlie No-Bottom:
Go to hell.

When it reached Gwynneth's ears she became a little anxious. Suppose her boys were moved to respond to this rallying call? All of the members of Kelvin's and Phillip's bands were still under-age. She admired the spirit of resistance in Cayerians, but thought that some ways of resisting should be left to adult Cayerians. *And nobody going have it to say, Look how that woman Gwynneth Cuffie send people chirren to fight with police for they to end up in jail and get police record to they name!* She sent a frantic message to Phillip and Kelvin that she would like to visit their bands on Carnival Sunday afternoon, with Mr Gaston.

In each of the two camps they encountered long faces and an atmosphere heavy with depression. Gwynneth and Gaston spent about an hour with each band, trying to cheer up the boys, and above all, entreating them not to come out on the road at any time over the next two days and get themselves into trouble with the police. They did not, and neither did any other citizens of Turagua or St Paul who would normally have taken to the streets at Carnival to make merry. In Kings Port, however, there was ruction. Some iron bands attempting to come out were stopped by the police. Some managed to parade on the streets for some distance, with crowds following, but were soon chased off under blows from police batons.

Not everyone was readily cowed. Revellers taunted the police, or pelted them with bottles and stones. "Is Charlie No-Bottom" resounded from street to street as the Black Maria carted people away and returned for more. People were arrested, some for just standing their ground, refusing to run when the police were chasing crowds away. People were beaten, detained at will, hauled before the courts, fined, or jailed.

As Gwynneth listened to the news on Carnival Monday night, her thoughts went to Kofi and his act of resistance, defending his drum with all his might that Kamboulay morning when they dragged him off and lost him away in jail. That was a decade or so before the battle royal of 1881 – the clash between the united front of Kamboulay bands and the huge contingent of police sent to drive them off the streets forever, or so the authorities hoped.

"Bless you," Gwynneth murmured. "Bless you, Papa Kofi. Look we Kamboulay still alive."

And the resistance was not over on Carnival Monday, 1942. In spite of the arrests and beatings and detentions in police station cells, some intrepid revellers came out on the following day. There was defiant parading again, and the Black Maria on busy patrol again.

Phillip and Kelvin and their band members were unhappy that they could no longer take the music onto the road, but in the days to come they would still be called upon from time to time to play at a contained function such as a house party, a concert, or a sports event. When they were not rehearsing for these performances, they would buckle down to sharpening their playing skills and further developing their instruments. Other iron bands did the same.

Kelvin also buckled down to the task of learning to read and write. He turned up faithfully for his session with Gwynneth in her schoolroom every Tuesday after work, and by July, she considered that he had acquired the most basic of the literacy skills needed to start music lessons – recognising all the letters of the alphabet; holding a pencil and guiding it across a page to form letters in a line. He was making great strides with reading – he had built up an impressive stock of words that he recognised on sight, and was bravely fighting his way through decoding whole sentences.

Yet he still had some way to go before he could be deemed fully literate. Gwynneth could sense, though, that he had grown in self-confidence as he progressed, and she suggested to him one day that he join the adult education programme held after hours at St Paul Government School. There he could improve his literacy to the point where he would be eligible to join the class that prepared students for the school leaving certificate. Gwynneth was gratified to learn that before the week was out, he had gone and registered himself in the programme.

After some months of music lessons, Kelvin and Phillip began to pass on this training to their band members. Later in the year, Ainsley arranged for Kelvin and Phillip, and one other member from each band, to visit Franklin's band, Squadron 7. Gwynneth and the four boys – Phillip and Learie, Kelvin and Reynold – were met at the Kings Port railway terminus by Ollie and Gaston.

They drove up King George Street to the outskirts of Morne Cabrite and parked near the bottom of Bedeau Lane. They walked up the lane to Ainsley's house, and then he led them through a maze of little winding lanes that sometimes turned into steps. This was familiar ground to Ollie, who was born in Morne Cabrite and had spent the greater part of his childhood there. On arriving at Franklin's home, they paid their respects to his parents in the gallery before making their way around the house to the backyard.

This was Squadron 7's base. The yard looked cramped and cluttered, but the band seemed to be operating comfortably in what space was left among the laden clotheslines, the washing-tub, dasheen patch, fig stool, rubbish-burning spot and other backyard fixtures. Some of the band members were sitting on the gnarled roots of an almond tree. While Ainsley was introducing the visitors, Franklin's father brought out a chair for Gwynneth.

Like Phillip and Learie, some Squadron 7 members had been experimenting over the past year and a half with putting notes on pans. Franklin gave a demonstration on a pan he was tuning to play the first line of "Twinkle, Twinkle, Little Star". The band had been asked to play at a birthday party, and another band member, Claude, had put two notes on a pan, just enough to begin the song "Happy Birthday to You". On the tuned pan, without any accompaniment, Claude beat out the melody for the words "Happy birthday", and the other band-members finished the line by singing "to you". They did this twice, and then they sang the rest of the song, playing a rhythm with their instruments to accompany it. During the performance, Phillip and Learie exchanged glances, and Phillip leaned towards Gwynneth to comment, "Just like we, Miss!"

The visiting boys were intrigued by the shape of Squadron 7's pans. On each one, the surface was pushed outwards, like a belly. On Phillip's paint pans, the surface had sunk inwards from the force of pounding to make the notes. Phillip was surprised to learn that this band had deliberately pounded the surfaces outwards, and he wanted to try out one of their pans. Franklin passed the sticks to him. The tips were wrapped with rubber – the same idea as San Miguel Warahoons had arrived at. Learie, Kelvin and Reynold also took turns at trying out the bulging pan, and all four of them found it to be an awkward exercise.

"Most of the iron bands I know," Franklin said, "that is how they making they pan."

He then showed them another pan he was working on. Its shape was convex like the others, but on this pan the surface was divided up by straight lines, like a round cake cut into slices. There were six "slices", each being the space for a note, but all the notes had not yet been filled in. The dividing lines were marked out with nail holes, just as Learie had suggested when he and Phillip were working on their new pan.

Squadron 7's bass section was a biscuit drum and a caustic soda drum with its surface divided into two halves that gave out two different deep sounds. They referred to that drum as the "du-dup", which, they said, was becoming very popular among the iron bands in town. Remembering that at Ainsley's birthday party in May 1939, Squadron 7's bass section was a biscuit drum and bamboo boom, Gwynneth asked about the bamboo. She learned that they had since dispensed with it. Now, three years later, their band was all metal.

Franklin and the other members present gave a short demonstration, playing the two bass drums along with a few other instruments. Kelvin was fascinated by the du-dup and asked to try it out. He decided there and then to get hold of a caustic soda drum and make a du-dup for St Paul Syncopators. Franklin gave him directions to the soap factory where he could get the drum. Syncopators had also been using a biscuit drum and bamboo boom from the day the band was formed, but Kelvin now contemplated doing away with the bamboo. He would put this idea to his band.

Phillip also decided to get a caustic soda drum and make a du-dup, but he was not in favour of giving up the bamboo boom. His greater interest, however, was in the tuning of pans. Franklin told them that Squadron 7 used to clean paint tins by scrubbing them out with turpentine, like Phillip, until they learned from a member of another band that the best way to remove the paint was to heat the pans over a fire. He pointed to the old coal-pot in a corner of the yard that he used for this purpose. "And then I realise that the heat making the metal stronger," Franklin said. "The pan I did tune before that, the notes fade away after a time, and the pan face start to dent and bust up. Now we heating the pan to tune it, and when it cool, it taking the pounding much better, and it keeping the sound of the notes."

The boys left Franklin's yard in high spirits, thanking Squadron 7 members for the time they had spent with them. They were happy to find that in many ways they were on the same track as this town band, and grateful for the new things they had learnt. Ollie and Gaston treated them to soft drinks at a parlour, run by an old school friend of Ollie's, before taking them back to the train station. The boys thanked their patrons for this most fruitful expedition. On the train going home, though, they did agree among themselves that one thing about the town bands that they were definitely not going to follow was the obzocky upside-down pan face.

25
"Let that girl go and drop her golliwog on the father doorstep."

In announcing that she was three months pregnant, Monica told Gwynneth that if they wanted her to leave the job, her mother would come and look after Mumma until they could find someone to replace her.

"Why? You feeling sick?" Gwynneth asked. "You doan think you going be able to work?"

"No, Tan Gwynnie, I feeling good. Nothing ain wrong with me. But I know people does fire girls when they find out they making baby."

"Well, we not so. Roy might make a fuss, but we will deal with him," Gwynneth assured her. "But what the father think about this? What the two of you plan to do?"

"The two of we? Tan Gwynnie, I doan even want he to know."

"So he not going to stand up with you?"

"Tan Gwynnie, the father is a nice man, a sweet man; but he wotless. He mother spoil he bad bad, and he not going to change. I stop expecting he to change, and I not going and saddle myself for life with no wotless man just because I pregnant for he. No, Sir! Last time I went and meet he, was to tell he I done with he. He start to cry long tears and beg me doan leave he. I just walk off. But I was pregnant already and didn know."

"You not going to tell him?"

"Nah!" Monica shook her head vehemently. "Elford is not a responsible man. He cyaan set no good example for my child. He have other children and I hear he does pass them straight in the road, or hide from them. Not my child. He not going get to mess up my child."

And then Monica addressed exactly the question that was going through Gwynneth's mind: "Tan Gwynnie, I doan know why woman does friend with man who they know ain no good. I cyaan believe how these kinda man could turn woman head so – make woman lost they senses and get stupid."

281

Gwynneth and Viola had a brief conference and decided that they would have to tell Roy, sooner rather than later. Viola was all for keeping him in the dark and letting him see for himself at whatever time Monica's belly started to show, but they both knew that this would mean more hell to pay. Better to get it over with. On his next visit to pay Monica, they diverted him to the backyard before he could enter the drawing-room. They made sure, however, to extract Monica's pay from him in the gallery, before nudging him back down the front steps and into the yard. There they had already brought out a chair from the schoolroom for him to sit on.

When they broke the news to him, he gave a start and blinked rapidly; then he tried to speak with a cold, in-charge voice: "Of course you're packing her back immediately to where she came from. Dismiss her and get someone else to take care of Mumma."

A wicked thought flashed through Gwynneth's mind. Monica and Mumma were sitting in the drawing-room. What if she dared him to go in and announce to the two of them together that he was dismissing Monica? She knew Roy would rather die; yet it would be foolhardy to make such a bluff. Suppose he obliged? He was beginning to rant, and in that state who knew what he was capable of? No point goading him. This was one time to handle Roy with kid gloves.

"What was she doing on her weekends off, going to town and servicing the Yankee armed forces? I don't want any whore taking care of my mother! I don't want any King George Street whore in this house!"

Gwynneth tried to stop him. "Roy! You cannot insult Monica like that!"

"And keep you damn voice down!" Viola hissed at him, as she moved to the edge of the bench, ready to run up his chest.

He continued: "Playing Miss Goody-Two-Shoes, Miss Holy-Mary, cyaan mash ants... Bitch! Hardly want to give a person the time of day, when all along, behind our back, you making fares?"

"Roy! Just stop right now!" Gwynneth leapt up off the bench. "I will not sit here and listen to you disrespect Monica. When you cool down we can talk, but nobody is getting dismissed. Monica gives your mother the best care we could ever want for her.

Mumma is very happy with Monica and you are not going to come between them."

Viola sat glaring daggers at Roy, until Gwynneth elbowed her and ordered, "Come on."

She got up and followed Gwynneth across the yard, into the house. They left Roy looking distraught. About half an hour later Viola looked out through the back door, and he was still sitting there on the chair, facing the empty bench. It would be some time yet before they heard the front gate slam.

The discussion was never taken up again. Roy would continue to bring Monica's pay every fourth Saturday, and on Gwynneth's suggestion, Monica would make herself scarce before he could finish climbing the gallery steps. He would sit and chat with Mumma for a while, then put the envelope with the money on the dining-room table, and leave.

Days before the baby's birth, they installed Monica in Gwynneth's room, and Gwynneth took Monica's place in Mumma's room, sleeping on the old canvas cot she had slept on for all the years at Catherine Street. Bernice, the mother of Gwynneth's godson, Garnet, had already sent over Garnet's crib, with a bag of his tenderly folded baby-clothes.

Gwynneth assisted the midwife, Mrs Noriega, in delivering the baby. Two days later, Monica's mother, Venus, arrived. She came armed with verveine, hog-plum leaf and a variety of other bush, all required for attending to the nursing mother and her newborn baby. She also brought two guards for the baby – the tiny sachet stuffed with washing blue, or asafoetida, that they would pin to his clothes, and his bracelet of beads – to protect him against maljo. Venus stayed a fortnight. In that time, not only did she take care of Mumma, Monica and the baby; she also took over as much of the cooking as Viola would allow. Venus could not be deterred.

The baby was christened at St Hilda's, attended by a crowd of godparents – Gwynneth, Viola, Ollie and Gaston. There was no shortage of names, either, for him. His grandmother, Venus, had sent his first-name, Joshua, out of a dream she'd had, right about the time she calculated to be the date of his conception. ("Hm," Monica murmured, rolling her eyes upwards. "My mother and

283

these dreams she does get.") The baby's two middle names, Elford and Kofi, were given by his mother and his godmother Gwynneth, respectively. Notwithstanding all of this, they continued to call him "Sonny" for that was what Mumma had called him the morning after he was born: "Son? Sonny? *Ou vini pou béni kay-sala?* You come to bless this house?"

When the baby stopped waking up in the night, Monica moved back into Mumma's room with him. A week or two later Roy visited. He stepped into the room to see Mumma, but instantly turned on his heel and went looking for Gwynneth. Mumma and the baby were both fast asleep, Mumma on the bed and the baby in the crib. Roy wanted the crib removed immediately, for that, along with the cot for the girl, was crowding his mother out of her room. Gwynneth and Viola were allowing the home to be turned into a choke-up shanty-town hovel, and so on. The dispute did not last long. Gwynneth informed him that it was Mumma's wish to have Sonny in her room, and that was that.

Sonny was born in June, so he was just a few weeks old at the start of the July-August school vacation, when Gwynneth was available to help take care of him during the day. She got hold of a fruit crate made out of spaced wooden slats and converted it into a day-bed for him. She lined it with a blanket, then placed a pillow in it for a mattress. They used it to cart him around and set him down anywhere on the compound while they worked nearby. This was mainly when Mumma was sleeping. As long as Mumma was awake, it was difficult to prise Sonny away from her.

Whoever was minding him while they cooked or washed the dishes would put him up on the pantry table where they could watch him from the kitchen. Monica put him on the backyard bench while she hung clothes on the line. Gwynneth and Viola placed him on the flower-garden bench when they went out to pull weeds. Or someone would take him out there and sit with him just for him to get some breeze. Out in the yard he would lie contentedly in his box with his eyes darting about trying to follow the fluttering of leaves and the swaying of branches on the greenery around him.

If on an evening he was restless, taking a long time to fall asleep when Mumma was already sleeping, they would take him out of the crib, put him in his box, and carry him out into the gallery where they sat around chatting. At that hour the drawing room centre table would be out in the gallery, and they would place him on it, having moved their drinks to the bannister. Soon he was going from hand to hand, lap to lap, with somebody patting his back, Ollie jiggling him on his knee, or Gaston cradling him and singing songs his grandmother used to sing to him, like "*Ba Mwen Yon Ti Bo*" or "*Dodo, Piti Popo*", until Sonny had become so drowsy that he could safely be put back into the crib.

One weekend during that school vacation, Gwynneth and Monica left Mumma in the care of Viola, Marjorie and Lennox, and took Sonny to Pilgrim for the first time. There, in his grandparents' house, Monica held a thanksgiving and had Sonny offered up. Monica and Sonny went back to Turagua on the Monday morning, but Gwynneth stayed on with Uncle Albert for the rest of the week. His daughter Lyris and one of his grandchildren lived there with him in the old house to which new spaces had been added over time. Cutty had built on the land, a stone's throw away from Uncle Albert, and so had Uncle Cecil's younger son, Dan. The compound teemed with the great-grand-children of Gang-Gang Sarah and Papa Georgie, some living there, as well as some living elsewhere but spending their school vacation there. Whenever Gwynneth stayed over in Pilgrim, she wondered why she didn't go there more often, for she always returned home invigorated.

At the reopening of school that September, Sonny was going on three months old. Gwynneth started taking him into the schoolroom when Monica had to go to the shop or the post office or run some other errand. Gwynneth would place him where he could see the trees outside, and he would lie quietly in his box for long stretches of time. The children were allowed a brief moment of fussing over him, but first had to go to the garden pipe and wash their hands with soap if they wanted to touch him. If he fell asleep, Gwynneth's pupils gained valuable practice at Working Quietly, Speaking Softly, and Treading Gently on the Floor. But naturally they sometimes forgot themselves and there would be lapses, which brought down the wrath of the whole school upon the offender.

One day Pamela and Eastlyn had a tug-of-war over a pencil-sharpener, which ended with Eastlyn roughly yanking the pencil-sharpener away from Pamela. The angry shriek that came from Pamela woke Sonny up in a fright. His whole body shuddered at the sound, his arms and legs jerked upwards, and he began to cry. Before the others could jump down her throat, Pamela, too, began to cry; she was heartbroken. Gwynneth had to console her by allowing her to help console Sonny: she picked him up and invited Pamela to pat his back.

Depending on what he met each time he visited, Roy would register one or another bitter complaint, always addressing said complaint to Gwynneth. (Of late he had begun to fear that Viola would do actual physical harm to him, and he longed for the courage to offend the vain bitch by saying to her that old age was making her more and more cantankerous.) If Monica was no-where to be seen and they told him she was feeding or changing her baby, he would complain that she was neglecting the duties of the job she was being paid for, and diverting her time and energy away from Mumma to the child. If Mumma was playing with the baby, the complaint would be that Monica was turning his mother into a nursemaid for her child.

Mumma could not get enough of this child, and Roy could not bear to watch. She would chat with him, sing to him and tell him stories. She would take his two tiny hands in hers and clap, singing:

> *Clap hand for Granny*
> *Till Mammy come*
> *Bring cake and sugar-plum*
> *And give Baby some.*

To add insult to injury, Mumma sometimes called the child "Roy", and even more hurtful, "Roysie-Boysie", his pet name when he was little. (Puppa had tried, without success, to make the family stop calling Roy by any pet name because, he said, petting him would make him soft; he was a boy and it was time to start toughening him up.) Another source of vexation for Roy was hearing Mumma say to the baby, "When you come a big boy, *Doudou*, you going in the College, just like Roy. But doan let them people make you stupid, you hear, Choonkulunks?"

Roy would have to turn his head away to sneer: *Hah! The yard-boy? In Ascension College? That and a lilac donkey coming down James Street you will never see. Look how fair-skin Gordon is and they wouldn let him in...* He would never forgive himself for not insisting that Helen go and register the boy for the entrance exam. Instead, it was Roy who went with him. Roy was sure that they had put some kind of code, some sign on the registration form to indicate that the candidate's father had the wrong shade of skin. Nobody could ever convince Roy that Gordon had failed that exam. Roy was prepared to go down on his knees and beg them to take his son into their school.

At every visit to Turagua, Roy just had to let it be known that his disapproval remained, that he objected with a passion to coming and finding the servant and her whelp still living there. One day he said to Gwynneth when it was safe to do so, Viola being out of earshot, "Let that girl go and drop her golliwog on the father doorstep."

It was not that he thought Gwynneth would be any less enraged by such talk than Viola. It was just that Viola's wrath had sharper teeth, was more terrifying. Gwynneth didn't waste any words on him. She took his hat down from the rack and handed it to him, threatening to tell Mumma what he had said, if he didn't leave immediately.

The next time he came, he met the front door locked, and Gwynneth standing with her fingers sticking out through the jalousie. Their conversation was carried out in vehement whispers.

"Just hand me Monica's pay," Gwynneth demanded.

"I will do no such thing," Roy replied. "Open the door!"

Gwynneth closed the jalousies on either side of the door and went inside. Roy sat himself down on a chair in the gallery, determined to wait it out. But after nearly an hour sitting there, he slid the envelope under the door and flounced off.

He came back a few days later, obviously to settle the score. They were not expecting him. When Gwynneth heard the gate and looked out, she quickly locked the front door and rushed to the back door to do the same. Roy began to rattle the front door and call for Gwynneth, then Mumma, then, as a last resort, Viola. Gwynneth came back and spoke to him through the jalousie. "You trying to break down the door? Eh? You want to frighten you mother?"

"Open the damn door," he demanded. "You don't own this house – you can't lock me out."

"So call the police. Give you mother a heart attack."

"You forgetting one thing, Madame. This house is not yours. In fact, no part of this property is yours. This property belongs to Mumma, Viola, and me. Remember? You are the one who is here on sufferance, not me."

"Oh, dear!" Gwynneth made her face into an expression of aching sympathy. "Mumma never show you the document? Maybe she couldn find you at the time. Man, you were scarce like good gold! Well, let me tell you. This house, this property, is as much mine as yours, dear little brother, no more, no less."

She opened the door to tell him about Mumma's deed of gift; then she left the door ajar and went back to folding the laundry she had just taken off the clothesline.

Puppa had disinherited Gwynneth. He had changed his will in the aftermath of the Grand Chemin march. They only found this out after Puppa died and the contents of his will were made known. Puppa had left the property to Mumma, Viola and Roy. Mumma wasted no time. Before Puppa was good cold in his grave, she went to the lawyer and had him convey her one-third interest to Gwynneth. At the time nobody saw any need to seek out the disappearing son and tell him.

Roy had to sit down in order to absorb this new reality. *If Mumma cut herself out, and gave her share to Gwynneth... then the property belongs to the three of us ... so, Gwynneth and Viola together own a larger share of the property than me!* He sat and mulled this over gloomily. After some time, he sought to console himself. His sisters were 16 and 17 years older than him. The two old bats were going to die before him, anyway, and the whole thing would then be his. He had made the mistake of saying to them one day (he must have had a drink or two), "This property could fetch a pretty penny in rent."

Since then, Gwynneth had lost no opportunity to accuse him of wishing all three of them dead – his mother and his two sisters. "The moment we kick the bucket, eh?" she would nag. "If you had half a chance, you would throw us in the Poor-House tomorrow morning, just so you could put in tenants and collect a fat rent every month. Money-money-money!"

At the time that Puppa bought the land, Turagua was a little backwoods settlement. "You could hardly even call it a village," Puppa used to say.

Man, Roy mused, *today this parcel of land, on its own, is prime property, and when you add in the buildings – four-bedroom house and annex, the annex that she calls her "schoolroom" but which could easily be converted into a neat little cottage...* His mood lifted. All of that would be his to pass on to Gordon and Freda. Of course, his children wouldn't want to live out here, but putting up the place for rent would raise their income...

He didn't bother to go in. He got up and left without a word to anybody in the house.

On his visits, now, Roy had nothing to say about Monica or her child. He pretended they didn't exist. However, it was obvious that such restraint was difficult for him to keep up. One day he arrived with rum on his breath. Viola and Mumma were sitting out on the gallery couch with the baby. Viola was playing a game with Sonny that she used to play with Roy when he was little, up until well past babyhood, so it was there in his memory of a happier time.

Viola was saying to the baby, "You so sweet and juicy, I could just eat you up!" and planting kisses on him.

Over and over she pressed her mouth on Sonny's belly and blew a blast of air. This produced a mild explosion which tickled him and made him shriek with scandalous baby-laughter every time that she did it. When Roy came into the gallery, Viola got up, and with Sonny on her hip, went in through the drawing-room door, so that Roy could sit with Mumma. His tongue loosened by the rum, Roy put God out of his thoughts and mumbled to Viola's back as she disappeared into the house: "The golliwog still here? When allyou going to send it where it belong?"

Mercifully, Mumma's hearing was not at its best that day, and Monica was in the backyard hanging out clothes. Viola, however, heard him. She came charging back through the door with a murderous scowl on her face. Roy put his hands in the air, exclaiming "Sorry! Sorry!" with more sarcasm than apology, then added, "I forget. Not the golliwog. The prince."

26
"And I doan want no snat in my funeral."

Sonny, walking now, was all over the house. They had to put some things up on the highest shelves – like the Flit gun, that held no end of fascination for him – or hide them away in cupboards that he couldn't open. They had already barred his way out of the house by placing wooden slats across the back door and the entrance to the gallery, as had been done when Roy started creeping. The adult Roy did not react well to this new provocation. The first time he encountered it, after marching as briskly as usual up the front steps, he came to an abrupt halt on the landing. There he stood and contemplated the barrier for a moment or two before firing a sudden kick and a swear word at it.

At the same time as Sonny started walking, Mumma started to go down. Her legs finally gave out, so she could no longer shuffle out into the drawing-room or the gallery on Monica's arm. She had to be lifted bodily. She was now so frail that Monica all on her own was able to pick her up and carry her without any difficulty. Now Mumma was choosing to spend more and more of her day in bed, where Sonny visited her regularly during his tours of the house. "Amma?" he would call out to her from the bedroom door. "Amma dodo?"

If she wasn't sleeping, he would go in, stand beside the bed and relay some pressing news to her in an incomprehensible tongue. And Mumma would nod and smile as though what he said was as clear as day. When he was ready to take a daytime nap, he would try to climb onto the bed with Mumma, but couldn't, and he would have to go and find his mother. He tugged at Monica's clothes, saying, "Lull donk," and she would come and hoist him up.

Mumma chatted with Sonny, almost in a whisper now. She would request, "*Yon ti bo, bay Mumma?*" and he obliged with a dribbly kiss on her cheek. She sang "*Dodo, Piti Popo*" to him, and he would put his two sucking-fingers into his mouth while his other hand played with her cheeks, her nose, her hair. Then he

291

held on to one of her ears, or laid his arm on her chest, as he drifted off to sleep snuggled against her; and she looked too happy for words.

But the time came when she seemed not to be fully aware of Sonny, or of anyone else, for that matter. Mumma stared blankly at everybody, seldom spoke, and had no desire to sit out in the drawing-room or gallery. Still, she made no protest when Monica or Lennox lifted her out to the gallery and put her on the couch to get some breeze. She willingly took a little porridge, juice and fruit that Monica would peel and cut up for her – mango, ripe-fig, pawpaw – but she had to be fed slowly, patiently. Lennox came over on evenings to help feed Mumma and turn her in the bed.

When Mumma stopped talking altogether, and on any given day would only consent to take a few spoonfuls of porridge and some water, they knew she had crossed a bridge. This was in early September, the first week of the new school term. Gwynneth would now take Sonny into the schoolroom with her more regularly, to relieve Monica, for the care of Mumma had become a more demanding task. But as soon as Sonny was ready to take his nap, he would drop whatever he was doing in the schoolroom and head for the house, where he insisted on being put into Mumma's bed. He seemed not to notice that Mumma no longer talked or sang to him, and he would cuddle up to her and hug her up just the same, as though nothing had changed.

Venus came and spent three days looking after her Nenn Estelle. On the fourth day she went home and returned to Turagua a week later with a larger bag of clothes. Two days after she got back, she went out to the schoolroom in the early afternoon to announce to Gwynneth that Mumma had begun to travel. Monica went to the Exchange and alerted Viola, who contacted Roy. He arrived later with St Anthony's priest in tow. On his way to the house he had gone to the presbytery to request that the priest come and give Mumma extreme unction. They were all taken aback, but they welcomed Father and invited him to sit in the drawing-room while they readied Mumma.

Monica tidied the bedroom while Venus sponged Mumma's face and tied her head. The priest was called in. He put down his bag and took from it his prayer-book, chalice, wine and cloth. He said the required prayers, and then asked them to raise Mumma's head a little. He leaned over and guided the chalice towards Mumma's face. Up till then she had been lying motionless with her mouth open and eyes closed, well on her way into the other world. She was breathing heavily through her mouth.

But suddenly, before the priest could manoeuvre the chalice into position to dispense the sip of wine, Mumma's mouth snapped shut and stayed tightly shut. She had no teeth and did not have her dentures in, so her lips were tucked away inside her mouth. All one could see was a line across her face, like a perfect seam. Father froze. His hands remained suspended, one holding the chalice and the other his white cloth, inches from Mumma's face. The poor man could make no headway.

Everyone was startled, except Mother Venus, who settled Mumma's head back onto the pillow and thanked the priest for his prayers. Before he was out of the gallery Mumma had returned to breathing with her mouth wide open, making a deep, rasping sound.

With all the people dropping in that night, Sonny was restless and objected to being put in the crib after he was fed, so they let him wander among them, hoping this would tire him out. They might have forgotten that he was at large, because he was so quiet. They were taking turns at sitting with Mumma to hold her hand, talk to her, sing her favourite hymns. Although she was beyond responding, they knew that she could hear all of this, and that she appreciated it. Now and again, as they scurried about like worker ants, there would be a time lag in the changing of the guard, and Mumma might be left unattended for a short time, never more than a matter of minutes, or so it seemed to everyone.

It was after nine o'clock when Gwynneth went into Mumma's room again. There was no one sitting on the chair beside the bed, but Sonny was in the bed, comfortably nestled against Mumma. The arm that was trying to hug her as he lay next to her could only reach part of the way across her chest, a regular sight. He was fast asleep. And there was silence in the room, no harsh, laboured breathing. Mumma was gone.

Nobody had put Sonny into Mumma's bed, they discovered,

neither Monica, nor Gwynneth, nor Viola, nor Venus. Sonny had learnt, that night, how to climb onto the bed, as he would demonstrate after the funeral home had taken Mumma.

Sonny was supposed to have gone to sleep hours earlier, in his crib which had been moved out of Mumma's room and placed, once more, in Gwynneth's room. He and Monica had been sleeping there since Venus arrived to take care of Mumma. They had tried, more than once, to put him to bed, but this was met each time with shrieking that rent the air, so they would take him out and let him walk about some more. Then Monica tried again. She laid him down in the crib and turned to go, relieved that he did not protest. As she opened the door to leave, however, she looked back. Almost half his body was leaning out of the crib, and one leg was on its way up to the rail. She quickly took him out again.

No wonder Sonny wouldn't go to sleep, Venus remarked. They had separated him from Mumma on this her last night on earth. They had insisted on putting him to bed in Gwynneth's room at the back of the house, while Mumma lay in her room at the front of the house. It had not occurred to anybody to bring Sonny to Mumma's bedside on this night; but Mumma was not going to leave without a hug-up from Sonny. They reproached themselves bitterly for not having been with Mumma when she breathed her last. Their feelings of guilt were allayed only by the thought that Sonny would have been there, cuddled up to her in that moment. Maybe that was how it was meant to be.

They knew that a person about to die might wait to "see" a particular loved one, before yielding to death. Papa Georgie had held out for two days, beyond earthly seeing or hearing, while the message made its way to his *doudou*-darling Estelle in Coryal and she made her way to Pilgrim. When she arrived at his bedside and threw herself on him, laid her head on his chest and wrapped her arms around his neck, she felt his heartbeat slow to a halt.

Mumma's instructions for her funeral were well known to all concerned. One of her favourite topics of conversation was her own death, and one of her favourite programmes on the radio was the death announcements. She enjoyed making up a death announcement for herself and performing it like the voice on the radio: "We have been asked to announce the death of Estelle Cuffie, formerly Casimir, mother of Gwynneth, Viola and Roy; grandmother of two; beloved daughter of George and Sarah Casimir, deceased; spiritual child of Mother Queen Charlotte des Vignes; sister of Albert and Cecil; aunt of Lyris, Cuthbert, Gracelyn, Wilfred and Dan; great-aunt of many; godmother of Venus Polydore; wife of Joseph Cuffie, deceased..." (When the time came, the actual announcement that they put on the radio and in the newspaper did give the names of Roy's children; otherwise there would have been hell to pay.)

Her instructions were very simple, and one of them had already been carried out: "Doan wait till I dead to send and call Venus." Mumma made it clear that her church had to put her down, not no Father-priest, so if they couldn't bury her in Pilgrim, then Pilgrim would have to come to wherever they were burying her. "And I doan want no snat in my funeral," she often said to Gwynneth, Viola, Roy, Uncle Albert, Uncle Cecil, Venus, Monica, Marjorie and Lennox. "Nobody is to cry for me." With that she would slide into song, and, in earlier years, dance:

> *I know where I'm going, I know*
> *I know where I'm going, I know*
> *Joy-bells are ringing*
> *Happy children are singing*
> *Come go to Zion with me.*

Or:

> *Row me over the tide, boatman*
> *Row me over the tide.*
> *Someone is waiting for me over there*
> *Boatman, row me over the tide.*

She was going to meet her parents, Sarah and Georgie, and all the others gone before her, so no need for anybody to cry for her.

They sent Roy to St Anthony's to make the arrangements for her burial in the churchyard. Mumma was no longer a parishioner of St Anthony's. She had turned her back on them twenty-seven years before, over the Shouter Prohibition Ordinance, and it was not long before Gwynneth had followed suit. Viola, the Nowherean, had ceased to be a St Anthony's parishioner at the age of 17, when Puppa found that he could no longer make her go to church, no matter how much he roared (and he was not at liberty to hit her). Only Roy seemed to still have a foot in St Anthony's. As a good Ascension boy he used to go to Mass on those weekends when he was home, and he had kept up some kind of contact with this church over the years.

Puppa, on his retirement, had leased a burial plot at St Anthony's for 50 years. Roy discovered, however, that according to their rules, Mumma's body would have to be churched at St Anthony's in order to be buried in their churchyard. Gwynneth worried that this would go against Mumma's wishes. Mumma had always assumed that her funeral service, conducted by members of her church, would take place right there at her home in Turagua, if not in Pilgrim, after which she would be buried in Pilgrim cemetery with her parents. But Venus did not think that a Catholic service would be too much of an offence to Mumma, as long as she was put down into her grave afterwards by her church.

"Since Nenn Estelle was a girl," Venus reminded them, "same strength she going in Shango-yard, so she going in Catholic church, just like plenty other people. Because prayers is prayers, and the more prayers, the better. We going give she a lil prayers here first, and nothing them Catholic do afterwards cyaan undo that."

They would hold wake for three nights. Phillip and his Uncle Chester were going to provide drumming, and for sure the side coming from Pilgrim would also walk with a skin drum or two. On the day of the funeral Mumma's body would be brought home for her last sojourn in her house. There they would hold some prayers before temporarily handing her over to the Catholic church. After the church service, even if the Father-priest needed to recite something at her graveside, the spiritual children of Mother Queen Lottie would have the last word.

The contingent from Pilgrim arrived, in time for the second night of the wake, bringing bags of ground provision from their gardens, and fruits. Queen was not with them. The church members had decided that the journey, this whole expedition, would be too much for Queen. She herself was not of this opinion, but heeded their advice, sending her gold brocade shawl that she loved the most, for them to place in Mumma's coffin.

For this period, they kept a lit candle in Mumma's room, and no one slept in there. Viola gave her room over to Venus, Monica and Sonny, and shared Gwynneth's room. Roy's room was commandeered to house what seemed to him an ever-multiplying number of fearsome head-tied women. He put up no objection whatsoever. *Not me and them witches*, he cautioned himself. *I not taking no chance.* Mother Venus gave him the jitters, and from the very beginning of her stay he had been very circumspect with her, almost obsequious, whenever contact with her could not be avoided. Some of the guests camped in the drawing-room and some in the schoolroom; and Marjorie accommodated two people in her home. For three nights the backyard rang with drumming, singing, and jovial conversation.

Mumma was brought home. Gwynneth and Lennox spread Queen's shawl over her chest and tucked it in around her shoulders. Viola went outside and cut some gladioli, Mumma's favourite flowers, and laid them alongside her in the coffin. Mother Venus lifted Sonny and passed him over the coffin, handing him to Gwynneth on the other side. A stream of people came through the drawing-room to pay their respects. Roy turned up alone. He explained that Helen did not believe in taking children to funerals. (Gwynneth calculated that Gordon would have been eighteen years old, and Freda, sixteen or seventeen.)

Mother Venus led the prayers, after which Mumma was borne out of the house by Uncle Albert, Roy (looking haggard), Lennox, Cutty and two other men from Pilgrim. The procession to the church made its way along Farfan Road, then took to the main road from Grant Trace corner. At Gwynneth's request it was led by the delegation from Mumma's friendly society, Heart and Hand, members draped in their green-and-gold sashes and holding their standards aloft.

The Father-priest was ill-equipped for the task of presiding over the funeral rites of Estelle Cuffie, formerly Casimir, spiritual child of Mother Queen Charlotte des Vignes. After the experience of trying to give Mumma extreme unction, which must have been daunting enough, he was now in his own church, conducting a Catholic mass, but it kept slipping out of his control. Father, like most of his comrades in the priesthood of Cayeri, was a native of somewhere in Great Britain, and was relatively new to the colony. He would never have witnessed Shouter Baptist worship, not even a roadside prayer meeting, for it was twenty-seven years since the Shouters had been driven underground.

What Father experienced that day was the delegation from Mother Queen Lottie's church now and again infiltrating their own rhythm into an unsuspecting Catholic hymn, and vigorously moving their bodies in time with that rhythm. Their singing overwhelmed and derailed the organist's accompaniment, and each time that this happened, organist and Father-priest quietly deferred to Pilgrim. The organist would rest her hands on her lap and sit with her head bowed, while Father just got a little red in the face, especially when some of these mourners escaped from the pews and danced in the aisle. Seen from the altar, the spectacle must have been quite unnerving for the Father-priest, and after the mass he made himself scarce.

The people from Mumma's church surrounded her grave and sent her off in the way that she expected, rocking St Anthony's austere churchyard with unaccustomed sounds of doption and goatskin drum and people catching power, all under the continuing reign of the 1917 ordinance as well as older laws against precisely what they were doing. Gwynneth reflected that in his heyday the irascible Father McVorran, now buried somewhere in this same churchyard and surely tumbling with indignation in his grave, would already have sooked the police on Mumma's funeral.

At one point during these final proceedings, Gwynneth caught sight of Uncle Albert with his arm around Roy's shoulder, leading him away. She kept an eye on Lennox. So far he was doing better than Roy. When they got back to the house, Lennox busied himself, helping to serve food and drinks to the company gathered there. A massive cooking operation had been started that morning, in the kitchen and in the backyard, under the direction of Mother Venus. She had left some of the younger Pilgrim men to finish it, while everyone else went off to the church service.

Just before six o'clock Gwynneth realised that she had not seen Lennox for some time, but she knew that he would not have gone home without excusing himself. She did a quiet search and found him sitting out on the backyard bench, staring into the dusk.

"You had something to eat, Lennox?"

"Not hungry, Tantie Gwynnie."

"All right. I will put aside food for you, *Doudou*. And I sure you tired. Come lie down in my room. I will make sure nobody disturb you there."

He went in willingly. Gwynneth fetched some juice from the kitchen for him, took it into the room, and found him curled up on the bed, sobbing. She put the glass down and lay on the bed with him, hugging him up and telling him how much he meant to Mumma, and how happy he had made her. "You brightened her life," she told him, "and Mumma will always be right near you, looking out for her little husband."

He managed to give a brief giggle.

"You can still talk to her, you know."

From time to time he nodded, or gave a choked "Yes, Tantie Gwynnie."

When she went back out, she took Viola and Marjorie aside and alerted them. Nobody was to go into the room unless they had good reason. If they had to go in, she cautioned, they should not turn on the electric light, but take a candle instead, so as not to disturb him. Gwynneth learned afterwards that a plot was immediately hatched between Viola and Marjorie. They waited until Gwynneth was settled in the gallery, chatting with some of the guests. Then the two of them slunk off to the bedroom and went in, with no thought of light, electric or otherwise, to sit on the bed with Lennox, hug him up, hold his hands and rub his back.

Between crying and laughing they talked about Mumma and how she could make all of them laugh, even when she couldn't get up off the bed, and how she must already have the whole of Heaven in uproar. They showed Lennox how, when he was a little, little thing, not even walking yet, Mumma used to hold him and kiss him on his forehead over and over, like a bird pecking him, and he would shriek with laughter. Lennox had, of course, heard that story (complete with the re-enactment) a thousand times, like all the other stories about Mumma and him when he was little and people called him "Ma Cuffie lil husband", but that evening it helped a lot to hear them again.

They tried to interest him in a plate of pelau, plantain and macaroni pie; they offered him sandwiches, coconut drops, fritters – to no avail. He was in better spirits, now, but still not focused on food. This alarmed them no end, for Lennox was an eating machine. Lennox could cuff down three plates of food, one after the other, in the time the average person took to finish one plate. To help him get back his appetite, Viola went out and drizzled a tot of rum punch into a glass for him. After all, he was seventeen years old now, old enough to go to work, and a very responsible young man.

The company had not yet begun to subside when Gaston intercepted Gwynneth on her way out of the kitchen carrying a tray of sandwiches. He took the tray from her. He peered in through the dining-room door and spotted Monica drooping with fatigue on a straight-backed chair. Gaston beckoned to her. She sprang up and came into the pantry, where she immediately tried to relieve him of the tray.

"Nah, nah, nah! Not you, Monica!" Gaston protested. "Just go and call another young person to serve these, please. You done tired enough already. Look at that strapping young fella holding up the drawing-room wall. Get him for me."

Monica went in, chuckling, for the "strapping young fella" leaning against the wall was just Vinnie, a boy from the church who, not too long ago, was a knobbly-kneed child running up and down Pilgrim Road driving a barrel-hoop with a stick. She brought Vinnie into the pantry. Gaston gave him the tray and then took on Gwynneth. "Come, lady. Let's go and sit down outside for a second. You tired."

He was drawing her along by the hand, towards the back door. Then he stopped and looked down at her feet. "Wait. What you have on, slippers? Put on shoes and meet me outside."

Gwynneth turned around and went in without argument. *A-a!* Gaston marvelled. *Taking orders just so? She must be really tired.*

Sleepwalking! And then she took so long to come back outside that he began to think she might actually have gone to her bed; but she came back out. Some of the flambeaus from the wake had been lit up again, for the benefit of guests staying in the schoolroom, so the backyard was not in complete darkness. The two of them sat on the bench, from where Gwynneth had earlier taken up Lennox.

"Gwynneth," Gaston said. "You seeing about everybody, but what about you? Is *your* mother we just bury, you know."

A shadow crept over her face, and she let out a long breath. "You right. I need a moment of peace and quiet, to catch myself. I wish I could hide from people for just a little while, like how I try to hide Lennox."

"Where you want to go?"

Gwynneth was startled. "You mean go from here?"

"Why not?"

"Well… I cyaan duck out just so…"

"Why not?"

"Hm," she said, then, after some hesitation, "Tell me if this is crazy, but I feel like I could just go and sit quietly in La Marina – on the veranda."

That grand old establishment had weathered time and war; indeed, war had raised its fortunes considerably. La Marina by night was now a muted, genteel club where Yankee officers from the Base could safely bring their wives. At La Marina there was little danger of the officers running into any of the colourful Cayerian ladies they might have wined and dined elsewhere in town. It was rumoured that the establishment knew all of the Cayerian ladies in question (like Flashy Mary, and Stella "Nice-Thing" Bascombe, and "Rita Hayworth"), and by a gentlemen's agreement between La Marina and the Yankee officers, such ladies were simply not allowed to enter the club, no matter who their escorts were.

The bitterness of the famous quarrel between Gaston and Gwynneth on La Marina's veranda, twenty-one years before, had been exorcised, and the nightclub was now one of their favourite haunts. It was one of the places they would sometimes visit as a party of four – with Viola and Ollie. Upon arrival they would scan the place for US servicemen, who could always be identified, in or out of uniform, by their loud talking. If there were a lot of them, Gaston would suggest choosing another club, but Gwynneth insisted that no Yankee invader was going to push her out of there.

They always hoped there would be no servicemen at all, for even if there were only one or two, Gwynneth would chafe the whole time about their boisterousness and their arrogance – their behaving as though they owned everything around them wherever they found themselves. If there were any servicemen, Gaston would steer the party to a table as far away as possible from them, for he was certain that Gwynneth would one day shout something at them, or she might suddenly fly up off her chair, rush over to one of their tables and get her hands on the throat of a US military man with a gun on his person...

"Not so crazy," Gaston remarked. "We're in September, and you want to celebrate the anniversary month of the La Marina Shoot-Out at High Noon, September the something, 1923. I bet you have a wicked alarm clock in your head that reminds you every year."

He got her to giggle. "So let's go and lime little bit in La Marina," he suggested.

"'Lime?' That's a youngpeople word, Grampa. Only young-people does 'lime'."

"So what you think we doing out here right now? We liming! And when you, me, Viola, Ollie, Marjorie and whoever else, sitting around the gallery, what you think we doing? We liming! Calling it 'liming' might be new, Grandma, but liming certainly is not new; and neither the word nor the lime is the youngpeople property. Let's go."

"You really think we could leave everybody and just run away?" Gwynneth was having second thoughts.

"And who, exactly, needs us here? You have an army of able-bodied helpers. Who needs you, or me, inside there? Nobody's indispensable, my dear. Let's go. And no time for nose-powdering or anything of the sort."

So, they left, Gwynneth feeling uneasy about this impromptu

move, but realising that going in to get her handbag (and maybe just glance in the mirror and make sure her appearance would not frighten the good patrons of La Marina) could scuttle the whole escape. Luckily, Gaston's car was parked at the side gate, on Wilson Trace... *But wait. "Luckily"? Is luck that park the car there? And making her take off her slippers and put on shoes, to step out into her own backyard?*

"Gaston! You wretch, you planned this!" She jabbed him with her elbow.

But the car was already coasting noiselessly down Wilson Trace. Gaston didn't turn the engine on until they had rolled across Farfan Road and got to where Wilson Trace flattened out, just before it met the main road.

Most of the Pilgrim visitors left for home the day after Mumma's funeral. Venus, Uncle Albert and three other members of Mumma's church stayed and held prayers every night up to her Nine Nights. They went home and Venus returned a month later to conduct Mumma's Forty Days service. Before she went back to Pilgrim, she and Monica helped Viola move into Mumma's room. They also installed Mumma's bed (now Sonny's) and Monica's cot in the "children's room" vacated by Viola.

One afternoon a few days later, Sonny went looking for Gwynneth and found her sweeping the kitchen. He tugged at her dress, took her hand and led her through the house to the bedroom where he now slept. There, with a beatific smile on his face, he pointed into the bed and said, "Amma come."

"Mumma? Where Mumma? You seeing her?" Gwynneth asked.

He nodded, and again pointing into the bed, answered, "Amma lull donk."

Then he relinquished Gwynneth's hand to climb up on the bed. Gwynneth stared, speechless, as he arranged himself along one side, put his two sucking fingers into his mouth, and went to sleep with his free arm stretched out towards the other side of the bed, which looked empty, but she understood.

27
"Where you going with Sonny clothes?"

Monica went into Kings Port every morning to look for work. On the first day she took the tram up to the Savannah and then walked to Brierly. On Tuesday she went through Primrose Hill, calling at gates in front of large, forbidding houses. If anybody came out it was likely to be a woman in cap and apron, or a man with leaves or bits of grass stuck to him, maybe with pruning-shears in his hand. Monica would ask whether the madam of the house needed anybody to clean, cook, wash, iron, or mind the children. She would be turned away with a sympathetic smile, or a cross look from whoever had come to the gate, for causing them to be sent on that long walk from the house.

Then, for the rest of the week, she visited every store on downtown King George Street, Albert Street and James Street, to ask whether they needed a store clerk, a cashier (for she knew book-keeping), or a cleaner.

In the second week she went north again, this time to Shadybrook, where the houses were bigger still and further apart than in Primrose Hill. But she had barely arrived and called at one or two gates, when her shoe let her down. The front of the sole separated from the top. It was impossible to walk in it, so she held it in her hand and walked to the next gate, with the other shoe on. The maid, on her way down the path, was already waving both her arms at Monica and saying, "No work here. No work."

But Monica held up the shoe, and asked the maid, when she came closer, if she could spare some string, please, for her to tie her shoe together. They had a brief conversation, during which the maid once or twice glanced back over her shoulder, as if to see whether the madam was watching. Monica told the woman her name and where she lived, and explained that she had been on the road looking for work since the week before. Now she would have to cut that short for the day and see how she could get the bust-up old shoe to stay on her foot so she could make her way back home. The maid, who said her name was Thelma, seemed to warm to Monica. "String, *Doudou*? I could do better than that for you. Wait."

She hurried back up the path and disappeared behind the building. After a while she returned with a paper-bag, out of which she pulled a pair of alpagats. "Take these," she said. "They old and dirty till you cyaan even see what colour they is. But they still strong. You know good alpagat doan mash up easy so."

Monica was overwhelmed. After days of refusals, brush-offs, people turning their back on her with a steups, one store-owner laughing in her face on being told that she had book-keeping experience...

"Thank you, Miss Thelma. I go bring them back for you. God will bless you."

Miss Thelma waved goodbye and hurried up the path, not waiting to see whether they fitted, for she knew that if alpagats were too big or too small, you only had to leave the back straps down and wear them like slippers. They were a little larger than Monica's feet, but that didn't matter. And now she had a bag to put the old shoes in, though they were probably beyond repair and should really be thrown into the nearest dustbin. The other shoe was also beginning to gape, and there was a hole, almost the size of a shilling, in the sole of each shoe. She had put a piece of cardboard into each shoe so that her feet would not touch the ground. Still, she would see if the shoemaker could resole them.

That afternoon Monica washed the alpagats, which revealed a beautiful pattern woven in tan, green and red. She decided that she would give the job-hunting a rest for a few days. It was time to buy a new pair of shoes; she would not wait for the shoemaker's verdict. But now she had no shoes that she could wear to town to buy the new shoes. She only had the sapats that she wore to do her errands in the neighbourhood. She showed Tan Vie the dilapidated shoes and asked her whether she had an old pair of shoes she could lend her for a day. Tan Vie lent her a pair from her stylish collection. (Tan Gwynnie called Tan Vie "Santapi" because of the number of shoes she had – enough to outfit a hundred-legged creature.)

The next day Monica made a beeline for downtown King

George Street where the cheapest stores were, and bought going-out shoes. Then she went over to James Street, and got on the tram. From the Savannah she walked up to Shadybrook again. There she delivered Miss Thelma's alpagats to her, as well as a bag of zaboka, gospo lemons and Julie mango from the out-of-season tree which insisted on bearing when there was no other mango in sight.

Having had no luck in the north of Kings Port, Monica planned to go, next day, to the western districts of Belair and Windsor Park. But that evening, Gaston told her about a temporary job at Cummings and Ramsewak, where his office was. He offered to recommend her, if she was interested. They were looking for someone to stand in for the cleaner, who had sprained her wrist and had to be off work for at least a month. Gaston also advised Monica to begin looking through the classified ads in the newspaper for employment on the Base, where the Americans were paying handsomely for housekeeping.

Monica went to town to be interviewed at Cummings and Ramsewak, some distance up Mary Street. They would have liked her to start on the following day, but she told them she needed one day to attend to some business before she could take up the job. She could start on the day after that, if they didn't mind.

After the interview she went back to downtown King George Street and bought a pair of washicong to work in. She couldn't very well walk about the people office barefoot as she did in the house, nor thump on their floor in her wooden-soled sapats. And it was clear that she wouldn't be able to work for eight hours in her new going-out shoes, either. She had walked up, down and across town in them, and now her feet were killing her. There and then she decided that she would not only wear the washicong on the job; she would travel to and from work in them. Not the most stylish wear for walking through the city, but *chou poul* – who vex, lost. Tan Vie, for a start, was going to have a fit.

She went to the terminus and got on the 4.05 train, the one she would be taking every day after work. She felt lucky that her work day would end at three o'clock so that she could take the 4.05 home. Most people working in town didn't leave their job until after 4.00 o'clock and had to take the 5.08 if they lived along the Eastern Line. On mornings she would have to take a bus, for she was starting work at 6.30 a.m., and there was no train that could get her to work so early. The first train to town in the morning left Turagua at 6.10.

There were a lot of schoolchildren on the 4.05, mainly high school students in their smart uniforms, looking a little stuck-up. They sat together in clusters and chatted in la-di-da voices. *Like if only them could go to high school.* She didn reach high school, but, for sure, her son... Abruptly she unfolded the newspaper and began to read. She had bought this newspaper in order to keep the next day's business out of her mind along the way. She read it through from the front to the back pages where the sports news was. Though she had no interest whatsoever in sports, she would read every word in that section. She went back through the paper and read some parts again, for there were still three more stops before Turagua: Canaan, Plaisance and St Paul.

Once she was home, Monica was all smiles as she told Gwynneth and Viola that she had got the job, and they were very happy for her. Then she went about her usual business of the evening – setting the table; bathing Sonny; feeding him and putting him to bed; folding laundry on the cot while Sonny fought sleep until sleep overpowered him. But when Viola put the food on the table and called to Monica to come and eat, she did not answer or come out of the room.

Gwynneth called, "Monica, where you?"

Still no response. The bedroom door was ajar. Gwynneth knocked and pushed it open. Sonny was asleep on the bed, and Monica was taking his clothes out of the drawer, putting them into a small suitcase open on the cot.

"Monica? Where you going with Sonny clothes?"

Monica turned towards her, tears streaming down her face.

"What happen to you?" Gwynneth asked in alarm. Then, lowering her voice to a whisper, she urged: "Let's come out. We might wake Sonny." She took Monica's hand and led her out of the room.

"*Bondjé!*" Viola exclaimed on seeing Monica's face. "Something happen?"

She rushed over to Monica, got her to sit on the couch, and sat next to her. Monica answered in a mournful voice and with eyes downcast: "Tomorrow morning I carrying Sonny home and leave him for Mammy and them."

She spoke as though Doomsday had finally arrived.

They were taken aback and just stared at her. But then Gwynneth found her tongue: "So you going to suddenly drop him in Pilgrim and disappear from his sight for how long? How you think he will take that?"

Monica looked even more stricken. "Not so good, Tan Gwynnie," she whispered, shaking her head. "He not going to take it so good."

"Then why he cyaan stay here with us until you get a steady job and a place to live? For that time he would be seeing you at least on mornings and evenings. That would be better for him."

"That is too much trouble for the two of you, Tan Gwynnie. You see how jipsy he get now – he cyaan keep still. Allyou go have to be running behind him all the time. He go wear allyou out."

"Trouble? Sonny is trouble?" Gwynneth asked.

"Well, you have you school to see about... He will get in you way..."

"A-a. I have him in the schoolroom almost every day since school start back. Since when he getting in my way?"

In the last days of Mumma's life, Sonny had started "going to school" with Gwynneth so that Monica could give Mumma all her attention. This arrangement had simply continued while Monica went out to look for work. Now, a month after Mumma's death, Sonny was practically a student in Gwynneth's school.

He had to be persuaded, though, that in school people were obliged to wear clothes, and that not even bareback was allowed. He had taken up a habit of pulling off his vest and pants whenever he felt hot. And, needless to say, he was no longer inclined to lie quietly in a box. He was everywhere, walking around the schoolroom to touch everything his arm could reach. Gwynneth and the children had moved things so that Sonny would not be able to reach anything that could break; fit into his mouth, nose, or ears; cut him; jook him; scrape him; or burn his skin.

After Monica began looking for work, Sonny couldn't go over to the house for his daytime nap, as there was no one there. With

Lennox's help, Gwynneth and Monica had put up a crocus-bag hammock in the schoolroom for him. It took some days to persuade Sonny at his nap-time that there was nobody at home. Gwynneth had to walk him to the house and stage a search. Together they would go from room to room, looking under beds and chairs and tables, opening cupboards, calling out, "Monica! Mumma! You there?" Only then would he cheerfully agree to go back to the schoolroom and take his nap in the hammock.

Now he would go and tug at the hammock when he conked out from exhaustion at mid-morning or early afternoon, having laboured at a variety of arduous tasks Gwynneth had set him, such as tearing up newspapers; filling a Klim tin with gospo lemons and then emptying them out again; shaking a Fry's cocoa tin with a handful of dry pigeon peas inside and its cover firmly pressed on; crawling in and out of a big cardboard box and sometimes pushing it before him like a wheelbarrow; working the counter – rattling and rolling its big, brightly-coloured beads, shifting them from side to side on the wires, and now and then trying to pull one off.

Monica sat on the couch with her head bent and her face in her hands. Her shoulders were shaking. Viola rubbed her back and offered to bring her some water. Monica wiped her face with her sleeve and held her head up. Her eyes were red. Gwynneth was already on her way to the kitchen to get the water.

"I would glad if allyou could keep him for me, just for the while, Tan Gwynnie and Tan Vie, because Sonny not ready to stay in Pilgrim if I not there. I doan want to put no burden on the two of you... Allyou treat me so good, I doan want you think I using you. But I doan know how I going to carry him there and just turn round and leave him..." Monica's face dropped into her hands again.

"Doan worry, Monica. Sonny is not a burden," Gwynneth said. "We would gladly look after him."

"Last time I carry him home for the weekend, I leave him with Mammy and them and I went and spend the weekend by my aunt in Beauregard. Long time I ain go and see her. Mammy say that child bawl. He bawl. He walk all over the house looking for me and bawling. He bawl till he get hiccups, till he get tired and drop asleep on the floor. Then he wake up and start bawling again. In the night he refuse to go to sleep. Dads and Sylvan had was to hold him and walk up and down with him, rocking him till he fall asleep. When I come back Sonny latch on to me and wouldn let go…"

"Doan worry," Gwynneth said. "We will take care of him." She was ready to cry, too, at the thought of Sonny in such dire distress.

Monica cheered up, but then looked worried again. "But what about Mr Roy? He will agree to that?"

"We will take care of *him*, too," Viola promised, fiercely. Monica had to smile.

The next time they saw Roy was on Latoussaint night, a month and a half after Mumma's funeral. He had not come to Mumma's Nine Nights, nor her Forty Days. Before coming to the house on this night he had gone to the cemetery to place his candles on the grave. There was barely room for him to place them, as the grave was already well lit up. Gwynneth, Viola, Monica, Sonny, Marjorie and Lennox had been there earlier, to place their candles and spend a little time with Mumma. And Puppa, lying in the same grave.

Other people, who were there to light up their own family graves, had come over to talk with them, and some placed candles for Mumma as well. Gwynneth knew that even after she and the others left, more people would make it their business to go and replenish the lights on the grave, mainly for Mumma, but there were still people of St Anthony's congregation who would also want to pay their respects to Puppa at Latoussaint. Next they went to the public cemetery to light up for Mr Fitz and Miss Amy, the two of them also lying in one grave.

At the house, candles were lighting the way up the front steps, and some were placed along the bannister of the gallery. Gwynneth never failed to light candles at home for Latoussaint, one each for Papa Georgie, Gang-Gang Sarah, Delphine, Kofi, Puppa, Tantie Grace, David, and now Mumma.

Roy arrived, and when he got to the landing at the top of the steps he met the contentious bars still firmly in place across the entrance to the gallery. He stood among the candle flames and roared, "Gwynneth!"

She emerged through the front door, asking, "Why the France you making so much noise out here?"

"And why the hell this thing still here?" Roy countered as he stepped over the barrier.

It took some arguing. They had it out in the drawing-room. No, they were not going to throw out Monica and her child. Monica was looking for work in Kings Port, and they had decided to let her stay until she found a job as well as a room to rent. Meanwhile, in return for boarding, she would wash and iron for them, and continue to help, generally, with the housework.

Roy was enraged. As he took his hat and stormed out, he promised them that he would be visiting regularly, to protect his property rights, since he was in danger of being evicted by squatters.

28
"And a very good nanny you are, my dear."

Monica's job at the lawyers' chambers lasted six weeks. The permanent cleaner returned, and Monica left with a glowing letter of recommendation from the firm. She had been looking through the classified ads for a job and for a room to rent. Without a steady job, though, she couldn't actually rent a room, so she had already responded to several job advertisements by post, with guidance from Tan Gwynnie in the drafting of her applications.

In the last week of November, Monica received an answer from a Mrs Kramer at Fort Roosevelt Base who was looking for someone to work as a nanny to her two children, as well as do some light housework. She responded and Mrs Kramer sent instructions for her to take the 7.00 o'clock bus on Monday, 4th December, from Kings Port to Fort Roosevelt, where she would be met at the gate.

Along the route, the bus took up and let off people at each stop; but on the last leg of the trip, everybody still on board was going to work on the Base. These passengers were let off at a shed outside the entrance. Most of them had their entry passes in their hands as they stepped off the bus. Mrs Kramer had advised her to sit in the shed if she got there before anyone showed up to meet her. Monica came armed with her primary school leaving certificate as well as her letters of recommendation from Gwynneth and the law firm.

It was not long before a plump white woman emerged from the gate and walked towards her, enquiring, "Monica Polydore?"

The woman introduced herself as Mrs Kramer and shook Monica's hand. They walked to the gate together. Monica would eventually get used to the sight of huge guns, and soldiers swarming in and around the two buildings with the roofed gap between them that they called "the gate", but on that first morning she cringed. She had to be thoroughly searched as she did not have a pass, not that having one would prevent her from being searched every now and then in the months ahead.

Mrs Kramer's car was in a parking lot on the other side of the gate, and she drove to the house, where they sat on the veranda to talk. There were toys everywhere.

Mrs Kramer called into the interior, "Cookie, can you bring us some juice?"

After a while Cookie came out, bringing a jug of dark red juice and two glasses.

"This is Mildred, our cook," Mrs Kramer said to Monica. "Cookie, this is Monica."

Cookie nodded. She set down the tray, eyed Monica suspiciously and returned inside. The juice was rack like green-plum, tying up your mouth. Monica learned later that it was called "cranberry".

Mrs Kramer then called out Angie and Jerome. The two children appeared in the doorway, and she introduced them. Angie was five years old and Jerome, going on three. The two of them stood around for a bit, studying Monica intently. Mr Kramer, or, as she would learn, Lieutenant Kramer, was at work.

The nanny, apart from supervising Angie and Jerome, would be expected to launder the children's clothes (Mrs Kramer said there was a "washing-machine" and a "clothes-dryer" for that purpose); clean their room; read stories to them; and take them to the park. A lady came in three days a week to clean the house and do the adult Kramers' laundry. The nanny's light housework would be to tidy the house on the days in between the cleaner's days, and to help Cookie by setting and clearing the table. Cookie washed the dishes. Mrs Kramer whispered to Monica, "She's gonna try to dump the dishes on you, Honey, but take no notice. That's *her* job. After you've cleared the table, you'll need to get back to your kids, to make sure they wash their hands and brush their teeth."

There and then she handed Monica a children's storybook, opened somewhere in the middle, and asked her to read a paragraph to her and the children, who were still hovering nearby. Jerome was driving two little toy cars on the floor and Angie was brushing a doll's hair. Monica didn't bat an eyelid. She knew it was a test. Despite Monica having shown the woman her school leaving certificate, she was testing her to see if she could read, and read well.

Just in case Mrs Kramer was also trying to find out whether she knew what a paragraph was, Monica chose a piece that started at the bottom of the page, where there were four lines of a paragraph, the rest of which was on the following page. She read that piece to let Mrs Kramer know that she could tell where a paragraph began and ended.

When she finished the reading, Mrs Kramer clapped her hands and said, "Excellent, Monica! Kids? Wasn't that great, kids?"

"Yeah, Mom," said Angie.

"Yeah, Mom," said Jerome.

Mrs Kramer drew her chair closer to Monica's to say to her under her breath, "The nanny's pay will be twenty-five dollars per month." Monica near fell off her chair.

Mrs Kramer hastened to add, "Your kind of dollars." (*Like I so dotish to think is Yankee dollars she talking bout*, Monica thought.) "But, here's the thing," Mrs Kramer was saying. "We want the nanny to live in. Weekends off, but every now and then we might ask you to stay over a weekend, and for that there's extra pay."

Monica's head was spinning. The ad did not say live-in. But it didn't say twenty-five dollars a month, either. She had to think quickly. Where else in Cayeri could she make twenty-five dollars a month with her present qualifications?

"I'll give you a little time to decide," Mrs Kramer said, getting up from the chair. She disappeared inside.

With twenty-five dollars a month, Monica reflected, think how much she could save towards commercial school, and in a much shorter time than she had thought possible. Mrs Kramer would have received a flood of applications. Monica guessed that she had already rejected some applicants because they could not read, or read very badly. But there would certainly be others waiting in the wings and holding school-leaving paper and recommendations, just like herself.

It was an opportunity to be grabbed with both hands. Living in would mean she did not have to find a room and pay rent out of her wages. And even if she did take a room in Kings Port, there was no reason why she couldn't have a live-in job. She hadn't planned to keep Sonny in town with her. He was not going to grow up in some little fowl-coop room with a dirty piece-a concrete yard where man peeing and dog messing. In Pilgrim, Sonny had a whole house, and big, clean yard to run about in. Sonny was going to spend his boy-days out in the country.

But he wasn't ready yet to go and stay with his family. Or was she the one not ready for that? The truth was that if she were to die suddenly, God forbid, and he had to stay in Pilgrim, in time he would settle down. Indeed, for the weeks that she had worked at the law firm in town and was gone for the whole day, leaving him with Tan Gwynnie and Tan Vie, he did not miss her. He waved her off with a bright smile each morning as she left the house (he was still at the stage of waving bye-bye the wrong away around, beckoning instead) and never asked for her all day. There was no latching onto her when she came back on evenings. He was happy as Pappy with his godmothers. If they were willing to keep him during the week for a little longer, she would take him to Pilgrim every weekend, until he got used to living there.

From the Base she would head for Turagua on Friday evenings and iron for Tantie Gwynnie and Tantie Vie the same night. She would get up early Saturday morning and do the week's washing, and then set out for home with Sonny. In a month's time he would know his family better. She had misgivings, but she could only hope and pray that Sonny would quickly settle down with Mammy and Dads and Malcolm and Sylvan. Cyrus, too, even though he was now living up in their grandmother Madlain's house.

Every night since Grampa died, one of the boys – Cyrus, Malcolm or Sylvan – would go up the road and sleep in the house so Gang-Gang Madlain wouldn't be on her own. Eventually she had agreed to Cyrus moving in permanently. He was the only one in the family who could cheerfully tolerate Gang-Gang Madlain's cantankerousness. "Cyrus is a blessed child," everyone said.

Mrs Kramer reappeared and Monica told her she had decided to take the job.

"Oh, that's wonderful!" She smiled brightly at Monica. "We like you. Don't we like her, kiddies?"

"Yeah, Mom," said Angie.

And Jerome: "Yeah, Mom."

The children were a little distance away, now, playing with some other toys. The floor of the veranda was strewn with toys, from end to end. *Allyou "kiddies" go learn to pick up allyou own damn toys; I promise allyou that*, Monica vowed to herself.

Mrs Kramer took her on a tour of the house. More toys, everywhere. She showed Monica the bedroom that would be hers. It was next to the children's room, which looked as though a hurricane had passed through. In the laundry Monica viewed, with suppressed awe, the two machines made for washing and even drying clothes. Mrs Kramer would show her, on her first day at work, how to use them. They walked through the kitchen and onto the back veranda. Cookie was sitting there, filling up most of a two-seater Morris chair, smoking a cheroot. She acknowledged Mrs Kramer and Monica by motioning towards them with her chin.

In the days to come, after Mildred's third attempt at getting Monica to wash the dishes, and her sly probing (also futile) to find out how much Monica was being paid, the two of them became fast friends. In their free time between chores, they sat out on the back veranda and limed, mainly discussing – in Patois when Mrs Kramer was likely to be hovering nearby – the inexplicable habits of the Yankee people, for example the ease with which they threw away good food every day.

Chirren could take one bite out of they bread-and-sausage, screw up they face, and *bam!* in the dustbin it gone. And every time the Kramers held a "dinner party", the amount of steak and salmon and potato and greens you had to scrape off everybody plate afterwards was enough to feed the five thousand. And wasn only good food they throwing away. Plate and cup with just a little chip on them, nothing to prevent you eating and drinking out of them – in the dustbin. Pot and pan with just a little hole that they coulda carry to solder – in the dustbin.

On Monica's first day at work, Mrs Kramer had asked her to start by cleaning the children's room. "It's a holy mess in there, Monica. A holy mess."

A waste-paper basket in the children's room was full to overflowing, and when Monica picked it up, she spied in it something made of cloth. It was caught between crumpled drawings; pieces of toys (a doll's leg, a yellow aeroplane wing); biscuit- and sweetie-paper; fig-skin; partially sucked-out orange

316

halves… She fished the cloth thing out. It was a little jersey, Jerome's size, striped red and white.

Thinking that it had, perhaps, fallen into the basket by accident, she took it to Mrs Kramer, who responded absent-mindedly: "No, I'm pretty sure I threw that in the garbage."

"But Ma'am," Monica insisted. "It is only missing a button. Nothing else wrong with it. I could sew on the button."

"Naw," said Mrs Kramer. "Dump it. Jerome's gonna outgrow it in no time at all."

Mrs Kramer was putting flowers into a vase, first trimming off some of the leaves and cutting down the stalks. Monica lingered. "Ma'am?" she said. "If it is to throw away, I could take it for my son, please?"

It was too big for Sonny, but she would put it away until he could wear it. The two boys were only one year apart. Mrs Kramer turned to her, looking a little confused. Then a light seemed to go on in her head.

"Yes, my dear. Oh yes! There'll be a lot more of those when I go through the kids' closet, and you can have them, too, if you like. The kids'll be getting new clothes soon. Do you know a little girl to give Angie's dresses to?"

Thus it was that from time to time, Monica left for the weekend taking with her a bag of children's clothes that would otherwise have been thrown away, when the little pants just needed the elastic changed, the jerseys a stain removed or a little darning, and the dresses a little tear mended, an open seam or a sagging hem stitched back.

Jerome's clothes were put away for Sonny, and Angie's divided between some little girls in Turagua and St Paul whom Tan Gwynnie knew, and some other little girls in Pilgrim. Monica also took away, with the hearty permission of Mrs Kramer, discarded toys; broken crayons; colouring books that reached the dustbin after only a page here and there had been partly coloured in; picture books and storybooks that were the worse for careless treatment, but would still gladden the hearts of little Cayerian children.

Mrs Kramer's plumpness, it turned out, was not all fat. Mildred had remarked jokingly one day that the madam was putting on some size and needed to stop eating so much potato, tapioca pudding, and ice-cream. Some weeks later, Mildred speculated aloud, "You think she giving you another child to mind?"

"What?" Monica's eyes widened. "Nah. Doan say that, girl. Not a baby on top of these two!"

It was not long before Mrs Kramer called Monica out to the front veranda and sat her down to give her the news that Angie and Jerome were getting a little brother or sister. Monica must have shown some involuntary sign of alarm, for Mrs Kramer patted her hand and assured her that the baby was the reason they needed a nanny, not for him, but for the two other children.

"You're the nanny for Angie and Jerome, and a very good nanny you are, my dear. Thank you. That frees me up to look after the baby. And you will know that looking after the baby starts with me looking after me while he's in there," and she patted her belly. "Now, from time to time we'll need to get a babysitter for him – like, say, I have to be out for a few hours. I could hire somebody just for that, but I would prefer to pay that money to you, if you're up to some extra babysitting?"

"Yes, Ma'am. Thank you very much."

"Good! Now please go and call Cookie for me, so I can tell her."

The fighting in Europe came to an end in early May, 1945, with the defeat of Germany. In Cayeri, it had been announced beforehand that VE Day would be commemorated with a two-day holiday during which the authorities would suspend the ban on street processions. This announcement set off a frenzy of preparation in the camps of iron-beaters. They had been driven underground for just over three years by the wartime ban, and had remained largely out of the sight and mind of most Cayerians. In those three years, their numbers had multiplied, their players had grown in expertise, and they had come to be called "steelbands". When, therefore, on the morning of Tuesday, May 8th, 1945, they burst out of their confinement and into a largely unwitting public, many citizens were startled.

There were residents of Kings Port who hurriedly shut their doors and windows, some not knowing what the sound was. They were frightened by what they heard and saw outside – bands of youths in motion, raising hell with what seemed to be mainly tin-pans. But the steelbands earned the admiration of the thousands of Cayerians who poured onto the streets when the sirens went off that morning, to celebrate the victory over Germany. Huge crowds jumped-up behind the steelbands for the entire two days, all over the colony.

For those who had heard and appreciated the iron band in its early days, before it was banished from the streets, its sound was even sweeter than before. Those citizens who had never heard or listened to the boys beating on old iron were surprised by their skill. Other music bands, string and brass, also played on the road for the VE Day celebration, but the steelbands stole the show. VE Day would thereafter be remembered by Cayerians as the "coming-out" of the steelband, never mind it had been out on the road for the first two Carnivals of the war.

Phillip's band went to St Paul on both days for the VE Day celebration, and so did some of the other steelbands which had sprung up during the war in Turagua, Oropuna, Canaan and villages further afield, not to speak of all the new bands in St Paul. Late in the evening of the first day, Lennox came home, tired to the bone, but enveloped in a cloud of euphoria. He just *had* to drop in on Tantie Gwynnie to tell her all about it before limping home to catch some sleep and hit the road again in the morning.

"Suppose I was up in England, eh, Tantie Gwynnie? Look how I woulda miss this! How I coulda leave Cayeri, go up in England, and miss this? Eh? You see why I cyaan go?"

He had finished school the year before, and were it not for the war, Louis would have lost no time in fixing a date for his son's passage to Southampton. In the aftermath of VE Day, Lennox received an excited letter from Louis saying that the war would soon be over, and in the meantime, he and Kate were making his room ready. Lennox asked Gwynneth to look over a letter he had drafted in response, explaining to his father, as gently as he could, that he had no desire to go to England and study. But, Lennox wrote, what he would like was to go up and visit his father as soon as possible. Meanwhile, he was planning to apply for a job advertised by the County Council, and if he got the job, he could pay one half of the fare.

319

Gwynneth suggested that he make the letter sound more like asking his father's permission to stay in Cayeri. But it was quite clear to her that to get this young man to leave Cayeri and take up residence in England, Louis would have to resort to extreme measures, like getting a court order, and a policeman to load him bodily onto the boat. Louis would also have to fight off Marjorie. Gwynneth did not think that Louis would really contemplate making Lennox move to England against his will. Louis was disappointed, but did not insist (to Marjorie's relief). He wrote back that he was very proud of his big son going to work, and offering to help pay his way to visit his father.

Lennox was taken on as a clerk at St Michael County Council, located in St Paul. He had expanded his garden and it was flourishing, to the point where he was selling his surplus of pak choi, yam and tomatoes wholesale to a vendor in the market. And he remained a steelband fanatic. Nobody and nothing could prise Lennox away from his life as it was.

After VE Day, Mrs Kramer called Monica into her bedroom, closed the door, and still felt the need to whisper. "My husband and I have talked about this, Monica, and we've agreed to ask you ... Now, this is just between us, okay? Not a word to Cookie, yet, right? The kids're very attached to you, Monica, and you take such good care of them. I hate the thought of switching to a new nanny when we get back home, and I don't think the kids'll like that one bit. How would you like to come with us to the States and continue looking after them?"

Monica was dazed. She knew the family would go back one day, and she took it for granted that she would then have to find another job. But to be invited to a job in America – how many of her friends in Pilgrim would faint with joy at such an offer! Like them, she had harboured ambitions of going Away at some point in her life, but now that this had fallen so abruptly into her lap, she realised that she had never really thought about what going Away would mean. Right now it meant picking up and going to work in a faraway place, where she didn't know anybody but the Kramers...

And what about Sonny? In her younger years, when the dream

of going Away swirled in her head, she didn't have Sonny. She would have to think about this, and talk it over with her family, including Tantie Gwynnie and Tantie Vie.

Gwynneth and Viola did not mince matters this round. They told her she would be very foolish not to take up this opportunity. Over there she could get to go to school – high school and then commercial school, if that was still her goal. In America there would be many other types of job training from which to choose. As for Sonny's fate, Gwynneth didn put water in her mouth to let Monica know what her thoughts were: she couldn't seriously be still planning to take Sonny away from them to leave him in Pilgrim. Monica did not put up any resistance, although she again spoke with anxiety of Sonny wearing them out as they got older. Gwynneth and Viola looked at each other and had a good laugh.

"How old do you think we are, Monica?" Gwynneth asked. "Don't worry. We also thought our grandmother was 'old' when we were little. But at that time Gang-Gang Sarah would only have been in her fifties, like us today. I know you think that is old, but we have plenty life in us still."

Monica's family in Pilgrim also encouraged her to take up the offer. On her acceptance, the Kramers immediately set in train the official immigration procedures for her to enter the country as a domestic worker in their employ.

Germany had surrendered, but the war wasn't over yet. As far as Mrs Kramer was concerned, however, bringing it to a close was a mere formality which would take place any day now, so she celebrated with a grand clearing-out of the children's wardrobe, chest-of-drawers, bookshelf and toy-box, which produced a large pile for Monica to take away. Monica had to divide it into instalments and travel with a bagful at a time over the next month or so of weekends.

Mrs Kramer had always talked with her children about "when we get back to the States", although Angie would have had no memory of such a place, and Jerome was born in Cayeri. Mrs Kramer had no doubt that the new baby, due in July, was going to be born "in the States". This was not to be. The baby (Alexander, already clipped to "Al") was a full month old the day the atomic bomb was dropped on Hiroshima. Less than a month after the Japanese surrender was signed, Mrs Kramer was ready to start packing. On VJ Day, September 2nd, 1945, Cayerians celebrated on the streets again, with steelbands at the forefront.

Monica left for New York with Mrs Kramer and the children towards the end of September.

29
"For all of those seventeen years, I was still your man."

They had been expecting a quarrel; there was no avoiding it. Roy came up to pick zaboka, for the price of it in Kings Port market was more than ridiculous. He knew that Monica had gone to America. Yet here he was, facing not only the bars still across the gallery entrance, but the whelp itself, standing in the front door, calling out to him excitedly: "Boy! Boy!" A most vexatious reception. The child was smiling up at him, so he suppressed the roar that was rising in his throat. "Go and call your Tan-Tan," he said to him, with all the calm he could summon.

But now Gwynneth, too, was at the door, hurriedly scooping up the boy as if to save him from some kind of monster who would harm a little child. The glare Roy turned on her spoke louder than words.

"Just a minute, Roy. Come in, and sit down," she said.

Gwynneth took Sonny inside and whispered to Viola, who called Lennox over to come and get him. Sonny trotted off happily with his best spar, "Nennox", leaving the bigpeople to do battle.

Roy called them crazy for keeping the servant's child, letting her exploit them. It was typical, he said – a clear case of low-class people preying on the "rich" and gullible. "Except that the two of you not rich!" he fumed. "How you intend to feed another mouth? Well, she pull a fast one on you. Put that child in the orphanage! She will let you feed him and clothe him, mind him till he big enough to help her, and then one day out of the blue she going to come and claim him. She not interested in him now, because he would be too much trouble up there. Up in America, and places like that, they doan have no Granny and Tantie and Nennen to help you mind you child, you know…"

For the moment they just listened to him rant. When they could get a word in edgeways, they assured him that nobody was pulling anything on them; *they* had insisted on keeping Sonny. They also advised Roy not to lose any sleep over how they would feed and clothe him. Sonny's mother was taking care of that.

"So," he continued, "the two of you going to have this boy tie-up in allyou skirt-tail – a boy growing up between two old tanties. He sure to turn out a faggot. Allyou want to bring shame on this family?"

"That is foolishness, Roy," Gwynneth responded, patiently, not raising her voice in the slightest. "If he is going to be a 'faggot' as you call it, then he already is, and will be, no matter who brings him up."

Eventually Roy seemed to run out of arguments, so he got up, Mumma's old cloth-bag in hand, to go and pick his zaboka. He pulled the cocoa-rod from under the house and headed up into the bush. He thought of how much he loved to walk into this canopied area when he was a boy. It was like walking into another world, where, between the foliage on the trees and the low shrubbery on the ground, the air seemed to be coloured green.

Gordon and Freda had also loved to go into the land when they were little. They used to plead with him and their mother, unsuccessfully, to let them spend school holidays or weekends with their granny and their aunties in the country, or even just to overnight there. Now, they had absolutely no interest in even visiting Turagua. In Mumma's last days he had to force them to come and see her. That was always a tussle, for Helen sided with them, asking him, in front of them, why he insisted on dragging the children all the way out there against their will.

Yet, this place was theirs, and maybe as they grew into adulthood, they would begin to appreciate it once more, as he did now. On the other hand, God forbid, they might cut down all these trees and build another house on this spot, for rent to strangers... Or, they might just sell it off... Then, an even more startling thought flashed into his mind, so startling that it made him sit down, on the empty bag, right where it lay on the ground.

He had settled into the assurance that this property would be his one day, and then would pass to his children, because his sisters had no children, and were too old, now, to have any. But suddenly, it hit him – Gwynneth and Viola had kept this child; they were besotted with him; and they owned two-thirds of the property. His part was only one-third. Suppose they should put God out of their thoughts and leave their part of the property to the whelp! This impostor would end up with a larger share than his children!

Almost sweating with panic, he calculated that Gordon and Freda would each be entitled to no more than one-sixth of their grandparents' property. One-sixth of what, by right, was theirs to inherit in its entirety. His children were going to be cheated out of the lion's share of their inheritance. They were going to be tied together in ownership with a total stranger and his hordes of needy relatives out in the backwoods, probably all just waiting to descend upon the place! What a nightmare!

He should have been minding his business. It had never entered his head that Mumma's share of the property might go to Gwynneth, or to anybody but himself. How could Mumma give it to her? He was Mumma's favourite child, for God's sake! He had paid for her care over the past four years. And he had two children – her only grandchildren. It was Gordon and Freda, Mumma's flesh and blood, who by right should inherit from her, not the servant's bastard. He would get a lawyer and challenge it in court, he would…

Roy realised that he was getting ahead of himself. Maybe his sisters were not even thinking about matters of inheritance, and perhaps such matters would never arise. Who knew how things would turn out? At any moment the child's mother could decide to send for him, whisk him away to America, never to be seen again here. Or, Gwynneth and Viola might have to give up on trying to mind baby in their old age, and give him back to his family out in the bush… One thing was clear – he would have to look after his business from here on; he would have to keep an eye.

Before the end of October they got a letter from Monica, telling them that she had arrived safely. She was feeling cold all the time, but Mrs Kramer kept saying to her, "No, dear, it's just a little chilly. It's not winter yet. This is the fall."

Mrs Kramer had given her a whole pile of sweaters, and she was wearing two and three of them at a time. Monica also reminded Gwynneth and Viola that her brothers would be only too happy to come and fetch Sonny, take him to Pilgrim to spend time with the family, and bring him back to Turagua. Sonny was very comfortable with his Pilgrim family, now, she assured them. He had spent almost every weekend in Pilgrim over the past year, and a week at Christmas, and she wouldn't like him to forget them now. She had warned her family not to spoil him, though, for they were completely dotish over him.

Gwynneth wrote back to say that she was taking Sonny to Pilgrim after Christmas. She planned to take him and Garnet to the Holy Innocents service at St Hilda's, and then take Sonny to Pilgrim on the following day. She would leave him to spend some days in Pilgrim, and Cyrus or Malcolm would bring him back.

"I hope they bring him back!" Viola fretted.

Nothing Gwynneth said would reassure her. Viola remained nervous that Sonny's family in Pilgrim might steal him. Gwynneth was planning to take the train with Sonny, but Gaston offered to drive them to Pilgrim, and she accepted.

Sonny was taking in everything, repeating, trying to imitate what he heard and saw around him.

One evening in the Christmas season, the parang side "Los Hijos de Carmen" visited the house. Viola opened out both halves of the front door, and they (household and guests) sat in the drawing-room, giving over the gallery to the paranderos. From the moment they struck up, Sonny went out into the gallery. The group sang and danced and played their instruments – mandolin, cuatro, shac-shac, tambourine, box-bass, toc-toc – with a vigour that rocked the whole house.

For the full length of the first song, Sonny stayed rooted to the ground with his face upturned, right in front of the lead singer, enthralled by her voice. Then, during the next song, he gravitated to one of the shac-shac players and stood, again, in awe. He watched the man's every move. He also began to copy the dancing actions of the players, even as he paid close attention to the shac-shac man's hands. After two songs, and Sonny still transfixed before him, the man, who had white hair like Uncle Ollie, bent down and held out the two shac-shacs to him, saying, "You want to shake the marac, Boysin?"

Sonny turned around and looked for Gwynneth. She smiled at him and nodded. Sonny turned back to the man and gratefully took the two shac-shacs from him. A new song had started up. With a shac-shac in each hand, Sonny crossed his arms on his chest and then dropped his left arm to a horizontal position across his waist. With a movement of the wrist, Sonny began to shake the shac-shacs in time with the beat of the music, all exactly as he had seen the man doing. The paranderos cheered Sonny on, and the man turned him around to face the drawing-room, where everyone clapped and cheered for Sonny as he shook the shac-shacs, danced, and even did a little singing, though he knew not a word of the songs.

The next song was "*Rio Manzanares*" and those in the drawing-room all sprang up and pushed back the furniture to dance the Castillian waltz – Viola and Ollie, Gwynneth and Gaston, Marjorie and Philbert. Lennox picked up Sonny, and waltzed him around the room, first getting him to give the shac-shacs back to the man. At the end of that song Viola put down Ollie and took up Lennox for the next dance, and then the two of them went into the kitchen to see about refreshments. Sonny had gone to Gwynneth, and Marjorie danced one more set with Philbert before joining Viola and Lennox in the kitchen.

Sonny was fast asleep on Gwynneth's lap when the paranderos danced their way out of the gallery, down the steps, and along the walk, all the way to the gate, singing their farewell, "*Somos caminantes, tenemos que andar…*" and, "Same time, but another year / I'm sorry, my friends, we are leaving / Same time, but another year…"

Sonny had spent his first two Christmases in Pilgrim. This year he would spend it in Turagua, and would be there for Holy Innocents' Day, in the week after Christmas. Gwynneth usually played the organ for the Holy Innocents' service, when children with their Christmas toys seemed to fill the church, outnumbering the adults who had brought them. Often, by the end of the service, she would be nursing a serious stiffness of the neck, the result of trying to take in the proceedings from a sideways view. The location of the organ – behind the pulpit and up against a side wall of the altar, with the organist facing the wall – was not the best vantage-point. Gwynneth did so enjoy the spectacle, and kept craning her neck to watch.

There would be bedlam in the church. Apart from children's chatter and laughter, babies crying, and their bigpeople trying to quiet them, there were sounds of toy drums, whistles, ra-ras, crying dolls, and all the other noise-making Christmas presents. Those with toy vehicles rolled them in the aisles or along the kneelers. Toddlers would be at large in the aisles. When it was time to line up, one pew at a time, and go to the altar for the priest to bless children and toys, Gwynneth would watch with amusement the corralling of headstrong two-year-olds on the loose, who giggled and shrieked as they fled on unsteady legs, with their bigpeople, arms outstretched, pursuing them. Most of the bigpeople would be just as amused as the little escapees they were chasing after, and, when they caught up with them, would scoop them up, laughing too, and maybe hug them up, kiss them, scold them a little, and cart them back to their places on the pew. But some bigpeople reacted with anger.

One Holy Innocents' Day, Gwynneth saw a woman, whom she did not know, bend down and repeatedly slap her lively, jolly little boy on the legs when she finally got her hands on him. The woman dragged the toddler back to the pew, she with her face in a tight scowl, the child crying his heart out.

Gwynneth had to restrain herself from abandoning the hymn she was playing and marching down to say something to the woman. Everybody in St Hilda's regular congregation knew that you couldn't rough up your children in the presence of Teacher Gwynnie. The incident would have spoilt the day for her had she not seen what Mr Forde did. He was sitting with his daughters in the pew behind the woman. He got up, took the whimpering child from the woman and comforted him.

This December, Gwynneth had given early notice that she would not be available to play the organ for Holy Innocents' Day, as she was bringing two of her godchildren to the service. Sonny took with him the toy truck that Ollie had given him for Christmas, and Garnet, now five years old, brought his favourite Christmas present, a hefty football. (Monica had posted a parcel containing toys for Sonny and Garnet, meant to be Christmas presents. The parcel would not arrive until well into January, but they were no less delighted with its contents when it came.)

As soon as the singing started, Sonny put aside his truck in favour of the hymn-book. Each time the congregation sang, he burst into song, too, and insisted on holding the hymn-book before him as he rendered an earnest stream of gibberish. In between hymns, he and Garnet took turns at rolling the truck on the kneeler. Gwynneth kept a firm hold on Garnet's football, promising that she would let them kick it around the lawn after the service. "For a little while," she stressed.

She assured them that they would get to play some more with it in the yard when they got back to the house, for Garnet was spending the whole day with them, and would stay overnight.

Gwynneth met up with Earline on the lawn. She had brought her youngest, Olive, and her neighbour's two little boys. Gwynneth and Earline sat on a bench and chatted, while Olive took charge of all four boys and Garnet's football. They had a good time kicking the ball, right up until Mr Scantlebury began to hover with his bunch of keys, ready to lock the gate.

Gaston arrived bright and early the next morning. Viola had promised him breakfast, and it was quite a spread she produced, to fortify the party travelling to Pilgrim. She also handed them a basket of food and drink so they could have their lunch along the way. Then she bade Sonny goodbye with more kissing and hugging-up than the occasion warranted, as though she was never going to see him again. On their way Gaston dropped Garnet off at his home. Then they headed for the route along the coast, rather than the inland roads which more or less followed the train line.

Gwynneth suggested they stop off at Tucupita beach, for she wanted Sonny to see the river-mouth. It was some distance down the beach, and as they walked Sonny picked up things – driftwood, sea coconuts, stones, now and then a hardy fruit washed in from another shore – and pelted them with all his might into the sea. He picked up seaweed and Gwynneth showed him how to pop the berries. After a while he began to flag, and Gaston stooped, saying, "Come for a kokiyoko, boy", so Sonny travelled the rest of the way slung onto Gaston's back.

They got to where the Tucupita river, in crossing the beach, had stopped to carve a heavenly bathing-pool of clear, sweet water in the sand, before continuing on its way to the sea. Sonny wanted to go into the pool, but Gwynneth promised they would do that another time. Somebody big would have to go in with him, she explained, but the bigpeople had not brought their bathing-suits. No, neither she nor Godfather Gaston could just take off all their clothes and go into the water. Little children could bathe naked at the beach, but not bigpeople. (Gwynneth was glad that he didn't ask why, for she had no ready answer for him on that score).

They collected pretty shells and stones on their way back to the car. There Gwynneth took off Sonny's clothes and let him play in the sand, as well as splash in the waters that rushed in, shallow, from the breaking waves.

Sonny was happy to see his grandparents, uncles and cousins, who greeted him with exclamations of joy. He settled easily into the household, and from his perch on Malcolm's shoulders waved away Gwynneth and Gaston as they left. A date was set for his return – the following Saturday, which meant a week's stay. Venus assured Gwynneth that one of the boys would bring him back, on Saturday, or earlier if he fretted to go home.

Gwynneth and Gaston went back to Turagua by the same route, but chose another beach as the place to eat their lunch. They sat on a fallen coconut tree trunk, and as they ate they looked out to sea, breathing in the ozone and listening to the sounds of the place. *Like one old, old couple with no teeth in they mouth, chewing they cud with they bare gum,* Gwynneth reflected, *and they doan even have to talk.* A chuckle must have escaped her, for Gaston turned and asked, "What?"

"Oh, nothing," she answered.

"Tell me, nuh. You locking me out again."

She told him. Gaston laughed uproariously, then countered, "I will say like Viola: Who 'old'? Speak for youself!" They looked out in a tranquil silence again. After a while, he said, "But yes, we *are* an old couple, of twenty-five years' vintage."

"Hmph," said Gwynneth. "How you get twenty-five years, *Konpè*? 1920 to 1923 is three years. 1940 to 1945 is five years. Three years plus five years equals eight years."

"Again, *Makoumè*, speak for youself. You spit me out and throw me away for seventeen years; but for all of those seventeen years, I was still your man. In my heart, anyway."

They finished Viola's mandatory picnic. In the basket they had found rice-and-peas, macaroni cheese pie, salad, cake, mauby... bless her. Viola was still matchmaking, a full five years after Gaston's reappearance. She seemed to think he would make good his escape at the slightest opportunity if she didn't do her best to keep the two of them together.

Viola had even said to Gwynneth once or twice, "Why you doan go and live with him?" which was odd, considering that Vie had given Ollie a pile of reasons for not taking up his invitation to ride off into the sunset with him and live happily-ever-after. Gwynneth was convinced, though, that in suggesting she move in with Gaston, Viola was only being Gaston's messenger.

But he had long given up any hope of Gwynneth setting up house with him. He had hinted at it a few times before he made the suggestion outright one evening. Gwynneth's response was, "The best life we will have together, Gaston, is with you living at you, and me living at me. We will appreciate each other a whole lot more."

They got up and strolled along the beach, until they got close to the rocky mass, more than twice their height, that jutted out across the sand, towards the sea. The tide was coming in, and there were only a few inches of beach still visible between rock and water. Gwynneth stopped in her tracks. "Eh-eh!" she said, shaking her head. "Too late. Tide will cut us off. We can go around there another time."

Gaston had gone a few steps ahead, but now he turned back. "So, you doan fancy being marooned on a beach with your old-man?" he asked. "What could be more romantic?"

And he mimed a sulk. She threw sand at him.

The Pilgrim run became a set outing, or "lime" as Gaston would have it. The two of them would take Sonny to his family in Pilgrim at least three times a year – after Christmas, at Easter and in the August vacation.

30
"And sing, Nenn Gwynnie! And sing!"

Fly couldn't light near this child. Nenn Gwynnie said he was born in her hand, and that was only one of the stories she loved to tell him and he loved to hear. Another was the book-story that had Flopsy, Mopsy and Cotton-tail in it. That story was really about their own-way brother Peter Rabbit who ran away and ate something named "radishes", but Sonny wanted to hear more about Flopsy, Mopsy and Cotton-tail, for he loved the sound of their names. So Nenn Gwynnie had to close the book and make up some adventures specially for this threesome.

In the end she took them in to live with Brer Anansi's many, many children. Then Sonny would squeal with delight when Brer Anansi, before he went off on each of his adventures, said in his talking-through-the-nose spider voice: "Bye-bye Madame Anansi. I gone. Bye-bye Flopsy, Mopsy, Cotton-tail, Doreen, Kalowtie, Olive, Satesh, Sylvan, Clydie, Fareeda, Garnet, Judith, Imtiaz, Lennox, Sonny and all my other pickney too numerous to mention. I gone, to come back just now."

But of all the stories she told him, from books or from her head, the ones he loved the most were the stories of The Little Boy Who Came to Bless This House.

On some evenings he would get to be out in the gallery in the bigpeople lime, sitting on Nenn Gwynnie's lap, and she might tell a story. If she should miss and just start up the story dry so, he would exclaim, "Tim-tim, Nenn Gwynnie, say tim-tim!" She would then have to stop and call out, "Tim-tim?" and he would answer happily *"Bwa sek!"* after which she had to start the story again from the beginning. And Sonny's eyes, fixed on her face, grew bigger and bigger as he listened with all his might, while his mouth slowly shrank into a tight little **o**.

Once upon a time there were three old ladies...

"Who 'old'?" Nenn Vie would object. "Speak for youself!"

... who lived in a land called "Cayeri". The three ladies were Estelle (that was Mumma) and her daughters Gwynneth and Viola. They had two dogs, Mirasme and Bubulups, and an all-colour cat named Queen Victoria, "Miss V" for short. Mirasme was as skinny as can be, and Bubulups fat as a pig. Miss V ruled over them both.

It happened that Estelle, the mother, got sick, and they had to get somebody to help them take care of her. So Gwynneth went to Pilgrim and got Monica.

Monica came to live with Estelle and Gwynneth and Viola, and there it was that she made a little baby.

Now, at this part of the story, Nenn Vie would sometimes look sternly at Nenn Gwynnie, because she never knew what outrageous explanation would follow. With each telling, Gwynneth seemed to wax more biological, and Viola found that her sister ought not to tell the child things not meant for ears as young as his. But steups, Nenn Gwynnie thought, why tell children damn foolishness? No child would ever hear from her that a human baby was something brought by some bird, or by the midwife, in her bag.

At first the little baby lived curled up and comfortable inside Monica's belly. Then, when he was ready to come out, out he came, straight into Gwynneth's hand.

By this time Sonny had scrambled down from Gwynneth's lap and stepped a few paces back, waiting. When she said "out he came" he dived at her, head first. She would cup her two hands and grab his head as he landed, to show how she had caught him when he dived into the world. Sometimes he stepped back again and positioned himself for another dive, begging, "Again, Nenn Gwynnie, again! Catch the baby again!"

And as he charged towards her, Gwynneth would have to cup her hands and be ready for his landing again, sometimes three and four times again before she was allowed to go on with the story.

Then the midwife took him and slapped his bottom to make him cry. The little baby gave a loud bawl, "WAAA!" and that was when he started to breathe.

Here Sonny would roll over for Nenn Gwynnie to give him a pat on his bottom, to which he replied with a gleeful "WAAA!"

When Monica carried her baby to Estelle's bed to show her what a nice little boy she had made, the old lady tried to raise up her head, but she wasn't feeling so well that day. So Monica put him to lie on Estelle's chest for a little bit and the old lady smiled happily with her mouth that had no teeth in it.

At this Sonny never failed to let out a throaty guffaw. Then Gwynneth had to say (or Sonny would remind her to say it) that the baby had no teeth either, and so he would roar with laughter again.

The first thing Estelle said to the baby was: "Son? Sonny?"
And then she spoke to him in Patois: "Ou vini pou béni kay-sala? You come to bless this house?"
And she was feeling up his cheeks and his forehead, his nose and his chin – like this – because she couldn't see so well. Every day Estelle and the baby held conversations. Estelle would ask him: "Who this little sonny belonging to, eh?"
Or she would ask: "Sonny? They make tea give-you, boy? And your mammy give you tottots? Mama-ou ba ou tété?"
The baby loved it when Estelle talked to him in Patois. He could only wriggle, and kick the air, and wave his arms about, but that was his way of answering.

Sonny sprang off Gwynneth's lap: "And sing, Nenn Gwynnie! And sing!" he reminded her, a little anxiously, because sometimes Nenn Gwynnie forgot parts of the story, and this part he didn't want her to forget. (The truth is that on evenings when Nenn Gwynnie was tired, she would do a little editing here and there to shorten the story).

Estelle would sing to the baby, too.

She would sing Scottish and Irish folksongs she had learnt when she was a girl, in school: "Where, and O Where, is my Highland Laddie gone?" and "Coming through the Rye" and "O Danny Boy". She sang songs she certainly hadn't learnt in school – calypsos, like "Nettie, Nettie" and "Run you Run, Kaiser William"; stickfighting lavway, like "When I dead, bury meh clothes / I doan want no sweetman to wear meh clothes"; or Patois songs, like "Ba Mwen Yon Ti Bo", "Congo Barra" and "Jouvé, Baré Yo". To make the baby go to sleep she sang "Dodo, Piti Popo".

Sometimes the old lady sang forbidden Yarraba songs, calling up Shango, calling up Oshun, calling up Shakpanna, Yemanja and all the good spirits.

Ye ye ye Yemanja yile …
Yemanja yile omi lodo …

And she would sing other holy songs for the baby, psalms and sankeys and such. She sang these in the Shouter Baptist way, for she never did give a damn about any police. Estelle couldn't dance on her feet as she sang, because she couldn't stand up for too long; but she could dance to the songs with her head, her shoulders, and her waist, and she could clap her hands. The baby's favourite one was "Going Down Jordan".

Going down
Jordan
We are going down
Jordan
We going to walk the heavenly road.

I have a sword in my hand
I going to use it now
I have a sword in my hand
Help me to use it well.

I going away

To watch and pray
Never to come back till
The Great Judgement Day-ay-ay-ay
I have a sword in my hand...

And Sonny danced and clapped his hands as he sang, lustily and without, as yet, much tune, but that didn't matter – Nenn Gwynnie held the tune. This chorus was one that could go round and round forever, and Sonny never got tired of it, so after two or three rounds Nenn Gwynnie would have to bring it to an end with one loud and final clap at "The Great Judgement Day". Then he climbed back onto her lap.

After the baby learned to walk, Estelle closed her eyes and went to meet her ancestors:

Row me over the tide, boatman
Row me over the tide
Someone is waiting for me over there
Boatman, row me over the tide

Monica got a job with the Americans down on the Base, and then she went to America (where, it was thought, the streets were carpeted with Yankee dollars). She let Gwynneth and Viola keep her little boy, because they promised to love him plenty, plenty, and take good care of him.

"And give him nice-pink-tea?" Sonny prodded.
"Nice pink tea," Nenn Gwynnie agreed.
"And dumpling?"
"Yes, dumpling, too."
"And Cokes?" Sonny pressed.
"Not too much Cokes. Cokes not so good for little children."
And so on through hopsbread-and-ham? And chilibibi? And juice? And red-sweetie? And condensed milk?... until Nenn Gwynnie chose to cut it short: "And the name of that little boy was?" And when everybody – Sonny, Nenn Gwynnie, Nenn Vie, and some evenings Uncle Ollie Cotton-head, or Olfala Gaston,

or Tantie Marjorie, or Tantie Earline – answered "SONNY!" he slid off her lap, clapped his hands and danced, ran and hugged each of them, and rolled on the floor for a bit.

Then he climbed back onto Nenn Gwynnie's lap and settled into the faint sweet-grass smell of her clothes. With his eyelids falling down he would stuff two fingers into his mouth while the other hand reached up, kneaded Nenn Gwynnie's face a little and then latched on to her earlobe, gently. There, as their murmuring voices enfolded him like rain on the roof, slowly he would sink into sleep.

"I am no monster, in spite of what you think."

Roy took up again the habit of appearing, out of the blue, in time for Sunday lunch, as in the first weeks of Monica's stay. Gwynneth and Viola wondered what could be the reason for this new haunting of the home, like a returning ghost, compared with his virtual disappearance in earlier years. Whatever his reason, after a month of his Sunday visits, Viola issued an injunction: "Every time you feel like eating Sunday lunch in Turagua, just pass in the market, please, Mister, so you could come with some beef or pork, not with you two hand swinging."

Now, on his Sunday visits, he ate with the household at the table, having steadfastly refused to sit and eat with "the servant" during the time that Monica was there. Often Ollie, or Gaston, or both of them, would also be at Sunday lunch. Roy found himself quite enjoying the men's conversation around the table, a pleasure he had denied himself, regrettably, when the servant was there.

In the time before and after lunch, if the other men were not there, Roy liked to sit in Puppa's chair and read the Sunday papers, or relax on the gallery couch so he could feast his eyes on the greenery outside, feel the breeze on his face, and just think. If the child approached him as he sat, he would take a swift look around, or cock his ear to gauge how far away Gwynneth and Viola were, before shooing him off as noiselessly as he could. (Even though they tried, whenever Roy visited, to keep Sonny by the side of one of them, or at least within their sight, they did have things to do in the house and around the yard, and they couldn't very well drag him everywhere with them.)

Mumma had a little bronze figurine, resting on a doily in the middle of the drawing-room centre table. It was a cherub in singing pose – head raised, mouth open, fingers on the strings of a lute held crossways before him. Sonny loved it, and he was allowed to take it up and play with it, for it was indestructible. The cherub had occupied this spot in the drawing-room of every house their family had lived in. All three children, Gwynneth, Viola, and Roy, had come into the world and met it there. Only late in their lives did they discover that it was originally Puppa's, given to him by Father Francois of Holy Family church, where Puppa was once an acolyte. He, in turn, had given it to Mumma, in Pilgrim, during the days of their courting.

One Sunday, Roy was sitting in Puppa's chair, reading the newspaper he had brought along with the meat, when Sonny appeared at the centre table, smiling from ear to ear. "Boy!" the child greeted him, and reached for Mumma's cherub.

Sonny's smile vanished as Roy lowered the paper and frowned at him, hissing: "Don't you dare touch that!"

Roy leaned forward and tapped Sonny lightly on the back of his hand. Sonny's smile returned at the prospect of playing this new game. He tapped Roy's retreating hand and giggled, putting his own hand back on the figurine for Roy to tap him again.

"And don't be damn rude!" Roy growled. "You hitting me?"

This was what made Gwynneth fly out of the kitchen, to find Roy with his hand suspended in the air, palm opened, as if ready to bring it down on Sonny.

"Ey!" Gwynneth called out, and she laid into him. "Ketch youself! You doan put you hand on this child! Watch me – when you and you madam have allyou kangkalang, doan come here to take it out on other people, you hear? This little child ain do you nothing! Go and talk to your stuck-up, unmannerly chirren."

Meanwhile Viola had come out into the drawing-room. Shooting a scowl at Roy, she snatched up the bewildered child and whisked him away to the kitchen. He soon forgot about the puzzling incident, for Viola put a basin of soapy water on the floor for him, took off his clothes and gave him an enamel cup and plate, a tumbler, and some spoons, to "wash".

On one of those evenings when Gwynneth allowed Sonny to stay awhile in the gallery with the bigpeople, she was reading to him, for the umpteenth time, *The Tale of Peter Rabbit*. There arose, that evening, a discussion about how Cotton-tail, one of Peter's siblings, would have got that name. Sonny wanted to know what "cotton" was (easier to answer than "What is 'radishes'?"). Viola went inside and brought out a fistful of cotton-wool to show Sonny. Then they looked at the pictures in the book again and agreed that each little rabbit's tail did, indeed, look like a ball of cotton-wool pinned on to its bottom.

Later that evening, Ollie arrived, and stood for a moment at the gallery entrance, wiping his feet on the mat. Sonny, by then drowsing on Gwynneth's lap, detached his head from its resting-place on her chest. He took his two sucking-fingers out of his mouth, pointed at Ollie's crop of white hair, and called out: "Uncle Ollie Cotton-head!" That became Sonny's name for Ollie. And his name for Gaston was "Olfala Gaston", which was what he made of the tongue-twister "Godfather Gaston". These two gentlemen, Ollie and Gaston, submitted cheerfully to their renaming; but Roy was not so accepting.

"Boy" was Sonny's earliest attempt at Roy's name. That was what he heard when Gwynneth or Viola called his name. To her dismay, Gwynneth had seen Sonny approach Roy, wag his finger at him and address him in a sharp, scolding voice: "Boy!" This was embarrassing to Gwynneth, because Sonny was clearly mimicking her and Viola in their dealings with their brother. Embarrassing to Gwynneth, amusing to Viola, but to Roy, infuriating.

Gwynneth worked hard at getting Sonny to say "Mister Roy", for she did not think that Roy would be thrilled to have this child claim him as "Uncle". The other thing was that Roy might be thinking his sisters had coached Sonny to call him a boy, for they had never put water in they mouth to tell Roy how immature they found him to be.

As it turned out, Sonny couldn't manage "mister". His earnest attempts at repeating the word after her only produced showers of spittle. He did shift, however, from "Boy" to "Yoy", so Gwynneth left it at that for the time being. Now Sonny took to welcoming Roy at the front door with ecstatic shrieking and jumping up and down like a chimpanzee: "Yoy! Yoy! Nenn-Gwynnie-and-Nenn-Vie, Yoy come!"

Sonny called his morning and evening cup of cocoa "my nice-pink-tea". On mornings he could be quite crotchety until he had gulped down his pink tea, draining the enamel cup that looked as though it had been through the war. (He indignantly refused to give up his battered cup and drink out of the fancy thing with teddy-bears on it that his mother had sent for him.) He would position himself on the little peerha placed just outside the kitchen door, and call out, "I want my nice-pink-tea!" This might be followed by, "Nenn-Gwynnie-and-Nenn-Vie! Where my nice-pink-tea?" and, seconds later: "Nobody not giving me no nice-pink-tea?"

Sooner or later an adult voice would float out from the kitchen, "Can I have my nice-pink-tea, please?"

He would dutifully repeat after the voice, but not without some pique. One morning, when the cup of cocoa did not appear with sufficient speed, even after he had used the required words, he suddenly called out, "For heaven's sake, can I have my nice-pink-tea, please!"

Gwynneth and Viola looked at each other and stifled their laughter. They decided not to make any fuss over Sonny's new turn of phrase, as it did not break any major rule of polite society that a two-year-old needed to know about. Sonny was only taking after his Uncle Ollie: "For heaven's sake, when the County Council going to fix that road?" and "For heaven's sake, Viola, hide the cake. I done fat enough already!" and so on.

They began to be cautious about what they said in Sonny's presence.

"Ladies and gentlemen," Gwynneth would remind the assembled gallery. "We have to be on our Ps and Qs. The Gestapo is among us."

Before long, somebody only had to whisper "Gestapo" for them to lower their voices, or stop a whole conversation in midstream. No bad-talking Roy and his poor-great bakra-johnny wife. No jokes about the woman Mumma used to call "The K-foot fool" who still came to the gate from time to time, Bible in hand, to preach fire-and-brimstone warnings to those not willing to be converted to the teachings of the church she belonged to. No mauvay-lang, generally, and no cuss-words, when Sonny was within earshot. They would have to get Roy to also heed this caution. But that was not all. Gwynneth resolved that she and Viola would have to exercise more patience with Roy.

She wanted to have this conversation with Roy, alone, minus Viola who was ready to just cuss him out and tell him to watch his nasty mouth around the child. On one of Roy's visits, Gwynneth asked Viola to keep Sonny inside for her while she took Roy to the schoolroom to talk. "Roy," she began. "Sonny is at a stage now where he can understand a lot of what he hears. We glad you love us so much that you finding the time to visit us regularly; but when you come here, you will have to be more careful about the way you talk to the child, and the remarks that you make about him in his presence."

"A-a. What remarks I make? You want to put me under censorship now? Next thing you will want to ban me from my mother house!"

"Roy. Roy. You call the child 'golliwog', 'tar baby', 'blackamoor', 'whelp', 'bastard'..." Gwynneth found herself going into a rant, so she pulled back and softened her tone. "Roy, you think I doan know what the bakra school did to you? You think I didn see how they full you up with hate for youself till you didn even want to look at you own face in the glass, Roy? Remember that? You didn even want to acknowledge you mother. She was seeing it, too, you know. She coulda see that she had lost you – lost her *doudou*, her sweet lagniappe child, to the bakra school. And she didn hold it against you. Now she dead and gone, with all of that in her heart."

Roy looked distraught.

"You have to promise me," Gwynneth appealed to him, "not to do the same wickedness to this child, not to undermine him as they undermined you. We doan want to have to hide him every time we see you coming, because then he will be afraid of you. Especially if you going to be barking at him like when he went to pick up the ornament the other day."

"So, no correcting him, eh? He can do anything he please, not so?"

"No, he can't. He has permission to play with that ornament. Roy, you *will* allow this child to grow up seeing himself as beautiful. You will allow him to love himself, and to be confident. I want you to promise me..."

"I want you to promise me that you and Viola not going to take my children property and give it to this child!" he blurted out, and then looked stunned at his own words.

Gwynneth was equally stunned. Her mouth fell open and she was speechless for a moment. "That is what you have against this child, Roy? But why would you even think such a thing?"

"Never mind," Roy said, and got up to go. He could have kicked himself. Clearly they had not given this any thought before, but now he had put the idea into their heads. "Never mind – you have my word. I won't do any harm to the boy. I am no monster, in spite of what you think."

Sonny soon learned to climb up on the drawing-room couch and turn on the radio, but if there was no music on it, only somebody talking, he would steups and turn it off. If there was music, he sat still and listened, and when a familiar song or advertisement jingle came on, he would spring to his feet to sing along and dance.

And they had to start locking the piano. Gwynneth was giving piano lessons again, and Sonny found this to be a most exciting activity. If he had his way, he would be most present at every lesson. He had to be enticed away by Viola, or taken over to Lennox and Marjorie. Afterwards, Gwynneth would let him sit beside her for a moment on the piano stool, just like the students, and play the notes. Sometimes Gwynneth would play one or two of his favourite songs and they both sang along.

One day Gwynneth forgot and left the piano open after lessons. It was not long before they heard, coming from the drawing-room, lusty singing accompanied by cacophonous piano sounds. Sonny had climbed up onto the piano stool. He was sitting naked, his fingers moving up and down the keyboard, as far as his hands could reach in either direction; and he was singing – what song they could not tell, but he was belting it out with great fervour. Given half a chance he would play the piano all day long, every day, but he knew better than to throw a tantrum when Nenn Gwynnie put the lid down and said, in her I-not-joking voice, "OK. That's all for today."

He had experimented a few times with tantrum-throwing to get something he wanted and they disapproved of. But that never worked. They ignored him completely. Once or twice they even put him out in the backyard ("To dry" Nenn Vie said), until he stopped kicking and screaming.

Sometimes when Sonny misbehaved, Nenn Gwynnie would send him to look for Nice Sonny, the well-behaved one. "Go and see if he in the gallery. If he not there, look outside, and if you see him going down the road, call him back. If you doan see him, stay in the gallery and wait till he come back from wherever it is he gone."

There were times when he put God out of his thoughts and resisted, using his favourite word: "No!" Then Nenn Gwynnie would lift him up and put him out in the gallery. He would bawl all the way out, and even after she went back inside and closed the front door, he continued to make a racket. She didn't open the door until he stopped. At other times he would go to the gallery without a fight, but not quietly. He would walk out bawling, for the worst thing was to be banished. Often, as he bawled his lungs out in the gallery, Gwynneth would have to ward off Viola. She felt sorry for him, and would whisper to Gwynneth, "Spare him this time, nuh."

"Eh-eh. Let him stay out there and think. It not going kill him."

If he went out willingly, Gwynneth left the door open. Sooner or later he would stand in the doorway and call out to her until she appeared, if she wasn't right there in the drawing-room. "Nenn Gwynnie?"

"Yes?"

"Me come back."

"Who that?" Nenn Gwynnie would ask.

"Is me, Sonny."

"Who Sonny?"

"Nice Sonny, Nenn Gwynnie."

"*Sé pa Sonny mal élivé?*" she would enquire. "Not bad-behaved Sonny?"

He was elated when she answered in Patois. It meant that things were good between them again, for that was their cosy language.

"*Non*," he assured her. "*Sé Sonny byen élivé.*"

"*Ah! Sé Sonny byen élivé! Vini Doudou!* Come, *Doudou*. Nenn Vie! Look well-behaved Sonny come back."

If Nenn Gwynnie was standing, he would run to her and hug her legs. If she was sitting, he jumped onto her lap and leaned against her, put his two sucking-fingers into his mouth and with his other hand would begin to knead her face.

They heard from Monica regularly. True to her promise, she sent money every month for Sonny's upkeep, and from time to time a parcel containing clothes, books and toys, some abandoned by the Kramer children, and some that she had bought. She sent beautiful picture-books, just right for Sonny's age, but so many of the images were nothing to do with his world that Gwynneth felt obliged to intervene. She took up pencils, crayons and a watercolour set from the schoolroom and converted some of the apples into mangoes or caïmites, pears into pommeracs or zabokas, and grapes into chennettes. She drew in here and there a coconut tree, or a fig tree with a bunch of bright yellow ripe-fig hanging on it. And she gave some of the humans a deep tan.

Monica's parcels always contained something for Gwynneth, Viola, Marjorie, and Lennox – chocolates, sweet biscuits, a brooch, a scarf, a smart-looking Yankee man-watch (to quote Viola) for Lennox. As Sonny neared his third birthday, Monica sent a letter with money enclosed, asking them please to take Sonny to a photo studio on that day, have his picture taken and send it to her. Gwynneth replied that she and Viola would put that money in the Penny Bank for Sonny and send his birthday picture as a present to her every year. Or, for as long as he was with them, Gwynneth reminded herself. Roy was right, of course – Monica could take her child at any time.

32
"Is like the story of Louis and Babsie all over again."

The red-letter day was at hand – July 1ˢᵗ, 1946. In this election of the Legislative Council, every Cayerian twenty-one years and over, rich or poor, male or female, would have the right to vote. Viola announced that she had no intention of bothering herself to go out and vote. She was not at all impressed with the high-sounding "universal adult suffrage" ra-ra, for she did not see how it would change anything. *"Menm bagay,"* she said. "Same old khaki pants." As for the candidates offering themselves to her choice in the County of St Michael, she dismissed them as three lochos: "Tweedledum, Tweedledee, and they brother."

The others intended to cast their votes, for what it was worth. However, they agreed with Ollie that this latest reform of the constitution was, once again, a mamaguy, a pappyshow, nothing near what people had been agitating for. It was no big step forward from the "reform" palmed off on Cayerians in 1922, a generation before.

"Certainly a far cry from Home Rule," Gaston pointed out. "We only voting to put in *part* of the government. The governor will appoint the rest, and he plus his appointees make up a majority, so he still in control! The governor will continue to be lord of the Leg. Co. and the long arm of the British government."

"And is still only well-off people can *sit in* our government," Gwynneth added. "Now everybody can vote, even if they doan have two farthings to rub together, but not everybody can go up for election to the Leg. Co. That is still only for people of wealth."

Ollie reminded them of the battles that had taken place in and around the franchise committee set up to decide whether Cayerians were fit to be given universal adult suffrage. "Putting labour representatives on the committee was only for show," he said. "They put them in after they did done make sure and stuff the committee with people who doan want to see everybody get the vote. And them committee members do exactly what they put them in there to do. Watch how much obstacle they throw in the way."

"Thank God for all the people on the ground keeping up the fight," Gwynneth commented, "unions, political parties, all kinds of groups…"

"And writers of letters to the editor, like Gwynneth Cuffie," said Gaston. "All of that is part of the pressure from the ground that make the motion get through."

"And by the skin of its teeth," Gwynneth noted. "Seventeen votes in favour, and sixteen against!"

Ollie persuaded Viola to go out on election day and exercise her right, if only to honour all the struggles Cayerians had waged, over the years, for political power. This was going to be the first time in their lives they could take part in choosing the government. "Doan mind is only half a loaf we get, this rounds," Ollie said to Viola. "The struggle ain done. We still fighting. One day we go take over we government from the British, and all of we go have the right to take part in running Cayeri business. One day."

Somewhere in the 1945 August holidays, Gwynneth had started talking more and more about her grand plans for retirement. She would be eligible for pension in 1948, but she might consider pushing her retirement to, say, 1950, if she lived to see that year. Why 1950? Well, it was a nice, round number; it would be the middle of the century and during that year Sonny would turn seven – he would be big enough for big-school. Gwynneth was talking about closing down her school at the end of 1950 (God-spare-life), thereafter to pursue, at her leisure: tutoring; giving piano lessons; expanding the story-book table and running it as a children's lending-library; forming, at last, the children's choir that would specialise in Cayerian songs; and publishing the songs that Moun Demmeh had collected in 1919.

Two of the core members of Moun Demmeh had migrated, and Edwin had died. Gwynneth was still in touch with some members, and she could, conceivably, muster them for the purpose of bringing out the songbook, as a lasting tribute to the work of the organisation. She was even thinking of forming a girls' steelband... Viola would only say "Hmph!" and roll her eyes at what Gwynneth saw as retiring to "rest her bones".

But the 1950 retirement date was not cast in concrete. Gwynneth sometimes hinted that she might close the school even before she became eligible for old age pension, and start living off private tutoring for schoolchildren, as well as piano lessons. The pension was a miserable pittance, anyway. "Two-three hours a day of private tutoring after formal school hours will bring in more than that pension. Is tutoring I survive on for the six years at Catherine Street. Now I have a roof over my head with no rent to pay. And then the war make all of we accustom to living frugally."

The war had also got people growing more of their own food (those who had not already been growing almost everything they ate). She did not foresee any danger of starvation, because the provision garden in their own backyard was flourishing, with expert help from Lennox, and they had a huge breadfruit tree up in the land, not to mention the other bearing trees.

When Monica left for America, in September 1945, Sonny had been "going to school" with Gwynneth for a year already. The distractions that Gwynneth provided for him in the schoolroom still held his attention for part of the day, but more and more he wanted to do things that the other children were doing. He sat between them, "writing" on a slate; solemnly turned the pages of a dilapidated storybook; stood among them and "counted" to a hundred; sang along with them in music time. And when he was tired, he would announce "Lull donk," and one of the older children would help him into his hammock to sleep.

At the start of the school term in January 1946, Sonny was two and a half years old. Gwynneth continued to put out a set of objects every day for him to handle, and she also let him roam at will about the schoolroom. But during the course of that year, Sonny became more and more interested in whatever those on the four-year-old bench were doing each day.

By June, when he turned three, he had abandoned taking his nap until after school, so engrossed was he in drawing and colouring on newspapers rather than tearing them up; sorting dried peas and beans into little heaps of black-eye peas, red beans, pigeon peas, split peas and jumbie beads; decorating his slate (for he now had his own) with a crowd of insect-like shapes meant to copy the row of letter **o**, or **t**, or **b** that Nenn Gwynnie had written across the top of the slate.

Towards the end of 1946, Gwynneth announced that she had made up her mind – the coming year, 1947, would be the last for the school. The others were flabbergasted. How could Gwynneth decide just so to part with her beloved imps? And why would she choose to forego, at this point, the income she gained from the school, when the pension, meagre or not, wouldn't start until April 1948? The tutoring thing seemed dicey to them.

"Meagre better than nothing," Viola argued. "Tutoring in town is one thing, but out here? You think Turagua have enough people with money to pay for private tutoring?"

"Yes, man," Gwynneth assured her. "Turagua, St Paul, Oropuna … We'll see."

There was no visible reason why Gwynneth couldn't keep her school open for another ten, fifteen years. She was healthy. She didn't look any more tired than the rest of them, all four of them either sixty-something or pushing sixty (not readily admitted by Viola) and not one of them about to retreat to the rocking-chair. They prodded Gwynneth until she revealed that in addition to all the other projects in her head, there were some things she wanted to get done while she still had all her wits about her.

She was going to put together into a book a selection of the letters she had written to the newspapers since 1916, most of them never appearing in the press. She would seek to have this book published. (Gaston clapped and exclaimed, "A book of living history!" She took a bow in his direction and went on talking.)

She wanted time to devote to writing. She was going to write some stories for Cayerian children, about Cayerian children, with illustrations done by Cayerian children (Gaston clapped again) and she might even write a novel for bigpeople. Now the others joined Gaston in cheering, "Raaay!" But then they began to prod her about the subject of this novel, and all she would say was, "Oh, just the story of a woman… And all you stop asking me all these damn questions, now. What the hell!"

Days later, when it was just the two of them, Gaston suddenly asked, "Will I be in the novel, Miss?"

Gwynneth did not immediately catch on, but then replied, "You? I said it's the story of a woman."

"Well, presumably this woman will have a boyfriend who is part of her story?"

"One?"

"Okay, boyfriends. But I think that as her life goes on, she settles on one?"

"Hmph," was all Gwynneth would say.

"Miss, doan be too hard on that fella, eh – the one she settle on. He may have made a bad start, but he ain turn out too bad in the end – what you think?"

"I think you doing too much presuming, Sir."

Gwynneth's change of plan (closing the school earlier – at the end of 1947) would involve putting Sonny into big-school before he turned five. The headmaster of St Hilda's Anglican, Mr Daniel, agreed to enrol him in the 1948 school year. Viola was not pleased.

"You putting the child in big-school when he is four years old?" she exclaimed. "You throwing him in the bamboo!"

"Four and a half," Gwynneth said. "At the beginning of the 1948 school year he will be four and a half years old."

It took a lot of talking to persuade Viola that Sonny would be fine. She had hoped that he would not have to leave Gwynneth's school until Standard 5, like the rest of Gwynneth's pupils.

Two Sundays after Carnival 1947, the conversation was what to do about Lennox. Marjorie was at her wits' end. Lennox was brooding, not eating, locking himself in his room, and saying very little to her. Veronica's parents had banished him. Gwynneth brought Ollie up to date.

"Veronica is Lennox girlfriend. Or *was*. She join the staff at County Council a few weeks after him, and from then on everything was Veronica. Day in, day out, 'Veronica this', 'Veronica that'. Lennox in love. And her family, it seemed, was very impressed with him. They thought he was the cat's pyjamas – inviting him to Sunday lunch, taking him on their beach outings, the mother starting to drop hints about wedding bells and grand-children… Until somebody tell Veronica father that he see Lennox playing in a steelband in St Paul, Carnival Tuesday. The father ban Lennox from setting foot in they house, and forbid Veronica to have anything to do with him, even threatening to pull her off her job, all for no other reason than Lennox is a steelbandman."

Veronica's family lived in a quiet village up in La Pastora Valley ("Behind God back," Viola sneered, when the parents started acting up. "Country-bookies.") Gwynneth had been planning to intervene on behalf of Lennox even before Marjorie begged her to go and talk to the parents. She asked Lennox if that was okay with him, and he was only too eager for her to go and visit them. Tantie Gwynnie was the one to talk them out of it. Gaston went with her.

This "visit" was chilly and brief. The mother shooed Veronica inside, seated the visitors in the gallery and went back in herself. The father came out and sat with the two of them. Gwynneth spoke in support of Lennox. Nothing penetrated this man's disapproving face.

"Is like the story of Louis and Babsie all over again," Gwynneth remarked to the company in her home gallery.

"And these two youngpeople working in the same office?" Ollie asked. "Not so easy to avoid each other. That must be very uncomfortable."

"We have to advise Lennox to steer clear of her, though, eh," Gaston warned. "That father – I doan like the look of him at all. No telling what he's capable of."

Marjorie looked startled.

"I had a chat with Lennox," Gwynneth said. "And from that conversation, I can tell you that Veronica well know what her father is capable of. Lennox say that Veronica, now, does look frighten to death whenever by accident the two of them eye make four, and if she find herself walking towards him, she will make a about turn and speed off in the opposite direction. He say she done cut him off already. And that is what hurting him. He find she abandon him too quick and easy, like switching off a light, the minute the parents order her to get rid of him. Veronica ain no Babsie!"

"How old are they?" Ollie enquired. "Not twenty-one yet?"

"Both of them will be twenty years old this year, not so? Lennox in July, and Veronica?" Gwynneth looked to Marjorie.

"She done make twenty already," Marjorie said. "October gone."

"Twenty years old. Serious, responsible workingpeople," Gwynneth fumed. "You handling the government business, earning you own money, and you parents can still have this kind of control over you life? You cyaan even choose you friends? And why they doan want they daughter to friend with Lennox? They know Lennox. They know he's a decent, respectful young man. Not a hooligan. Not a criminal. They know him, and they like him. But they acting out of prejudice, not reason. The world will have to think over what is the legal age of adulthood, *oui*! Nowadays a twenty-year-old is not a child!"

Viola steupsed at the folly of these parents-from-behind-God-back, and spoke with vexation: "This might be the time for Lennox to go up by his father and cool off."

All agreed, happy for this way out of the mess.

"Problem is, though, he only been on the job one year and some months," Gwynneth pointed out. "He won't be entitled to much vacation leave."

"But if this thing affecting him so bad, it might be wise for him to take no-pay leave," Viola proposed. "He ain have no chirren to feed, and he have a roof over his head. One month no-pay leave ain go kill him. Better he lose money than he lose he mind from tabanca."

"He could afford to take no-pay leave, *oui*," Marjorie said. "He well making he lil money from he garden and putting it in the bank. I hope he agree to a holiday up by Louis, for he will have a good time with he father and forget about them people. I cyaan bear to see how hard he taking this thing."

Within a matter of weeks, Lennox was off to Birmingham, early one morning, lugging a suitcase heavy with Cayerian confectionery and other things to eat that Louis loved – made and packed by Viola and Marjorie. That night Marjorie did not sleep much. She could not put out of her mind how forlorn he looked at the airport. He could barely stretch his mouth into a smile when Tan Gwynnie made a joke about his overstuffed suitcase and the bulging bag over his shoulder, "Boy, they well load you up with food, eh? Like is the Sahara desert you heading for!"

When Marjorie fell asleep, she dreamed Lennox landing in England to find that it was really a desert, and there was nobody in sight, until Veronica appeared on the far side of this wide expanse of sand. He called out to her, but she turned and fled.

Next morning Marjorie went in to work, put down her lunch bag, and said breezily to her boss, "Lil-Aleong, *Doudou*, I coming back just now. I have to go and do something."

Marjorie was the only employee in the shop who could call Old Man Aleong's son by the pet-name the community had given him. She stopped a route taxi going towards St Paul and got off in front of the County Council.

Marjorie had never met Veronica's parents, but she knew, even before this thing happened, that she did not like them – the father because he was a damn ass, and the mother for letting the damn ass get away with he stupidness. Lennox had talked about Veronica a lot, and the topic of her family had come up quite often. He had told her how the father behaved when Veronica's godmother gave her a note to take to her parents, saying she was willing to put her godchild through high school. Veronica badly wanted to go to high school, and her godmother was offering to stand the cost – fees, books, uniform, season ticket for the train, down to lunch money and pocket money. The father threw the note aside and said, "If money going to spend for a child to go to high school, in this house that child will be one of the boys."

And the mother ain say a word. Well, the godmother leave she house, quite in town, and come up in La Pastora to deal with the father. He, now, with all he big-mouth and fat-talk, all the in-charge he in-charge, he fraid this woman. He boil down like bhaji. Why? Because she big – she was the matron in the hospital. And on top of that, she fair-skin. The damn-fool father does bow down to high-colour people. And then, when Veronica finish high school and pass she exam, he doan want the girl take no job. Keep the girl home for a whole year, until – next big kangkalang – the godmother had was to come up this side to take a lag in he tail again. Now he threatening to make Veronica leave she job.

Inside the Council building, Marjorie stood at the counter and searched the pool of people sitting at desks. Before she could pick her out, Veronica shot up from her seat and began walking briskly to one end of the counter, where she lifted up the flap to let herself out.

"Good morning, Miss Marjorie," she said under her breath. "We could talk outside, please?"

Her voice was nervous. She led Marjorie out into the yard at the back of the building. Marjorie dived right in, although Veronica had opened her mouth to speak.

"So what really happening, girl? You have my child in one helluva state. I put Lennox on the plane yesterday morning..."

Veronica jumped. "He gone?"

"So you didn know he going up in England to see he father?"

"Somebody tell me that, yes. But I didn know when! You mean Lennox couldna even send a message to let me know? To say bye-bye dog, I gone?"

"He say you turn you back on he – you cut him off..."

"No, Miss Marjorie!" Veronica's reply was a shriek, but then she looked around her anxiously and returned to almost whispering. "Is *he* that cut *me* off. Lennox know that my father have a spy inside that office, and if he hear I was talking to Lennox, he will make me leave the job and stay home. But still Lennox keep coming to my desk to try and talk to me. We have a plan that until I reach twenty-one years, he could just come and meet me by my godmother, for I does spend one weekend in every month there. He was meeting me there all the time, before this.

"When I reach twenty-one, I going to leave my father house and stay in town by my godmother until I could get my own place to live. That is why I cyaan afford to lose this job. I doan want nobody mind me; I saving up to support myself. When I am twenty-one, my father cyaan make me leave the job. I will be twenty-one in October. That is only six months from now. But like Lennox cyaan understand that he will spoil everything if he doan stay far from me in the office. Everything will work out if he could just have a little patience!"

Marjorie leaned her head to one side. "That is all? So you ain cut him off?"

"No, Miss Marjorie. I wouldn't cut off Lennox!"

"But he doan know that. Girl, see about you business, eh," Marjorie said, digging in her purse. She fished out a slip of paper. "Look here. This is he father address. Write to he. You doan want he get so mash-up with tabanca that he decide to stay up there with he father and ain come back. He father wouldn't like nutten better."

Veronica's eyes widened, and her face began to crumple.

"Doan cry, *Doudou*. Just see about you business. Man doan always behave like if God give them sense. Sometimes you does have to think for them. Write to he *today*. Post it *today* – post office right next door to you work." She gestured towards the adjacent building. "Now go back inside before they fire you and mash-up allyou plan for real." And to herself she thought, with a steups and a chuckle: *Allyou youngpeople just too damn happy, oui!*

Marjorie turned and headed back to Turagua to start her day of shelving goods in the storeroom, measuring out and packing flour, rice, dry-peas and sugar into one-pound, two-pound, and five-pound paper bags, and helping Lil-Aleong in the rumshop section. There she served customers and washed glasses. Lil-Aleong also depended heavily on her when it came to sorting out rowdy or belligerent drinkers.

33
"Hush you mouth! You want something to cry for? Here!"

In the Christmas vacation of 1947, Gwynneth began to get Sonny ready for big-school. She bought his reading-book and exercise book, and packed them into the brightly-coloured Mickey Mouse schoolbag Monica had sent. Gwynneth took him to the tailor, to be measured for his Anglican School uniform, and Mr Worrell told her to bring the cloth after Boxing Day. She would begin drilling Sonny, also after Christmas, to answer to the name "Joshua Polydore". And they decided they would wait until the last moment to buy his school shoes, lest his feet outgrow them before school opened.

The whole plan fell down, however, when it came to cutting his hair. Sonny's hair had never been cut. They had kept it plaited in cane-row, Viola renewing the plaits every weekend. Now he sat squirming on a chair at the bottom of the back steps, with a piece of curtain draped around his shoulders. Viola had the comb. She had started undoing his hair. Gwynneth stood by with the scissors. The little cloth bag that Venus had made for them to put the cut hair in was hanging by its drawstring on the chair back. But Gwynneth began to feel palpitations coming on. "Stop, Viola," she said, weakly.

This was too drastic an action. Gwynneth felt as though they were preparing to sacrifice an animal. She could not proceed with this.

"What, now you sending him to big-school in plaits? For the chirren to call him 'girl-boy'?" Viola asked.

"No," Gwynneth replied. "We not sending him to big-school, not yet."

"Ah!" was all Viola said, and she set about re-plaiting the two cane-rows she had undone.

Having changed her mind about sending Sonny to big-school in the new year, Gwynneth would now have to think what next. She had been really looking forward to closing her school at the end of 1947, as fondly as she would always remember what had been a priceless twenty-one and a half years with her rambunctious imps.

She could teach Sonny at home, but she didn't like the idea of a child being schooled entirely by himself... Her decision was to send word out that for the 1948 school year *only*, she would enrol a class of five- and six-year-olds. This offer was gratefully taken up by some families who had been obliged to enrol their infant children all the way over in St Paul. They were happy to pull them back and send them to Teacher Gwynneth.

Towards the end of the 1948 August vacation, Learie brought a message from Phillip, asking if she could come, please, and hear something he was rehearsing for an upcoming engagement. San Miguel Warahoons and St Paul Syncopators had developed to a level that Gwynneth could not have imagined when she first took these boys under her wing. They needed no such tending now, but still sought her out to share with her, Gaston and Ollie the pride of their every new achievement. Their numbers had grown; each of the two bands was well over twenty members strong. Both were doing well in steelband competitions held in St Paul and in Kings Port. They had become quite skilful at tuning pans.

The music training from Teacher Gwynneth had served the Warahoons and the Syncopators in good stead. As part of this training, she had taught Phillip to play the recorder flute, and he had taught it to those band-members who were interested in tuning, so that they could sound each note and reproduce it accurately on the pan. Each of the two bands had invested in its own recorder flute.

Gwynneth was happy to learn that in Kings Port (and no doubt elsewhere in Cayeri) there were other people who had adopted steelbands and exposed them to music training. These bands were coming up with innovations which spread to others. Steelbandmen, generally, had gone beyond making a pan with a few notes on it just to play a bar or two of a song. They were now putting more notes on their paint tins and sweet-oil drums, and playing whole pieces. Those pans that were tuned to produce melody had come to be called "ping-pongs."

357

From the beginning, however, tuners had been using only the eight-note diatonic scale, mainly because they knew of no other. Steelbandmen were only just becoming acquainted with the richer chromatic scale. Just as she had foreseen, melody was taking on more and more importance. Phillip was well ahead of many a town band. He had learnt about chromatic and diatonic scales long before most tuners in town began to put thirteen notes on a pan. When he felt that he had fully mastered the science of tuning pans, he had turned to the challenge of making a ping-pong that carried a full chromatic scale.

Instead of getting a new pan just yet, he would use the sweet-oil tin on which he had already put the eight notes of a diatonic scale, placed around its edge. The middle of the pan-face was clear. Over a period of months Phillip and Learie had worked at putting the additional notes needed to make up the chromatic scale into that middle space. Gwynneth had followed the under-taking through Lennox, who went up on some evenings and sat in on tuning sessions. This ping-pong would come to be the *pièce de résistance* of the San Miguel Warahoons steelband.

The first time she had heard Phillip play the finished instrument was at St Hilda's Orphanage Christmas concert in early December 1947. On that occasion, the band played the choruses of "Jingle Bells" and "Joy to the World". Then Phillip played unaccompanied, on his thirteen-note pan, verse and chorus of "O Holy Night" to a marvelling audience. Gwynneth spoke with him afterwards.

"That was a beautiful performance, Phillip! Now I want you to consider making another big step forward. Moving to the chromatic scale is quite an achievement, and now that you have a wider range of notes, I want you to think back to something we talked about when we were doing the music lessons: *harmonising*. Remember? I notice you have three ping-pongs in the band, all playing the same notes. Just think what a difference it would bring to the sound of the band if you could arrange some harmonising."

Phillip remembered Teacher Gwynneth first talking to him and Kelvin about harmonising at a point in their music lessons when they had become thoroughly versed in notes and scales and key, among other things. They had learnt to name each note and enter it correctly on a music sheet. They could read a tune and play it on the piano and the recorder. Then she had moved on to harmonising, showing them on the piano what it meant; but in those days they had little use for that knowledge. Kelvin had only just started tuning a pan; Phillip had one paint tin with three random notes on it, and another with five notes just to play a line from the chorus of one song.

After the 1947 Christmas concert, Gwynneth had offered to do a few more sessions with him and Kelvin in the new year, when she expected to have more time, with the closing of her school. She wanted to teach them, if they were interested, about composing a counterpoint. In the new year the school was not closed, as she had planned, but Gwynneth kept her promise. The two young men took to this training like ducks to water. Gwynneth realised that they both had a natural ear for harmonising a melody.

They could just *hear* a counterpoint in their heads to any melody line. She would play a melody on the piano, and when she played it again, either one of them was able to sing, off the cuff, a counterpoint that produced a very pleasing harmony. But that was not enough for Teacher Gwynneth. She thought they should be equipped with some of the basic rules of counterpoint, and she also wanted to get them into the habit of identifying and writing down the notes of the counterpoint melody – or anything else they might compose.

"Make sure you teach everyone who joins your band to read music," she said to them again and again. "It is time that your bands move towards becoming *orchestras*, playing harmonised music. Work out different parts for the ping-pongs, and do your musical notation. That way, everybody will be clear what they're supposed to be playing, and you won't get wrong notes – clashing sounds that will spoil your harmony. Not many steelbands have made that move as yet, but in the end they will all see how much sweeter the music is with harmonisation."

Some steelbands in town had recently taken to using 55-gallon petroleum drums, discarded by Fort Roosevelt Naval Base, to make their ping-pongs. In the 1948 Carnival season Kelvin and some friends went to a fête in town where the music was provided by a steelband. The major attraction in the fête was this broad-faced pan that all by itself could easily drown out the sound of the other ping-pongs in the band. Kelvin spent so much time hovering near the band to observe this impressive instrument that the girl he had invited to the fête was quite displeased and flounced off, fuming.

On the way back to St Paul he got an earful from her, but he barely heard. He was too excited by this new pan. He had spoken with the player and learned that the reason it was louder than all the pans they had been using so far was that it was made of harder metal, which also made it sturdier, not so easy to mash up. And the notes held longer – they were not readily knocked out of tune as could happen with the lighter tins they had been using.

Kelvin lost no time in contacting Phillip. They hired Mr Sylvester and his rickety, wheezing truck to take them to the dump outside the Base. There they got themselves six of these large, sturdy oil drums, three for each band. They sawed off the bottom segment of each drum at about nine inches, and made that into a ping-pong, sinking the face inwards, as all bands now did. Kelvin and Phillip had never warmed to the convex pan-face.

On the last weekend in August 1948, Gwynneth and Gaston went up to the palay to hear the piece Phillip was rehearsing. What they heard there was a most sophisticated performance by Phillip and Learie playing "Ave Maria" as a duet, on two pans made from thrown-away petroleum barrels, each pan with no fewer than seventeen notes. Learie played the basic melody, and Phillip, a descant that Gwynneth described as "heavenly". She and Gaston stood up to applaud, and she to hug-up these now towering young men with gruff voices who would always be "Gwynneth's boys".

On Boxing Day 1948, Gwynneth, with some trepidation still, asked Gaston to cut Sonny's hair. Gaston did so without batting an eyelid. Gwynneth collected the precious clippings into Venus's cloth bag, and that was the end of that. They took his picture to send to Monica.

The time had come for Sonny to get used to his going-out name. All through the rest of the Christmas vacation Gwynneth drilled him so he would remember to stand up and say, "Present,

Miss" when the teacher called out "Joshua Polydore?", for that would be him. (Joshua Elford Kofi Polydore, to be exact.) But up until that morning when they put him in his blue shirt and khaki pants, stiff from starch and ironing (Viola's eyes filling up with water, the old fool), and his first pair of white washicong, he was just Sonny, their eyeball. Some called him Gwynneth's Shadow.

Sonny was five and a half years old when he entered Anglican School in January 1949. He had already learnt everything there was to be learnt in First and Second Primer, and could easily have gone straight into Standard 1, but Gwynneth did not think it would be best for him to be placed in a class where the average age was eight years. She therefore had him placed in Introductory.

On his first day he sat looking around, taking in the bigness of this schoolroom, and all these children! There were children filling up this oversized schoolroom from one end to the other. Then the teacher said "Roll-call!" and he knew what that meant, so he tuned in to her voice and fixed his gaze on her. She was calling out names, and he had to listen for his going-out name, Joshua Polydore. He began to recite it in his mind, *"Joshua Polydore, Joshua Polydore, Joshua…"* But his head swivelled again, because the children sitting with their backs to him, with a teacher of their own, had suddenly started a chattering and seemed very excited at something, so he wanted to know what it was.

Suddenly he realised that his teacher had stopped calling out names. He turned his eyes back to her. She had raised her head from the book and was searching with her eyes for somebody. And all the children right around him, facing his teacher, were looking all about, too, turning their heads this way and that. His teacher did not look pleased. "Joshua Polydore?" she asked, impatiently. There was a steups in her voice.

Sonny jumped up from his seat, shrieking, "Present, Miss!" a little too loudly. The children breathed a laugh, as though they were glad that she had found him, just in time, before something bad could happen; but the teacher smiled, too. (Later in the term Sonny would catch on: Miss had only been pretending to search for him, in order to teach him that he must pay attention. At roll call one day, Miss kept calling out Doris Beresford's name, and

361

searching all around with her eyes, even looking behind her and up in the air. All the children were saying, "Look she there, Miss! Look she there!" and indeed Doris Beresford was right there in the second row, not too far from Miss, just too busy quarrelling with a boy behind her who was kicking her bench.)

Now Sonny planted his elbows on the desk and held his face firmly in his hands to prevent it from turning away again. He stared intently at the teacher, determined to listen with all his might. His face was turned towards the teacher but his thoughts began to drift away to Nenn Gwynnie and Nenn Vie; to Lennox and Tantie Marjorie; to Pilgrim and his cousins, his uncles, Gang-Gang, and Papa… when he heard the teacher call out, "Sonnylal Premchand?"

A boy stood up. Without thinking, Sonny shot up again, and exclaimed to the teacher, "I name Sonny, too!"

All the children giggled, and the teacher's mouth was trembling with trying not to laugh, but then her mouth spread out into a wide grin. The other boy was standing, looking uncomfortable. The teacher said to Sonny, "Okay, Sonny-Too. Look you twin-brother, Sonnylal," and she pointed her chin at the standing boy. "Or maybe we should call you-all Sonny-One and Sonny-Two." The teacher smiled warmly, and the children, including the two Sonnys, giggled.

At recess time Sonny was caught up, willy-nilly, in the stream of children pouring out of the building. He knew what "recess" meant, but this jostling bewildered him. He realised, with some alarm, that he could not move of his own accord; they were pushing him along, pressing closer and closer around him. He cried out, "Ey! Allyou squeezing me!"

He heard his teacher's voice above the children's noise: "Lynnette! Hold that little boy's hand. Take him for water and to the toilet."

A big girl elbowed her way towards him and grabbed his hand. She moved him along, shielding him from the pushing and shoving, and then they were out in the yard. She led him past the children lining up for UNICEF milk and biscuits, past the wild crush at the standpipes, straight to the row of latrines at the back of the building, and waited for him. Then she took him to the standpipes, where the crowd now looked a little less fearsome. After he had got a drink of water, Lynnette took him to the long bench just outside the front door of the building, and ordered the children sitting on the bench to make room for him: "All you come on! Dress round!"

To Sonny she said: "Stay there until you hear the bell. That mean, time to go back inside."

With that, she turned sharply and went about her business, swinging her limber arms.

At lunchtime Nenn Gwynnie appeared, as she had promised, bringing food for him. Many of the children had gone home for lunch; others ate around the yard or the playing-field. There were only a few children indoors, eating at their desks, like Sonny. Gwynneth stayed with him for the whole lunch period, peering at him for any clues that would tell her how he was faring in this new place. She had gained nothing from asking him outright, "You like big-school?" for his answer was a swift nod and nothing more, as he tackled his dumplings. He did not look in any way distressed when she waved him bye-bye at the gate, and she made her way home with a sense of great relief.

That afternoon Sonny tried his best to listen to his teacher only, and block out all that was going on in the sea of children and teachers around his class. He did not miss his turn to stand up and read aloud from the Introductory reading-book that, weeks before, he had read from cover to cover. He copied the sums Miss wrote on the blackboard into his exercise book and set about working them out.

Then, a loud crack, a cry of pain, and a bawling from the other side of the aisle, a little way behind his class. Sonny's head swivelled, but he couldn't find the child. He turned his face to his teacher, with a questioning look… But his head swivelled again at the sound of a sharp, snarling voice: "Hush! What you crying for? Hush you mouth! You want something to cry for? Here!"

And he was just in time to see a teacher with her hand upraised, holding a ruler, and the hand coming down – another loud crack – and the child cried out again. Sonny was seized with fear. He began to wail as he stood up and tried to get out of the stuck-together bench and desk, but he couldn't. He was locked in by children sitting on either side of him. Panic allowed him to climb onto the desk, crawl to one end of it and jump off, all of this before any of his bench-mates could react to his daring action. They were puzzled; they could not think what was making him so frantic. They looked at the floor under the desk and didn't see any snake or scorpion or anything else that could have frightened him. And they were uneasy, for the consequences of his daring could come down on all of them.

The whole school fell into a nervous silence as Sonny sped howling along the narrow aisle and headed for the door. He ran outside, across the yard and through the gate, where he stood, crying, looking right and left along the road, not sure which way was home. His teacher appeared behind him and tried to calm him down, but he shook off her hand and began shrieking, "I want to go home! Nenn Gwynnie! Nenn Gwynnie!"

Somebody alerted the headmaster that there was ruction at the school gate, and he came out. By then the teacher had already persuaded Sonny that Nenn Gwynnie would soon come for him. It was after half past two, not far from the end of the school day. When the teacher related to Mr Daniel what had happened, he held his head and said, "Oh Lord. Miss Cuffie is not going to like this one little bit. Which teacher was it? Miss Corbin, nuh?"

Sonny's teacher, Miss Telemaque, nodded. She was, herself, quite shaken by the episode.

"I thought so," Mr Daniel sighed. "Please go and tell her I want to see her right now."

Sonny was still whimpering, but he agreed to go and sit in Mr Daniel's office and wait for Nenn Gwynnie, while Miss Telemaque went and got his school bag.

Viola wanted Gwynneth to take him out of the school immediately and teach him at home. Viola was so het up that Gwynneth did not interrupt her ranting. Eventually, though, Gwynneth shook her head.

"Sooner or later we going have to send him to school, Vie. We cyaan keep him in a cocoon forever. We will let him stay home for a day or two. Then I'll take him back. No teacher will put God out of they thoughts and beat Sonny. I settle that with Mr Daniel before I put him there. And I try to make Mr Daniel see that he could have that conversation with all his teachers and get them to stop beating the children, because he himself is not a beater. He doan believe in beating children. He is a kind, thoughtful man, but he ain moving no mountain. He is Mr God-rest-the-dead. 'Too great a leap for the teachers.' And, 'What will the Inspector say?' And 'The parents *expect* you to beat they children. People genuinely think that good parents and good teachers are those who beat children…'."

Gwynneth sighed, heavily. She would have to reflect on the matter before going back in to talk with this headmaster. She couldn't really criticise Mr Daniel for not wanting to take on that fight. She knew just what he was up against, for she had fought that fight.

34
How we going to keep them down?

In her childhood Gwynneth had attended four different primary schools, in places all over the colony – Morain, Coryal, Lakpat, Trois Rivières – wherever Puppa was posted. Like every one of those schools, Oropuna Government School, where Gwynneth did her first teaching, resounded daily with weeping and wailing and gnashing of teeth, brought on by the crack of whips and belts and rulers on children's skin.

This was just normal, everyday school noise which did not turn any heads. The only beatings that interested anybody enough to make them look in that direction were the ones in which a schoolmaster doubled a boy over a desk, pulled the boy's pants down, and with a thick leather belt or tamarind whip, near flayed the skin off his bottom which was exposed for all to see. Benchings (witnessed by the whole school) were not an everyday occurrence and were spoken of in hushed tones.

She would carry in her head for the rest of her life the sound that came from her Standard 5 classmate at Lakpat Government School, Freddie Quamina, piercing the hush that surrounded his benching. Freddie was a skinny boy, with a head that seemed too large for his body. All his teachers thus far had agreed that he just could not learn, but Mr Taylor seemed to think that it was just stubbornness and laziness. Gwynneth caught sight of the terror in Freddie's eyes as Mr Taylor, having chased the other boys off the two benches, Freddie's and the one in front of his, lifted him off the floor and slammed his body over the desk. There he remained, like a broken stick, bent at the point where his legs were joined to the rest of him, and uncomfortably keeping his head up.

Mr Taylor's belt came down on him again and again with an awful crashing sound. Usually boys would try to salvage some shred of their dignity by not crying, not giving a whimper during this experience. It was a feat at which some of them succeeded. Freddie gripped the backrest of the bench in front of him as his whole body jerked with each blow; but he kept his silence. The whole school held its breath.

Suddenly Freddie let out an eerie high-pitched squeal, a piglet sound, that startled everybody, including Mr Taylor. It did not resemble any human sound that Gwynneth had ever heard. The teacher's arm remained suspended in mid-air for a moment before it brought down a last blow on the boy. After that he released him. Gwynneth remembered the incident vividly, but never could recall what error in his exercise book had earned Freddie that particular assault.

Gwynneth had always wanted to be a teacher. In 1901, Puppa was transferred from Lakpat to Trois Rivières R.C. School, and there Gwynneth finished her primary school education, going through Standards 6 and 7. Then she was taken on as a pupil teacher at Oropuna Government School. She spent the early years at Oropuna doing silent battle with Miss Munroe, the senior teacher who supervised her. Miss Munroe kept warning her that the children would get out of hand if she didn't get serious with them. She noted with alarm that Gwynneth had no strap or whip, or anything to beat them with; furthermore, this pupil teacher was doing too much smiling and chatting with the children.

"You are their teacher, not their friend," Miss Munroe scolded, and later handed Gwynneth a tamarind whip. Gwynneth accepted it meekly, took it home and broke it into many little pieces.

Gwynneth was only fifteen years old, not in any position to argue with Miss Munroe, so she listened quietly, with a placid face, to all of the woman's admonitions, not answering her, but not budging, either, on her refusal to beat the children in her charge. Miss Munroe became very frustrated with her. She called Gwynneth recalcitrant, rebellious, and bent on turning the children into some little renegades like herself. Whenever the noise in the schoolroom, shared by ten classes, became louder than usual, Miss Munroe blamed Gwynneth's class. "Spare the rod and spoil the child! What happen, you too lazy to beat them? You will be held responsible for these children's misbehaviour."

On more than one occasion Miss Munroe came close to slapping her. She only changed her mind, Gwynneth thought, because this pupil teacher was the daughter of Joseph Cuffie, headmaster of Trois Rivières R.C. School, whom it would be prudent not to anger. It was, no doubt, for that reason also that Miss Munroe did not simply have her dismissed. That would have been very easy to do; pupil teachers were expendable material. But not Mr Cuffie's daughter.

Instead, Miss Munroe took to visiting Gwynneth's class far more often than she did the other pupil teacher's. And each time she dropped in on Gwynneth's class, she would stand and slowly run her eyes over every child until she found one who, she said, was fidgeting. That child would be slapped, or hit with Miss Munroe's ruler, and loudly berated for the whole school to hear. Gwynneth would be screaming inside her head: *You old witch! You doan know little chirren cyaan keep still for long? You know anything about little chirren, you old soucouyan?*

Gwynneth was determined to some day get into Teachers' Training School, and she vowed that when she came out as a trained certificated teacher, wherever they posted her, she would go into that school and make them stop beating children. She would seek out parents and teachers who were also against beating children, and invite them to form a group that would work towards the abolition of child-beating in Cayeri...

At Oropuna she passed her pupil teacher exams for the Third Class and Second Class certificates, with Puppa helping her prepare for each exam. Now Miss Munroe was off her back. Gwynneth applied to Training School, and took her place in the queue. She taught at Oropuna for two more years, waiting to be admitted. Miss Munroe, who had withdrawn into a resentful silence around Gwynneth, breathed *Good riddance* when she heard that the unruly girl had got a place at Training School.

When Gwynneth came out of Training School, she was appointed to St Paul Government School. She was assigned to the Standard 3 class which, along with Standard 2, sat at ground level right in front of the stage. The space up on the stage was shared by Standard 4 and Standard 5, the latter taught by Headley Burris. For her sins, Gwynneth's class was right under Mr Burris's. By the end of the first week she knew that she would have to steel herself, either to keep her mind fixed only upon the children in front of her, or, to take action.

Routinely, at the end of every lesson, every day of the working week, Mr Burris lined up all the children who had misspelt words in dictation, or got wrong answers in mental arithmetic, or stalled speechless and trembling in the middle of reciting a poem by heart – all those who had made mistakes during the lesson. The hapless offenders, on reaching the front of the line, had to hold out one hand with the palm upturned, the hand that was in less pain than the one struck in an earlier lesson. Burris would pick an instrument from the array on his table – guava stick, tamarind whip, leather belt, ruler, electrical cord – and dish out lashes into the children's hands. The blows were laced with insults: "Dunce!" "Nincompoop!" "Ignoramus!" "Stupidee!"

Children waited anxiously in the line, squirming, wringing their hands, shifting from one foot to the other. Early in the term, a girl, waiting in line to be beaten, peed herself and stood frozen in the pool that collected on the floor. Another child was sent to the headmaster's office to get a floor-cloth. Meanwhile Burris tried, without success, to get the rest of the class to laugh at the girl, still standing in her pee, crying. What warmed Gwynneth's heart was that no matter how much Burris taunted the girl, her classmates went into a stony silence after one or two obedient snickers had shrivelled and died.

Daily, Gwynneth bit her tongue and bided her time. She couldn't make so bold as to walk into the people school and immediately start criticising, especially as nobody else seemed the least perturbed by what was worrying her. But she knew she would not be able to hold it in for long.

She considered speaking to the headmaster, Mr Seignoret. How could she be sure, though, that he was not of the same ilk as Mr Burris? Many headmasters were. *Most* headmasters were, including Puppa. And Mr Seignoret did sometimes carry a whip in his hands clasped behind his back as he went on his usual slow, attentive walk from one end of the schoolroom to the other, picking a class at random for inspection of the children's exercise books. The headmaster might just dismiss her as a news-carrier…

At the first two staff meetings, Gwynneth had been very quiet, but she made up her mind that she would say something at the next one, the last staff meeting scheduled for that term. But what would she say? For days she composed and discarded versions of the comment she would offer. She didn't want it to sound as though she was preaching at her colleagues, or scolding them. But at the staff meeting, all her judicious preparation came to naught, for what fell out of her mouth was not what she had carefully planned.

Mr Seignoret began the meeting by expressing concern about the dismal performance of pupils at arithmetic, in most classes, especially Standard 5. "A few teachers seem to have found the right formula for teaching arithmetic," he noted, "and Standard 3 is an outstanding example. Miss Cuffie, I hope you will agree to share your secret method with the rest of the staff?"

Before Gwynneth could give any kind of answer, Mr Burris piped up, announcing that he had a plan to improve his pupils' performance at arithmetic: "I have told them that they will get two lashes for every sum they get wrong…"

Gwynneth flew up out of her seat, and not waiting for permission to speak, or for Burris to finish speaking, she blurted out, "But you can't get children to learn by beating them!"

Just as abruptly she sat down, with an apology for speaking out of turn.

"Not at all, Miss Cuffie," Mr Seignoret answered. "It *is* your turn. Would you mind coming to the front to speak?"

She did mind, but nevertheless walked up to the front and faced the staff, with the headmaster standing at his desk beside her. "Children just don't learn at their best when they are in fear and in pain," she said. "As a child I could not learn arithmetic because of fear. My teachers couldn't beat me because my mother had forbidden it. Yet in arithmetic class, with the teacher beating my classmates all around me, my brain would seize up from fear. I eventually learned arithmetic because my father took his time with teaching me at home, patiently, and without licks. My mother wouldn't let him hit me."

"So," Mr Seignoret mused, "you're saying that, in your experience, flogging can actually prevent a child from learning? Interesting. What about bad behaviour – you don't believe in punishing children for bad behaviour, either?"

"With all due respect, Sir, 'punishing' does not mean beating. If children misbehave, they must face consequences. And for me, Sir, getting a beating is not one of those consequences. There are many other ways to make children think about something they have done."

There was dead silence. Her colleagues sat looking at her with a kind of pity, as though they feared for her mental health; but she soldiered on. "You realise how much beating there has been in our history already? It's seventy-five years since we came out of slavery, and we still whipping our children like the overseers whipped our ancestors. We really want to take that forward, from generation to generation, into our future?"

Gwynneth then attempted to go back to her seat, but Mr Seignoret asked her to hold on for a minute. The teachers found their voices and warned of the dire consequences (on the scale of Sodom and Gomorrah) that would follow from her unholy thinking. Mr Burris opened his mouth and shifted to the edge of his seat to say something, but Mr Seignoret held up his hand to silence him, throwing him a look of annoyance. Burris closed his mouth (like a gasping fish, Gwynneth remembered thinking) and shifted back on the chair.

She could see that Mr Seignoret was intrigued by her point of view, but during the meeting he would not be drawn into any to-beat-or-not-to-beat argument. He made a closing speech, exhorting the teachers to always be mindful of their duty to teach the children well. He expressed the hope that St Paul Government could maybe win a college exhibition one day, but insisted that exhibition or no exhibition, *all* the children who came in through the school doors must leave with a sound education.

Through all of this, Mr Seignoret kept Gwynneth standing by his desk, and at the end of the speech he turned to her. "Miss Cuffie," he said, "you are welcome to share your views with your colleagues on the use of corporal punishment, at the first staff meeting next term."

Despite the startled glances this announcement drew from said colleagues, Gwynneth agreed. Mr Seignoret wished the staff a happy Easter and restful vacation.

It seemed to Gwynneth that the headmaster was permanently

371

irritated with Burris. She guessed that the mantra repeated by Mr Seignoret at every staff meeting, about giving *all* the children a sound education, was thrown at Burris, above all. One of Headley Burris's first actions on being assigned to Standard 5 had been to set a test, for the purpose, he said, of "separating the wheat from the chaff." Only the bright children, those who stood a chance of winning a scholarship, would be in his exhibition class. The rest could be put back into Standard 4, he suggested, or sent to Standard 6; or they could be gathered into a new class, to be called Standard 5B and given to the pupil teacher.

According to the story told by teachers, Mr Seignoret first got wind of this when the newly-appointed Burris came to the office to present his list of the students he would allow into Standard 5A, *his* exhibition class. The headmaster had to close his office door before tearing up his list and exploding at him: "Not in this school! We don't do that here. I don't give a damn what they do in any other school. Here, you will teach every last one of these children, right to the end. Yes, we know that for some children, sitting the exam would be an unnecessary torture, so, a month and a half before the exam, we determine which pupils should not be sent up. Meanwhile, you will continue to teach the *whole* class, *all* of the children, with equal diligence, and down to the last day."

After the staff meeting, two teachers sought her out, almost furtively, to thank her for what she had said about beating children. Miss McKend waylaid Gwynneth at the school gate that afternoon and asked, apologetically, if she could walk with her to tell her something. She told Gwynneth that she had never felt good about hitting children, because she could never forget how it felt to be beaten as a child. She had used the strap because that was what was expected of teachers, and she really didn't know any other way of handling children. That was how she, her siblings and her cousins had been handled by the adults in her family.

But, she said, she was not comfortable with beating children, and had simply decided one day that she would stop, and try talking with them more. Yet putting away the strap made her feel as if she was guilty of breaking some rule. She could not get rid of that doubt, even though her pupils were doing better. Their schoolwork improved, and their behaviour. "What I find, Miss Cuffie, is that in talking with them, I get closer to them, and now they just eager to please me and make me proud – not out of fear, but because they feel that I care about them. After what you said in the meeting, I will stop doubting myself. I know now that I am on the right road!"

The next morning, another teacher, Mrs Cumberbatch came to Gwynneth's table at recess and spoke under cover of the din outside. She was already a rare bird – a Mrs among all the Misses on the staff. In her youth she had taught at Canaan Government School for eleven years and earned a good reputation as a teacher. Then she got married, and had to leave the job forthwith, as per the regulation that said a woman could not be married and working in the Government Service. When, however, there was a dire shortage of certificated teachers in St Michael County, Mrs Cumberbatch was called back out to teach. She had only been at St Paul for one year before Gwynneth joined the staff.

Then Mrs Cumberbatch revealed to Gwynneth the other oddity about herself – she, too, was against child-beating. She spoke of her own three children. "The first two, man, I blaze them with licks for tea-breakfast-and-dinner, just like I beat the children I used to teach in school. By the time the third child born, I just too tired to beat anybody. I never beat that last one. I handle him in a different way and I can see the difference between him and my first two. He is my best child, and I will never forgive myself for the way I handle my first two children. Was a real injustice I do them and the schoolchildren I teach in the past. I would like to see teachers stop beating people children, and handle them with more love. But these teachers in here?…" and she steupsed.

A day or two after the staff meeting, Mr Seignoret called her into his office. "Go ahead and put your case against corporal punishment," he said. "But I can see that in your class, the question does not arise. Your handling of the children seems to make corporal punishment irrelevant. Very interesting. Well, you may have discovered already, at your young age, that those who work hard and work well get more work piled on them, while idlers idle undisturbed."

He had stopped, and was looking at her with a hopeful expression on his face, as though waiting for endorsement. Gwynneth nodded and smiled politely at what seemed like a compliment, but she was not sure where the headmaster was heading.

"You are someone living before your time, Miss Cuffie, and I am hoping that you can nudge these teachers forward into a new attitude to children and a better understanding of education. What I would like you to do in the first meeting next term is to speak some more about why corporal punishment is a bad practice. After that, I'm going to call an extraordinary staff meeting, probably in the following week – the sooner the better – in which I would like you to focus on the topic of good teaching. It is good teaching, like yours, Miss Cuffie, that will cancel out beating, and of course, will give children a sound education. You ready to take on this extra work?"

"Yes, Sir. And thank you."

Before the school closed for the Easter vacation, Gwynneth spoke with Miss McKend and Mrs Cumberbatch, seeking to enlist their aid. She wanted them to speak at the meeting about their experiences and their feelings on the matter.

Both women were very reluctant. They felt that they would achieve nothing but bring ridicule and ill-will upon themselves. They were not sure the other teachers had noticed that they did not beat their pupils, and certainly neither of them had drawn their colleagues' attention to what would be seen as delinquency on their part. They had never even shared their views on the subject with each other. Neither Miss McKend nor Mrs Cumberbatch was ready for the other teachers to be showing them bad-face and washing they mouth on them.

~

As she reflected, now, on how to handle the situation with Sonny, she noted with dismay that everything she had said to the teachers in her first year at St Paul Government School, 1913, still needed to be said in 1949 to the teachers of St Hilda's Anglican School, and to teachers and parents all over Cayeri. Now, more than a century after Emancipation, there had been no change on that front. Children still lived under the whip. Cayerians continued to uphold child-beating like a religious faith.

Gwynneth mused, tiredly, that fighting the British was easier than this struggle. Cayerians had defeated slavery. They had won the right to form trade unions. They had won the right to vote. Cayerians were going to achieve self-government eventually, she was sure, and then even independence, one day – full political independence. Was that day going to come to the descendants of an enslaved, brutalised people, and find them, God forbid, still beating their children, passing on the slaver's whip?

~

Gwynneth's views on child-beating had jolted her colleagues at St Paul Government School, and then the headmaster added insult to injury by inviting her to talk about it again at the next staff meeting. At the meeting after the Easter vacation, when Mr Seignoret called on her to speak, the hostility the teachers had brought into the room grew thicker by the minute. You could cut it with a knife. When she paused to invite discussion, there was nothing but stony stares, until Mr Burris asked, "Can I speak, Sir?"

He delivered a speech of his own, the content of which boiled down to "Children have to be corrected! You have to cut they tail!" And he looked around the room for the grateful adulation that was due to him. One or two teachers, hidden in the back row, gave a tentative little clap, but the others could not be roused to show their approval in any spirited way. They sat, as cowed by the mere presence of the headmaster as their pupils were cowed by the presence of their teachers.

Gwynneth put up her hand, and Mr Seignoret nodded to her. "So, does 'correcting' mean 'beating'?" she asked Burris. "When an adult does something you disapprove of, or makes a mistake, do you beat that person? Your wife, for example? You does cut her tail when you vex with her?"

Burris began to puff up. Gwynneth knew that she was crossing a line, going into the man's family. Remembering this scene, Gwynneth winced at her indiscretion. In that distant period of her life her mouth didn have no cover. Discretion was not her strong point. The headmaster could have stopped her, but he obviously didn't care to. *I will really have to learn to behave myself in these situations,* young Gwynneth thought, but pressed on, regardless. She knew that he was married, because he wore a wedding band, but did Burris and his wife have any children? Young Gwynneth did not know, and did not need to know.

"Or, when you tell her something and she forget, or she mix-up you children name – calling Jenny 'Denise,' or calling Joey 'Frank' – you does cut she tail?"

"Of course not," Burris answered, outraged. "I respect my wife!"

"Oho! So you don't respect children."

Mr Burris did the fishlike gasp again. Other teachers began to thaw out of their resentful silence. A period of near-hysterical babble ensued as they vented their worst fears, to each other, or to no one in particular. Gwynneth's translation of their worst fears was: *If we cyaan beat them, what we going to do with them? How we going to keep them down?* Or, it was as though the ground was being cut from under their feet and they saw themselves falling into an abyss where children ran riot and overpowered adults, a vision no doubt shared by slave-owners with regard to their stock … Suddenly Mrs Cumberbatch's voice was heard, rising angrily above the chorus of doom. "Allyou talking like if chirren is demon! Chirren is people, too!"

The teachers turned to stare at Mrs Cumberbatch. By the time she had finished speaking, Miss McKend had gathered her courage, and she also spoke up. The two of them looked relieved after they had spoken. The other teachers now turned to stare at Mr Seignoret, as if looking for rescue. But Mr Seignoret kept out of it and held his tongue until the end of the meeting, when he announced that in the following week, Miss Cuffie would discuss with them some elements of good teaching. They now stared at him in disbelief and dismay.

Over the next few days Gwynneth got sour looks, cut-eye and cold-shouldering from some members of staff, notably Mr Burris and some of the older teachers. Miss McKend and Mrs Cumberbatch also attracted the displeasure of their colleagues, but were now past caring what they thought. Mr Seignoret was coming out of his office more frequently than before to walk the aisle between the classes. Gwynneth noted that he no longer walked with his whip. Moreover, although he had not pro-nounced on the matter of corporal punishment, Gwynneth realised that for the duration of his tour, not a hand would be raised against a child in any class. Even Burris would put down his weapons until Mr Seignoret went back into the office, the same Burris who had always made a point of dishing out blows when the headmaster was around.

When there was a staff meeting, school ended early, and the teachers took their chairs with them to the headmaster's office. There they would place them facing the headmaster's desk. Except for Marlene, the pupil teacher, they were all grown men and women, but they all seemed to be jostling for the back row. For the extraordinary meeting that Gwynneth was scheduled to lead, she asked Mr Seignoret if the chairs could be placed in a circle. He looked a little confused, but agreed.

Teachers traipsed in, half-carrying, half-dragging their chairs, already signalling protest on their faces and in their movements, only to be told of a change in the arrangement of chairs. A moment of deliberate chaos ensued, with the most disaffected ones seemingly unable to figure out what a circle was. But there were others who quietly set about forming the circle with their chairs. Mr Seignoret held up his hand to make the complaining ones stop their noise (which included the prolonged scraping of chair-legs on the floor). When he began to take their chairs from them one by one, to personally complete the circle, the remaining protesters fell in.

The meeting began with an onslaught of vehement and expansive praying from Miss Giles. Mr Seignoret brought this to a premature end, cutting in with a loud "Amen" as he seemed to suddenly catch on that she was stretching it out on purpose, to cut down on meeting time. But then he delivered a speech that went on even longer, and made Gwynneth squirm with discomfort because it was all about her! She silently fumed throughout. *Yes, Mr Seignoret, this is just what I need, right now. Go ahead and give them grounds to accuse you of favouritism, and me of currying favour with you. Thanks for getting these teachers' backs up before throwing me into the ring to be eaten raw...*

"Teachers, let me introduce to you Gwynneth Cuffie. You have already made her acquaintance, but I would like to recommend that you look at her more closely, that you observe her teaching, as I have been doing. Here are one or two of my observations, points you might want to discuss with her and learn more about, because what I have asked her to talk about is not corporal punishment; I have asked her to speak on the topic 'Good Teaching'.

"I know you've observed that Miss Cuffie walks around her class unarmed – no leather strap or guava branch in her hand. Yet her pupils are not unruly, and they are doing well in their schoolwork! How can that be?

"All her children come to school every day, give or take some rare absences. Quite remarkable, isn't it, given our problem of poor attendance. Her children enjoy their time in school. I have never heard the sound of a child crying in her class. But I regularly hear the whole class laughing, teacher and all.

"The few in our midst who have had the benefit of attending Training School will have been introduced to some of the methods used by Miss Cuffie, but let's be honest – many teachers leave that training behind when they graduate. We just lapse into the way that we were taught when we were children in school. We turn back the clock. Well, time to move forward. We need to use the skills we were taught, and we need to share them with our colleagues. That is what today's staff meeting is about.

"And speaking of helping each other learn, Miss Cuffie gets her children to work in pairs. You may have heard her say to her class, 'Work with your neighbour.' Or, she might shuffle the class to pair off children of different ability. The children put their heads together to work out sums; to go through the reading lesson before they are called upon to read aloud; to inspect each other's handwriting… And Miss Cuffie visits each pair of children, checking on their progress; helping them through any difficulty they might be having; encouraging them and praising them for their work.

"Miss Cuffie brings old newspapers and magazines from which the children cut pictures to use for different purposes. She brings storybooks for them to read; she reads stories to them; she gets them to tell stories from their own lives and to write them down, with help from their classmates.

"And there is so much more. But lemme hush and siddown, *oui*, and hand over to Miss Cuffie now, before some-a allyou kill me dead with cut-eye."

His closing pleasantry actually touched off a ripple of laughter around the circle! It lightened the mood. Mr Seignoret did not get much cut-eye, and they did not eat Miss Cuffie raw. Some of the teachers seemed to warm to the novel experience of sitting in a cosy circle with the headmaster at a staff meeting. Some showed interest in what Gwynneth had to say, posed questions, and joined in the discussion. There were those who did not participate but felt obliged to put away their scowls for the moment, because, sitting as they were, everyone could see everyone else's face. (Mr Burris's attempt at adjusting his face into a cooperative expression was a study).

And so, it grew. From the following week, the younger teachers started seeking out Gwynneth for advice, asking her to look over their lesson plans, or to come and watch them teach a lesson and tell them what she thought of it. With Mr Seignoret's blessing, teachers could also leave their class working independently on an assignment and go to observe Miss Cuffie's teaching.

The headmaster was now walking the floor more and more, and there was markedly less beating of children. But poor Mr Burris remained unable to embrace, or even to conceive of any other *modus operandi* than what he had inherited. Mr Seignoret had not issued any formal edict against the beating of children. There was, after all, no law against it. Children were not covered by the law of assault and battery. As it was under slavery, where man, woman and child were fair game for assault and battery, so it remained for children, long after the abolition of slavery. At St Paul, Burris and the other objectors remained free to continue with their practice; but it was clear that in the new climate of the school they were feeling some pressure to lay down the whip and seek other ways.

One day Mr Seignoret asked Gwynneth if he could have a word with her in his office. She went to see him at lunchtime. He expressed his appreciation for her work. He said it was lifting the performance of teachers (those who had chosen to work with her) and hence the children's performance. He talked enthusiastically about what he was seeing in those classes, but still seemed to be avoiding comment on the matter of corporal punishment.

But then he gazed past her and said, as if talking to himself, "Helluva thing. Who would have thought beating children was something to debate? Like debating whether the sun would rise and set every day. Never gave it a thought. Part of being a child is getting licks… Part of being a teacher is beating children so they would learn, or so they would behave. That's what we inherited. But Miss," and he turned his attention back to her, "how startling, after thirty years of teaching, and bringing up your own children, how startling to learn, to see with your own eyes, that it was quite unnecessary to use violence. That you may have done a better job without it! Helluva thing."

Gwynneth mumbled something sympathetic.

He nodded and waved his hand absent-mindedly. "You notice I keep my mouth out of the debate. I haven't said Yea; I haven't said Nay. But now I am ready to do something. I have to be careful, though. If I ban licks, those who still want to hit the children and insult them will be blue vex, and they will take it out on the children. If they can't beat them, I feel they will insult them even more."

He would seek, instead, to draw all the teachers into what he had already named "Miss Cuffie's Programme", a rubric that Gwynneth knew might not sit well with the objecting teachers.

She stayed on after school the following day to help him work out a plan. Mr Seignoret was not in favour of imposing any blanket decree. Offending the teachers was one thing, but their revolt could set the Inspector of Schools on him, and he knew for sure that Mr Scipio was not somebody who thought that the rearing of children could proceed without licks. However, Mr Seignoret was willing to risk imposing one rule: Teachers would have to abandon the idea that licks helped children to learn.

"No teacher must use corporal punishment as a teaching method," he said to Gwynneth. "I am thinking of putting up a plaque that says, 'What makes children learn is good teaching, not licks'."

Hm, Gwynneth thought. *More provocation for the objectors. But steups, that might help to light a fire under them.* However, what she

380

said out loud was, "You would have to be careful where you display that. The inspector, the parents, and the teachers themselves might see it as fomenting rebellion among the children..."

"You're right. Not a good idea. But it is something I would certainly want to say to the teachers, at every opportunity. Of course I want to also stop the beating of children for bad behaviour, but it would be better to make a change as drastic as that in stages. What do you think of this: I could ask the teachers to send children to my office for misbehaviour, instead of hitting them? I might have to call on you, though, for advice on what to do with them."

Gwynneth nodded. "Certainly, Sir. But I think we already agree that the first thing to do is to talk with the child and try to find out what is at the root of the misbehaviour. There is always a root cause; but the cause is not an excuse. While we must do what we can to remedy the cause, the misbehaviour must result in fitting consequences..."

"Aha!" Mr Seignoret spoke with mounting enthusiasm. "Next staff meeting, Miss Cuffie, let us focus on Fitting Consequences. That, I think, will clinch it, for some of the teachers still think that not hitting the children means leaving them to do whatever they please and letting them get away scot-free."

Over the next few days, Mr Seignoret would speak with all the teachers, one by one, in his office. He would commend those who were already adding to their repertoire of teaching skills by taking advantage of Miss Cuffie's programme. Those who were dead set against it would be asked to try out at least one of the methods Miss Cuffie was recommending, and discuss the outcome, either at a staff meeting, or with him, privately in his office, if they preferred.

Staff meetings would become a fortnightly instead of monthly affair, with a built-in session for sharing ideas on teaching and the handling of children, as well as colleagues talking about their day-to-day classroom experiences and any difficulties they might be having. Gwynneth suggested that in those sessions, anyone who still wanted to defend the use of corporal punishment should be free to do so, for this would be a chance for their arguments to be answered and their fears allayed.

The meeting remained something of a battleground for almost the whole of the second term, with hostilities only beginning to noticeably wane just before the August holidays. The Christmas term proceeded without too much contention, and at the end of it, the teachers got together and organised a Christmas party for staff, something never before done at this school (not in anybody's memory), at which they honoured Gwynneth in speeches and in song. The young pupil teacher delivered a heartfelt oration.

"Miss Cuffie's programme" she began, and nobody bristled or steupsed; instead, they laughed indulgently for a long moment, so she had to begin again. "Miss Cuffie's programme has made the school a brighter and happier place for children as well as teachers…"

And Miss Reid, whom Gwynneth had secretly named "Old Misery", did have quite a pleasant singing voice. She sang for Gwynneth:

> *Where'er you walk*
> *Cool gales shall fan the glade.*
> *Trees where you sit*
> *Shall crowd into a shade…*

Before the close of school for the Christmas vacation, Mr Seignoret asked Gwynneth to take over Standard 5 in the new school year. He also asked her to take charge of the new pupil teacher joining the staff in place of Mr Greenidge who was retiring. Mr Burris was assigned to Standard 6, which made him ill, it would seem, for on being informed he took two days' sick leave.

Now, after all that dredging up of history, what, exactly, was she going into St Hilda's to say to Mr Daniel?

35
"Teach us to see you in every child."

Gwynneth did not immediately see the usefulness of having dredged up the St Paul experience. She continued, that Monday afternoon, to agonise over putting Sonny into primary school. Should she go against her better judgement – withdraw him, and school him at home? Or send him back to St Hilda's and for the next six years keep harping on the message that nobody must beat him?

But that would be no solution to the problem Sonny faced. There was no danger of anybody beating him. It was the beating of another child, accompanied by the teacher's cutting words, that had shocked and distressed him, and children were going to be beaten in the school every day of the week. And if Sonny was upset by this, what about the children at the receiving end of the licks? Was it really enough to protect Sonny alone, and to hell with the rest?

She thought of how it felt for her and Viola to be the only children in the school who were never beaten. The other children found it most unfair. They assumed it was because their father was the headmaster – this headmaster who did not hesitate to drop a lash on any child, in any teacher's class, as he patrolled the school, any child except Princess Gwynneth and Princess Viola. Little did their schoolmates know that the authority protecting them was not the imperial headmaster at school, but their mother, invisible, at home.

It would not do for Sonny's schoolmates to see him as a favoured child, enjoying special treatment, and hold this against him. She and Viola had each other when their schoolmates shunned them, but Sonny was alone. Gwynneth yielded now to a thought that had been trying to emerge and discomfit her for longer than she cared to acknowledge. This niggling thought was that issuing directives to headmaster and teachers that they must exempt Sonny from beating was a shamelessly selfish act on her part. She was forsaking the other children, and at the same time throwing Sonny in the bamboo.

Of course, sending him to St Paul Government School would have been the easy way out, if the school was still the place she had left years before. There, the most committed teachers had held out for years against beating children, even after Mr Seignoret retired. But Mr Seignoret was replaced by a succession of headmasters whose main equipment for exercising authority was the whip, and as Gwynneth's cohort of teachers retired, one by one, the beating had easily crept back into the school.

She felt suddenly tired. Defeat washed over her. Why would she want to take on, once more, and at her age, this heritage of violence that had been bred into her compatriots? She would have to leave that fight to a future generation. All she could do was protect Sonny. And her mind fled, again, to her last resort – schooling him at home. That evening she shared her anguish with Gaston.

"So tell me why you can't get this school to move away from corporal punishment, as you did at the other school?" he asked. "Give me one good reason."

"Reason one: I am not on the staff at St Hilda's, and reason two: Mr Daniel is not Mr Seignoret."

She was placing Mr Seignoret next to Mr Daniel and remembering Mr Seignoret with admiration because he was willing to take the leap. Then it struck her that Mr Daniel was further along the road in his thinking than Mr Seignoret was when she first came into his school. Mr Seignoret had taken child-beating for granted all his life up until then. Mr Daniel already understood that beating did children no good. Maybe all he needed was help for him to act on his understanding.

Before her conversation with Gaston was over, she knew what she was going to Mr Daniel to say. She was going to say that she would be willing to help him, in any way she could, to make his school free of corporal punishment. She would tell him about the steps taken at St Paul Government School when she was a teacher there. Of course, she was not a member of staff at St Hilda's, but if he was willing to bring the change, she would leave it up to him to decide how to use her help. She would go and see Mr Daniel the very next day, Tuesday, in the afternoon.

Gwynneth and Sonny spent Tuesday morning at home together. Before going outside, Sonny had some chocolate tea and Nenn Gwynnie had coffee. Then they shelled corn and cut up coconut, which they went and scattered it in the fowl-run, among the flapping and squawking fowls. Next, they pulled up some weeds in the garden before the sun could climb too high in the sky.

For breakfast they put two eggs to boil and then decided to also make chokha. They would eat their egg and chokha with the roast bake that Nenn Vie had made before she left for work. (Nenn Gwynnie was not lucky with making bake.) They took the coal-pot outside, to the bottom of the back steps, where they roasted the beigan and some tomatoes. Sonny did not like beigan – stewed, fried or chunkayed – so with his egg he had tomato chokha, while Nenn Gwynnie had both tomato and beigan chokha with hers.

After breakfast they went back outside and took down the clothes that had been left on the line overnight. They brought them inside and folded them, sitting on the drawing-room couch. And all the while they talked, mainly in Patois, as Gwynneth had found that when Sonny was upset, talking with him in Patois always helped to comfort him. They talked about Sonny's bad experience of the day before, and how some bigpeople hit children because they didn't know better… Gwynneth assured him that no teacher at the school was going to hit him, and promised that she would work to get the school not to hit any children at all, for she had done that once, in another school.

Sonny told Gwynneth how the teacher had given him the name "Sonny-Too", and how the whole day she only gave them easy work to do, so he got everything right, and she turned the pages of his exercise book and said, "Joshua, you are a bright boy!" He also told Gwynneth about the big girl who had taken care of him, saving him from getting squeezed up between all the children rushing out for recess. Gwynneth decided she would suggest to Mr Daniel that at recess time the youngest children could stay in their seats until the bigger ones had got out.

"So what you think about going back to school tomorrow?" Gwynneth asked. "Suppose Miss teaching something new, something that you doan know about already?"

Sonny pondered for a moment, then nodded.

Gwynneth had an arrangement with the Sookram family that if she had to be out during the day (before Viola, Marjorie or Lennox came home), Sonny could go up and stay with them. He loved spending time there. Kalowtie had two nieces and a nephew – Vashti, Priya and Satesh, all a little older than him, but to him, great fun, and they loved it when Sonny came to play. Sonny had known Kalowtie for as far back as he could remember, as the big girl who brought the milk on mornings. Sometimes she would call out, "Sonny! Look I bring you milk for you, *beta*."

If she wasn't too rushed with making her rounds, she would sit on the back steps with him and chat for a while. Kalowtie was now almost nineteen years old, and whenever Sonny spent time at her home she was the one officially in charge of him. Gwynneth had gone to Sookram with the idea of making it a formal nanny job that she would pay Kalowtie for, but Sookram would not hear of it. "Neighb," he insisted, "you bring am come play with me grandchirren them, any time you want. No pay, Neighbour."

Gwynneth and Sonny had lunch, and then she took him up to Kalowtie's family for the afternoon. On the way there Gwynneth promised him that before he went to his bed that night, the two of them would play some duets on the piano, and sing.

Mr Daniel welcomed Gwynneth, but remained ill at ease until she told him that Sonny was coming back to school the following day. He apologised, again, for the distress that Sonny had suffered, and told her that he was, himself, very troubled by the incident. Indeed, he felt that it had affected the teachers as well. A sombre mood had come over them. Not a child had been hit all morning, and the school was quiet, even subdued. He gave a wry chuckle.

"I suppose they've never met a child who did not see being beaten as par for the course!" he said. "Miss Cuffie, I am ready to fight this thing, you know. I've spoken to Miss Corbin, not for the first time, about the crude and heartless way she speaks to the children, on top of beating them. She is not the only one, but she's the worst. I have made her turn in that ruler, and the strap that hung on her chair. I told her that when she needs to measure something, she can borrow the ruler from me. But this is just a beginning. Where do I go from here?"

"I will tell you how we proceeded at St Paul, Mr Daniel. You will decide what you can use from that, or whether you will make a plan of your own. I am willing to help; you just have to tell me how."

The next morning Sonny was taking a long time to get dressed, but Gwynneth tried not to make too much of it. He did have a tendency to be dreamy, particularly when getting ready to go out. He would wander out of the bathroom and stand in front of the sink, apparently deep in thought, before he slowly reached for his toothbrush, then the toothpaste. After that he might stand motionless once more. Eventually he would come to life again and go through the motions of brushing his teeth, slowing to a halt now and again with the toothbrush in his mouth and his hand on the toothbrush handle.

Or, Gwynneth might go into the bedroom and find him seated on the edge of the bed, staring straight ahead with one shoe in his hand like an absent-minded old man. She hoped that his slow movement this morning was just his normal dreaminess and not reluctance to go back to school.

They got to the office early, as Mr Daniel had requested. He sat Sonny on his lap and chatted with him for a while, reassuring him that he would be safe at school. Then Teacher Marva came in to get the bell, and Mr Daniel asked Sonny if he would like to ring the bell for school to start. Teacher Marva was the designated bell-ringer, but Mr Daniel sometimes invited a child to ring in the morning or afternoon session of school.

Teacher Marva took him outside the office door, and explained to him that they had to ring the bell six times. She was going to help him with the first three rings, and then he would do three rings on his own. She clasped his hands over the handle, then her hands over his, and guided the ringing while she counted: "One. Two. Three." Then she let go, and Sonny boldly executed three chimes, also counting aloud: "One. Two. Three." He beamed at Gwynneth.

Mr Daniel had decided to lead the morning prayers that day, and to invite Gwynneth. Before they left the office, Gwynneth spoke briefly with Sonny, in Patois. This made him more relaxed and even cheerful. Mr Daniel told Gwynneth afterwards that he was both amazed and touched by that gesture. In his childhood, he said, the adults in his family would only use Patois in the presence of the children in order to shut them out of "bigpeople conversation", never in order to communicate with them. And they certainly didn't expect the children to speak to the adults in Patois!

Gwynneth took Sonny to his class, while the whole school rose and turned to Mr Daniel with a resounding "Good morning, Sir." Mr Daniel stood in the aisle and solemnly read from the Bible:

> *Then were there brought unto him little children, that he should lay his hands on them, and pray, and the disciples rebuked them. But Jesus said, Suffer the little children, and forbid them not, to come unto me: for of such is the kingdom of heaven. And he laid his hands on them, and departed thence.*

At the end of the reading he raised his head and did not speak for what might have been a full minute, as slowly and gravely he perused the gathered school that seemed to be holding its breath.

He broke the silence: "Let us pray." He bowed his head and everyone followed suit. "Heavenly Father, we thank you for all these precious children you have placed in our care. Teach us to see you in every child. Speak, Lord, and make us listen. May our daily example be Jesus's love for children, that we may always be kind to our little ones, treating them always with understanding and respect. May each of us resolve to stay our hand and our tongue whenever we are tempted to do harm or cause distress to any of these young ones whom you have entrusted to us. Make each and every one of us a good shepherd to your children."

On the following Monday, Gwynneth visited Mr Daniel's office again. He had decided to mount a programme similar to the one carried out in St Paul, adding some ideas of his own. Reverend Fields had given his support to the plan, which Mr Daniel called "Learning Without Licks". He was still trying to decide on a teacher who could shoulder some of the responsibility for leading the venture. Gwynneth asked him to consider Teacher Evie – Evadne Thom.

It was Teacher Evie who had founded the thriving Brownie troop at the orphanage, and, years later, was still running it, lovingly and tirelessly. A familiar sight in the village was the zigzag moving line of little girls in brown, with Teacher Evie at the front, making their way purposefully to the church, or to the savannah, or to God-knows-where, chatting and chirping and singing as they went. Evadne was a stalwart of St Hilda's church, a pleasant, smiling person, but a wrango when necessary, and some of the staff at the orphanage, the ones known for ill-treating the children, had met the wrango side of her. She gave them hell.

Mr Daniel was happy for Gwynneth's recommendation; he had already been thinking of asking Miss Thom. He proposed, as a first step, to speak with every teacher, individually, before calling them all into a staff meeting. Gwynneth agreed to speak at this meeting, and to be part of the programme as it unfolded.

At the meeting there was little or no hostility directed at Gwynneth and her message. This was not because there had been any revolution in the attitude of Cayerians to corporal punishment. Teacher Gwynneth was known to most of the staff at St Hilda's, and they had the greatest respect for her. But they gave off the same scepticism, the same anxiety and sheer dread as the St Paul teachers at the suggestion that children could be held at bay, or be successfully taught anything, from arithmetic to acceptable behaviour, without licks.

It was an exhausting meeting, but Mr Daniel was optimistic. By the end of it, the teachers had moved to the stage of curiosity about how this miracle could be performed – taming children and getting them to learn what was required by the primary school syllabus, all without laying a finger on a child. Over the coming weeks and months, Gwynneth would work with Mr Daniel and Teacher Evie. Gwynneth made herself available to the school at least one afternoon in every week to hold sessions with the staff, in which teaching strategies, ideas, experiences and problems were shared. She gave practical demonstrations, looked over lesson plans and mentored individual teachers.

Some teachers admitted to Gwynneth that, at first, putting down their whips and their rulers and their leather belts made them feel handicapped. It was a difficult time for them, but gradually they would find themselves making the change.

On Sonny's return to school, Miss Telemaque had put him and Sonnylal to sit together. She suggested that Sonnylal could look out for Joshua at recess time, because Sonnylal was six years old and had been in big-school since ABC class. Joshua, she said, was only five, and new to big-school.

"Oh no," Sonny piped up. "I have five and a half years!"

And this time Miss Telemaque giggled openly along with the class.

The name "Sonny-Too" stuck on him. After Nenn Gwynnie had worked so hard to teach him his going-out name, all his classmates called him "Sonny-Too", and his teacher mostly called him "Joshua". It was only at roll-call time that he became the person who was named "Joshua Polydore".

The two Sonnys roamed the schoolyard together at recess; went to drink water and to pee-pee after the big children had moved away from the standpipes and the latrines. Next, if either of them had been given a penny for recess, they hurried to the lady at the gate and scrutinised her tray, pondering whether to buy stewed tamarind (sweet or sour, or a bit of both), or chilibibi, or kaiser ball, or bara-and-channa… At the end of the school day, Sonnylal waited at the gate with Sonny-Too until Gwynneth came, and then the three of them walked up the road together. They parted company at the corner of Grant Trace and Farfan Road.

After the first fortnight, Sonny told Gwynneth that she didn't need to bring lunch for him any more. He wanted to take his lunch to school in a paper bag, like Sonnylal and others in his class. Gwynneth agreed, and Viola was happy to pack lunch for him every morning. The two boys ate lunch together at their desk, exchanging some of their food, except when Sonnylal had beigan or Sonny-Too had beef.

Before long, Sonny began to suggest that Nenn Gwynnie should stop taking him to and from school. He could walk with Sonnylal. She agreed, nervously at first, for the way to school involved crossing the main road. But then Sonnylal had been making his own way to and from school since he was in Second

Primer. He and half the school population, the half that lived north of the main road, had survived years of crossing it to get to their school and back again, without the help of adults. And anyway, it wasn't as though the main road, on its way through sleepy Turagua, was anything like the broad ribbon of highway the Yankees had put down in the war, a mile or so to the south of them, where hardly a minute passed without some vehicle flying along it.

Still, she started by taking him to Grant Trace corner in the morning, to meet Sonnylal, and then in the afternoon going back to the corner to stand and wait for him. This was her routine for only three or four days before Sonny began to press her to let him walk to Sonnylal's corner and back by himself. She gave in reluctantly, though on the first morning when he walked off by himself, she did stand outside the gate and look up the road until she saw Sonnylal take his hand at the corner.

That afternoon she fought against and overcame the urge to go out into the road and see if he was on his way back. Instead she hovered in the gallery, every now and then leaning over the bannister to crane her neck towards the east. And, on that afternoon, Gwynneth abandoned her post for a moment, as there was a pot on the fire. When she came out again, Sonny was on his way up the gallery steps. He held up to her a leafy stem with bunches of ixora along it, broken off from somebody's hedge. The one in his other hand was for Nenn Vie.

36
Roy was thrown by the child's boldness.

Roy seemed to be sliding back into eating by himself when he visited. He would eat at the table with them sometimes, and sometimes in his room. They soon realised that it was when Gaston or Ollie was there that Roy would be present at the table, but never when it was just the three of them – Gwynneth, Viola and Sonny. If neither of the men turned up, then the minute the cooking was done, Roy would take a plate from the wagonette, go into the kitchen to fill it with food, and take it into his bedroom. The first time he appeared at the kitchen door with empty plate in hand, Viola had puffed up, hissing at him, "Nobody ain coming and dipping in no pot in this kitchen!"

But Gwynneth made peace. "Vie," she said. "Let him go ahead and dish out his food, nuh. Look at that nice piece-a pork he bring for us!"

Since then, Roy felt free to serve himself before the food reached the table, rather than wait until everybody had got up and then go to the table to eat alone, as he used to do when Monica was there. He had taken to spending most of his visiting time in his room, unless the men were there. Sometimes he disappeared into the land, armed with a phial of citronella oil for the mosquitoes (or, if it was late afternoon, the sandflies), and the folding chair that he and his family used to take to the beach, back in the days when they used to go the beach together.

Talking with Viola in the kitchen one morning, discussing Roy's behaviour, Gwynneth remarked (carelessly, by her own admission), "Hm. So you think is Sonny he hiding from, now?"

To her dismay, Sonny immediately appeared at the kitchen door. "Yes, Nenn Gwynnie?" was all he said.

It turned out that he was simply presenting himself, because he had heard her say his name. He seemed not to have heard the rest of what she said, for he did not ask who was hiding from him, or any other embarrassing question. With great relief, and in her most coddling voice, Gwynneth asked him, "You want some juice, *Doudou*?"

Sonny was going on six when Roy started eating separately again. He would not be forced to humour this brat. He would have to stop sitting in the drawing-room, or the gallery, or any place where the boy could corner him. And sitting at the dining table with him and Gwynneth and Viola was a perfect trap; the doting old bats would probably come down on him like a ton of bricks if he didn't respond as they thought he should to the little intruder's prattle. He would have to go back to eating his lunch by himself. But he didn't want to disrespect the men when they came to lunch, by seeming to cold-shoulder them. And he wanted to chat with them, so he sat at the table when they were there; it was worth the discomfort of having to pretend he was okay with the irritating child up in his face.

As the child grew older, it was not so easy to just shoo him away or ignore him. He was changing from stage to stage at an uncanny rate, or so it seemed to Roy; but then he reflected that it may have been the same with Gordon and Freda when they were little. They were just so grown up now (and so independent) that he must have forgotten. Every time Roy returned to Turagua after a longish absence, he would encounter what seemed to be a new child, much more mature than the one he had last seen, until, suddenly, the child was no longer a toddler. This older child was looking him in the eye with an unnerving candour, and insisted on speaking to him, in spite of the stony expression with which this was met. Roy was thrown by the child's boldness.

It did not help that he was now addressing him as "Mr Roy". The child had long dropped the babyish "Yoy". That name, and "Boy", had been aggravating enough. But "Mr Roy"? He didn't quite know how to take this new title. It made him feel curiously alienated, even diminished. It turned him into a stranger in his own home, made him out to be an unfamiliar and less-than-welcome presence. Trust Gwynneth and Viola to do a number like that on him. The child called the other men "Uncle" and "Godfather", but he, who was born in this house (unlike his sisters) and raised in this house, was "Mr Roy", an outsider to be kept at arm's length. The old bats had put the boy up to it.

The old bats, meanwhile, were quite relieved that Roy was choosing to make himself invisible for such a large part of the time he spent at their home. The less contact between Roy and Sonny, the better. In recent years their keenest worry had been the effect Roy could have on the child.

At the sight of the child, Roy's face seemed to twist into a scowl. When Sonny was in the drawing-room with Roy, one could hear, from the adjoining rooms, the freezing silence, or the low growl that was Roy's answer when Sonny approached him enthusiastically with his news for the day, such as, "My mammy send new shoes for me. You want to see?"

And they didn't put it past him to be saying hurtful things to Sonny, when they were out of earshot, that would scar the child for life. Now they were becoming less nervous, as there seemed to be little opportunity for Roy to mistreat Sonny. But now Gwynneth worried that Sonny would notice Roy was avoiding him, not a pleasant thing for a child to experience. He could wonder why a grown person, whom he saw as a member of his family, did not want to have anything to do with him. He would conclude that he, himself, was somehow at fault – that there had to be something wrong with him to make Roy not like him. Something that made him unlovable. How was she going to handle that?

Yet Sonny did not seem the least perturbed. He still greeted Roy at the door, but no longer sought to engage him in conversation. He would just go back to whatever he was doing – reading a book; putting together a jigsaw puzzle (his mother kept him amply supplied with storybooks, toys and every kind of puzzle); playing the piano; helping Nenn Vie in the kitchen… He seemed to have lost all interest in Roy – *thank you, Jesus,* Gwynneth thought.

One afternoon he asked, "Nennie, why Mr Roy so boring?"

("Boring" was a word Sonny had been using liberally ever since he encountered it in a storybook and got Nenn Gywnnie to explain what it meant.)

Gwynneth was alarmed. She thought the moment had come. This must be Sonny's way of asking, finally, why Roy didn't like him. Still, she had to be sure she wasn't jumping the gun. "What you mean, Sonny?" she probed.

"He only staying in his room all the time. He doan like to talk?"

"Well, he likes to come here to rest. He works hard all week, you know, and he gets very tired. It's so nice and quiet here, much quieter than in town, and much more beautiful. He just finds that this is the best place in the world to come and rest."

Gwynneth, girl, you real good. You win all cockfight. She marvelled at this nifty little web she had spun, off the cuff and without batting an eyelid. She had prepared a different response, a long conversation for the moment Sonny showed signs of being hurt by Roy's rejection. She had been planning to explain to him that people who are unhappy are not always able to be nice to other people, and *koté-si koté-la*... And she had another neat response ready for when, inevitably, he would have asked why Roy was unhappy.

But Sonny had already moved on to reviewing the momentous events of the school day, as he did every afternoon. He and Sonnylal had both got all their sums right. Miss had written "Very good" in their exercise books. A bird had flown into the school, messed on a child's reading-book, and flown back outside. And as he told of the high point of his day – the sada roti, curry channa and bhaji that Sonnylal had brought for lunch that day – Sonny licked his lips, rubbed his belly and grinned from ear to ear.

Gwynneth was hoping to enrol Sonny in the school's Cub Scout troop as soon as he turned seven. She started to talk with him about it at the beginning of the new school year, when he was six and a half and he and Sonnylal moved up into Standard 1. But Sonny showed no interest. Every time Gwynneth brought up the subject, he would explain, patiently, that he didn't want to be in Cub Scouts because Sonnylal wasn't in Cub Scouts. She related this to the others one evening, and Viola told her to stop harassing the boy with Cub Scouts. Both Ollie and Gaston agreed with Viola. Gwynneth gave up, reckoning that in a few years' time he might be willing to join the Boy Scouts instead.

Sonny was more interested in joining St Hilda's church choir, although he described church in Turagua as "boring", unlike church in Pilgrim, which was one of the things he looked forward to every school vacation.

And every school vacation, as Sonny went off to Pilgrim, Viola would fuss for days about two things. One was her enduring fear that his family in Pilgrim might steal him. Secondly, she was not happy about Sonny being taken to Queen Lottie's church where the police could attack at any moment and harm him. Gwynneth did not share this anxiety. In all the years that the church was up on the hill, the police had only visited once, never to return. The lookouts gave good warning, and everybody present evacuated in time, according to plan, so that the police found no one to harm. In any case, Gwynneth pointed out, she had never heard of a child being harmed by police in the act of raiding a Shouter church. And, she reminded Viola, police raiding Shouter churches was about to become a thing of the past.

"Hmph," Viola said. "You believe that? Ollie think he cousin could work wonders, but that motion ain going nowhere. The Leg. Co. will throw out that."

"Doan say so, girl," Gwynneth replied. "The wind changing. Plenty people, high and low, supporting the Shouters now. People admire how they stand up to persecution. Thirty-something years, holding on to they faith. Refusing to give it up. And Ollie cousin stick with them. He ain let them down. He will work on them other men in the Leg. Co."

A member of the Legislative Council, a Portuguese Cayerian who Ollie swore was a fifth cousin of his (and who was just as corpulent as Ollie), had taken up the cause of the Shouters. Some leaders of the faith, vigorously campaigning against the ordinance, had put up yet another petition for its repeal. Ollie's cousin took it and tabled it in the Leg. Co. That was months ago; a select committee was still deliberating on the motion. Gwynneth was certain that they would approve it, so that it could move to the stage of debate.

Gwynneth had taken Sonny with her to choir practice at St Hilda's one Saturday afternoon when he was five years old, arming him with storybook, crayons and colouring-book. These would remain untouched, however, for Sonny joined enthusiastically in the singing for more than half an hour, and then had to be laid out full length on a pew to sleep.

By the time he was six, he had become quite involved in the

proceedings, and Gwynneth had to give him a hymn-book so he could read and sing the actual words along with the choir. When he started asking to "really join the choir", she had to think through this request. The youngsters in St Hilda's choir were all twelve years and older. What would Mrs Knight think of having a six-year-old added to her "crosses" as she called them?

"But you in the choir already, Sonny," Gwynneth tried to convince him. He was not fooled; they had not invited him to sing in the choir for Sunday morning service.

"So you want to leave Nenn Vie to do all the cooking by herself every Sunday?"

Sonny thought about this for a moment before he answered, "Well, I doan have to sing in the choir *every* Sunday, Nenn Gwynnie. Only sometimes. And then Godfather Gaston could come and help her cook."

Mrs Knight was quite tickled at the thought of Sonny officially joining the choir. As a matter of fact, she told Gwynneth, she had been planning to talk to her about letting him do a solo from time to time in the Sunday morning service. He had a beautiful voice, she said, could hold a tune better than many in the choir, and obviously loved to sing. "To join the choir would be too hard on him, though. Full members have to come out for the regular practice, then come out every Sunday morning unless they sick to dead... You cyaan lay all that on a little child. And if you give him any ease-up, those crosses would want to know why they have to follow the rules and he getting away. Better he just continue to come to choir practice with you for the time being, whenever he willing, and sing now and then at Sunday service. Let the boy have he boy-days."

Gwynneth explained "honorary member" to Sonny. He was satisfied with the explanation, and thrilled at getting to sing at Sunday morning service. Mrs Knight put him through some training and rehearsal every time he came to choir practice with Gwynneth. Sonny began to sing once a month at Sunday morning service – in the choir as well as solo – and he was booked to sing at that year's Harvest Fair concert. At home, the company in the gallery would sometimes ask for a short recital before he turned in for the night. He obliged, with them acting as his chorus.

He sang at a wedding in the church one Saturday afternoon, and then requests began to come in for him to sing at wedding receptions. Gwynneth declined, with apologies. "Too much of that can lead to overexposure," she argued, "the kind that turns a child into a performing monkey, like that little American girl – the little force-ripe movie star."

Viola came to the defence of the little force-ripe movie star. Gaston and Ollie did not enter that discussion, but then Gaston asked Gwynneth, "So you wouldn't consider letting Sonny sing on Auntie Jenny's programme?"

Viola was most enthusiastic about this suggestion, and Gwynneth agreed. Auntie Jenny she saw as a kindred spirit. Auntie Jenny's Children's Talent Show was a fixture on Radio Cayeri every Sunday afternoon. It was the work of an intrepid woman who had been running this operation for years, drawing out children to sing, recite a poem, tell a story, or play a musical instrument, on the radio. What endeared Auntie Jenny to Gwynneth was that she encouraged and warmly welcomed onto her show children who could perform Cayerian items. From the beginning, Gwynneth had commented that this show would prove to be an important nursery of Cayerian artistes.

Auntie Jenny attracted some disapproval from the hoity-toity, but that was no surprise. She soldiered on, regardless. One lady reported, in an indignant letter to the newspaper, that she did not let her children listen to this programme because they were likely to hear children singing "calypsos and other songs in bad English." Indeed, she complained, the very theme song for the show was in the form of a calypso – no grammar. What was the world coming to? Children should be encouraged to stick to the edifying English, Irish, and Scottish songs they had learnt in school, or the American songs they heard on the radio every day.

The fact was that British and American songs had been pretty much the only ones heard on this show, until Auntie Jenny went on a campaign of sorts, appealing to parents and grandparents to teach their children the old Cayerian songs. As a result, more and more children were going on the programme to sing these songs, many of these children having learnt them only from listening to Aunty Jenny's Children's Talent Show.

Auntie Jenny had also raised eyebrows when she opened the door for children to play the steel drum on her programme, long before the instrument had gained any respect at all from the hoity-toity. This had inspired Gwynneth to write a letter to the newspapers congratulating her, and rebuking her detractors. The letter was never published, but Gwynneth sent a copy to the radio station, and received a gracious acknowledgement from Auntie Jenny.

Sonny chose the song "*Mwen Sòti Anho*". They rehearsed for two weeks, Gwynneth accompanying him on the piano. After the show Auntie Jenny hugged him up and kissed him, and asked Gwynneth if he could do a guest appearance at her Christmas programme. Gwynneth readily agreed, for that was months away – no danger of overworking him.

Gwynneth started planning for Sonny to perform a parang song at the Christmas show. Mr Jeremy's son played the guitar with as much skill as he played the violin; she would get him to accompany Sonny on the guitar… She could bring together a small group of children, maybe from St Hilda's school choir, to be his chorus, and one of them could play the shac-shac. All of this brought to mind her pending project of forming a children's choir to sing Cayerian songs.

Truth be told, most of Gwynneth's nine retirement projects were still pending, a year and a half after the "retirement". Two of them were not, strictly speaking, projects. They were her livelihood. She was coaching schoolchildren facing official exams, and giving piano lessons, three afternoons a week, during the term as well as in the vacation periods. As she had envisaged, her students came not only from Turagua, but also from St Paul and Oropuna. On Tuesdays, she had primary school children preparing for the College Exhibition exam, and on Wednesdays, high school children preparing for the Senior Cambridge exam. The piano lessons were on Thursdays. (And Sonny, who had already been playing the piano for about two years, was now officially one of Gwynneth's music students, preparing for The Royal School of Music grade exams.)

But neither children's choir, nor songbook, nor children's lending library, nor girls' steelband, nor compilation of letters to the press, nor stories for Cayerian children, had as yet got off the ground. What had taken her over almost entirely – half of her daytime hours; much of her thinking time, day or night; and a large share of her energy – was her "story of a woman" novel. The book had grown a title: "The Life and Times of Eunice Walker".

Gwynneth had become so absorbed in this work that it made her feel, at times, that she was neglecting some major obligation, throwing aside some pressing responsibility to others in order to indulge herself. But once she sat down at her table on a morning, Sonny dispatched to school, fowls fed, plants watered and four-legged residents petted, Gwynneth banished all guilt and self-reproach as she lost herself in the writing. Not that this was any holiday. She had not expected it to be plain sailing, and it was not.

Often a whole morning's work would yield nothing but a measly paragraph, so much so that a page or two meant a fruitful morning, cause for celebration. Now and then the product of a whole morning's writing effort was the changing of a word here and a line there in what she had written on a previous day, with the story not moving forward one inch, even if she stretched the morning to 2.00 o'clock. Sometimes she had nothing at all to show for the morning. Inspiration could dry up completely; and then it was best to get up and go do something else, like make an early start to her afternoon of housework and preparation for the private lessons class of the day.

But Gwynneth was not daunted. The briefest of letters she had written to the press over the years could take hours to perfect, so obviously a novel could not be written overnight. The slowly growing sheaf of foolscap that was her "story of a woman" lived in a box under her bed, wrapped in old newspaper – camouflaged, she had no idea why. Nobody was likely to go looking under her bed for her manuscript, as curious as they were about it, every now and then seeking to pry out of her some clue about this mysterious novel.

As for her other projects, she realised that her mind had put them aside for the time being. A voice was telling her that nothing was wrong with taking time off for herself. *You ain kill no priest.* Some of the projects could safely be undertaken by others. Happily, there were many more labourers in the vineyard, now

– the vineyard of Cayerian culture. Gwynneth noted with pride that those she knew of were mainly women.

One woman, a schoolteacher, had for years been collecting stories from the Cayerian oral tradition and was now putting them into print for children. Not too long ago another woman had founded the first Cayerian dance company. Yet another woman had formed a choir that was singing forgotten Cayerian songs. That was an adult choir, but Gwynneth Cuffie was not the only person in the whole of Cayeri who could one day form a choir of children and teach them Cayerian songs – someone else could have this idea and make it happen.

She thought of the exercise book with the lyrics of Cayerian songs dug up from oblivion by Moun Demmeh, and the music sheets she had prepared, all sitting in the box under her bed for thirty years. Every choir in the land, she reflected, could avail itself of this material, and add these songs to their repertoire. It was time that Moun Demmeh's "Songs of Cayeri" be brought forth. However, unless other members of Moun Demmeh could take charge of that project, the songbook might have to be shelved for some time yet, along with the children's choir – indeed, with everything else but her "story of a woman".

She would give herself another year or so before stepping back into the fray. She was no longer fifteen, the age at which she had taken on Miss Munroe at Oropuna Government School and waged her first battle for change in her corner of the scheme of things.

37
… And give us the victory /Again and again

They had already heard the good news by word of mouth, but still they cheered and clapped when it was announced on the radio in the evening. The Legislative Council, after deliberating and debating for a year and a half, had voted to repeal the Shouter Baptist Prohibition Ordinance. Sonny was almost eight years old. Gwynneth let him stay up for the conversation in the gallery that evening.

The Shouters had won. For over three decades the authorities had waged a relentless war on them, trying to stamp out their faith. But the Shouters had kept right on worshipping in their way. It did not matter how many of them the police arrested, beat up, hauled before the courts, fined, or jailed. It did not matter how many Shouter churches were demolished. They had stood their ground.

Queen's spiritual children were always harking back to events in the particular history of their church, and Sonny had heard, again and again, the story of The Lion of Judah Mystical Tabernacle moving up the hill so that the police wouldn't mash down their place of worship. This piece of history lived in his imagination as another intriguing Bible story, like Noah's ark, floating safely with all those animals packed into it, or baby Jesus sleeping in a cowshed on his bed of dry grass (which, Sonny had learned, was the meaning of "hay").

He had heard many of the stories of the church from his uncles. Malcolm and Cyrus were born in the time of the ordinance, so they did not know any other church than the one up the hill, surrounded by thick bush. They had never been to prayers in the building behind Mother Queen Lottie's house, but, like all members of Queen's church, Sonny's uncles knew the history of the church before it was outlawed. They felt as though they had lived through every piece of that history, and increasingly, as he grew older, so did Sonny.

~

Queen and her church had pretty much ignored the ordinance until the police struck at Leader Benjamin's church, over in Clancy, one Sunday morning, and then at Mother Ruth's church in Beauregard the following Sunday. Those two attacks were the warning to Queen that it was time to go up into Lokono mountain.

Like other Shouter Baptist churches, they would have to hold service after dark. Baptism would have to be even earlier than fore-day morning. The coldness of the water would then be just another tribulation to make them strong in their faith, Queen said. They would still baptise people in Beauregard river, but they would have to choose a different spot. They would have to follow the river deeper into the bush and find a place, well off the beaten track, to hold baptisms. As for moving the church up the hill, they would build an enduring tabernacle up there, not keep on holding their service week after week in any flimsy now-for-now shelter. "We building to stay up there for a generation, if need be," Queen said.

And so it was. Shouters would remain in the wilderness for thirty-three years and four months.

The whole church went up the hill on the Saturday after the attack on Mother Ruth's church. They chose one of those flattish parts of the mountainside where the ground seemed to recline for a moment, as though Lokono was taking a short rest before continuing upwards to the sky. They laboured for the whole day. Some cooked, some went up and down the hill to fetch drinking water and whatever else had to be fetched, and some worked on preparing the spot. They had brought with them cutlasses, hoes, pitchforks, shovels, and a luchette borrowed from Mr Mohammed. The church was very grateful to Mr Mohammed, for without the luchette, the work would have been much harder and would have taken much longer. The spot was not entirely flat. It was a gentle slope, and the task was to dig down at its upper end and level off the ground some more.

By nightfall they had cleared the bush and trees, dug down a bit and begun the levelling. Queen consecrated the spot and held service there on Sunday evening, in a circle of trees and high bush. The following Saturday they finished preparing the ground, and put up a joupa where they would hold service for the next few Sundays, until they could fence the compound. As time passed,

403

this joupa became a church with tapia walls and carat roof. Then they built a modest palay and chapelle.

They decided they would not put on a mourner-room. Apart from the smallness of the space, they would not want to leave anybody up there for several days and nights, not in those times that were so dangerous for Shouters. It would be safe enough to continue putting down mourners in the room on Queen's home compound. There was nothing about going on Mourning-Ground that could attract the attention of the police, for that was the quietest thing that Shouters did – as quiet as the graveyard.

As soon as Malcolm and Cyrus were old enough, they joined the ranks of the lookouts. They took turns with others at standing on the inside of the gate, or patrolling the fence. They kept their eyes peeled in the pitch-dark night for lights winking through the bush, and listened for the sound of footsteps coming up the hill. There were false alarms, with the lookouts rushing in to warn the church because they thought the police were on their way, and the church springing into action to evacuate, needlessly, but better safe than sorry.

The church had a clear plan for escape. Members of the congregation would quickly snuff out every candle and the one flambeau that the church allowed itself. Then they would wait in complete silence and stillness, ready to file out through the hidden opening at the back, if any police should seek to break into the compound. They would take the flambeau with them, for it would still be giving off pitch-oil fumes from the newly-extin-guished flame. Those fumes would signal to the police that the congregation had just left, would not have got very far from the place, and could still be caught. Officers could also hit upon the idea of using the pitch-oil in the church's own flambeau to sprinkle the place and set it on fire.

On one occasion, a crashing sound in the bush, accompanied by a cuss-word, did turn out to be the police. The congregation were already poised to flee when the officers found the main gate. One member of the raiding posse was spewing cuss-words and quarrelling about these devil-worshippers who had made him bruise his knee and sprain his wrist in trying to break the fall. When they pushed the gate down, shouting "Police! Everybody here under arrest!" everybody was either crouching or sitting in the grove of black sage further down the mountain, listening to them. (For Sonny this was the best part of the story; he always laughed uproariously at the thought of police up by the empty church, shouting at nobody.)

The church members waited in the black sage, listening; but there were no sounds of destruction coming from the compound. Indeed, there were no sounds at all. The officers seemed not to have lingered. On the other hand, they could be up there still, lying in wait, so the church members slowly rose to their feet, tiptoed down the other track to the village, a route more treacherous than the one the police had used, and scattered to their homes.

Some time later, a policeman from Clancy station whispered to Queen's brother that the party of officers, having shone their torches around the yard and into the open buildings, had decided that it was an abandoned place, not worth the sweat to break it down. Their mission was to arrest miscreants, and since they could not find any to arrest, they turned tail and got to hell out of there. In making their way back down the mountainside, they carefully avoided the boulder on which Corporal Regis had come to grief.

~

The ordinance was repealed on a Friday, and the very next day, Gwynneth and Sonny headed for Pilgrim. All over the colony, all weekend, Shouter churches were preparing to hold thanksgiving.

The first thanksgiving had already been offered, on the pavement outside Government House, under the windows of the Leg. Co. chamber, moments after the repeal. Some leaders of the faith who had been foremost in the campaign against the ordinance were keeping vigil there, when someone came out of the building and revealed to them the outcome of the vote. Immediately, people in the gathering took up their bells and filled the air with ringing, while prayers and singing erupted for all to hear.

The Shouter Baptist roadside meeting had all but disappeared from the Cayerian landscape for more than three decades, because it was an arrestable offence. Gwynneth declared it a fitting return that this Shouter Baptist roadside meeting was held in the centre of the capital, on the very doorstep of Government House, a stone's throw from Police Headquarters and from the courts of law.

On the train, before he started to get drowsy, Sonny repeated to Gwynneth the old story of the police coming up the hill to the church. And, as he drifted off to sleep, Gwynneth told him, again, about the days when she and Nenn Vie, as little girls, used to go to prayers in the church behind Queen's house…

When they got to the Polydores' home, only Sylvan and his grandfather were there. Venus was up at Queen's home compound, directing preparations for the thanksgiving service, and, from the evening before, Malcolm and Cyrus had been part of the crew bringing the church back down from Lokono mountain. Members were bringing down, for now, only as much of the church's paraphernalia as would be needed for them to hold thanksgiving.

Sonny wanted to run up the road immediately and join them, but Gwynneth told him he had to eat first. Viola had packed frybake and accra for them, *and* there was food waiting for them at the Polydores. Venus had instructed the household to leave lunch on the table for them, although no message had been sent to announce their coming (no point – they would have got to Pilgrim before the message did). Sonny quickly polished off everything on his plate so he would be allowed to go up with Sylvan. Gwynneth knew that she would be of little use, just yet, in the work taking place at the church. She needed to rest for a bit, so on their way there, Sylvan and Sonny settled her in at Uncle Albert's.

The sacred buildings in Queen's yard had been preserved for all of the over thirty-three years of exile, awaiting the day when the church would come home. Never doubting that this day would come, the members had been leepaying the floors and walls, renewing the carat, and constantly, scrupulously, cleaning. These buildings had not been standing idle. The palay had become a liming-spot for young members of the church, including those who lived with Queen – her deceased brother's great-grandson and some descendants of the sundry children she had taken into her care in her younger days. Through all the years of the prohibition, the church building had been used for baptism instruction and for meetings as before. Likewise, the mourner-room had continued to be used for its intended purpose.

Queen was now 93 years old. Right up to their very last service on the hill, the Sunday before the repeal, she had trudged up Lokono on her own steam, slowly and painfully, flanked by a retinue of sturdy youth, but refusing to be carried.

To all intents and purposes, Venus had been the head of the church for the past few years, but Queen was still carrying out, when she was able, and with Venus's help, the duties of a person whom the Spirit had given the charge to found a church. Queen was still attending to pilgrims on Mourning-Ground; laying hands on the sick; preaching; instructing candidates for baptism. She had stopped baptising people, though, for she had to agree with her spiritual children that, at her age, going into river-water in the middle of the night would be just looking to get ague. If she went to a baptism, she stayed on the river-bank with the rest of the congregation and lent her voice to the singing.

The thanksgiving service was held on Sunday morning, in the old church that had been waiting patiently for the return of its congregation. Many of them had never been to a service in there, though they would have entered the building to help clean it, or for baptism instruction. There were some present who could only barely remember what it was like to hold service in broad daylight. The younger members had no memory at all of such a thing. Today the church was dressed up with palm branches, balisier, croton, flowers of many kinds, beautiful cloth draped everywhere, the table piled high with offerings of fruit, vegetables, bread, cakes, drinks, sweets… It was a most joyous morning, with clamorous bell-ringing, drumming, singing, people embracing each other… Gwynneth felt a pang of sadness that Mumma had not lived to see this day.

Sonny had taken his leave of Gwynneth as they entered the church, and gone to sit with the other children, on one side of the altar. The drummers were sitting on the other side. At a certain point in the service, Gwynneth saw a drummer relinquish his place and beckon in the direction of the children. Immediately Sonny got up and walked over to take the man's place. More than once he had mentioned casually to Gwynneth and Viola that in Pilgrim they let him beat drums in church, and Gwynneth had treated this news just as casually, assuming it to be a case of the drummers humouring a little child. But Sonny was playing the drum, a skin drum that was just the right height for him, with the confidence of an old pro. Gwynneth was overwhelmed with pride to realise that Sonny was an official, expert drummer of Queen's church.

Queen spoke. "Chirren, I thank God that I live to see this day. We fight the good fight and we conquer injustice. We come back home. Lion of Judah Tabernacle come down out of the wilderness…"

The joyful sounds that greeted this declaration turned to murmurs of distress when Queen continued, "So now I could close my eye."

With a mischievous grin Queen sought to comfort them. "Doan fraid. I ain going nowhere before God call me. And until he call me, Lottie on holiday. Now is Mother Polydore allyou going have to deal with. After Mother Polydore speak here this glorious morning, anybody else who want to bring a word will get up and talk. I want to hear somebody say they glad for Mother Lottie how she live to see Shouter set free, and how she on her way to her higher home now, happy and at peace, going to meet all who gone before this day break. Like Sister Estelle, who I dream up to last night. Teacher Humfrey. Mother Grace. Leader Gareth. Nurse Irene. Mother Myra…"

And Queen slid into song: "There is no city on earth for me to dwell … / There is a city over yonder…"

Ignoring the muffled sighs and wails coming from the congregation, Queen raised another hymn: "In the sweet by-and-by / We shall meet on that beautiful shore…"

Everyone sang, but not with the vigour she would have liked, and when the song came to an end, she conceded, smiling, "All right, all right. I know. Is not wake we keeping. Is thanksgiving. Mother Polydore, come and talk to you church. Give them comfort."

Some members formed a little circle around Queen and Mother Polydore. Queen took off her shawl and draped it over Mother Polydore's shoulder, and then anointed her. The bell rang out, followed by drumming and singing. And Mother Polydore, before she addressed the gathering, raised a singing that chased away the lurking shadow:

The Lion of Judah
Shall break every chain
And give us the victory
Again and again.

~

It was the first Sunday in May 1954, the thirty-sixth anniversary of the meeting in which Moun Demmeh's "cultural reconnoitre" had been conceived. Ainsley had rounded up the small core of Moun Demmeh stalwarts who still kept in touch with each other, and invited them to his home to plan for the publication of "Songs of Cayeri". It was the first Sunday in May 1954. There were seven of them besides Gwynneth and Ainsley. Edwin had died, and Kenrick and Ravi had migrated – Kenrick to Britain, Ravi to Canada.

Gaston was part of this gathering, at Gwynneth's request. She had shown him the manuscript of the songbook one evening. He looked through it and then asked her in a near to scolding voice (but she decided that she deserved it), "So you been sitting on this treasure for how long? The first thing we have to do is duplicate it, before the pages start to disintegrate. We just lucky the termites and the silverfish ain do the job already."

He would help to get the pages typed, with carbon copies, and Gwynneth would write out duplicate sheets of the music.

The gathering thrashed out concerns such as where the money would come from for printing, given their experience with *The Cayerian Review*; who would own and issue the songbook, since Moun Demmeh was still, officially, an illegal organisation; and what to do with funds collected from sales of the book.

Gaston was a great help. He spoke of different possibilities. "There are organisations in the metropolitan countries," he said, "that are interested in less-known or endangered cultures around the world. They offer grants for projects of conservation or archiving within these cultures. Moun Demmeh could apply for a grant to have the songbook printed. Or, you could approach a publisher, who would not need to be paid. The publishing house would recuperate the cost of production by selling the book, and pay royalties to its owner, i.e., Moun Demmeh."

On the question of ownership, Gaston advised them to consider setting up a trust, with themselves as the trustees. "You can continue to use the name 'Moun Demmeh' for the trust, if you make some change to the full title. The name of the banned organisation was 'Moun Demmeh Social and Cultural Society'. I suggest that you change it to something like 'Moun Demmeh Cultural Trust', which would make it a new entity, not under any prohibition. The purpose of the trust would be to get the book published; to receive the proceeds of its sale; and to manage these funds. The trustees would have to decide what to do with the funds."

"One choice would be to put the money towards future reprinting of the book," Raj suggested.

"And maybe also print the cookbook," said Joycelyn. She was the one holding the recipes they had gathered in 1918 and '19. "We have enough material there for us to print a booklet of Cayerian cuisine; but of course we should first review what is there, and maybe add to it. Is so sad, though, that we didn get to put out any of the material we gathered, except for the bits we put into the *Review*. All that information, still not published – Cayerian bush medicine; Anansi and *Konpè Lapen* stories; proverbs and more. To think that most of this has never come to light... Maybe we should do some digging, some scouting around to find out whether any of it did survive."

"Hm. Where to start with that?" someone asked.

"Well, we had certain members leading in the different areas of culture," Joycelyn said, "but I cyaan remember who led what, apart from Gwynneth for the songs, and for the recipes, me and Ravi."

"When we were putting together that issue of the *Review*, I think it was Kenrick who brought a folder of proverbs," Ainsley recalled. "We could write to him."

"If we still have a chance to get our hands on the material we gathered, that would be great," Sylvia said. "If we doan find it, no sweat. Now we seeing a new generation on the path of 'cultural reconnoitre'. The work continues. More people interested in gathering our old stories, for example, some that so far have been handed down only by word of mouth."

"Yes!" Gwynneth said. "You-all remember the question David

asked: 'Where is the great novelist, playwright, or poet of this colony who will choose to look inwards and write from within Cayerian life?' Well, bringing forth our stories from the oral tradition is part of what will fill that gap. And now we also seeing a modern Cayerian literature springing up, Cayerians 'writing from within' our world since the thirties, publishing and earning high acclaim in the metropolitan countries. Not many Cayerians have even heard of them, but one day, one day, these works will become part of our education. Our people will see themselves in that mirror, and gain a stronger sense of themselves from their own fiction, as people do in other societies."

The company took stock of progress made in the recognition of Cayerian culture – especially the arts – in the years since those early efforts of groups such as theirs to chip away at the oblivion and contempt surrounding it.

The Cayerian Dance Company was well established, and so was *Vini Chanté Ansanm*, an exuberant choir of voices old and young, devoted to singing Cayerian songs. Aunty Jenny's Children's Talent Show was growing from strength to strength. Calypso tents were flourishing. Carnival was attracting more and more tourists. And just two months before this anniversary meeting, a huge advance: the steelband had mounted the colony's most prestigious musical platform: The All-Cayeri Music Festival! At last!

The steelbands had multiplied and were now to be found all over the colony. They were being invited to perform in high places, such as the Governor's Residence and the Hotel de Versailles… Some night clubs with an uptown clientele engaged small steelband stage sides, or soloists for cabaret performances. Bands had begun to go on tours abroad, where they played at world-renowned concert-halls.

Gwynneth marvelled at the level of expertise their craft had reached. She had not been able to keep up with all the intricate orchestral developments achieved by steelbands, including the two young bands that she, Gaston and Ollie had taken on as protégés. "Me, I quite content, now," she said, "just to sit back and listen with pride when *any* steelband music play on the radio. But the fighting! The foolish, foolish violence among those men in town! That is what preventing them from getting all the respect they deserve for their achievements. Let's hope the Association can really help to keep the peace."

The violence, Ainsley pointed out, was fuelled by rivalry between some Kings Port steelbands. It was landing steelbandmen in the courthouse and the jail. Recently, though, with the help of supporters and advocates highly placed in the social order, including Ollie's cousin in the Leg. Co., peace had been brokered and the bands had got together to form their own umbrella body – The Cayeri Steelband Association. For the moment, however, the reputation built by warring steelbandmen in Kings Port hung over the whole steelband fraternity. Lennox's situation was a case in point, and Gwynneth told the gathering about the experience of this young man with his girlfriend's parents.

The anniversary gathering paid tribute to the woman in Kings Port who had recently formed a steelband comprised of young women. A few months before that, Ainsley pointed out, some of the inmates at the Girls' Reform School right there in Morne Cabrite had been allowed to form a small steelband that not many people knew about.

Gwynneth was happy for these two developments, for thus far it was pretty much only boys and men who were involved in the bands (except for here and there a jamet who did not give a hoot what people would think of a woman being in a steelband, and the big-hearted women who, like Miss Verna, readily sheltered a homeless band). One day, Gwynneth was sure, it would become a perfectly normal thing to see girls and boys, men and women, together making music in steelbands.

"Let's not overlook the liberation of the Shouters," Sylvia said. "That is a major milestone on this journey we charting. Remember our *Review* had two editorials about religious persecution – the ban on Shouters and the government not recognising Hindu and Muslim marriages. Today the colonial government has had to accept that in Cayeri religion extends beyond what was brought from Europe."

"People had to wring that change out of them," Raj commented. "Took them decades. Muslim marriages officially recognised in the thirties; Hindu marriages in the forties; and the ban on Shouters lifted at the start of the fifties."

Before they moved to the social part of the meeting, they observed a moment of silence for David and Edwin. They went on to reminisce about the meeting of May 1918 – the lively discussion on culture; the abrupt and disgruntled departure of Johnstone, soon to be followed by some of those who shared his opinions; the impromptu pot of oildown... It was at this point that Ainsley made a surreptitious exit and returned from the kitchen carrying an iron pot. He placed it on the dining-room table and invited everyone to dig into some "anniversary oildown".

The celebration that ensued took in Ainsley's birthday, only a month away, as well as the renewal of Moun Demmeh's mission.

38

"We know the real, true-true Roy is still in there."

Just as they suspected, all was not well with Roy on the home front. He was visiting more frequently. They were seeing him, on average, twice a month, usually on a Sunday, but sometimes he spent the whole weekend. He would arrive looking dispirited. Now and then he greeted them from the gallery with slurred speech and a heartiness that soon fizzled out. Viola removed her rum punch from the wagonette and stored it in her room.

On these visits, Roy still kept pretty much to himself, coming out to eat only if the men were there, but mostly holing up in his bedroom. Part of his time he spent sitting immobile in Puppa's chair in the drawing-room, or slumped into the gallery couch. Sometimes he positioned himself like a watchman out on the backyard bench.

One Sunday morning Viola heard him arrive at the gate and come through the front door. Gwynneth was at church. Viola looked in through the dining-room door to acknowledge his "Good morning" and saw him collapse into Puppa's chair with a great heaviness. It gave her a jolt, for what she saw was Puppa flopping into that same chair in the corner, one evening twenty-six years before, only dragging himself out of the chair to take to his bed for good. She lingered, peering at Roy, but he didn't look sick, or drunk. She sighed and went back into the kitchen.

Sonny, who was sprawled on the drawing-room couch, reading, had already sat up to say "Good morning, Mr Roy," and then resumed his comfortable position with his book.

After some minutes had passed, Viola heard Roy's voice. "Sonny-Boy," she thought she heard him say. "Bring some water for your Uncle Roy, nuh?"

Sonny appeared at the kitchen door, and Viola handed him the glass of water, making no comment on what she might have heard. She reported it to Gwynneth later that day, and Gwynneth was sceptical, too. But since Sonny thereafter began referring to and addressing Roy as "Uncle Roy", while Roy actually began to acknowledge Sonny's presence and call him "Sonny-Boy", they concluded that Viola might have heard right.

It was not until weeks later that Viola mentioned to Gwynneth how Roy had plonked himself down in the chair and how much it had reminded her of what may have been the last time Puppa sat in his chair. Viola spoke of Roy's action in a matter-of-fact, even light-hearted way, relating how she had felt like asking him, "If your ass was a egg, now?"

Gwynneth, however, was worried. "And you didn ask him what was wrong?"

Viola steupsed. "I have time with Roy and his foolishness? Whatever wrong with him, he bring it on heself."

Gwynneth decided she would take Roy aside on his next visit and talk with him. They had not seen him since that Sunday – more than a month ago, she reckoned – and she thought of getting Gaston or Ollie to check on him at his office, to make sure he was all right. Then, one Saturday morning towards the end of October, a car they did not know stopped at the gate. Sonny called Gwynneth, and as she came into the gallery, a young man was emerging from the driver's side of the car. He seemed exasperated. He waved at her and called out, "Good day, Aunt Gwynneth."

That was when she recognised Gordon. He came through the gate and walked briskly up to the house. Gwynneth was alarmed. "Something happen to your father?" she asked.

Gordon turned around and called to the car, "Dad! You not coming out?"

Viola was now in the gallery, too.

"Mummy hit him with the frying pan," Gordon announced. "Damaged his wrist. She was aiming for his head and he put up his hands to block the blow. He's on sick leave and he asked me to bring him here." He turned again and shouted, "Dad!"

Roy shouted back at him, "A little help out here, nuh! That would strain you?"

Roy had been struggling to get himself out of the front passenger seat. Now he was out, and Viola gasped at the sight of a cast on his right arm. Roy leaned against the car door to close it back. Then he began a futile tugging with his left hand at the back door handle, but gave up when Gordon joined him beside the car. The two of them snapped at each other briefly, their words inaudible from the gallery.

Gordon opened the door, dragged a large bag out of the back seat and took it up into the house, while Roy made his way up the walk at a slower pace. Gordon stayed long enough to install Roy in his room, leaving him lying on the bed. Gwynneth and Viola managed to detain Gordon in the gallery for a moment as he bustled out. He had to be back in Kings Port before eleven o'clock, so he gave rapid responses to their queries.

"She says *he* was about to hit *her*, and he denies it. They're just at each other's throats all the time. Anyway, I have to go. Bye, Aunt Gwynneth. Bye, Aunt Viola."

The two of them stood rooted to the spot even after the boy had driven off. Viola was seething. "That wicked bitch!" she exploded. "And those dragged-up, heartless children!"

Gwynneth reminded her that Roy was in the house and might be hearing her.

Viola lowered her voice. "I *know* they treating him bad. What, they think he doan have nobody? They think he's a stray dog? Eh?"

She became speechless and stormed inside.

After a day or two of agonising over whether she should say anything, Gwynneth knocked on Roy's door and asked to have a word with him. She went in and sat side by side with him on the bed, just like in his high school years, when he was home during school vacations and would rush into his room after a scorching blast of disapproval from Puppa over one thing or another. She or Viola would go in after him and try to comfort him. Sitting now with the hurt wrist cradled in his other hand, Roy was morose, not inclined to talk, and Gwynneth was not inclined to give up too much of her precious time coaxing him into conversation, so she went straight to the point. "This hitting incident, Roy," she began. "You know that Mumma didn't let anybody hit you, so I can't imagine you hitting your wife…"

Roy was jerked out of his silence. "That young snake told you that I hit his mother?"

416

"Well, not exactly…"

"Gwynneth, I have never hit Helen, or Gordon, or Freda. Helen is the one always reaching for something to hit me with, or pelt at me – a pot, a shoe, a book, even a bottle – and in front of the children… Teaching them to disrespect me. 'Thank your lucky stars neither of you got his colour,' she says to them. 'One golliwog in the house is enough'."

He clammed up, and looked away, as though he felt he had said too much. Gwynneth got up, placing her hand on his shoulder to hoist herself to her feet. "Make yourself comfortable, Roy," she said. "Make yourself at home."

For the time that Roy stayed with them, Viola waited on him hand and foot, drafting Sonny into this operation. It was so pathetic to see Roy trying to butter a slice of bread or stir his tea with his left hand that she instructed Sonny to keep an eye out for him getting into such difficulties, and help him. Roy soon began to call Sonny his "right hand man", thanking him profusely, every day, for being helpful to him. Gwynneth pitched in, but drew the line when it came to laundry. She got Roy to pay Miss Ivy, who took in washing for a living, to come and collect his clothes once a week and bring them back washed, ironed as necessary, and all neatly folded.

In the first week or so they would now and then come upon Roy sitting in the gallery, staring off into space, his face sagging, and his wounded arm pressed against his chest. But daily his disposition improved. He relaxed and became quite talkative and sociable, almost jovial, especially when Ollie and Gaston were there. They took him out one evening on a man-lime. They went to a bar in St Paul, not the classiest of joints, they warned him in advance, not a place where he would meet any other Ascension old-boys; but Roy had such a good time that he was in seventh heaven whenever they invited him out again.

About a fortnight before Christmas, Gordon turned up at the gate. His mother had dispatched him to bring Roy home because Empire Bank's Christmas dinner was coming up. That was a premier social event of the year, at which it was very important to be seen. It was held at the Hotel de Versailles. Empire's staff members and clients who were prominent business owners came out with spouse or fiancé on the arm, and dressed to kill. The newspaper photographers would be there, and with any luck, you and your other half could end up smiling out from the Who's Who page the following Sunday.

Helen was obliged to skip the bank dinner that year, for Roy would not budge. He told Gordon to go back and tell his mother he was spending Christmas with his family. The cast was off, and he was able to help with some of the lighter Christmas cleaning of house and yard. Christmas was on a Tuesday that year, so the preceding weekend was devoted to putting away the house. On the Saturday, Lennox came over and helped them take the Morris chairs, the centre table, and the dining-room chairs out into the gallery. There Roy and Gwynneth sandpapered them and did most of the varnishing, while Lennox and Sonny got down and scrubbed the drawing-room and dining-room floor.

Next morning, Roy varnished the remaining pieces of furniture, and in the afternoon he and Sonny applied polish to the floorboards. Both of them on all fours, Sonny started from the dining-room end, as it was easier for him to go under the table, while Roy started from the front door, and they met, triumphantly, in the middle of the room. Now it was time to shine the floor.

Viola brought them each a glass of juice, and went out to Mumma's garden to pick seasoning before dark. Gwynneth was out. She had gone with Gaston to Christmas dinner at his workplace. Roy took up the broom that was used for shining the floor, its brush part wrapped in an old jersey, but immediately he seemed to have second thoughts. He leaned the broom against the wall, saying to Sonny, with an air of excitement, "Lemme show you something!"

He hurried to his room, and after some rummaging, came out with a fraying towel. He put it on the floor, stood on it, and began to skate on it along the floor boards. He told Sonny that when he was a boy, perhaps a little older than Sonny, his big sisters allowed him to shine the floor in that way, using discarded old clothes, while they worked with the wrapped-up broom. Sonny needed no persuasion to take the towel and begin shining the floor with the towel under his feet, leaving Uncle Roy to push the boring broom.

But then, Uncle Roy seemed to have another brainwave.

"Coming back just now," he said, and rushed into his room again. He returned, this time with socks in his hand. "Now, lemme show you what they *didn* allow me to do. Here, put these on."

He handed Sonny a pair of socks and sat to put on the other pair. "One Christmas I put on socks and come out to shine the floor with my feet. I get a good lil run before they notice was my good school socks I had on, in a mess, sticky and stain-up with floor polish, threads unravelling... not fit to wear again. Well, pardner, when they realise what I doing, they start to quarrel. 'When you get a job and could buy your own socks, Mister, then you could do that!' Well, now I have a job and I could polish the floor with my socks! Let's go, Sonny-Boy!"

Viola, still out in the yard, began to hear riotous sounds coming from inside the house and thought she should investigate. As she walked up the back steps, she could hear them singing, with Sonny carrying the tune, "We wish you a merry Christmas..." Roy was tone-deaf and couldn't hold a tune to save his life, but that had never discouraged him from bellowing a song at the top of his voice. Viola tiptoed across the pantry and peeped in on them: Mutt and Jeff, their feet in socks, skating, shuffling, dancing from one end of the room to the other, and round and round the dining-room table, singing now, "Jingle bells, jingle bells..." Viola tiptoed back out and went to finish what she was doing.

Early on Christmas Eve morning, Lennox came over to help with lifting the furniture back into the drawing-room, and then went home to help Marjorie put away their house. Roy and Sonny stripped the cushions and put on the new covers. Then they gathered up all the ornaments from the wagonette and the centre table, and carried them into the gallery to clean them. Mumma's singing cherub was always cleaned with Brasso, and that smell, mingling with the smell of floor polish and varnish, had remained, for Roy, part of the aura of Christmas. It now assailed him with an almost painful memory of happiness.

In the evening, Gwynneth put up the new curtains before going off to service at St Hilda's. Meanwhile Roy and Sonny helped Viola with the orgy of cooking that every year began on Christmas Eve, to be interrupted only by the need for the cooks to catch some sleep before they continued next morning.

Marjorie and Lennox joined them at the large spread that was Christmas breakfast. Just before they had all finished eating, Roy excused himself from the table and disappeared through the door to the pantry. Soon they heard a tinkling sound approaching from that direction. Roy came back into the dining-room wheeling a boy's bicycle – shiny red – and playfully ringing its bell. Sonny gaped.

"A-a! Well look what I find in my room!" Roy exclaimed. "Like Father Christmas lost his way and put it in the wrong room? I doan think is me he bring it for – lemme see…" He scratched his head and made a clowning attempt to get onto the saddle. "Nah. It too small. Well, we only have one little boy here, so must be him Father Christmas bring it for?"

Sonny glanced around the table as if to find out who Roy meant. Gwynneth and Viola were trying their best to look surprised. Sonny turned his gaze back to the beautiful vision. Here was his heart's desire, but he could only sit and stare open-mouthed at it.

Roy beckoned to him. "Come, Sonny-Boy. Take your vehicle."

Sonny came to life and sprang off his chair. As he made his way towards the bike, Viola enquired, "Sonny? What you say to Uncle Roy?"

"Thank you, Uncle Roy!" Sonny said, rushing to encircle Roy's waist in a tight hug-up.

"Lennox, you want to give him a little practice outside, on the front walk?" Gwynneth suggested.

Lennox picked up the bike and headed for the front door with Sonny following close behind, almost tripping over his own feet.

In the early afternoon, Marjorie and Lennox brought over the dishes they had cooked, and Gaston and Ollie joined the company for Christmas lunch. Roy had the time of his life that Christmas Day. He made a little speech at the table, thanking everyone for their care, and promising to be a better brother to his big-sisters Titta and Lolola, and a better uncle to Sonny-Boy. He explained, needlessly, that "Titta" meant "sister," and joked that they could now stop barricading the front door whenever they saw his car pull up at the gate.

Roy's sick leave would end early in the new year, so he had arranged to get a lift back to town with Gaston who was coming to lunch on Saturday. Before he finished up his packing that morning, Roy went to Gwynneth's room.

"Thank you, again," he said to her, "and sorry for all the trouble."

"You know we never could resist looking after you, Roy."

"Believe me, Gwynneth, I didn't come up here expecting to be looked after. You could have ignored me, paid me no mind at all – I was quite prepared for that. God knows I don't deserve your help, because..." He hung his head. "By 'trouble' I mean not only your putting yourselves out for me these past two months. I mean all the years of trouble, all my adult years, so-called, when I made myself a really bad pain in the ass to the two of you. I can do better."

"We know," Gwynneth said. "We know the real, true-true Roy is still in there," she tapped on his chest, "and we would like to see more of him. Doan be a stranger, now."

"Thank you, Titta," and he hugged her till he near squeezed the breath out of her.

39
"I am Shouter Baptist and Anglican."

Quietly, without warning, Queen had gone her way. The month of May was dry and scorching. The little sprinkles they were getting now and then would leave no mark on the soil, nor bring any comfort to the leaves that were curling with thirst. Rainy season was nowhere in sight, no matter how high the cigales pitched their screeching. On evenings, one or another of the youngpeople would hold the bucket and walk with Queen as she made her way slowly around the yard, dipping the calabash in the bucket and giving each of her beloved flower-plants a little water to save them from drying up entirely.

Then, one night in early June, Queen's great-grand-nephew Gerald was woken up by spray blowing in through the window. It was then he realised that rain was drumming heavily on the roof. He knew that Queen's window would also be open because of the heat, so he got up to go and close it.

He could barely make out her form on the bed. Her lamp was burning dimly, and the oil was low. He turned the wick up a little. Queen was not lying on her side, curled up with her cheek cupped in her hand. Instead, she was lying on her back, stretched out to her full length. Her hands, with fingers neatly intertwined, were resting on her middle. It was as though Queen had laid herself out for burial.

The rain was tapering off. Gerald sat with Queen for a while, mustering what fortitude he could to go and wake up the whole house.

Monica was now living on her own, renting a room in Harlem and working at a hot-dog and hamburger counter. The littlest Kramer, "Al", was now at school, like the two older children, so the family no longer needed a full-time child minder. Mrs Kramer still called upon her, though, when she and her husband went out at night, and Monica would go and babysit all three children, even if it meant missing one of her night-school classes. That was a major sacrifice on her part, for Monica didn' make joke with her classes, the road to her high school diploma.

But she was always willing to help out the Kramers. They had shown her *so* much kindness, over all the years she had spent with them. And she knew that Mr Kramer could not persuade his wife to go out with him, on what he still called a "date", unless Monica came and stayed with the children. Nor would Mrs Kramer leave Angie, Jerome and Al with anybody but Monica.

For the past year or so a man named Terence had been regularly cropping up in Monica's letters. Ordinarily, Monica was not one to talk out her business. In the eight years she had lived in America, she had not said much to Gwynneth and Viola about boyfriends. She wrote once about someone called Walter taking her to a show at Carnegie Hall, and this she only mentioned because Carnegie Hall was a place she had heard Gwynneth speak about.

Another time, she had Gwynneth and Viola laughing with her description of Travis, whom she had dumped because he ate like a pig. You could hear Travis eating from blocks away, she said, because of his loud snapping and slurping. And if you were bad-lucky enough to be sitting in front of him as he ate, you could see right into his wide-open mouth where the food he was chewing looked like vomit; pieces of it might even fly out and hit you in your face.

Her letters to Gwynneth and Viola, though, had always been tinged with anxiety about the two of them perhaps getting overwhelmed with looking after Sonny. Almost every other letter carried the refrain: "I hope he is not getting to be too much for you", or, "Just let me know if you want Mammy and Dads to take him over." When that anxiety began to irritate Gwynneth, she simply stopped trying to reassure Monica that Sonny was no trouble at all, that they loved him and were happy to have him. And whenever irritation got the better of Gwynneth, she sent Monica words to the effect that she must stop thinking of them as two decrepit and dotish oldpeople, for Sonny was keeping them young.

With Terence in the picture, Monica's letters were mostly

light-hearted and chatty. Yet a new anxiety seemed to be creeping in. Sonny was about to go into Standard 5. Nobody in Monica's family had gone beyond primary school, and not only was she determined to pursue high school education herself; Sonny *had* to go to high school, whatever it took. And what it might take was bringing him to America as soon as he finished primary school. Up there, she wrote, every child could go to a high school, free of charge. Gwynneth replied that Sonny was very likely to win a college exhibition. Monica was sceptical. For all of her schooldays, the thought of winning a college exhibition had never been anything but pie in the sky, a thought wasted.

Gwynneth sought to give her hope, writing to her:

> *There are some 200 college exhibitions offered now, and Sonny is a bright child, doing very well in school. Let's wait and see if he gets an exhibition. Then you can decide, not forgetting that you should also ask him what he wants to do.*

The mention of what Sonny might want or not want to do was enough to trigger an upsurge of Monica's anxieties. Suppose Sonny did not want to leave Cayeri? Suppose he did not want to come up there and live with her? She dreaded the moment when she might have to tear him away from the people and the life he was accustomed to, distressing him and Tan Gwynneth and Tan Viola and the rest of his family in Pilgrim. That was not going to be an easy thing to do.

She would be happy if indeed he could get an exhibition and go to high school in Cayeri, but to Monica, that was as likely as winning the sweepstake. Every year, on a soggy wet-season morning, a small grappe of children would be bundled onto the bus at Pilgrim Road corner, and then the train at Clancy Halt, heading for San Pedro to sit the college exhibition exam. It was only the very brightest pupils in each year's crop of Fifth Standard children who were sent on this journey; yet no Pilgrim child had ever won an exhibition. Monica was glad to hear that the government was now giving so many scholarships, but 200 out of how many thousands of children still did not guarantee Sonny a place in high school.

Then, in a letter to Gwynneth, Monica piled on her newest

worry. She and Terence wanted to get married, but she was holding him off, telling him she had to think about it some more. Terence was a kind and generous man, and he seemed to accept, even admire, that she would always be in charge of her own life, as her mother was, and, for that matter, his mother was. On one occasion Monica had warned him, in so many words, that he could never own her, and his response was a very calm "I know." He was neither surprised, nor amused, nor vexed. His reaction was reassuring to her. Nothing in his behaviour had ever suggested, anyway, that he thought he could own her.

It was one of the movies she had seen in New York. Perhaps she was going to the movies too often. She had seen more movies in the time she had thus far spent in the States than in her whole life in Cayeri. Often it seemed to her that the women in the movies were not sufficiently in charge of themselves. They were too easily ruled by their men. And, somewhere along the way, she had watched a particularly disturbing story in which a woman allowed her husband to completely take her over. He refused to let her have a job; he cut her off from her family and her friends; he banned her from going anywhere without him; he talked to her as if she was stupid, and didn't let her have an opinion of her own.

That movie had stayed with her, leaving her with the feeling that certain things needed to be said to a man, sooner rather than later, so that it would always be clear who she was.

Monica worried about bringing in Sonny. Some nights she lay awake, seized with apprehension. Perhaps if Sonny was a little child of two or three… but you could never be sure how things would turn out between an older child and a stepfather. Sonny would be eleven and a half years old when he finished primary school… and Terence a complete stranger to him… Worse yet if Sonny didn't want to be there, couldn't settle down, only wanted to go back home… He could make life difficult for Terence and herself, and what, then, would be Terence's attitude to Sonny? How would he treat Sonny?

If her son couldn't get a high school education at home in Cayeri, then she would have to put aside getting married, and persuade him to come up to America so he could get to go to high school. She had to see about her child. Set him on a good road to the future. Sonny would get used to living with her; she was not a stranger to him. They had been in contact with each other for all of the years she had been away, thanks to his godmothers reading her letters to him, writing for him, and sending his drawings to her. Then the drawings began to have a word or two on them, written by him. Later on he was filling half an exercise book page with words – three sentences or so in huge, dancing letters, and decorated with drawings. Now he wrote all his news to her, in a handwriting that was better than hers. If Sonny had to come to New York, he would be well able to keep in touch with his family in Turagua and in Pilgrim…

If Terence didn't understand her putting off the wedding plans, and decided to break with her, then *chou* that. But Gwynneth suggested that Monica talk to Terence about her dilemma before she did anything as drastic as calling off the plan to get married. That would not be fair to him. She would be throwing away a good man, without even giving him a chance. Gwynneth also asked Monica to consider that she might one day come to hold it against Sonny if she were to throw away Terence because of him, a burden no child should have to bear.

Put all your cards on the table. I will assume that Terence already knows you have a child over here. I can't imagine you keeping that from him. Let Terence know all the complications you think you are facing now. You can't keep this poor man dangling on a string while you wait to see whether Sonny will have to come and live with you.

Of course Terence knew about Sonny. There was nobody who knew Monica and didn't know about Sonny. Pictures of him adorned all four walls of her room, the door, the edges of her mirror, the two panes of the one window… And Terence had helped Monica pack, wrap and tie up the boxes of clothes, books and toys that she sent home for Sonny's birthday, for Christmas, and from time to time during the rest of the year. She had shown Terence one or two of Sonny's letters that she was particularly proud of.

Monica followed Gwynneth's advice and started the conversation with Terence late one evening, after her night-school classes. They talked until well past midnight. Her fear that he might be driven to ill-treat her child did not go down so well with him. He was hurt, and he told her he was hurt, but he didn't make a big drama out of it. He just sighed and gave a quiet little speech. "Monica," he said. "Remember what I told you about my daddy. You're forgetting that the man who helped my mother bring me up is not my father. He came into our home when I was nine years old, not two or three, and I couldn't have a better daddy."

In the end he suggested that he and Monica get engaged. They could wait to get married, but what could not wait, he said, was getting her out of that cramped room, with the dingy bathroom placed way down at the end of the dingy corridor and used by an untold number of other people. The two of them could share an apartment. If Sonny had to come to New York, they could try all three of them living together. If it didn't work, and if she still loved him and wanted him in her life, he would move out of the apartment and go back to being her visiting man. If Sonny got the scholarship for high school in Cayeri, they could then get married – if she still loved him and wanted him to be a permanent part of her life.

Monica was very touched, but had to look at him closely to make sure that he wasn't just being sarcastic, because of the thoughtless hurt she had laid on him. But she knew in her heart that going to such lengths to be sarcastic to her wasn't like Terence. This was a serious solution he was offering. That very night they set a date for the engagement – a date that would give them enough time to find and move into an apartment where they could announce their engagement to a few friends and celebrate with a little party.

At the reopening of school in September, Gwynneth took Sonny and Sonnylal into her Tuesday afternoon class of children preparing for the following year's college exhibition exam. Sonnylal's family responded with regular deliveries of produce from their garden – the best of their carailie, beigan, bodi, anything they reaped. They also brought cooked food – sada roti filled with tomato chokha, pumpkin, channa, bhaji or potato, for they knew that these were among Sonny's favourite things to eat. This thanksgiving would continue even after the two boys entered secondary school.

On Sundays, Gwynneth always bought the newspapers on her way home from church, at a vendor's stall outside the market. But one Sunday morning in the Christmas term, before she could even get ready to go to church, let alone buy the papers, an acolyte of St Hilda's arrived at the house to say that the list of exhibition winners was in the Sunday papers, Sonny's name was there, and Reverend Fields wanted St Hilda's three exhibitioners to come to the service that morning. At the sound of Gwynneth's shriek, Viola rushed out to the gallery, followed, sleepily, by Sonny, and the shriek that she let out was even louder than Gwynneth's.

Viola lost no time in starting to cook, for this day's lunch could not be any ordinary affair. She was sure that the others would be coming up to celebrate. Gwynneth called out to Marjorie and Lennox, and they rushed over to congratulate Sonny, smothering him with hugging-up before Viola roped them into the cooking. Roy was the first to arrive. He brought a choice cut of pork, and a carite – Viola's favourite fish – from Kings Port market.

While those at home cooked up a storm, Gwynneth and Sonny were in church, where the three exhibition winners from St Hilda's school were being honoured. Mr Daniel stood with them before the congregation and called out their names – Joshua Polydore, Sonnylal Premchand and Jennifer Subero. Then he announced that he was going to put up a scroll of honour on the wall at school, and their names would be the first to go up on it, as they had brought the first college exhibitions to St Hilda's. He also called out the names of the teachers who had taught them from First Primer to Standard 5, and thanked them.

"And special thanks," Mr Daniel said, "to Teacher Gwynneth Cuffie, not only because she gave one of our exhibitioners his earliest schooling, but because of the great change she has brought to our school over the past six years, working as a voluntary assistant. She has certainly lifted up St Hilda's Anglican School."

The congregation stood up and applauded the scholarship winners and their teachers, and Reverend Fields blessed the three children. The choir led the church in singing the hymn that had been added to the order of service when the news came out that morning:

Now thank we all our God
With heart, and hands, and voices...

Gwynneth and Sonny came home to a house that was bustling like Christmas Eve. Indeed, when they stepped in through the front door, Lennox and Roy were putting up last year's Christmas curtains in the drawing-room and dining-room, under instructions from Viola. There was the smell of cake baking, and excited voices coming from the kitchen and pantry area, where Viola directed her cooking crew of Gaston and Marjorie. Ollie arrived a little later with a bottle of champagne.

An agreement was made among the bigpeople, before they sat down, that at the lunch table no one would say anything bad about Ascension College. Monica had sent word, when Sonny entered Standard 5, that she would want him to go to Ascension (in the event, in the unimaginable event, that he should win an exhibition). Any bad-talking of Ascension could take place later, in the gallery, when Sonny would be out.

Lennox was taking Sonny and Garnet to the 4.30 show at Regal Theatre in St Paul. It was a double: *Peter Pan* with *Ambush at Tomahawk Gap*. The second title gave Gwynneth a little shiver, but she was not too alarmed. Sonny knew how to watch a western, no matter how loudly the audience around him cheered and clapped and stamped their approval with their feet as the star-boys heroically massacred droves of pesky Apache. More than once she had taken him to see a film that was doubled with a western, and on each occasion the two of them had discussed the western afterwards, so that Sonny could understand what the history was and who, really, the heroes were, and who the villains.

At lunch, the bigpeople made congratulatory speeches and drank several toasts from their glasses of champagne, as every last one of them spoke and at the end of the speech called upon the others to drink to Sonny's health. Sonny was allowed some cherry brandy mixed with water in a tiny shot glass, a privilege which

Gwynneth, Viola and Roy had enjoyed once a year, from Sonny's age onwards, at Christmas. Everyone clapped and drank another toast when Viola prophesied that at the end of his high school career, Sonny would win the Island Scholarship, which would take him to university in England.

Sonny, innocent of the taboo on bad-talking Ascension at lunch, announced that Sonnylal's family had chosen Government College because they did not trust Ascension. They had heard stories of Hindu and Muslim boys being pressured by the school to become Catholics. There was silence around the table, with everyone looking to Gwynneth for direction. Viola broke that silence.

"Best you doan tell them that your family is Shouter Baptist!" she blurted out. "Put 'Anglican' for your religion. You christen in the Anglican church."

"But it's not against the law, now, to be a Shouter Baptist," Gwynneth pointed out.

"I know," Viola said, "but that ain stop people looking down on Shouters, disrespecting them, ridiculing them. And son, you know if they give you any bad treatment there, I will have to go and burn down that school!"

Amid the laughter, Gaston observed, "Well, Vie, if they treat Sonny bad, God help them, I doan know who will get there first with the matches and the pitch-oil, you, or your sister."

"But Nenn Vie," Sonny argued, "I want them to know I am a Shouter Baptist."

Viola made a last bid: "Well, just tell them 'Baptist' so they could think is London Baptist you mean. I still feel, though, that to avoid any fuss, you could put 'Anglican'. That is the Church of England, another whitepeople religion. They will respect that more than any African or Indian religion."

"So I can't tell them I am both? I am Shouter Baptist and Anglican."

The conversation was suspended while everyone pondered how this would sit with The College of the Ascension, until Gwynneth spoke. She looked a little dazed. "Yes, Sonny," she said. "That is what we will put on the registration form. And they cyaan do you a thing. Let them know who you are."

Monica had sounded him out on the question of which school he preferred, Ascension or Government College. Sonny had no opinion on either institution. He fell in with his mother's choice, especially as his grandparents, too, were awed by the very thought of Ascension College.

Sonny was a little disappointed that he would not be going to the same school as Sonnylal. Gwynneth reminded him that he and Sonnylal would be travelling on the same train morning and evening, as well as walking up James Street together on mornings. He could wait for Sonnylal after school and the two of them could walk down to the railway station together. And it was not as though they were going to stop visiting each other at home, and playing football in the savannah, or any of the other things they did together.

The following Saturday, Gwynneth and Sonny went to the Premchands' home to attend the puja held in thanksgiving for Sonnylal's success. On Sunday morning, Sonny, Gwynneth and Viola, driven by Gaston, set out for Pilgrim. Venus was holding Sonny's thanksgiving that afternoon, in the church. Just as he had been given a share of the puja offerings to take home after the prayers held for his friend, Sonny made sure to get a thanksgiving bag from the table to give Sonnylal.

Ascension would not have been Gwynneth's choice, given Roy's experience in that place. Yet she did not put up any argument. She would not interfere with Monica's right to make the final decision. But Gwynneth would be watching The College of the Ascension like a hawk.

431

40
"Know your place!"

Gaston was going with Gwynneth to register Sonny at the school. He had invited himself to accompany them. It would not do, he said, for Sonny's career at Ascension to begin with a shoot-out on registration day between the student's guardian, one Gwynneth Cuffie, and whoever was the unfortunate soul placed behind the registration table. He would go with them to place himself between said guardian and any agent of the school who might do anything to vex her. All in the gallery agreed. They also agreed to the "conscience clause" letter, proposed by Gaston, to protect Sonny from being caned at this school. "And," Gaston added, *sotto voce*, "thereby protect Ascension College from the wrath of Gwynneth."

He explained that in English history, people who did not want their children to take part in Church of England worship at school could invoke something called a "conscience clause" to get them exempted, on the grounds that it would go against their families' religious beliefs. "We could present the school with a declaration," he said, "worded something like this: 'Inflicting corporal punishment on this student would violate the principles held by his guardian on the treatment of children. Any misconduct on this student's part for which caning is prescribed by the school must, instead, be referred to his guardian for her attention'."

A loud "Hm!" came from Roy. "Good luck with that! In my time only the rich boys were exempt from caning. Their conscience clause was their family's money and skin colour. I don't know how much has changed at Ascension on that score."

Registration day was Sonny's first practice run for travelling to and from school. Gwynneth took him to town on the 7.00 o'clock train and walked him up James Street to the college. Gaston was waiting for them outside the gate.

Sonny found the aspect of Ascension a little intimidating. First, the thick, high wall (which looked like how he pictured the wall of

Jericho in the Bible), stretching along the pavement for what was his idea of a mile. Then, inside, this vast expanse of concrete yard, where marble angels and humans (saints, maybe) with hard stares either looked down from their high pedestals, dwarfing even Nenn Gwynnie and Godfather Gaston, or looked straight ahead, into the air before them, as though there was nobody passing below.

The man to whom they were sent didn't look at them too much, either – at first. They sat facing him while he went through Sonny's registration form. Now and then he threw them an irritated glance. Then he lifted his head and looked at them with clear and full-blown irritation, to ask, "Shouter Baptist *and* Anglican? Which is it?"

Gaston, sitting next to Gwynneth, became nervous and put his hand on her arm as she leaned (more like lunged) towards the man. " *'It'* " she said, "is just what you see written there."

The man winced. Gwynneth was still bending forward, glaring at him. He fidgeted, sat up and straightened the little stack of forms in front of him. Gaston told the gallery afterwards that it was her schoolmistress voice, scolding a pupil in the Queen's English, that put this man on his Ps and Qs, for up till then what the man was seeing before him was a black, free-place boy with his black, poor-ass and most likely illiterate family members.

At the end of their encounter, Gaston handed the man the "conscience clause" letter, which was in a sealed envelope, and said to him, "Please give this to the principal. My office will deliver a copy to the dean of discipline."

The next expedition to town was to buy Sonny's books and uniform. Part of Gwynneth's purpose on this trip was for Sonny to learn the way from school to Ollie's drugstore and to Gaston's office, so that he could go to either of them in the event of an emergency during the school day. Again, he and Gwynneth travelled to town on the 7.00 o'clock train and walked up James Street to Ascension. Then they walked across the two blocks to King George Street and went downtown to the drugstore, "Luzia's", named after Ollie's grandmother.

Shopping for the schoolbooks took up most of the time. Apart from their having to go to more than one bookstore, at each of those stores Sonny would disappear among the shelves to look at books, while Gwynneth lined up at the counter to pay. She would then have to find him and almost drag him out of the store. Their last stop was Cumberland's, to get Sonny's tie, blazer and shirts. Monica was sending everything else. She had written to them, listing all the items she had packed into a box and already posted – khaki pants, merinos, underpants, socks, shoes, handkerchiefs, raincoat, bookbag, pencils, pens, notebooks…

They went to Gaston's office and put their parcels into his car trunk, for him to bring up later. The three of them went to lunch at The Coal-Pot, and afterwards Gwynneth took Sonny to join the Public Library. She had enrolled him in the St Paul branch when he was eight years old and there was nothing left in the house that he had not read, or attempted to read and put aside because it was "too boring". At that age he was already reading both of the daily newspapers (or more accurately, those parts of the papers that were of interest to him).

The children's section of The Public Library in Kings Port was an inviting space on the upper floor of the building. Sonny's face lit up at the sight of the shelves lining the walls, packed with books, many times more books than there were in the St Paul library, children's and adult's sections combined. In Gwynneth's childhood, the Kings Port Public Library looked very much like the current St Paul branch – a modest wooden structure, raised a little off the ground by stumpy concrete supports. It was nothing like this grand, two-storeyed edifice of ornate bricks, with verandas and arches and balustrades, where Sonny was now feasting his eyes on books. But Gwynneth had been just as thrilled when, at the age of seven, she first entered the old Kings Port Public Library. In those days, the children's section was more like a children's corner, compared to this room that seemed to occupy most of the upper floor.

Puppa had never ceased to drum it into his children's heads that they must *read, read, read*. From their earliest years he gave them storybooks for their birthdays and for Christmas. They were living in Coryal when Puppa brought Gwynneth to town to enrol her as a member of the library and arm her with her own library card. Going to town from Coryal meant quite a journey. You had to walk out to the main road and wait for the bus to Wellington Junction, where you would get on the train and ride for what seemed like forever. Every three weeks, early on a Saturday morning, Gwynneth and Puppa would make this journey to town for her to return a book and borrow another, as well as browse and read until it was time to leave for the train station.

Gwynneth always looked forward to being let loose among the bookshelves for what would have been almost two hours, during which she could read two or three storybooks for her age group, or one fatter book meant for a higher age group. Puppa waited patiently, sitting in the adult section to read the day's newspapers, walking the pavement in front of the building, or standing as if on guard outside the door. Two years after Gwynneth joined the library, Puppa took Viola along and enrolled her as well. Then, through the years at Lakpat, he continued to escort the two of them to town to make use of the library. Later on it would be Roy, when they were living in Turagua and the journey to town was much shorter.

Now Gwynneth sat on a chair in the veranda outside the children's section and let Sonny browse to his heart's content. When he was done, they still had some time to spare before the 4.05 train, so they took the tramcar up to the Botanic Gardens, where they strolled among the beautiful greenery and sat for a bit on one of the benches, before taking the tramcar back downtown. When they got off the tram, Gwynneth took Sonny across to Albert Street, to show him the bus stand, in case he ever needed to take the bus home.

Monica's parcel arrived, and Sonny had to dress up in his uniform so Lennox could take some pictures of him to send to her.

On the first day of school, Sonny met with Sonnylal at Turagua station and they travelled to town together. They parted at the gate of Ascension, and Sonnylal continued on his way up to his school. Sonny entered the gate of Ascension College and then stood stock still. On registration day, which was in vacation time, the big concrete yard had been near empty, with just the new first formers, each with a family member or two, trickling across it on their way to or from the hall. Now the space was teeming with whiteboys, such a lot of them milling about that he felt as though he had stepped into another country, or had somehow got sucked into the screen at Regal Theatre. He had never seen so many real-life, moving whitepeople all in one place.

During that first week, the new students were invited to choose an extracurricular activity. Sonny's form master wrote the list of clubs and groups on the board, and passed around a sheet of paper for them to write down their choices. "This does not mean that everybody will get what they choose," he advised. "Put a first and a second choice; but again, not everybody can be accommodated where they would like to be. You might not get your first choice, nor even your second."

A day or two later the placements were pinned up in all the Form 1 classrooms. At break time, students gathered around to check, and this produced a mixed buzz of excitement and disappointment. The new students did not yet know each other. They had not finished matching names with faces, so it took them another week to see the full picture. The Creole and Indian boys began whispering to each other about what they were seeing. Some of them had put their names down for Sea Scouts, but not a single one of them had been placed there. Those who signed up for Sea Scouts had all been assigned to Cadets, whether or not they had given Cadets as one of their choices.

It turned out that the boys whose names appeared on the Sea Scouts list were all white or well off. It also became clear that the lawn tennis courts were only for such boys. Other boys who had chosen lawn tennis had been given football or cricket. This, they discovered, was the case across Forms 1A, 1B, and 1C.

Sonny had only put down one choice – the choir. He was offered football. The time slot allocated to extracurricular meetings was 3.00 – 4.30 p.m. That would mean missing the 4.05 train, and going home on the 5.08. The form master had not said that extracurricular activities were compulsory, and Sonny was not prepared to be getting home late one day in every week for the sake of football, so he had no intention of joining. He played football in Turagua savannah almost every weekend, with Sonnylal and other boys from Anglican School, or with Lennox's friends. And not being chosen for the choir caused him no pain. He was an honorary member of St Hilda's choir, and when, in a few months' time, he turned 12, he would become a full member.

On the following Monday, during the roll call period, Jainarine

Dass steeled himself, stood up, and asked Mr Superville why he, Leon Walker, and Conrad Harewood had not been allowed to play lawn tennis. Mr Superville did not bat an eyelid. "Of what use will lawn tennis be to you boys, outside of school?" he asked. "Are your parents members of the Country Club? Are there tennis courts in your neighbourhoods where people like you can enter as you please?"

What flashed into Sonny's head was the incident that took place in front of Turagua Estate Staff Club, when he was nine years old. Lennox had taken him to the quiet patch of road, a cul-de-sac, outside the club to ride his bicycle. The tennis court was at the road's edge, enclosed by a high wire fence. There was nobody on the court at first, but then some whitepeople went in and started to play. Lennox and Sonny drew close to the fence to watch for a bit. Immediately, some angry black men in uniform, waving batons, rushed out into the road, shouting, "Get from here! What allyou doing here? Scram! *Marche!*"

When they got home and told Nenn Gwynnie and Nenn Vie, there was something of an uproar, during which Nenn Vie asked them again and again, "They say '*marche*'? You sure? *Bondjé*, they think is dog they chasing? Well, them is the dog, you hear? Them is Laurent pot-hound…"

Gwynneth, thereafter, made it her business to take Sonny out there to ride as often as she could find the time, for that was the government road, not Massa Laurent property.

Mr Superville was still talking. "And I suppose that those of you who did not get into Sea Scouts will want to know why not. Well, again, I will ask you a question or two in return. Do your parents own boats? Does your family go boating? Does your father make donations to the college? Know your place!"

The boys he targeted were crushed with embarrassment. None of them would dream of answering back to the teacher, for their parents would near murder them if they were to get themselves expelled from the great Ascension. At break time there was an indignant discussion among the affected students, and this became even more indignant when one of the town boys offered, for those who did not know, the folkloric explanation of what the Country Club was. He said it was a high-class recreation

437

place in Windsor Park, where they had somebody standing up by the gate with a shop paper bag the colour of khaki, and if your skin was darker than that paper bag, they didn't let you in.

On hearing of Mr Superville's responses to the boys, Nenn Gwynnie was silent for a long moment before she asked, "And this teacher is a black man, not so?"

Sonny answered "Yes, Nennie."

Gwynneth became pensive again. Then she said, as peaceably as her contempt for the man would allow, "Stay out of his way, Sonny. Just do your work, and don't let him throw you off course."

She talked about the incident later with Gaston, who at first expressed surprise. "But I know this Superville fellow, or I met him when he was a child. I know his father, Herman," he said. "We were in primary school together. When did Herman's son become a social snob? Herman came from very humble beginnings. Grew up in LaCour Danglade. His mother was a domestic in a Windsor Park house, and his father, a City Council scavenger. That's the grandmother and grandfather of this Mr Superville, the teacher pouring upper-class scorn on people chirren.

"Herman was so proud when his boy won an exhibition! He came to the office with the newspaper to show me his name on the list of exhibitioners, and insisted, 'Man, come by me this evening and take a drink on the boy head!' I did go to his home, where Herman was making speeches, refilling glasses, calling out the boy to introduce him every time a new guest arrived. Herman was just beside himself with joy. Well, the high school he chose to send him to was Ascension, and thereby hangs a tale!"

In their first French class, the teacher asked whether any of the boys spoke Patois. Sonny's hand shot up. Mr de Verteuil quelled the giggling that broke out. He was quite used to such reactions from students in his first class with them. "What is there to laugh at?" he asked. "You're really just showing how ignorant you are of your own heritage."

One very confident whiteboy, who sat sprawling in his chair, snorted, "Patois? That is hog language."

"Is that so? And what is your name? Sit properly before you answer me, young man."

438

"Kent Peschier… Sir," the boy replied, in a sullen voice, as he reluctantly shifted his position on the chair.

"Oh, really?" the teacher said. "Well, your Uncle Roland speaks Patois beautifully. I'm sure you've never heard him call it 'hog language'. He has more sense than that."

The boy seemed to shrivel under Mr de Verteuil's glare.

"Your ancestors and mine, French families, came here almost two hundred years ago, Kent Peschier," Mr de Verteuil said. "It was your ancestors and mine who brought Patois here, young man, because they brought the people who were the creators of Patois – the blackpeople. And some of the whitepeople arrived in Cayeri speaking Patois as well as French. Even today, some of your relatives and mine understand the language very well. I, for one, am proud to be able to speak Patois. I learned it from my nanny, and I am very grateful to her." He turned away from Peschier and asked the class, "*Ki moun ankò ka palé Patwa?*"

Then, pointing at Sonny, he said, "Young man, translate that into English for your classmates, please."

Sonny obliged: "It means, 'Who else speaks Patois?'"

Another boy rose from his seat to say, "*Mama-mwen i ka palé Patwa, Misyé.*"

"*Bon! Épi ou menm? Ou pa ka palé i?*"

"*Mama-mwen pa vlé mwen palé sa, Misyé.*"

Mr de Verteuil shook his head slowly, sadly. Then he seemed to throw off the sadness.

"Okay," he said. "Now we'll translate that whole conversation into English, from the top. Tell me your names." He was pointing at Sonny and the other boy who had spoken.

"Joshua Polydore, Sir."

"Conrad Harewood, Sir."

"Polydore, you will act as Mr de Verteuil." He smiled as he spoke, so the class felt free to laugh. "And Harewood, you will act as yourself. Let's go!"

Sonny started the dialogue: "Who else speaks Patois?"

"My mother speaks Patois, Sir," Harewood replied.

"Good! And yourself, don't you speak it?"

"My mother doesn't want me to speak that, Sir."

The class was still sitting in silence, feeling some measure of awe, and coming to understand, now, why Harewood's last response had appeared to sadden Mr de Verteuil. At his suggestion, they gave a hearty round of applause to the two translators. The rest of that day's French class was devoted to talking about how, in the eighteenth century, planters in the French Caribbean had been encouraged to come and settle in Cayeri. Mr de Verteuil got the boys into a discussion of what things these immigrants had brought into the Cayerian heritage.

Before the end of the class, most of the boys were willing to join in singing, led by Sonny, *"Ba Mwen Yon Ti Bo"*. It turned out that some of them knew the lyrics of the song, and all of them were familiar with the melody. And, just before the period came to an end, three more boys in the class, one of them a whiteboy, felt it was safe to confess that they understood Patois.

Three weeks into the term, a teacher called Sonny aside after Friday morning assembly. Sonny had been aware of him standing among the teachers who lined the edges of the hall to keep order. This teacher had been peering into the Form 1 rows as though searching for a particular student. His eyes had eventually fastened on Sonny, who was singing lustily, unlike his classmates around him. Many of the boys were nonchalantly mouthing the hymn, or singing with no desire to be heard, while others seemed not to know the words. Gwynneth had been teaching Sonny some of the most commonly-used Catholic hymns, so that he would be well prepared for assembly and for those occasions when students were taken across to Mass at the Church of the Ascension.

"What is your name?" the teacher asked Sonny, as the assembly drained away towards the classrooms.

"Joshua Polydore, Sir."

"And which form are you in?"

"Form 1B, Sir."

"Polydore?" The teacher's forehead creased. "Did you put your name down for the choir?"

"Yes, Sir, I did."

"I don't remember seeing a Polydore on my list."

"They put me in football, Sir."

The teacher cursed under his breath. Sonny heard the words "damn foolishness!" The rest was inaudible.

"Do you belong to a choir elsewhere?"

"Yes, Sir. St Hilda's Anglican Church."

"There you go!" the man fretted. "There you go! You have a beautiful voice, and a trained voice. And they put you in football. Have you joined the football club?"

"No, Sir."

"Then you're welcome to join the school choir. I am Mr Henderson, the choir master. We've already started rehearsing for the Inter-College Festival, but it's not too late. With your level of training, you can just jump in. I'll bet there's nobody in that bunch they've sent to me who could ever sing a solo like you. Wednesday afternoon, 3.00 o'clock, in the hall. I will notify your form master. Come to the staff room today and collect your song sheet."

Preliminaries for the Inter-College Festival of Song were two and a half months away. Rehearsals had begun in the Christmas term, for it was an event taken very seriously by the school, as indeed by all the competing schools. This year, it was of particular importance to Ascension. They had suffered a serious blow the last time the competition was held, two years before. Ascension College had experienced the indignity of being knocked into third place by one of those establishments that they referred to as "fly-by-night high schools". The hurt could only be healed by a resounding victory this time around.

Over the years the Championship Cup had pretty much become the rotated property of the three schools seen as the only bona fide colleges. These were: The College of the Ascension; "Government College" (correctly, Prince Albert Edward College); and "Presbyterian College", or "Prez" (correctly, Canadian Mission Boys' College). Also seen as a force to be reckoned with was "Girls' Anglican High School" (correctly, St Agnes Girls' High School). In the two previous years of the competition, 1951 and 1953, Girls' Anglican had placed fourth. (Maria Regina Convent High School had never taken part in the festival. The nuns had not yet managed to convince the Mother Superior that entering a competition with boys' schools posed no danger to the modesty of their girls).

Considered to be at a tolerable distance behind the "real colleges" were the Government Intermediate schools. And bringing up the rear was a tail of schools, the "Blandins" and the "Alleynes" and the others – deemed third-rate; accused of having been set up by half-educated charlatans; and (it was said, scornfully) filled with the children of those who didn't know better, or couldn't do better. It had been assumed all along that these upstarts entering the competition did not have the slightest chance of getting within reach of the Cup. Their participation only served to stretch out the preliminaries, tediously; most of these schools did not survive into the semi-finals. Cockroach in fowl dance, some said. So for one of them to move up and wedge itself between Government College and Ascension, pushing Ascension down into third place – that was humiliation.

It was rumoured that at the staff meeting following that competition, there were calls for Ascension to appeal the results; demand that the adjudicator hand over the judges' score sheets; and investigate whether the school that came second (nobody would even utter its name) had broken any of the festival's rules. Mr Henderson would have none of it. He scolded the meeting.

"So we lost. Let's face it – this is liable to happen when you stuff the choir with children who can't sing to save their lives. Indulging them, sending them to me just because they come from this or that 'important' family – high on the social ladder, and Catholic, of course. Turning down boys who can really sing, because their pedigree doesn't suit you. As choir master, I don't see religion, I don't see class, I don't see colour. I only hear voice."

At break time, Sonny went to the staff-room entrance. Mr Henderson came out and handed him a page with the lyrics of a song. "This is the choral set piece. We'll be rehearsing it on Wednesday. See if you can learn the words by then."

"Sir, if you will lend me the music sheet, I will learn the tune as well, by Wednesday."

Mr Henderson cocked his head to one side. "Really? You have somebody who can read the music for you?"

"I can read music, Sir."

Mr Henderson was ecstatic to learn that Sonny was the holder of a Grade 3 Certificate from the Associated Board of the Royal

Schools of Music, and that his godmother, with whom he lived, was a piano teacher.

"Wonderful! Wonderful! You come from a musical home!" he said, and then did some more swearing under his breath at the fools who would bar such a student from the choir and want to throw him, instead, into football.

41
"Are you sure, Polydore?"

Monica sent a wedding picture and a generous chunk of wedding cake. In her letter, she said the only thing that could make her any happier now would be to see her child and hug him up. For that she was saving to come home for Christmas.

As the picture was passed around the gallery, Viola commented, "Nice man, eh? He look like a young Gaston."

"Excuse me," Gaston replied, looking to the right and to the left and behind him. "And where do you see an *old* Gaston?"

Ollie's amusement gave way to a worried look. "Seriously, though," he said, "allyou know we cyaan let Roy see that picture. We doan know that he ever get over Monica. That boy went through a bad tabanca."

"Tabanca my foot!" said Viola. "Roy didn have no real feelings for Monica. She was just another good-looking craft he thought he coulda meddle with."

Gaston was shaking his head. "You wrong, Vie. I can tell you that the boy was seriously in love. Bounce he head, poor fella. And look what happening to him at home, now."

For a moment they were all silent, acknowledging Roy's misfortunes. When the conversation resumed, they agreed that in addition to more sympathy, more understanding, and more love from all of them, what Roy needed was a good bush-bath.

Helen had announced to Roy her decision to move to America with Gordon and Freda. Friends were warning that Cayeri was about to be taken over by the low-class blackpeople, the riff-raff, and that it would be wise to get out before it was too late. The rabble-rouser they called "The Scholar" was forming a political party in time for the 1956 election. If he should win the election, and get through with his "self-rule for Cayeri" plan, God help whitepeople. Crapaud smoke they pipe. Had she not heard the calypso which predicted that they would soon find themselves bowing down before blackpeople and calling them "*Mister Nigger*"?

Most of Helen's white school friends had edged away from her years before, after it became impossible to keep Roy a secret any longer. She had heard, from those who were still talking to her, that whitepeople were packing up with their families to migrate to Australia.

Twice the same awkward situation had arisen.

Judy Rostant said to her one day, "Australia is the best bet, girl. Lots of land, wide open spaces, plenty of opportunity for your children…"

And, on another occasion, it was Petra Knaggs who advised, "Why don't you go to Australia, Helen? The US is such an uncivilised place. Ugh! Talk about the Wild West!"

They had each become very embarrassed as it dawned on them that Helen could not migrate to Australia unless she left her husband and children behind. Australia's immigration laws would not allow the likes of Roy, Gordon and Freda to settle there. (Not that Roy was part of the plan – Helen had every intention of leaving her husband behind when she left Cayeri.)

Within a few weeks Mr Superville had become Sonny's personal tormentor. Sonny had very little chance of following Nenn Gwynnie's advice to stay out of his way. The man was his form master, so he faced him twice every day, morning and afternoon, for roll-call. On top of that, Superville was his history teacher, so they met again twice a week for a 40-minute class.

Mr Superville's first grievance was the "no caning" request, too easily accepted, for his liking, by the school administration. Who did this boy's people think they were? He had never heard of any family in Cayeri named "Polydore" with the social standing to warrant this kind of special consideration. Then, contrary to the ruling of the Committee for Extra-Curricular Activities, Joshua Polydore was in the choir. Mr Superville was not a member of that august committee, but he felt personally aggrieved at this boy from nowhere coming to flout its august authority.

Mr Henderson had notified the committee, and the form master, about his recruiting Polydore into the choir. The committee had accepted the choir master's decision, especially when he explained that this boy was likely to bring the Cup back to the college. Mr Superville, however, continued to be offended. At first he would just frown at Sonny when he got to his name on the register. Eventually, however, Mr Superville could no longer contain his grievance. As he marked the register one morning, he got to the name just before Sonny's, called it out, "Fazal Mohammed?" and then put down his pen with a throwing action. He fixed his eyes on Sonny. "So, Mr Polydore, the Shouter Baptist, you worked some obeah to get your choice, eh?"

The class sat up, their interest piqued. Those seated in the front rows turned around to glance at Sonny. There was some muffled sniggering, during which Mr Superville picked up his pen, made a mark in the register and went on to call out Stephen Quesnel's name. It did not escape the notice of the class that their form master had not called out Sonny's name. This intrigued them even more. The front rows turned around again to peer at Sonny, then turned back and tried to read Mr Superville's face.

Sonny was also left staring at the form master, puzzled, until the thought came to him that it must be about his getting into the choir. He put his hand up and held it straight up in the air while Mr Superville deliberately went all the way down the register to Hollis Wint before he finally lifted his head and asked gruffly, "What is it, Polydore?"

"Sir, I didn't work obeah to get into the choir. Mr Henderson invited me to join, Sir."

Mr Superville narrowed his eyes and said, "Are you sure, Polydore?"

This response became a habit. Now and then at roll call, when Sonny answered "Present, Sir," Mr Superville would raise his head and shoot at him, "Are you sure, Polydore?"

He would do it also in History class.

"Polydore!"

"Yes, Sir?"

"In what year did Christopher Columbus make his fourth voyage to the New World?"

"In 1502, Sir."

"Are you sure, Polydore?"

"Yes, Sir."

Sonny held off reporting the obeah remark at home, for that would only serve to rile up and distress everybody. He did not think he should tell them, either, about Mr Superville constantly singling him out and trying to make fun of him – or confuse him? Maybe all of this was to do with throwing him off course, as Nenn Gwynnie had warned.

The whole class could plainly see that their form master had declared war on this one student. Sonny knew that his classmates were on his side because their faces became grim and not a snigger was heard when Mr Superville made snide remarks to him or about him. Outside the classroom – in the corridor and out in the quadrangle – some of the whiteboys would offer Sonny a shy smile, or wave at him, while some approached him to express their opinion on the matter.

"Why Supermanicou picking fight with you, man?" Mendes asked. "Why he can't leave you in peace?"

And Laughlin offered comfort: "Don't bother with the manicou, eh, Polydore. He just looking to make himself feel big."

Before Sonny entered the school, Gwynneth had asked Roy and Gaston to scope out what arrangements existed for Ascension students to have a proper meal at lunch time.

"Well," Roy reported, "not much has changed from my time. The school dining-room is still there, serving a hot lunch to students whose parents can afford it. In my day that meant pretty much whiteboys only. I hear that the students now refer to it as 'The Waldorf Astoria'. It is still far beyond the reach of any but the really well-off students, but nowadays that might include a coloured boy, here and there, whose father is a doctor or a lawyer. Some of the wealthy town-boys are picked up in cars and taken home for lunch. Some bring food from home, prepared and packed by the family's servant, and they eat in the hall, sitting in groups. Me, I used to go 'home' to Mrs Gouveia's boarding-house for lunch."

"Students who live within walking distance might go home for lunch," Gaston observed, "especially those living along the near side of Morne Cabrite. Some of those who live outside of Kings

Port eat at the homes of women around the town whose liveli-hood is cooking and serving lunch to schoolchildren and workers – a whole little industry going on there. Some of the neediest students go to The Helping Hand Shelter, run by Olga Frederick's organisation, where schoolchildren can get lunch for six cents, if they can afford it, and free of charge if they can't."

"The indefatigable Olga Frederick," Gwynneth said, "not only breaking down barriers put up to keep women out of govern-ment, but also actively engaging in social work."

Gaston's informant was a young clerk at his office, Kenneth, fresh out of Ascension. He spoke about the school's tuck shop.

"From what Kenneth says," Gaston reported, "the tuck shop is not very useful to boys whose lunch money is small. For them, the sandwiches sold in the tuck shop for lunch are way too expensive. Those boys can't afford more than one, and one can barely fill a bird's craw, according to Kenneth. On top of that, they find the tuck shop's dainty sandwiches to be bland to the point of tastelessness.

"So you have students turning their backs on this 'English food' as they describe it, and going up to the Savannah, or across town to King George Street. There they can buy food that suits their taste as well as their pocket, from pavement vendors or from parlours – good, heavy, bellyful roastbake, frybake, sada roti, bara, or hops-bread, with properly seasoned fillings."

Roy chuckled. "In my time, such a thing was out of the question. Boys in Ascension uniform caught patronising such enterprises would face punishment, for that was a major offence!"

"It is still officially frowned upon by the school," Gaston confirmed. "But with recent increases in the number of exhibi-tions, there's been an increase in the number of free-place boys. Ascension has no alternative to offer these boys for lunch, so I reckon the school may have to turn a blind eye."

"Or, they could get the tuck shop to start offering some affordable Cayerian choices for lunch," Gwynneth said. "How difficult would that be? Anyway, I doan think we want Sonny roaming about Kings Port in the middle of the school day looking for food."

The decision was that Sonny would take a light packed lunch

to school, and have a more substantial meal at home on evenings. This plan would be largely ignored by Viola. She insisted on getting up early and making lunch for him, often putting pot on fire to send him off with what amounted to a full-fledged, sit-down-at-table plate of food.

"Nenn Vie," Sonny tried to convince her, "you doan need to get up fore-day morning just for me. I could make sandwiches to carry to school."

"That's not enough for a growing boy," she would counter. "And unlike you, I could go back to my bed after I make your lunch, and sleep whole day if I want, because I doan have to go to work any more. I am now a lady of leisure."

He thanked her every morning with a kiss and a hug-up before he set out for the train station.

At the beginning of the year, Sonny and other free-place boys of Form 1B who brought their lunch to school had stayed in the classroom at lunch time, each boy eating at his desk, because none of them knew anybody in the school with whom they might go and eat lunch in the hall. One day, Sonny persuaded these classmates to go into the hall with him at lunch time and stake out a spot. Thereafter, like other students, they would take some chairs off the stacks in the hall and place them in a circle, to sit together, eat, chat and lime for the duration of the lunch hour.

Before long, they were joined by some students from 1A and 1C who shared their sense of being "outsiders" and "underdogs". In talking about their experience at Ascension, they did not always find it easy to pinpoint or voice the source of their trouble, for not everything was as clear-cut as only whiteboys getting into Sea Scouts and lawn tennis. They told of teachers who threw hurtful words at them. But there was more that was not spoken – a pushing away, a you-don't-belong-here, a slighting... From their huddling conversations, they learned that others were having similar experiences, across the board.

Boys nodded in recognition when one student related how, in class time, his hand might be the first to go up when a teacher posed a question, but if any whiteboy's hand also went up, the teacher, routinely, would call upon the whiteboy, instead, to give the answer. Sonny pointed to the other side of that coin. More than once, he or another black student had put up his hand to ask a teacher a question, and had to wait for quite a while before the teacher chose to notice him. Then the teacher might snap a one-sentence or even a one-word answer and move on. But when other students, white or well-off, asked questions, the teacher would go all out, giving elaborate answers and asking solicitously, "Do you understand?" or, "Is it clearer now?"

Sonny learned that one or two black students in 1C had also had the experience of their form master sometimes not calling out their names as he marked the register. Instead, Mr Baker would glance at them and silently record their attendance, calling out the names up to and after theirs. There were many complaints about this form master, Mr Baker, a white Cayerian who was the literature teacher. A student from 1A, Keith Vincent, reported that in class they were learning about the different types of poetry – the ballad, the sonnet, the limerick, the ode, etc. Mr Baker was telling them that poetry began as something people sang, or chanted, and that even in modern times, the lyrics of songs could be seen as poetry. Vincent put up his hand and asked, "So, then, Sir, calypso is a form of poetry?"

Vincent said that you could almost feel a cold breeze entering and filling up the classroom as the teacher prepared to answer, putting down his notebook, taking off his glasses and drawing himself up to his full height. "Poetry? Don't make me laugh!" Mr Baker said. "Calypso is nothing but doggerel, often obscene dog-gerel, composed by an illiterate clown, in bad English, taking pot shots at his social superiors, promoting disrespect for authority."

The boys' sense of being unwelcome followed them even into the tuck shop, where, some complained, it was not unusual for the whiteboy standing behind you in the line to get served before you.

Yet they had to admit that the majority of their white class-mates did not show them any particular malice. For sure, there were those whiteboys who did not hesitate to make known their contempt. By and large, however, the white students just seemed oblivious to them, not deliberately ignoring them or snubbing them, just operating in a different world that floated at some distance above the reality of other students. Sonny found, though, that most of the whiteboys in his class were polite to him and some were quite friendly.

Peschier was not one of these. He showed arrogance towards students and teachers alike, of every hue. He was restless. It seemed he did not want to be in school, and made this clear by being obnoxious. He walked with an entourage that included Creole and Indian students. One day at break time, for the amusement of his entourage, he put his foot out and tripped a black student, Horace Weekes, who ended up sprawled on the ground in the quadrangle. Weekes sprang to his feet, cuffed Peschier in the chest and ran like hell, with nobody pursuing him. The upshot of that incident was that Weekes was caned. Peschier was not.

The preliminaries for the Festival of Song were scheduled to take place in April. Before Sonny's first meeting with the choir, he had learnt the set piece, and rehearsed it with Gwynneth accompanying him on the piano, although Gwynneth steupsed and grumbled that she couldn't understand why, on the brink of Cayerian self-rule, a Cayerian Festival of Songs would still be making young Cayerians sing nothing but British pieces. The choral set piece was:

> *How many kinds of sweet flowers grow*
> *In an English country garden?*
> *…*
> *Daffodils, heart's ease and flox*
> *Meadowsweet and lady smocks*
> *Gentian, lupine and tall hollihocks*
> *Roses, foxgloves, snowdrops, blue forget-me-nots*
> *In an English country garden*

… and so on.

Mr Henderson had already made his final selection of students who would be in the festival choir. From among these he had chosen five boys who were being considered for special parts: the duet; the solo backed by a small chorus group; and the solo within the full choir performance. Therefore, when Mr Henderson introduced Sonny as another student auditioning for a special part, the choir reacted with a murmur of surprise tinged with disgruntlement, but the choir master proceeded to the full choir rehearsal, in which Sonny performed the solo part.

At the end of it there was complete silence, until Mr Henderson asked what they thought of the solo, and the students broke into applause. The choir master then summarily announced that in the prelims, Polydore would be the soloist for the choir's performance; Polydore and Medford would sing the duet, and in the category solo with chorus, the five candidates for special parts would form the chorus, with Polydore as the soloist. The choir applauded again.

While there was a set piece for the choir's performance, and another set piece for the duet, each school had to make its own choice for the solo with chorus. A song had been chosen for this last category. Yet Mr Henderson asked Sonny if he would like to suggest one. Sonny replied that he would need time to think about it.

"From next week onwards," Mr Henderson announced to the choir "rehearsals will be twice a week – Wednesdays and Fridays. Next Wednesday, Polydore will put in his suggestion for the solo with chorus, so that we can make a choice and submit it to the festival committee for approval."

In discussion with Gwynneth later that evening, Sonny decided on the Patois song "*Diwi Dou*". The next day he went to Mr Henderson at break time with the suggestion. Mr Henderson asked him to sing a verse of the song.

"Beautiful! And what language is that?"

When Sonny told him, an excited smile spread over the choir master's face. "Good idea – a local song, and in the old language! I've heard of Patois, but I've never heard it spoken. Can you bring me the lyrics of this song, double quick? The deadline for submission is just around the corner. And they'll probably want a translation, too. You'll sing it for us on Wednesday, and then we'll see about the musical notation."

"We have the music sheets for it at home, Sir. My godmother is making a songbook."

"Oh, splendid, Polydore, splendid! We're all set, then! And that songbook will be something to look forward to!'"

For Gwynneth it was painful to hear that Mr Henderson had never heard Patois spoken. "How long has he been in Cayeri?" she asked Sonny.

He didn't know, but he told her that Mr Henderson (who was also the geography teacher for the upper forms), had been choir master at Ascension for the last two inter-col song festivals. Since the festival was held every other year, he had to have been there for at least four years.

"Four years, and never heard anybody talking Patois?" Gwynneth exclaimed. "Then Patois really in danger of dying out altogether!"

Ollie sought to ease her mind. "Oh, it might just be that the man got adopted, or more like kidnapped, into white Cayerian circles from the moment he landed, as often happens to expatriates who come to work. He may not have had any chance to meet the rest of Cayeri."

The song was approved by the choir on the following Wednesday. Rehearsal time was given over to Sonny sitting at the piano, teaching *"Diwi Dou"* to his chorus of five, with the whole choir sitting in. They hummed along as Sonny got the chorus group to first practice the melody as he played it on the piano again and again. Mr Henderson remarked that whether or not the festival committee approved it, Ascension choir would have learnt a beautiful Cayerian song.

At Friday morning assembly in the same week, the principal gave a speech that had become an Ascension ritual – the Friday-before-Carnival warning. Carnival season was nearing its climax. Calypso and steelband had practically taken over the radio for the past month or so. Gwynneth, Gaston, Viola and Ollie had together been making the rounds of the calypso tents. They had never taken Sonny to the tents, not only because the shows went on late at night, but it was in the tents that you were likely to hear the kind of calypso not made for the ears of children.

But on weekends, Sonny and Gaston, usually accompanied by Ainsley, were among the people who went around crowding the steelband yards to hear bands rehearse for Carnival. Those visits were a thrilling experience for Sonny, adding to the excitement with which he looked forward to that year's Carnival Tuesday…

"We are aware," Father D'Abreau was saying, "that more and more college boys have been hanging around steelbands, mixing with the unsavoury characters that engage in this activity. Let me remind you that we don't expect to see any Ascension boys parading through the streets in any steelband on Monday and Tuesday next week. You know full well that the only reason school is closed on those two days is the difficulty everyone would otherwise experience in getting here – making their way through streets clogged with disorderly revellers. The situation presents not only obstruction, but danger.

"If you feel that you must take part in the revelry, there are decent bands that you could follow, made up of only people like yourselves, bands which take precautions to ward off the mob. Bear in mind, however, that Carnival Monday and Tuesday are not public holidays, and you really ought to be in school. Therefore, a better use of your time on those two days would be study or meditation, so that on Ash Wednesday you are able to get up and come to school. Any student absent on Ash Wednesday will have to show a doctor's certificate indicating that he couldn't come to school because he was at death's door…"

The hall gave a perfunctory laugh at the yearly "death's door" joke. Some boys exchanged knowing glances. It was common knowledge that Ascension boys were visiting steelband yards in places like Jericho, Morne Cabrite and even Bourg Ravine, but the identities of these boys were closely guarded by their peers. Ascension boys, some from the milieu that the principal called "decent", were playing the pan, or just stealing away to the yards of the "mob" to drink in their music.

Sonny listened to the principal with growing alarm. Ascension boys not allowed to play in a steelband at Carnival? This was definitely not a ruling to tell Nenn Gwynnie about! She had given him permission to go on the road with Phillip's band for this year's Carnival in St Paul, under the care of Lennox. The permission was only for Carnival Tuesday, because Carnival Monday was too long a day, starting fore-day morning with Jouvay, and going until the players were ready to collapse with fatigue on Monday night. He would go with Lennox on Tuesday, and if Lennox wanted to stay out until Last Lap on Tuesday night, he would have to put Sonny on the train or the bus home before dark, for Sonny had school the next day.

Over the years Sonny had become a regular visitor to Warahoons yard with Lennox. He had learnt to play all the different pans, and now and then performed with the band at public events, but he was eager to go on the road with them. Gwynneth had promised that he would be allowed to when he reached the age of twelve. This Carnival he would be four months away from his twelfth birthday, but in December, when the 1955 Carnival season was launched, Gwynneth said to him that he shouldn't have to wait until Carnival 1956, a whole year later, to go on the road. By Carnival Tuesday 1955, she pointed out, he would be a high-school student travelling to and from Kings Port without any adult holding his hand.

She said that he was also proving himself to be as responsible as any twelve-year-old, and more responsible than some. "But you see that room of yours?" Nenn Gwynnie said, with a distinct change of voice, and going from complimenting him to glaring at him. "That is where you falling down in responsibility, and you will have to do better. I tired talk to you about that pigsty. Clean you room! Not a lick and a promise. Clean it and tidy it, and keep it clean and tidy! If you cyaan keep you room in a fit state, you not going to no Carnival with the band, and furthermore, you will have to start sleeping in the drawing-room, for you will not have a room of your own if you cyaan keep it in a proper state."

"Okay, Nenn Gwynnie," he said, meekly, and went to work immediately on the room. He was not going to risk losing the privilege of going on the road. Nothing must get in the way of that. His Carnival Tuesday was already in danger, what with Father D'Abreau's ban hanging over his head. Suppose Nenn Gwynnie should hear about the ruling? He cleaned the room as he had never cleaned it before. Maybe if he made it really spick and span, Nenn Gwynnie might be so happy that even if she heard about Ascension's ruling, she would let him go out with the band all the same.

Come to think of it, if news was to reach Nenn Gwynnie ears about the principal bad-talking steelband and forbidding Ascension boys to take part

455

in it, she would get blue vex, for sure, and she might send him on the road with the steelband just for spite, to let them know what she think about they ruling, Sonny reflected; but of course he knew that doing a thorough job on his room was the better guarantee.

Warahoons practised for Carnival on most evenings during the Christmas vacation, but when school opened, Sonny could only go to practice on Saturdays. Gwynneth drew the line at his going up San Miguel Road on evenings after school, to return home in the night. Phillip had assigned him to the tenor pan section, and Sonny kept the pan at home to practise during the week. Sonny was determined to play this pan on the road with Warahoons on Carnival Tuesday. He was offended at the way the principal had spoken about pan players, and he had no qualms about defying him.

Sonny thoroughly enjoyed his first Carnival beating pan on the road, giving not a thought to the principal and his ruling; nor to the form master determined to make him feel he was nothing; nor to Mr Baker and his clear contempt for all the black students.

Then it was back to school on Ash Wednesday. And on that day school was decidedly a place of discomfort. Form 1B had a history period on Wednesdays, and just for spite (the boys were certain) Mr Superville chose Ash Wednesday to spring a history test on them: "Write on the life and achievements of <u>one</u> of the Great Explorers – (a) Sir John Hawkins, (b) Sir Francis Drake, <u>or</u> (c) Sir Walter Raleigh." Two days later, before morning roll call, Mr Superville called Sonny up to his desk and said to him, with a voice and a face that suggested he was about to burst with offendedness, "Wait for me outside Father O'Malley's office, this afternoon, right after school!"

"Sir, I have choir practice at 3.00 o'clock, Sir."

This response pushed Mr Superville into a hissing rage: "You will present yourself at the dean's office, as instructed! You think you have some kind of privilege inside here, eh?"

Father O'Malley, a priest from Ireland, was the first formers' dean of discipline, so Sonny, and those of his classmates who were within earshot, wondered what this could be about. At break time Sonny went to the staff room entrance, asked to see Mr

Henderson and informed him that he would be late for practice because of an appointment with his form master.

When school was dismissed in the afternoon, Sonny went and sat outside the dean's office. After a while Mr Superville arrived, huffing and puffing. He knocked on the door and motioned fiercely to Sonny to follow him inside. The meeting with the dean was short, and not a good experience for Sonny's form master. Mr Superville showed Father O'Malley Sonny's history test script. Sonny caught a glimpse of the front page, with the first sentence underlined in angry red ink. Father O'Malley seemed to read only that sentence before he looked up. Sonny had written: *These great explorers were actually great plunderers, pirates and slave traders.*

"Well, weren't they?" Father O'Malley asked Mr Superville. "Were they not plunderers and pirates and slave traders? What is the misbehaviour – is this boy rude to you? Is he disruptive in class?" He looked at Sonny. "Young man, you are excused from this meeting. Please wait outside."

About five minutes later, Mr Superville emerged from the office and hurried away. Father O'Malley stood in the door, beckoning to Sonny. "Here you are, young man," the dean said, handed Sonny his essay and closed the door.

Sonny had chosen to write about Hawkins, pioneer of the British slave trade, who was the first to take captured Africans to the "new world" as cargo. He transported his captives on a ship named "Jesus" and exchanged them for bags of sugar. At the end of the essay was a grade in red ink: 20%. That had been crossed out with blue ink, and below it was a new grade, in blue: 75%.

At roll call the next morning, Mr Superville delivered a vague and ominous lecture on the danger of people running behind a politician who preached revolution, in short, a Communist. "No matter how many letters he might have behind his name, you have no business getting caught up in that," he warned. "Leave that to those who are uneducated and easily misled. You are not empty-headed sheep. You are college boys; you can think for yourselves. History may be interpreted in different ways, and those of you whose forefathers were brought to these shores by the slave trade should ponder on the darkness from which you were rescued by that first intrepid explorer."

The Scholar had, indeed, taken the population by storm. His series of public lectures, which began as a fairly staid Public Library affair, had grown and spilled out into Columbus Square, just across the street, and The Square became the University for All. People brought their children to look upon the face of this blackman who had performed with excellence in the whitepeople's most esteemed university, quite up in England. People declared this Cayerian blackman to be a genius, more intelligent and more knowledgeable than all the whitepeople who ruled over Cayerians, from the estate overseer right up to the governor.

People brought their children to hear The Scholar's confident voice rolling out over The Square, transmitting to them rare wisdom about themselves, drawn from his research on Cayerian history. At home they made their children listen when his speeches were carried on the radio. They made them read his articles in the newspaper. Some named their newborn babies after him. People got a sense that the coming of this man had brought all previous struggles to a head – the valiant resistance of the first Cayerians to their conquerors; uprisings against slavery; Kamboulay riot; Hosay riot; water riot; workers rising up in 1919 and 1937; and all the years of agitation for the right of Cayerians to take the running of their affairs into their own hands.

42
"That is all that leff from the Great-House"

Rehearsals for the Song Festival continued into the Easter holidays. The first week of the vacation was "choir camp" for those singing in the festival. They came in on mornings, as for a normal school day, but all had to bring their lunch from home, as there was no dining-room service. (Most choir members were students who had lunch in the school dining-room – aka "The Waldorf Astoria" – during the term.)

For that week, choir members spent the better part of each day at the school, living together at close quarters – rehearsing, chatting, eating, and relaxing (sometimes by horsing around) in the periods of rest between sessions. Rehearsals went until late afternoon, when Mr Henderson would drive Sonny down to the train station for him to get on the 5.08. Sonny was the only boy in the choir who had a train to catch. Were it not for him and his crucial role in their festival performance, rehearsals might sometimes have gone on an hour or so later, for everyone else was picked up in a car afterwards.

One day rehearsal went on so late that there was no chance of Sonny catching his train, so Sonny's duet partner, Larry Medford, got his father to drive Sonny all the way home to Turagua. In telling Gaston that Sonny had struck up a friendship with a whiteboy, Gwynneth remarked: "You see why they have to keep black-hen chicken out of they school clubs?"

"Yep," said Gaston. "Dangerous business for their chickens to get such a close view of ours!"

Larry was a Form 2 student. During choir camp, he and Sonny ate their lunch together. When one day they began talking about their plans for the August vacation, Sonny told Larry he was going to spend most of it in Pilgrim.

"Pilgrim?" Larry asked, in what was almost a shriek. "You know Pilgrim?"

"Yes. My grandparents and my uncles live there, and my cousins…"

"So you know where Beauregard is!" Larry exclaimed. He seemed quite excited.

"Yes," Sonny answered. "Beauregard is near Pilgrim. You been there?"

"My Uncle Maxwell – really my great-uncle – living in Beauregard, in the forest, all by himself."

"Really?" Sonny said. "I doan know him."

"I been there many times, with my father and uncles. Last time I went, I was ten years old." He paused for a while, looking wistful. "They always ending up in a quarrel, with them trying to rag him up, to make fun of him, saying, 'You too old for this foolishness, now, Uncle Max. Time to stop playing Papa Bois.' And Uncle Max would only say, 'I tell allyou I not coming back. Leave me in peace, nuh.'"

"He living in Beauregard forest?" Sonny asked, sceptical.

"Yeah. And three years now like they just not bothering to go and see him. Like they give up on him. Whenever I ask Daddy if we could go and see him, he says, 'When you get older, Sir, I'll be glad to drop you off at the station so you can take the train and go spend your holidays with Papa Bois.' He saying it as a joke, but one day I going to do just that – get on the train and find my way there."

Sonny felt sorry for his friend. Larry had such a happy memory of visiting his Uncle Maxwell that he longed to go back again. He spoke about bathing in the river, catching crayfish, rocking in a hammock strung from the roof of a cool ajoupa in the yard, walking a long way through the forest with Uncle Maxwell to get to the best starch mango tree. And before they left for town, he and Uncle Maxwell would go out again into the bush, but only a little way beyond the yard, to look for places where the hens were laying their eggs. The visiting family members always brought with them a basket or two, buckets, and some crocus bags, and they would go back to town with all these receptacles full of mango, zaboka, Gros Michel fig and yard-fowl eggs.

"If you get to go and see him in the August holidays," Sonny said, "You must come by me in Pilgrim." And because Larry was still looking downcast, Sonny added, "My godmother says that I'm almost old enough for her to start putting me on the train to Pilgrim by myself. Maybe your father will let you go with me."

Sonny got some more of Uncle Maxwell's story from Nenn Gwynnie. He learned that the forest in which Uncle Maxwell Medford lived was once a thriving cocoa estate that belonged to a man who must have been Larry's great-great-grandfather, William Medford. He had two sons; and Mumma, who had helped to look after Sonny when he was a baby, had also looked after those two boys when they were little. Nenn Gwynnie knew their names – Christopher and Graham – for Mumma had sometimes talked about them. One of them would have been Larry's great-grandfather, but Nenn Gwynnie didn't know which one.

Christopher and Graham were sent to school in England, and when they came back as young men, they didn't want anything to do with any cocoa estate. They didn't want to live in the family house on the estate, or even in Beauregard. They called the area "the back of beyond". Their father was afraid they might leave Cayeri and return to England, or migrate to some other place, like Australia, so he set them up in business in Kings Port: Medford Bros. Import & Export Co. Ltd.

The sons of Christopher and Graham inherited the family business, and one of these sons was Maxwell. But, one day, out of the blue, Maxwell disappeared, leaving a letter on his office desk to announce that he had gone to Beauregard. Where in Beauregard, nobody knew, for by then the Medford estate had long gone to bush, the grand family house on the edge of the estate had crumbled to dust, and only the oldest people in the area remembered anything about the Medfords.

It was during the war that Maxwell Medford had walked out of the world he was living in, and, as far as anyone could tell, had settled for good into the life of a maroon, deep in the jungle that Medford estate had become. Legends swirled around the idea of this whiteman in the bush who remained largely invisible and undisturbed. Most people had never laid eyes on him, so not everybody believed he existed.

Gwynneth didn't know how much of this history Sonny's friend had been told by his family, so she was careful not to say too much to Sonny. There were some things Sonny did not need to know, although he was likely to hear some of them sooner or later in Pilgrim. Gwynneth didn't think he needed to know, for example, that people said the whiteman was really a lagahou that came out at night in the guise of a human, to go and prowl. Others saw Maxwell Medford as just a man coming out at night to visit a lady in Beauregard village.

It was easier to believe those who said that the whiteman went into the village now and then to buy things like pitch-oil, matches and soap, and to take a drink with the men who had helped him build his bachie of tapia and carat. It was also quite conceivable that he would appear from time to time in San Pedro, as some people said, dressed in an old suit and felt hat, doing business at the post office, the warden's office, or a hardware store. Some insisted that it was in San Pedro that he visited a lady, not Beauregard.

Helen and the children flew out. They went to Canada. Pulled up roots – lock, stock and barrel – and turned their backs on Cayeri. Roy felt justified in going ahead with a decision that had started to form in his head ever since the time he spent in Turagua with his injured wrist. Now, he felt, there was no need to agonise any longer about passing on his share of the Turagua property to Sonny. He sought Gaston's advice.

In the middle of their conversation, with Gaston laying out for him what steps could be taken to give Sonny a stake in the property and ensure that nobody could evict him, Roy stopped listening. "Too complicated," he said. "Let's make it simple. I cannot imagine my sisters leaving their share of the property to anybody but Sonny. Whatever their plan is, I am gifting my part to him, while I'm alive. We can't leave Helen any opening to do mischief."

As it turned out, Roy's sisters had already approached Gaston for advice on the same question. Gwynneth and Viola had told Gaston that, until recently, there was no other plan for the future of the property their parents had left them but that it would automatically pass to Roy. When Sonny was two years old, Roy had expressed the fear that Gwynneth and Viola would somehow push his children out and give the property to Sonny. Gwynneth had sought to reassure Roy that they had no such designs.

But now, Sonny gaining a free place at Ascension College had put a new complexion on things. It meant that he was going to be with them (God-spare-life) for the next five years, or seven if he went on to do the Higher School Certificate. Indeed, it could be eight years if he did so well that the school kept him on an extra year to give him a shot at the Island Scholarship for higher education. Now it was their turn to be worried about ownership of the property.

"What will happen to Sonny when we gone?" Gwynneth fretted. "That could be years from now, and it could be tomorrow."

Gwynneth and Viola had never allowed themselves to take it for granted that Sonny would grow up with them, and they didn't want to begin presuming now. But they suspected that even if he went abroad to study after high school, he would turn out to be a homing pigeon, like Gaston, or Lennox for that matter. Lennox had travelled to England twice to visit his father, and on each occasion returned without hesitation to Cayeri.

Whatever the distant future might bring, the property was going to be Sonny's home for some years to come, for as long as they were alive, at any rate, and they had begun to think that he should have some legal right to be there. They had no desire to push out Roy's children. All they wanted was to leave their part of the inheritance to Sonny, or, better still, transfer their part to him before they should close their eyes. And they believed that their part was worth, at the very least, the value of the house and the portion of the land on which it stood. They wanted him to inherit the home in which he was born and had spent his childhood. But they were worried. They couldn't put it past Helen, never mind she was all the way up there in Canada, to have Sonny booted out of the house.

Thus it was that they were asking Gaston's advice on whether the property could be legally subdivided, in their lifetime, so that Roy's wife and children could inherit Roy's share as a separate property. The land was, after all, more than an acre. There must be some equitable way for Roy's entitlement to be passed on to his natural heirs, and for his sisters to do what they wished with theirs. Gaston was making enquiries along these lines. He let them know that such a process could take a long time, assuming the authorities would even allow it. "There are some restrictions," he explained, "on what you can do with leasehold Crown lands. But tell me, do you want to keep this matter from Roy, or do you intend to inform him?"

Gwynneth and Viola looked at each other, and then turned to Gaston, without an answer.

"Hm. You think it might be awkward?" Gaston asked.

"We really doan know how Roy will take this…"

"I will tell you," Gaston revealed, "that Roy has the same concerns as you about Sonny's future, so the three of you should talk about it. I can be there if you invite me."

Gaston and Roy came up to the house the following evening.

Gwynneth and Viola thanked Roy warmly, again and again, for his decision. Then Gwynneth said to him, "I want you to consider a different way of doing this, Roy. Cutting yourself out of your inheritance at this point in your life is kind of drastic. You doan know what the future will bring. Rather than signing it over to Sonny now, what if you *will* your interest in the property to Sonny, instead, so that you can still make use of it for years to come? Unless you're thinking of going abroad?"

"Haven't ruled it out," he said.

"Well, whether or not you go abroad, you might want to come and spend your retirement here, on this spot where you were born and raised. And if you stay in Cayeri, you might want to build a lil something – I doan want to say 'bachie' because, again, who knows what the future will bring? But you might want to build a little weekend retreat up in the bush, surrounded by your mango and your zaboca and all the other trees. You used to love going up into the land when you were a boy."

A warm smile spread over Roy's face. "Yes, I did," he said. "And I still do. This is a great idea, Titta, and I will give it some serious thought."

Gwynneth knew that he genuinely wanted to help secure Sonny's future, and they would never be able to thank him enough. But what she had not said aloud was that there was some hastiness in the route he wanted to take, brought on, perhaps, by spite – aimed at Helen.

The Song Festival was held at the Atlas theatre. It began with preliminaries in the second week of the Easter holidays: full choir on the Tuesday, duet on Thursday, and solo with chorus on Saturday. Sonny was singing in all three categories, and Nenn Gwynnie came to town with him on all three days to be in the audience. They got there early every day, ahead of the crowd. Mr Henderson had said to Sonny beforehand that he would like to meet his godmother, so, on the first morning, Sonny steered Nenn Gwynnie to a seat in the front row and went in search of him.

The choir master came and with reverence shook Gwynneth's hand, then sat down beside her, first asking, "May I?" Sonny went off to muster with his choir-mates, and Mr Henderson talked with Gwynneth until the theatre began to fill up.

Five schools, including Ascension, were sent forward to the semi-finals, to be held the following Saturday, one week after the reopening of school.

On the first morning of the new term, Ascension's choir was rowdily applauded at assembly, and Sonny singled out by the principal for special mention. In 1B's roll call period right afterwards, Mr Superville marked and closed his register, got up and made to leave the room.

"Wait, wait, wait, Sir!" Stollmeyer was on his feet, his open palm upraised. "A-a! So we not going to clap Polydore?"

Mr Superville had stopped in his tracks at the first sound of Stollmeyer's voice, and the obsequious smile appeared on the teacher's face, the one he always presented to whiteboys, whatever the tone in which they spoke to him.

"Okay," he said, meekly, and stood by as Stollmeyer led the class in a round of applause for Sonny.

After the semi-finals, the three schools going forward to the finals for the Championship Cup were Ascension, Girls' Anglican and Government College. The choir was again honoured at morning assembly, and in the classroom of 1B, Mr Superville had to suspend roll call and wait, pen in hand, while the class cheered and clapped and thumped on their desks in celebration of Sonny.

The finals were at the end of the third week, on the Saturday. On Friday morning a special assembly was held, at which the choir performed its three items for the school as their dress rehearsal. This was a tradition that allowed the whole school to cheer on their choir just before the finals, for there were not enough seats at the theatre to accommodate everyone who would have liked to attend.

Ascension's choir restored its school's reputation at that year's championship. Sonny was sent on stage to accept the Cup, to the sound of a standing ovation. The midday news on the radio carried a report of the event, and Viola and Marjorie immediately set to work cooking up a celebration for that evening.

On Sunday morning a picture of Ascension's choir appeared in one of the newspapers. There, in a sea of white faces and one or two brown ones, was Sonny's round, shining black face with its thick crown of hair that Gwynneth steadfastly refused to suppress. The article that accompanied the picture was headlined: **Young Soloist Stars at Festival.**

In literature class that week, Peschier was at the centre of a whispered conversation at the back of the room. It included muffled giggling and the passing of notes. It was distracting everyone, but Mr Baker seemed to have no interest in putting an end to it. Suddenly the noise reached a crescendo, in what was unmistakably Peschier's voice: "Oh, *shit!*"

All eyes turned to him, but he and his accomplices had their heads bent, each studiously looking into his *Merchant of Venice*. Mr Baker pounced on the black student sitting two desks in front of Peschier – Dennis Cateau.

"You!" Baker snarled, pointing at Cateau. "Stand up!"

"Me, Sir? I didn't…"

"Yes, you! Not another word from that latrine-mouth! Don't bring your barrack-yard behaviour here. This is not Bourg Ravine!"

Cateau was shocked into silence. There was a low rumble welling up in the classroom, but nobody seemed ready to stick his neck out, for the offence was a grave one, and Baker could try to pin it on somebody else.

Sonny spoke. "Sir, that was not Cateau…"

Baker was so taken aback that all he could do was sputter, "Who do you think you are?"

"I am Joshua Polydore, Sir."

"Well, 'Joshua Polydore, *Sah*'." (Baker regularly caricatured students whose speech did not suggest Windsor Park or Shadybrook.) "Don't let the little moment of fame go to your head, eh? Give you people an inch and you want to take a mile. Just get out of my sight. Get out!"

Now the rest of the class found their voices, some saying, "It wasn't Cateau, Sir!" others saying, "It was Peschier, Sir!" and "Unfair!" and soon the whole class was chanting "Unfair! Unfair!"

Baker's face turned red, and he barked at Sonny, who was on his way out of the classroom, "Polydore! Get back to your seat!"

He ordered the class to start reading, silently, Act 2 of *The Merchant of Venice*. After about fifteen minutes of students "reading" and their teacher sitting at his table glowering at them, the bell rang for the afternoon break. Mr Baker got up and walked out of the room without a word, and immediately the students turned on Peschier. For the whole of their first term at Ascension, classmates had dealt with this boy by giving him a wide berth, because they found him to be so poisonous. Now they quickly surrounded him and started to upbraid him for not owning up, and for letting Baker take it out on Cateau and Polydore. Peschier got up, shoved and elbowed his way through them, and headed for the door.

Before they went out for break time, some members of the class converged to try and figure out why Baker had so quickly backed down. One boy, who had an older brother in the school, told them of an incident that had taken place two years before, news of which had reached the press. Mr Baker had been hauled over the coals by the principal after Dr Keith Armstrong, the father of a black student at Ascension, lodged a formal complaint about Baker calling his son "just another baboon in human clothing". Baker was quite likely living under a warning since that time, and would know that an incident like the day's fracas could do him no good.

Sonny felt bruised by Baker's attack on Cateau and on him. And when he put that together with Superville day by day trying to chip away at him, he began thinking that he should perhaps ask Nenn Gwynnie if she could have him transferred to Government College. He had been telling Sonnylal about some of the "outsider" experiences he and his friends at Ascension were having, and Sonnylal listened wide-eyed, for he had never witnessed any such thing at his school. For one thing, there were many more Creole and Indian students, as well as teachers, at Government College than at Ascension, so Sonnylal did not have the same sense of not belonging.

But the more Sonny thought about the idea of a transfer, the more convinced he was that he couldn't just run off and leave the other boys who were also not having a good first year at this school. They depended on each other a great deal (and particularly on him, he could sense) to brave the situation as one body. It was for this reason that Sonny had resisted being siphoned off into one or another clique within the choir. How could he now turn his back on his friends and escape to the safety of another school?

He was not going to deliberately pick fights with Baker or Superville, or any other teacher. He would do his schoolwork well, as Nenn Gwynnie expected him to, and not let anybody throw him off course. But he couldn't promise anybody not to stand up to unfairness. And although Baker's attack was the most outrageous thing to have happened thus far, he would keep it from Nenn Gwynnie all the same.

In the week before August vacation, the choir held a last meeting. It was a celebratory meeting, looking back at their triumph in the inter-college championship; but they also turned their attention to their next challenge. The All-Cayeri Music Festival, like the Inter-College Song Festival, was held every other year, the two competitions taking place in alternate years.

As important as the inter-col festival was, and as ecstatic as they were about having got "their" cup back, the All-Cayeri Music Festival was the more prestigious event, the higher height for them to attain. Music Festival was the Big Cup, held at the grandest of venues – the Pantheon theatre. It was scheduled for March of the following year, so the work would have to begin in the very first week of the Christmas term.

On the last day of school, Larry came looking for Sonny to tell him – and he could barely hold down his excitement – that his father had agreed to take him to see his Uncle Maxwell, *and* to visit Sonny in Pilgrim, one Saturday in the holidays. Sonny gave him directions to his grandparents' home, also telling him that once they got to Pilgrim, they could just ask anybody for Polydore. He also told Larry that he would be in Pilgrim for five weeks, and gave him the dates.

Gaston and Gwynneth took Sonny to Pilgrim, as usual, and as soon as they left, Sonny started questioning his grandparents about the Medfords. The Polydores were intrigued that Sonny would have ended up as the schoolmate of a young Medford. And Sonny couldn't wait to tell Larry that Papa knew his Uncle Max! But days and then weeks went by, Sonny's time in Pilgrim was drawing to a close, and still no sign of Larry and his father. Sonny feared that his friend was going to be let down – his father was not keeping his promise.

Then, on the fourth Saturday of his stay in Pilgrim, Sonny and Papa were sitting in the gallery, Papa still digesting his lunch before heading back down to his garden, when they heard the running engine of a car that had stopped outside the hedge. Sonny made his way down to the gap. On seeing him, Larry rushed out of the car, looking as if he could just burst with joy, and Sonny, just as excited, blurted out, "My grandfather knows your Uncle Maxwell!"

"Really?" Larry exclaimed.

He and his father had just arrived from Kings Port, and they had not yet visited Uncle Maxwell. Sonny brought more chairs out into the gallery, and Gang-Gang came out to meet the visitors. As soon as the introductions were over, Larry, turned to Papa and shot the question at him, "You know Maxwell Medford, Sir?"

"Yes, man," Papa replied. "When Mr Max first come, he was staying by his friend in Beauregard, one Mr de Gannes. I used to work for Mr de Gannes at the time, so he send me with some other fellas to help Mr Max clear the spot and build. Mr Max is a good man. Long time I ain bless my eyes on he. Tell he for me Isaac Polydore send to say I wish him the best."

"Or, you could come with us and talk to him yourself," Mr Medford said. "We were hoping you would let Joshua come with us; but even better if both of you could come."

"All right. Let me just go inside and put on clothes." Papa was in his merino and yard pants. He changed his pants, put on a jersey and a cap, and picked up his cutlass on his way out.

The road to Beauregard, Old San Pedro Road, ran through almost continuous forest, but now they were turning off into a narrow dirt trace.

"It used to have a sign say 'Medford Trace', right there on the corner, from since I was a boy," Papa reported. "Mr Max take it down." Then he added, with a chuckle, "He say he doan want nobody know he address."

Medford Trace was a cul-de-sac, and Larry's father drove to the end and parked. They walked back a little way to find the opening – easy to miss – that was the beginning of a track into the forest. A short while after they started to make their way, under tall trees and through flourishing undergrowth, Papa stopped and pointed out to Sonny a high, ghostly mound some distance to their right, draped with vines. Papa went towards it, clearing a path with his cutlass, and the boys followed him. When they got to the mound he began pulling and chopping away at the vines to reveal two curved staircases forming an arch, except that whatever had once joined them at the top was gone. The boys counted fifteen steps on either side – two flights of concrete steps, dark with mildew, eerily ascending to nowhere.

"That was the front step," Papa informed them. "That is all that leff from the Great-House."

It turned out that Sonny was not the only one being informed. No one in Larry's family had ever drawn Larry's attention to what Papa was showing them. The two boys stood looking up in awe at the stairs. They got back onto the track and continued walking, with Papa now and then lopping off the tip of an overhanging branch, so the branch could lift itself out of the way. It was a long hike in. They walked in single file, for this was no more than a goat track. They had been walking for an age when they heard a dog bark, still some distance away. As soon as they could actually make out the clearing through the trees, Larry's father began to call out: "Uncle Max! It's Robert and Larry, with Larry's school friend and Mr Polydore from Pilgrim!"

He did so because he knew Maxwell had a hunting gun, ready and waiting to be used on human intruders.

"All right!" a voice shouted back. "Heard you! Doan wake up the lions and tigers!"

They finally stepped into the yard, to be met by three pothounds who charged at them, barking and baring their teeth. But then Uncle Max emerged from his joupa and called out to them, "Okay, fellas. Good doggies!"

The dogs withdrew and ran back towards him. He patted them, and they turned into frisky oversized puppies cavorting around him. He greeted Larry's father, asking him with a perfectly straight face: "So, Robert, is the war over yet? Who won, Hitler or Churchill? I hope it wasn't Hitler!"

Then he warmly welcomed Papa, throwing his arms around him and slapping his back. "Ey, Poly, man! Good to see you! And Larry! Boy, I thought they ship you off to boarding-school in England."

He hugged up Larry, ruffled his hair, and then stepped back to inspect him. "Look at this handsome young man, nuh! When they come out here without you, boy, I doan even want to see them. I keep asking for you, and they just keep giving me excuses."

Larry turned his head abruptly and faced his father with a murderous look that foreshadowed hell to pay afterwards. So his family had not stopped coming to visit Uncle Max. They had just been sneaking off and leaving him behind! (As Sonny learned later, Larry's father admitted to him, on their way back to town, that Larry's aunties did not think his Uncle Max was a good influence for him to be exposed to.)

"And this is your friend, son?" he asked, holding out his hand to Sonny.

"Yes, Uncle. This is my school friend, Joshua Polydore."

"School friend? At Ascension? Awful place, especially for boys like you, Joshua. Why would your folks send you there? This is one of your grands, Poly?"

Papa nodded proudly, perhaps taking the comment on Ascension as just friendly picong.

While Uncle Max was engaged in greeting his visitors, a little ginger-haired shabeen child wandered out from the joupa, rubbing sleep out of his eye, and attached himself to his leg. Except for the mop of frizzy hair on his head, the child resembled Larry. Uncle Max picked him up and kissed him.

"Stevie, say 'Good afternoon'." Stevie wriggled with shyness and buried his face in Uncle Max's chest. "His mother let me keep him for the weekend. He's a handful! Come sit down, Poly and Robert. Younger men, feel free to roam. The lions and tigers sleeping. They went liming and fêting last night, and now they cyaan wake up. So allyou safe."

Uncle Max had dada-head, matted into strands that hung like *liane* on a tree. He wore a merino and cut-off dungaree pants, and walked barefoot. His house was one room, raised off the ground by posts that were knobbly tree trunks. The small shed at the bottom of the house steps was his kitchen, where he had his coalpot and fireside for cooking. The men went into the ajoupa. The two visitors sat on the bamboo bench running around its edges, and Uncle Max in the hammock.

He lived on a river bank. The ajoupa directly overlooked a clear, slow-moving stream. Larry took Stevie's hand and the three boys walked down the short incline to the water. It was shallow enough for them to wade right in. The little boy started a splashing and gleeful shrieking. Their clothes got wet, so Sonny called up to Papa for permission to take off their jerseys and play in the water for a bit.

When, eventually, Larry's father called out to the boys that it was time for him and Larry to get on the road back to town, Larry was not persuaded. Their water games were in full swing, but Sonny came out of the river, taking Stevie with him. Stevie toddled up to the joupa to join Uncle Max, and Sonny waited for Larry at the water's edge. Larry's father came down the path and promised to bring the boys back one day.

"When?" Larry asked, in a sharp tone.

"Soon," his father said. "At the very latest, for your birthday."

Larry then waded out of the water, still eyeing his father askance.

43
"I am still going to be watching like a hawk."

It was the first day of the new term, early September. As they waited for assembly to begin, the hall resounded with the excited chatter of four hundred schoolmates who had not come together in six weeks. Father D'Abreau eventually mounted the stage, and they wondered why he looked so grave. He waited for a minute or so while the hush spread to the four corners of the hall. Then he welcomed them back to school. After he had led them in saying the school prayer, he took up a page from the lectern. "The following students of Form Four," he said, "please pay attention."

Father D'Abreau read out three names. In front of the whole school, he announced that these boys were suspended for two weeks, because they had been seen playing in a steelband on the streets during the Discovery Day carnival in Kings Port. He told them to get their belongings, go to their dean of discipline to each collect a letter addressed to their parents, and go home.

Discovery Day fell in the August school vacation, so Sonny was in Pilgrim, far from the sight or sound of its celebration. The Discovery Day carnival nearest to Pilgrim was miles away in San Pedro. Not that he would have gone to it. Nenn Gwynnie took a dim view of people celebrating the day when Christopher Columbus stepped ashore on Cayeri and opened the gate, she said, to the barbaric, rapacious onslaught of Europe. "And '*discovery*?' How the *France* Columbus coulda 'discover' a place that had people living in it already?" she would rant. "Those people discover the place centuries before he reach! Or, maybe them wasn 'people'? Them was just part of the fauna of the land, like the gouti and the guana in the bush, so nutten wrong if you just kill them off and take the land. 'Discovery Day' my ass."

The three fourth-formers left the hall, with all the other students craning their necks to get a glimpse of them. The principal continued with the proceedings of the assembly. Sonny did not hear much more of what Father D'Abreau had to say that morning.

As soon as he got back to the classroom, he wrote down the names of the three students, to what end, he wasn't sure. He sat through the first two morning periods, distracted and quietly fuming. When the bell rang for break time, he stayed put, still trying to think through this latest episode. Cateau and Harewood, on their way to the door, realised that Sonny was still sitting at his desk. They turned back and went to him, and the three of them vented angrily about the suspension, straining to keep their voices down.

By lunch time, Sonny had made up his mind. He had had his fill of this place. He packed his book bag and went first to Father O'Malley to ask his permission to go home because he wasn't feeling well. Next he sought out Mr Henderson and announced to him that he had decided to leave the choir, for he was no longer willing to sing for the school.

Mr Henderson gasped, but then tried to stay calm. "It's the suspension of the boys, isn't it?" he asked. "I know. I don't like it one little bit, either. Do these cloistered priests know that the steelband is part of the All-Cayeri Music Festival – the highest forum for musical excellence in the land? You can't go higher than that! Instead of suspending students for playing the pan, we ought to be looking to start an Ascension steelband orchestra, don't you think? Other schools will, sooner or later, so why couldn't we be the pioneers?"

He got a reluctant smile out of Sonny, who was just turning to go about his business.

"Look, son," Mr Henderson held Sonny's shoulder. "Don't give up on us yet. There's a staff meeting this afternoon, and I intend to raise hell in there."

"I not singing for this school, Sir. Sorry."

His next stop would be Gaston's office. Sonny marched over to Mary Street and up the two blocks, still fuming. He came out of his thoughts only when he had to cross streets, and when he entered the lawyers' building, for he had to remember his manners as he stood before the clerk who would let him into Gaston's office.

"A-a! Sonny? Like you breaking *bish!*" Gaston joked, but his smile faded when he saw the look on Sonny's face. Gaston sat him down to find out what could have tightened this boy's face into such a picture of vexation. Sonny told him about the suspension of the boys, his decision to leave the choir, and the discomfort he and the other black students were feeling. Gaston listened with growing concern, for Sonny, normally a placid child, was quite upset, and getting more and more worked up as he spoke.

"Doan worry, son." Gaston's voice was gentle. "We'll have to tackle this. First thing, you remember the names of the three students?"

Sonny produced the piece of paper on which he had noted the names, and Gaston complimented him on his presence of mind in writing them down. "Go on home, Sonny. I'll come up later." He went into a drawer and took out a dollar. "Here. Take the bus home. I doan know if there's any train you can get at this hour, but it certainly wouldn do for you to be waiting around till 4.00 o'clock. Change the dollar by getting something to eat at the bus stand. The conductors doan like passengers giving them paper money. See you later. And on the bus, practise smiling. You doan want to give your Nenn Gwynnie a heart attack when you arrive with that vex-face!"

Sonny tried his best to relax his expression.

"Nice!" Gaston cheered, with a big grin. "Continue working on it."

As soon as Sonny was out through the door, Gaston took up the telephone and called a friend who worked at *The Listener*. He gave him the story, but did not give him the boys' names, and asked that he not expose their identities even if he found out who they were. Nor should he reveal Gaston as his source of information, as he intended to go into the school and talk with the authorities, and this would jeopardise his approach to them.

Gaston had a court appearance in the early afternoon. When he got back to the office, the clerk had already gone through the telephone directory and listed the phone numbers of people with the same surnames as the boys – thirteen numbers in all. Only one of these yielded a result; Gaston reached an aunt of one of the boys, Edison Bobb. (It turned out that none of the three students' homes sported anything as luxurious as a telephone.) Gaston told the aunt why he was trying to contact the parents, and after indicating to him, with an expletive or two, her opinion of the College of the Ascension, she readily gave him directions to the boy's home. It was a start. He would get the other students' addresses from Edison.

Before he set out to visit the boys' families, Gaston phoned Roy and, briefly explaining why, asked him to come up to Turagua that evening. This matter was cause for a panchayat.

Edison Bobb's mother eyed Gaston suspiciously. He had introduced himself to her and offered legal assistance, without any charge, in the matter of her son's suspension. What he proposed was to speak with the school authorities on behalf of all three boys, and get the boys reinstated immediately, without going to court, if possible; but, with the parents' permission, he would go to court, if it came to that. The mother did not immediately warm to the idea. She apologised for asking, but wanted to know why he was taking this on. When, therefore, he went on to the two other homes, he was prepared for the scepticism, and explained without being asked what was in it for him. "Well, for one thing, I am a patron of two steelbands," he let it be known. "Also, I have a godson at Ascension, and I am not happy with the discrimination that takes place in there. It is a problem we have to solve."

The parents agreed wholeheartedly with this statement, but were afraid that their sons would be victimised as a result of Gaston's intervention.

"Look," he said. "My godson is in Form 1. He will be there for at least five years. For those five years, and beyond – for as long as it takes – I will be like a tick in they tail. I am not going to represent these three boys and then look away. This thing has been going on for generations – discrimination against students who are black, or coming from the underclass. Time for it to stop."

Two of the boys lived in Morne Cabrite, and the third lived a little way out of town, in Montecristo. This was two or three stops along the Eastern line – on the way to Turagua. Perfect, Gaston thought. In speaking with these families, Gaston found out that all three boys had their parents' permission to go downtown to the Discovery Day carnival, to roam the streets looking on at the parade of costumed bands, and perhaps take a little jump-up in one or more of the bands, just as some of the adult members of their families would have done when they were younger.

The Morne Cabrite families knew that beating in a steelband might have been part of their boys' outing on Discovery Day, and had no objection. One of the fathers said that the steelband his son was playing in had its base in a neighbour's yard, just around the corner. He had known most of the fellows in the band since they were babies.

The parents of the boy out in Montecristo were surprised to hear that their son had played in a steelband on the road, and might not have given permission, but they were adamant that this was a matter to be settled by the family, not the school. All three families were critical of the school for not speaking with them instead of just sending a notice. "Like if the boy is a criminal getting a summons," Edison's grandmother fumed.

The families were also worried about the loss of school time.

Gaston proceeded to Turagua, having got the permission of all three families to go into the school the following morning and represent them. Roy had arrived earlier, had spoken with Sonny, and had just finished ranting to Gwynneth, "Get him out of there! They will try to break his spirit!"

Roy was not entirely reassured by the plan Gaston announced – to go in and accost those in charge at Ascension.

Gwynneth had been startled by the sight of Sonny coming through the gate that afternoon, hours before the usual time, dragging himself along in a way that was not him. She thought he had been sent home, but he told her that he had left the school voluntarily.

"Left the school!" she exclaimed, close to panic. "*Bondjé,* you expel youself?"

"No, Nenn Gwynnie," he answered in a patient voice, as though he were the adult, reassuring a child. He sat down and wearily told her about the day's events, then began to spill out other stories of upsetting incidents at school that he had thus far kept from them.

"You should have told us, Sonny. You should have told us," was all she could say, in a stricken voice, again and again.

She suggested that he bathe, eat something if he wanted to, and then write a report detailing the incidents. Sonny went to his room and did not emerge again until he had written five notebook pages of reporting. This was the document that they now showed to Gaston, who took a quick read. Sonny wanted to send it to the newspapers as a letter to the editor, but Gwynneth had advised him against that idea. It would not help for him to be accused of bringing his school into disrepute.

Gaston agreed: "That would not be a good move, Sonny. It would give the school ammunition to use against you. This information *could* get into the papers, yes, like when your Mr Baker made a remark to Dr Armstrong's son, a couple years ago, insulting all blackpeople. But the story shouldn't come directly from you to the press. There are ways and means of making these abuses public, if it comes to that. The first step, though, is a formal complaint to the school authorities. I want you now to write a fair copy of this report, with two carbon copies. Address it to the principal. Nenn Gwynnie will show you how to set it up. Good work, Sonny."

Gaston laid out for the others the arguments he intended to take to the school the next day. "Four points," he said. "First of all, the 'rule' under which these boys have been suspended is nowhere to be seen in the handbook given to students at registration. Secondly, the school cannot properly claim jurisdiction over students outside of school and school hours, when they are not in school uniform. Next point, the school is seeking to prevent Cayerian students from participating in what is an important cultural activity of their native land. And as a corollary to this point, the school is also condemning all Cayerians who are involved in developing an indigenous musical instrument, the value of which is now widely acknowledged."

He would put two demands on the table. "The suspension is a blot on these boys' school record, and it must be expunged. And the students must be reinstated immediately, because two weeks out of school is a serious setback for students about to enter the year of their Senior Cambridge exam."

He would also raise the underlying issue of discrimination against students who were not white, or upper-class. He would

478

suggest to the school authorities that the population of Cayeri had become less tolerant than in the past of that long-standing problem with Ascension.

"Hm!" said Roy. "You're an optimist. Why would Ascension be inclined to give a hoot about what the population thinks? That would be like the elephant worrying about the opinion of the grass that it walks on!"

"That was in your time at Ascension, Roy," Gaston countered. "Since then, we have had 1919, 1937, 1946 and, today, on the horizon, The National Party of Cayeri. Things are not the same."

Next morning, Tuesday, the story of the boys' suspension was in *The Listener*. Trust Calvin to go and snoop. He had lurked at a safe distance from the school gate – one block downstream on James Street – so he could catch Ascension boys going to the train or bus station, or to Morne Cabrite and other plebeian destinations, and interview them.

Calvin's article reported the facts of the story, down to the name of the steelband the boys were playing in. He had also solicited the views of the students he waylaid on James Street, regarding the suspension of their colleagues, and their indignant reactions became part of the story. The piece was juicy enough to irritate those in authority at Ascension, so Gaston did not expect a warm welcome on the other end of the line when he phoned the school that morning and announced that he wished to speak with the principal on the matter of the suspended boys.

The voice on the phone asked Gaston to hold on, and whispered to someone whose answer was not decipherable – it came over as a growl. The first voice returned to Gaston to ask whether he was a newspaper reporter, and Gaston identified himself, again, as a barrister-at-law. Father D'Abreau was not immediately available, but the vice-principal could speak with him. Gaston requested an appointment with either the principal or his representative, that afternoon.

The principal met with Gaston at 1.00 o'clock. Gaston put to him the parents' concerns and his own concerns as a lawyer retained by the families of Edison Bobb, Wayne Calliste, and Lincoln Harriot. The principal chose to give a cynical answer.

"Those families can afford a lawyer?" he asked, almost chuckling, or so Gaston felt.

"No, they can't, but rest assured, they *have* a lawyer," Gaston replied. "Let's cut to the chase, though. The school can avoid legal action by reinstating these students as of tomorrow morning, and removing any record of the suspension from their files. I am willing to wait while your office prepares letters to this effect, for me to deliver to the parents."

Father D'Abreau hesitated, then raised his voice a notch. "Are you a lawyer, or just a troublemaker? You can't just walk in here and make demands…"

Gaston interrupted him. "Father, it might be worth your while to have a look at this statement from one of your students. He is my godson and I know that he is very disenchanted with Ascension College."

The principal scowled at him and read the first page, then turned to the end to find the name of the writer. He found it, blinked rapidly and began to read again, from the top of the second page. Gaston waited, and only spoke again when the principal had finished reading the whole document. "Doesn't smell nice, does it?" Gaston said. "Rampant prejudice on the one hand, and privilege on the other. We're not in the nineteenth century, Father, nor the early years of this century. You might want to consider the new political climate – the mood of the citizenry in this Year of our Lord 1955; a nationalist movement sweeping the colony; self-rule within our reach… What we were subjected to in the past, because we had little power, will no longer be tolerated."

Father D'Abreau tried to interrupt, but Gaston did not stop. "This child's complaint doesn't do much for the image of the school, or the Church, does it, Father? Especially in the light of these unjust suspensions. So, can I wait for those letters? It has to be this evening, for those boys to be back in school tomorrow morning. As for my godson, you can look forward to a visit from his guardian, Gwynneth Cuffie, concerning the behaviour of two specific teachers towards him and other black boys. Those two teachers are named in his report – his form master, Mr Superville, and Mr Baker. Nasty business!"

"And I must tell you, Father, the boy's guardian is a person not blessed with the gift of patience. You could easily wake up tomorrow morning and hear that she has transferred him to Prince Albert Edward College. I wouldn't put it past her. And even if she doesn't... Apologies, I forgot to mention my godson's first response to this situation, a hasty response that no one has as yet been able to talk him out of."

And Gaston told the principal about Sonny's decision to leave the choir.

This was news to the principal. Sonny had not told anybody at the school except Mr Henderson, and it seemed that Mr Henderson had chosen not to give life to the bad news by repeating it to anyone else. At Monday's staff meeting he had railed against the suspensions and the school authorities' attitude to the steelband, which he called "a formidable invention in the world of music", but said nothing about the contact he had had with Sonny hours earlier.

Perhaps the choir master hoped that Sonny, having slept on his decision, might have changed his mind by the next day. Or that his godmother, evidently a music-loving person, might have persuaded him to stay in the choir and sing at Music Festival. The school authorities, therefore, had been blissfully unaware of Sonny's defection. Father D'Abreau responded after a heavy pause.

"You are making it sound like blackmail, Mr Boniface. That is not called for. We are reasonable people. Young Polydore is a valued member of our student body, as you can well imagine, and we will investigate the abuses he has reported. Meanwhile, I'll need to consult with others – I cannot make a decision by myself about the suspended students. If there is agreement that we should accede to your request, the letters will be delivered..."

The three suspended boys were back in class the following morning, Wednesday, and the story that made its way around the whole school, from lunch time onwards, was better than a Saturday matinee featuring a John Wayne western:

At the staff meeting on Monday afternoon, Mr Henderson blasted

481

the principal and the fourth formers' dean of discipline for suspending the students, and the whole staff for allowing it. Polydore's father, or uncle, or grandfather, or something, came in yesterday and threatened to take the principal to court unless Bobb, Calliste and Harriot were allowed to come back to school right away. Just like how Roger Armstrong's father came in year-before to blast the principal about Baker insulting his son. Polydore was absent yesterday and again today and that is because he has transferred to Government College in protest against the suspension of the three boys. He will therefore be singing for Government College in the Music Festival, which means that Ascension's choir is in for a licking. Polydore's aunt, or grandmother, or godmother, or something, came into the school this morning to take on Baker and Superville. She chew them up fine fine...

Neither Gaston nor Sonny knew that Gwynneth would make her visit on that day. Neither did Gwynneth, until that very morning. She had kept Sonny at home on Tuesday, for he remained distracted, even depressed, not at all eager to go to school. She thought it just as well that he not be at school when Gaston went to meet with the principal, as she did not know what to expect out of that encounter. This morning she had to go to Sonny's door twice and call him before he got up; and then she had to go back a third time, because even though he was awake, he was taking a long time to come out of the room.

The night before, Gaston had come up and told them that the suspension was off and the three boys were going back to school in the morning. Sonny had retired to his room for the night, considerably cheered by this news, and Gwynneth went into the room to talk with him. He told her then that he had thought about it, and was willing to stay in the choir. He would sing at Music Festival.

When he finally emerged in the morning, Gwynneth asked him whether he was having second thoughts.

"No, Nenn Gwynnie." He shook his head. "I just tired, Nennie. Today is Wednesday, and that means I have to sit in front of Mr Superville three times for the day – morning roll-call, history class, and afternoon roll call. And then, after school today is choir. I not ready, yet, for all that, Nenn Gwynnie. I doan have Baker until Friday, and I hope this whole thing will die down by then. Let me stay home one more day, please, Nennie. I will go back to school tomorrow."

Gwynneth sat up. *Superville and Baker! Of course! This is not over! Those two still have to be dealt with!* How could she just throw Sonny back to the wolves? The incidents he had told them about were serious offences – misconduct on the part of teachers, that actually made them unfit to be teachers – and the principal had been informed via Sonny's written report. What action had been taken by the school authorities? What action did they intend to take?

By the end of her conversation with Sonny, Gwynneth had made up her mind, and Viola was happy to endorse her decision. Gwynneth would have to go in and make it safe for this child to enter that place again. She joked with Viola that if she could make some headway, they might not need to burn down the whole school. Gwynneth readied herself and set out, while Viola looked forward to pampering Sonny for a second day.

The little clerk sitting nearest to the door was clearly not impressed with the image of this person standing before her. Gwynneth had greeted her with "Good morning, Miss," and waited. The girl lifted her head once to look at her, and then went back to whatever it was on her desk that had been occupying her before Gwynneth's arrival. No words. No "Can I help you?" No "One minute, please." Just a little red girl seated at a desk doing something or the other in the most unhurried way, and a black woman, elderly, waiting on her feet in front of the little red girl's desk. It was like registering Sonny, all over again. This place might need burning down after all.

Gwynneth gave her a minute or two before speaking again: "Excuse me, Miss. Are you seeing me, or am I invisible?"

The girl looked up and asked, "Yes?"

"I would like to see the principal, please."

"You have an appointment?"

"No, but I will wait until he can accommodate me. All day, if necessary."

"Hm," the girl grunted, and motioned with her chin. "That's

the principal's secretary over there," and she returned to her dawdling.

The secretary's desk was at the opposite end of the room, outside a closed door. Gwynneth strode through the room, saying "Good morning" to all the people seated at desks, most of whom responded in one way or another. The principal's secretary offered her a seat and asked her about the purpose of her visit.

"I am Joshua Polydore's guardian, and I would like a word with the principal."

The secretary went in to Father D'Abreau and he came to the door to invite Gwynneth in. Before she followed him inside, Gwynneth said to the secretary in a loud voice, "Thank you for your politeness, Miss." Then she turned towards the little clerk at the door and spoke to her across the room: "Young lady sitting by the entrance, you need to learn manners."

Father D'Abreau had a nervous smile on his face. He welcomed Gwynneth, and with some anxiety, asked after Sonny. Taking from her purse her letter of excuse for Sonny's absence, she assured him that he would be back out to school on the following day.

"And can you please let Mr Henderson know for me, before the end of the day, that Sonny will be back at choir practice next week. Now, Father, before my child returns to your school, I would like to speak with two of your teachers – Mr Superville and Mr Baker – for I am not sending him back in here to be further abused and undermined by them. Those two are not the only ones abusing the black students; they are just the worst. I pray that you will acknowledge and take steps to root out this problem across the school. Talk with your staff. But Superville and Baker I would like to meet face to face. Can you arrange that for me? And I would like to meet with them in your presence, please."

The principal had no objection to granting this request. Indeed, Gwynneth thought he seemed eager to throw the two men in the bamboo. He sent for them right away. Gwynneth knew that Baker had already brought the school some unwelcome attention, with the Armstrong affair getting into the newspaper. As for Superville, Gwynneth could only imagine the grovelling toady that black fool turned into before this whiteman, D'Abreau, who was his boss. She did not expect that Father D'Abreau would have any high opinion of him, either. It was clear that the principal was not willing to defend either of these two gentlemen, and was quite happy to let an angry parent loose on them.

Baker swaggered into the room, wearing a look of utter contempt – eyes narrowed, nostrils flaring a little, and mouth formed into a smirk – but as he took his seat, Gwynneth could see that his face was turning redder by the second. Superville tiptoed in looking cowed, too seized with apprehension to speak. Father D'Abreau introduced Gwynneth, and with a wave of the hand, invited her to speak. In her mildest voice, and with a deadly smile, she opened the meeting with the question, "So you think, the two of you, that the black students in this school are fair game for any kind of disrespect and mishandling you might choose to inflict on them, eh?"

On Thursday morning, news got around that Polydore had returned to school, which meant that he had not transferred to Government College after all. The three suspended fourth formers tracked him down at break time. They found him at the entrance to the staff room, in conversation with Mr Henderson. The three boys waited patiently for their turn to shake Sonny's hand and speak with him.

And at lunch time, a flood of students, of every hue, came to the hall also to shake his hand and thank him for his action. Some came into the hall to pay their respects to him and then went to get their lunch; others came after they had eaten, took chairs from the stacks and sat down, eventually forming a new circle around the one in which Sonny and his first form colleagues sat. Some boys stood around and joined in the intense discussion that would go on until the bell rang. Larry was there. After choir camp in the Easter vacation, he had become a regular visitor to their lunch circle, dropping in to lime after he had taken lunch at the "Waldorf".

The discussion was a venting that jumped from topic to topic: race prejudice, class snobbery, discrimination, privilege, disrespect for a people's culture, colonialism, inequality, and general unfairness. On the following day, Friday, the lunchtime visitors came back to drive the discussion further. What, they asked themselves, were they going to do about any of this?

Suggestions began to fly. Sonny put up his hand to suspend the discussion. "Anybody with paper to spare?" he asked. "Gimme a page or two, and a book to press on. Let's make a list of these ideas."

A notebook was passed to him from somewhere in the gathering, followed by the voice of the owner: "Write in that, and then you could take out the pages."

Some of those present advocated joining the Youth League of the NPC – the National Party of Cayeri – that was set to be launched early in the new year. A Form 3 student suggested that those who saw themselves as underdogs at Ascension should instead become watchdogs for fairness, and be prepared to write up and report every experience of discrimination that they suffered.

A sixth-former pointed out, indignantly, that there was a whole programme on the BBC World Service, broadcasting literary works by writers from the West Indies, including Cayerian writers. "These works are being introduced to the world," he pointed out, "but here, not a word about them in literature class, and not a single West Indian book in the whole school library. They have to put West Indian literature on our syllabus!"

All those present agreed that the impromptu event they were participating in should become a regular activity. Someone put forward a name: "The Lunch Time Forum". Another boy found that the term used by the third-former, "Watchdogs for Fairness", could also be considered for this purpose. It was agreed that they should gather more suggestions for the name before making a choice.

The bell rang, bringing the lively meeting to an end, by which time Sonny had collected an impressive list of suggestions. The one that had produced the greatest excitement and readiness to act was his call for the school to make an addition to its official list of extracurricular activities: a steelband club. Sonny assured them that Mr Henderson would give his full support. In the last minutes of that lunch hour, the idea of campaigning for a steelband club was adopted as the first project of the gathering.

Those present agreed to reconvene on Friday of the following week to plan the campaign.

At home that evening, the gallery lime deliberated upon the events of the week. Viola was concerned that Sonny could get into trouble with the authorities at Ascension. "Watch you step with them, eh. All now they must be looking for excuse to put you out of they school."

Sonny was sitting on the bannister. He got down and went behind Viola's chair to squeeze her shoulders and give her a hug-up. "Yes, Nenn Vie. I know. But they cyaan get away with that so easy, now."

Ollie agreed that Sonny and his comrades should tread carefully. "But never on tiptoe!" he hastened to add. "You not there on sufferance. You have every right to be there, and to speak out."

Roy tried to convey how he felt. An old score settled... a deep wound that could now heal... He spoke almost reverentially: "You and your schoolmates are doing what my generation could not. Thank you, Sonny-Boy."

"So, Teacher Gwynneth," Gaston prodded. "You still not telling us what you said to Messrs Superville and Baker in your tête-à-tête with them?"

"Nah!" Gwynneth responded. "You doan want to know. What was spoken in that room is between me, the two miscreants, the Father-priest and the doorpost. You doan want to hear what I said to those two. Suffice it to say, they get the message. Now is for the youngpeople to take it forward. And that does not mean that I am going to doze off. I am still going to be watching like a hawk. Go brave, Sonny, you and your schoolmates. Go brave!"

ABOUT THE AUTHOR

Merle Hodge was born in 1944, in Calcutta Settlement, Carapichaima, Trinidad and Tobago. She was educated up to secondary level in Trinidad and Tobago, and then at the University of London. She is a language arts teacher; a cultural and social activist; and a writer. She has taught at secondary schools and tertiary institutions in the Caribbean, including the teacher education programme of the Grenada Revolution, and in the USA. She is active in the women's movement, and a co-founder of Women Working for Social Progress ("Workingwomen"). She has published two novels: *Crick Crack, Monkey* and *For the Life of Laetitia*; short stories; papers in international journals; and a textbook, *The Knots in English: A Manual for Caribbean Users*. Among her areas of interest are language and family in the Caribbean. Merle Hodge lives in Trinidad and Tobago.